TIDES OF TIME

LUNA JOYA

CITY OWL
PRESS

TIDES OF TIME
The Legacy Series, Book 1

CITY OWL PRESS
www.cityowlpress.com

Cover Design by Mibl Art. All stock photos licensed appropriately.

Edited by Tee Tate.

For information on subsidiary rights, please contact the publisher at info@cityowlpress.com.

Print Edition ISBN: 978-1-949090-45-1

Digital Edition ISBN: 978-1-949090-46-8

Printed in the United States of America

To Patrick,
My Happily Ever After

CHAPTER ONE

Magic and family drama sucked Cami in the same as riptides. Sometimes, she could spot them coming on the horizon. Other mornings, like today, they swept her away without warning. Such was life in a legacy witch lineage with all its rules and expectations.

She pushed through the staff door of the emergency animal hospital and blinked against the blinding Southern California sun after another all-night shift. She scanned her surroundings as she'd done everywhere for the last year, balancing her backpack on her hip so she could fumble through it. Had she forgotten her sunglasses? She jumped at the approaching squeal of tires, her scattered nerves fraying. Her older sister's Mini Cooper skidded to a halt less than three feet away from where she stood.

She scrubbed her hand over her face. Why was Delia here? Shouldn't she be at work? Her courthouse was an hour away in Los Angeles traffic. So why was she here shoving open the passenger door?

"What the heck, Deals?"

Delia met her gaze. "Mina's missing."

Just like that–*riptide*.

Cami jumped into the car and dumped her bag on the floorboard.

"More like she's temporarily lost." Swinging her sleek blonde ponytail over her shoulder, Delia slammed the car in reverse and shot out of the parking lot. "She slipped unsupervised."

Cami sucked in a breath. Their youngest sister's power was slipping through time. Mina's body would move in the location as it was today, but her mind traveled to see a different time through another person in the same geographic space. Scenery changes after the psychic impression made for perilous slips. "Where? When?"

"She toured a historical mansion last night courtesy of a USC alum." Delia spat the last words.

"Focus." They didn't have time for sibling or college rivalries. "Mina's slip?"

"Right." Delia shifted gears and raced down side streets toward the ocean. "She followed a woman named Sunny Sol out of the mansion. I ran a search on the name. It came back to an actress from the 1920s and '30s. Mina trailed Sol along the bluffs down to the beach."

"The bluffs?" Panic shot through Cami, and her own powers thrummed in response to the strong emotion. Mina had chased an actress from old Hollywood along steep cliffs? Mudslides and falling rocks could've easily changed the landscape over the decades. Mina wouldn't have been able to distinguish the past surroundings from her present ones.

"Don't get me started." Delia switched lanes. She barely squeezed between a bus and a truck.

Cami grabbed the handle above her head. "We can't find Mina if you get us killed with your crazy driving." Her older half-sister might be the ultimate protector, but Delia drove as though her little race car had its own force field.

"Mina sent a 911 text fifteen minutes ago. Luckily, I was already in Santa Monica interviewing a witness for a trial next week." Delia slid a look her way. "I knew your ringer would be off so I called her back."

Cami spent every hour either at the animal hospital, cramming for board certification, in the ocean, or sleeping. She'd graduated with honors from the top veterinary medicine program in the country last year. Her psychic affinity for communicating with animals helped, but she still had to put in the work. Her vet residency didn't leave much free time. As a deputy district attorney, Delia understood long hours.

"I figured I could catch you before you left work." Delia streaked through a yellow light. "Mina's phone died before she told me where she was. She forgot to charge it."

Typical. Mina could be flighty handling the basics of life.

Delia swung a hard left onto the downhill ramp for the Pacific Coast Highway, locally known as the PCH. "You'll have to use your call to find her."

No. Cami's chest tightened. She didn't tap into her elemental magic, and there was no way she could tell her sisters why. She—the quintessential "good girl" Donovan sister—had broken the first rule of magic. There'd be no coming back if others discovered why she'd really walked away from her element.

"I wouldn't ask if it wasn't the only way without spending hours driving up and down the coast hoping to find her." Delia's stone-faced glare gave nothing away, but her voice had softened. "You and I don't know spell craft. There's only one person who could whip up a locator spell in an instant, and I didn't think you'd want me to call her."

"Ama." Cami sighed. She couldn't call Ama. Her mother, a powerful spellcaster, would ask too many questions if she discovered Mina had chased a historical psychic vision alone. Mina didn't need a one-way ticket to magical mommy guilt trips. It was bad enough Delia knew. "We're not telling Ama."

She fingered the pendant at her neck, similar to the one all four sisters wore. Ama had spelled the charms to warn them of danger. Hopefully, Mina had hers on.

"She called from the shore. I could hear waves and seagulls." Delia swerved into the turning lane and pulled into a beachfront parking lot. She stopped the car. "I know you and your element had some kind of a falling out a year ago."

Each of the four sisters had a call to an element. Cami's was water. She could manipulate it, communicate with it, cause damage with it.

It hadn't been a simple breakup with her element. She had nearly killed a man with her connection to water. So much for *harm none* with magic. While she'd gone to the beach daily since then and surrounded herself with its comfort, she hadn't let herself give in to her power. Not when she'd abused and then refused it.

But her sister needed her. She swallowed back the fear of what might come if she tapped into that big source again.

She unbuckled the seatbelt and tugged her stained scrubs off, stripping down to a threadbare graphic T-shirt and undies. She wadded the work clothes into her backpack, slid a pair of shorts on, and switched Crocs for flip flops.

Delia opened her door.

Cami stopped her. "Why don't you keep your couture, 'dry clean only' self in the car?" She didn't want anyone witnessing her return to her element, because what if it all went wrong?

Delia paused with her hand on the door. "Want some privacy?"

She bobbed her head, checked her necklace, and climbed out. The ocean breeze snagged her short curls. "Give me five minutes."

"Hey, Cams?"

She ducked into the open car window.

"If you can't do this, it's okay." Delia unlocked her phone screen. "I'll keep trying in case Mina finds a way to charge her phone."

Cami took a deep breath. "I've got it." If only her voice hadn't wavered.

Stepping onto the sand, she slipped off her shoes and strode toward the water's edge. She wouldn't risk this but for her sisters.

While she longed for her elemental magic to soothe and guide her, the very same source could rebuke her for misusing her power. She feared its condemnation. It'd be too much, but Mina needed her help. She leaned down, sweeping her fingers into foam on the wet sand.

Fighting doubt and worry, she reached for her magic and sent a tentative call to her element. The ocean responded in warm welcome without judgment, and she forced back the urge to tap fully into her power.

Oh, how she'd missed this.

She wanted to walk into the waves and savor each precious lap against her skin, to let the water bathe away the fear and darkness she'd carried. The need to link to that tidal power pulled her in, promising absolution she didn't deserve. She had to focus on Mina before she lost herself to the water's beckoning homecoming.

She pushed past the water's thrum of longing and expectation until her power conjured images of Mina waiting at the water's edge further north. Cami breathed a sigh of relief and gratitude along the connection.

"Thank you," she whispered and said a reluctant goodbye. With a single glance over her shoulder, she hurried back to the car and jumped inside. "Found her. Head north."

Delia tore out of the lot and zipped across three lanes of traffic. She smacked the steering wheel with her palms when they got stuck at another red light at the busiest intersection on the PCH in Pacific Palisades.

Gas stations, grocery stores, and a restaurant jammed together in the precious real estate across the street from the shore. Cami craned her neck to check the signs as they passed through the intersection and accelerated. Corraza's Restaurant.

"If Mina has slipped, she'll be starving." Each sister's magic had a price. Mina's had always been hunger. "We can head back here if they're open."

"I'll check once we find her."

They passed beneath a pedestrian bridge next to a steep set of stairs cut into the bluff.

"Here," Cami said. "She's close by, near the water's edge."

Delia flipped a U-turn in the parking area of a large Spanish-style building with arched entrances and windows below a hexagon-shaped center. "Go. I'll catch up with you."

Cami jumped out of the car and sprinted for the water. Her power called to her, directing her. She hopped the concrete barrier and raced across the sand, searching for her sister. Perched on a rock jetty, Mina stared over the waves.

Cami called out, relieved when her sister turned with clear eyes, not the dazed obsidian dilation of magic.

Mina ran a shaky hand through her hair. "You came for me."

"Always." Cami stooped to pick up her sister's hooded sweatshirt and sandals tossed nearby. She studied the strain in Mina's eyes, the dark smudges beneath. "Were you out here all night trailing Sunny Sol?"

Mina took her hoodie and gave a weak smile. "Hazards of slipping. I should've known better than to be curious."

"When I think of what could've happened to you." Cami slid her eyes closed.

"I couldn't resist, and then I got pulled in too deep."

She knew all about the overload when magic overwhelmed logic.

Mina's lips twisted. "Do you ever want to be normal? No elemental powers? No psychic ability?"

Cami wanted a lot of things: to stop looking over her shoulder; to have a good man adore her without going crazy stalker abusive on her; to have her hard work correct the bad choices she'd made so she wouldn't doubt every new one; to not have to worry about their family's magic.

She nudged Mina. "Come on. Let's go save Delia from ruining whatever designer shoes she's wearing. We spotted a place to eat a mile back. Maybe they've got pancakes."

Minutes later, Cami half-dragged her younger sister through the glass doors into Corraza's Restaurant to find a table while Delia parked the car. The swift change from bright sunlight to the darker interior had Cami blinking behind sunglasses she'd borrowed from Delia.

If only the dimmed lighting and dark glasses could excuse her gawking at the man behind the front podium. All muscles and tanned skin, he looked up from his notes, and his gaze locked on her face.

The exhaustion of back-to-back shifts must have caught up to her. Or the cost of her magic decided to crash into her as it did for Delia, who'd black out from using too much.

Cami bit back a groan. She'd drawn so hard on her psychic ability to connect with animals last night and then her elemental magic this morning, she should've expected her powers would demand replenishment. Her magic craved fulfillment from a hot guy. *This* hot guy. She'd probably leaked the desire all over him. She swallowed, shoving down the need as best she could with the powers calling for collection of a debt owed.

With one hand bracing her sister, Cami tugged her sunglasses into her tangle of curls and blew out a breath. Feeding Mina was top priority. No more sexy daydreams about a handsome guy.

The fleeting second she'd given in to the fluttering in her belly had been the best part of her week. Time to return to the reality of her witchy family.

CHAPTER TWO

SAM CORRAZA'S MORNING HAD STARTED OFF IN THE CRAPPER. NOT literally. Though with the industrial-size garbage disposal dripping underneath the massive kitchen sink, the stench was about the same. No plumbers had been available on short notice, so it'd been up to him to plug the leak. Such was the glamorous life of restaurant ownership, but Corraza's meant everything to Sam.

He'd finished minutes before the breakfast rush, praying his patch job would hold until he could get a plumber out. The kitchen had swarmed with activity for hours by the time Sam shrugged a collared button-up over his undershirt. He pushed through the swinging door to the dining area and headed toward the host stand.

He needed to work out table arrangements for a big group arriving soon. After scratching quick notes, he lifted his head to double-check his counts. That's when *she* walked through the sunlight streaming in the front door.

She had hourglass curves and a riot of chin-length curls in every possible shade of brunette. Her face tipped up toward his. All that wild hair framed strong cheekbones and a pouty bottom lip begging to be kissed.

When she slid her sunglasses into those curls, he stared even harder. *Her eyes.* They were enormous pools of molten gold. He'd never seen that color in a woman's eyes. They couldn't be real. She blinked, dark lashes fluttering before she glanced toward the tables and then back up at him. Sunlight shifted across her face. Those huge golden eyes were real.

She checked every face in the room, gripping her keys and gnawing her lower lip. Worry filled those beautiful, tired eyes. What could've happened to make her so cautious?

Seriously, he needed to get a grip. Thinking with the wrong head at the restaurant led to disaster. He glanced to the strikingly similar woman next to her with darker eyes and longer curls. She was pretty, but she didn't draw him in like the first.

"Welcome to Corraza's." He recited the same welcome he'd given for years.

"A table for three?" Those golden eyes darted over the crowd. "Something with a little privacy, if you have it?"

Sam snagged three menus and led her to a booth tucked in the alcove at the end of the bar. Led them both, he corrected himself.

Golden Eyes waited for the other woman to slide into the same seat of the booth. She angled herself so she faced the front door. Her shorts hugged all the right places and revealed smooth olive skin. A faded graphic shirt stretched across her breasts, screen-printed with the cover of a children's book.

"Here are your menus. I'll be happy to answer any questions you have." The practiced words rolled off his tongue even as his mind bounced between not staring at her chest and not asking her name.

A tall blonde slid into the booth opposite Golden Eyes. "Leave us," the newcomer told him.

Golden Eyes whispered a harsh word across the table followed by exchanged hot glares with the blonde.

He took a step back at the nonverbal standoff between the three women. Sisters. Had to be. Only family could rile someone so quickly. What would it have been like to grow up with family so close they didn't need words to communicate? He'd gotten to know his own siblings pretty well the past five years, but these women must have been tight their whole lives.

Returning to the rhythm of his job with some distance from Golden Eyes, he sorted out servers and mixed drinks for customers at the bar. He could've passed the women off to an employee, but he didn't. He headed toward the booth with three waters.

Golden Eyes stood and pushed the other dark-haired woman to go clean up with quiet assurances she'd remember her order.

"I'll go with her," the blonde said. "Same for me."

The two women walked around the corner, leaving Golden Eyes alone. Sam settled the glasses on the table with a soft clink.

"Hi, I'm Sam."

"Nice to meet you, Sam."

He could swear he'd seen a spark of interest there. "And you as well, um...?" He trailed off, hoping for a name before he slipped up and did something dumb like calling her by her eye color.

"Cami."

"Cami." He savored the name before tilting his head in the direction the other women had gone. "Sisters?"

"Were we obvious?" She dipped her chin and lowered her lashes.

The inference hadn't been tough with the familiarity, affection, and even the annoyance

the women showed each other. Sam wiped a spot on the table that wasn't the least bit dirty. "I haven't seen you here before."

She shook her head, and the curls flew. How could she be so adorable and seductive all at once? His body reacted to her like it did to the ocean when he paddled out on his surfboard, excited to discover what came next with the uncertainty if it'd be a smooth ride or an unexpected thrill.

"I saw the sign from the road and took a chance." She waved a hand toward the busy tables. "Looks like I made a good choice."

Sam grinned at the double meaning. Sure, he wouldn't mind if she'd only been talking about him, but Corraza's was his life's work. The fact she liked it was all the better.

He gestured toward her shirt. "The book where the kid got sent to bed without supper for being bad. He becomes king of the monsters, right?"

She glanced down. "Something like that."

"I loved that book as a kid." He didn't add how he'd read it every night and wished for the comforting parental love the character found at the end of the book. Sam had grown up without the same and moved on.

He steered away from the loneliness he'd shared with the characters in the story to focus on the fun part. "Nothing like an ocean escape to wild adventures in your own bedroom." He hadn't filtered the thought before saying it out loud. Great. Now she'd think he was a creep.

She tilted her head, studying him with a half-smile on her pretty pink lips. "How very true."

He cleared his throat. "I hope you and your sisters came hungry."

She huffed a tiny chuckle. What would her real laugh sound like? Would it be loud or annoying? Maybe quiet or cute?

"We are always hungry."

"I can't have that." He crouched down with the pretense he needed the table as a writing surface, but really he wanted to be closer to her. "What will it be?"

She scooted toward him with the menu. When she ordered enough food to feed six starving lumberjacks who'd been lost in the wilderness for weeks, a piece of his heart melted. He loved when a woman wasn't bashful about eating. Especially when it came to his food.

He focused on her order and not the glint of a delicate gold chain sliding at the curve of her neck. "Want a drink? Orange creamsicle mimosa with ice cream is my specialty."

"Creamsicle anything sounds divine." The side of her mouth curved wistfully. Was that a dimple? He'd have to get a real smile from her to know for sure.

"Divine, huh?" He should stop stalling and get back to the kitchen. "What can I get for your sisters?"

"Coffee, please. One black. The other with cream, sugar, and cinnamon if you have it." She paused. "Heavy on the cinnamon."

Sam recognized the recipe from surfing trips to Baja. "Brown sugar?"

She blinked. "How did you know?"

"Lucky guess." He caught movement out of the corner of his eye.

Her sisters. "A creamsicle mimosa, a black coffee, and a *café de olla* coming right up."

He straightened as her sisters walked toward them. The younger had a playful bounce, the older a regal stroll. Neither moved like Cami's serious stride.

Sam put the order in and headed into the kitchen. He grabbed ice cream from the freezer to whip up her specialty mimosa. At least three more orders would come the minute customers watched him bring the drink out. He needed to concentrate on maximizing sales and quality at Corraza's to keep the business on top. He didn't have time for a woman in his life. But he'd sure like to make some time for Cami.

CHAPTER THREE

CAMI LEANED TO GET A BETTER VIEW OF SAM WALKING AWAY. BROAD shoulders tapered to a slim waist, and the edge of a tattoo peeked from his rolled shirt sleeves. She'd fit right in the cut of muscle at his shoulder. His chocolate eyes shone several shades darker than her own. The way the skin around his eyes crinkled when he smiled mesmerized her. The man even smelled good, like the ocean mixed with rum and bay leaves. She licked her lips.

"What a cute butt," Mina chirped.

Cami jerked, worried she'd been caught gawking. Mina obviously didn't have any such anxieties. She slid into the seat and beamed.

Her sisters looked amazing. Cami sniffed her own shirt, wondering if it smelled like sweat or animal stench from the night before. "Did you two invoke one of Ama's glamor charms in the bathroom?" she teased after checking for people within earshot.

Mina snickered. "Not all of us have crazy bed head."

Cami reached up. The wind this morning had frizzed an already unruly riot of curls sticking out in all the wrong ways. Why had she slept on it damp yesterday? Because she'd been at the clinic all night with no plan to flirt with a handsome man afterward. She'd worn the crumpled *Where the Wild Things Are* shirt that should've been tossed a few dozen washes ago under her scrubs. It bordered on transparent now. She winced at her fashion disaster.

"Mina, do I need to remind you we both came from work to fix your screw up?" Delia lowered her voice to a whisper for the last words. "She had to use her element to find you."

"Good." Mina crossed her arms. "It was time you were done with your ridiculous vow of magic celibacy or whatever you call it. We've already got Delia with her no-powers-unless-absolutely-necessary policy."

Cami couldn't even respond before Delia gave their sister a glacial glare. "Discretion is how we protect the family. Don't be a brat. Try a little gratitude."

"Sorry." Mina fidgeted with the straw in her water. "It's not like the rest of us can compare with your rocking the ancient fertility goddess lineage anyway. Wish I'd inherited that from Ama."

Ama had passed the Nahualli legacy on to Cami and Mina, like she had their dark hair and severe lack in the height department. Their older half-sisters Ruby and Delia looked like their mother, a tall, blonde from an old witch family but with no viable powers. The dad the siblings shared came from generations of magical Donovan women.

Delia lifted a shoulder. "Can't say I'm not a tiny bit jealous to have missed out on that DNA jackpot."

Despite what her sisters said, Cami wondered if having the magical mother lode was a curse some days. "Completely your imagination." She didn't want to talk about whatever price of her powers she might be emanating subconsciously.

Mina huffed. "Please, every guy in here can't stop staring at you."

"Shut up." Delia stretched a hand toward Cami's. The psychometric flexed her fingers briefly before making contact. Delia could read secrets and memories from connecting with skin or unfamiliar objects. She didn't touch anyone outside of family if she could avoid it because she never knew what awful surprises she might see. "Can't you see Cami's worn out? She needs refueling, but she put you first."

Mina's face crumpled, and she leaned into Cami. The loving

connection from both sisters seeped into her, taking the edge off her magic. Her price for magic was more complicated than Mina's hunger or Delia's exhaustion. She needed affection, freely given. Sometimes, sleep had to suffice.

A server brought platters loaded with food and two coffees to the table. Delia snatched her hand back to the safety of her lap, but Mina stayed close by.

Maybe they could have a quiet breakfast. Not likely with Mina.

"Our ripped waiter? He's your type." Mina drowned her pancakes with syrup and dug in. "Hot, interested, available. Did I mention hot?"

"I don't have a type," Cami said, taking the syrup before Mina used it all. She poured for Delia. One less thing for her sister to touch. "Even if I did, I'm too busy for distractions right now."

"All part of your life plan?" Mina mocked.

"Yes." The life plan had pulled Cami together after she'd escaped her abusive ex-boyfriend Neil. She might carry the invisible scars of that mistake forever, but she had a successful career and bright future as long as she stuck to the plan.

"I like the life plan." Delia wiped her mug and silverware with a spelled cloth from her purse before neatly cutting her pancakes into squares.

"Her plan is dumb." Mina shoveled in another mouthful.

"My plan gets me through." It kept her away from magical interferences like this. A little while longer and she could crash at her studio apartment for a few hours before work tonight.

Mina shook her head. "Neil," she bit out and swore.

Cami started like a scared rabbit. "Where?" She'd checked the restaurant when they walked in and had steadily scanned the crowd before she'd become preoccupied with Sam. How had she missed the one person she constantly feared running into?

"He's not here. I'd have already told him off if he was." Mina's jaw clenched.

"You and me both." Delia pulled out her phone.

Mina sipped her coffee. "I meant Neil is the reason for your life plan. You used to be flexible and fun. You rolled with the punches."

Cami flinched. Rolled with the punches, indeed. Her family didn't know the violence Neil had resorted to when she couldn't be controlled through words alone. "Things didn't go so well the last time I got off plan."

"Not your fault," Delia said, scrolling through text messages.

Cami wondered some days. She should've seen the signs. Maybe she could've avoided Neil altogether. "Still, life's safer this way." She was sure of it. She'd stick to the plan. A tattooed, tanned, devilishly handsome guy wasn't in it.

Time to change the subject to something else Mina would care about. "The woman in your slip? The one you risked danger to follow? What was she like?"

Mina picked through the fruit on the side of her plate to eat the blueberries first. "Sunny? Feisty actress in her twenties. She had platinum hair in ringlets, this pouty little Cupid's bow, and a magnetic smile. Exquisite golden goddess perfection."

Cami nodded and tried to focus on Mina. Not on Sam, who'd returned from the kitchen with her mimosa or the way his black hair was shorn short on the sides with longer curls on top. She couldn't stop staring even as he stood in front of her. The corners of his mouth tipped up. Busted.

"Can I get you anything else?" His tone implied he was offering more than a drink. She sipped through the straw and knew she should look away from him, but he simply waited there, close enough to touch. His gaze narrowed on her lips before flicking back to her eyes.

"That looks tasty," Mina said. She nudged Cami with a knee under the table. Hard.

Cami ignored the hint, savoring the drink in a luscious mouthful of yum. She hummed in satisfaction. "It's delicious. Thanks, Sam."

"No problem. Everyone doing okay this morning?"

Cami paused. Rescuing her witchy family and struggling to suppress her own powers? Not exactly an okay kind of morning. Delia's brow arched, but she had her phone to her ear, listening to messages.

"Oh, you know, *Sam*." Mina drew out his name like she'd learned a secret between them. "Sister fun. Cami loves the ocean."

What was her sister doing? Really? *Now?* When they had just talked about the frizzy mess that was her hair?

Sam angled toward her. "The beach is the best place to start a morning. Am I right?"

"I try to go every day." Blocking her powers, she could be surrounded by the source. Seeking its solace in the weeks and months after she'd gone too far. Let it know she'd made it out even if she couldn't fully come home to the ocean. "Only a half hour or so after work or before studying. Ow." Cami stopped and flinched from the swift kick to her foot.

"She paddleboards in her free time." Mina sounded like a bad dating ad.

She wanted to crawl under the table. *Sisters.* Thank goodness Delia didn't join in.

"Cool, I surf most mornings. And I work a lot." He glanced at Cami. "We have that in common."

What else could they find in common? His focus on her didn't waver, and his steady attention brought a thrill of anticipation.

"Cami can surf. You any good with a board, Sam?" Mina asked in the long silence.

"Some days." He looked back to Cami. "When the waves are right."

She almost fanned herself. All the waves between them felt right.

Delia hung up. "Mina, we gotta go in ten minutes. What's the deal with Sunny Sol?"

Cami opened her mouth to say something to her sister about getting so lost in her work she didn't notice anyone else. But Sam cut in. "Sunny Sol? The actress?"

Mina's eyes widened. "You know who she is?"

"Of course. Her café was about a mile up the road from my restaurant, and the garage where her body was found is now a morbid tourist attraction."

Delia tapped a finger against her mug. "Your restaurant?"

Sam nodded.

"Sunny Sol had a café?" Cami asked before Delia could interrogate him about his security system or finances.

"Sure." He snagged a coffee pitcher from a passing tray and topped off Delia's mug. "Sunny owned an upscale restaurant too. The building for both is only about a mile away. Arches and a hexagon center. You can't miss it."

She shifted in her seat. They'd U-turned in the parking lot of Sunny Sol's café earlier. "You know anything else about her?"

Sam looped his thumbs in his pockets. "They called her the Sunshine Sweetheart. She starred in over a hundred films before her maid found her body in her car."

"Mabel." Mina's shoulders drooped. "Her maid's name was Mabel."

"That's right." Sam stopped to answer a quick question from staff. "A lot of people believed Sunny had been murdered. Maybe by her jealous lover or her abusive ex-husband."

Cami swallowed hard. The poor woman. To have not one, but *two* scary men in her life. Cami had never recovered from Neil and what'd happened between them during their last fight. She lived in dread of him showing up again. "How'd anyone know Sunny's ex abused her?"

Sam's jaw clenched. "Because he was a jerk and a con man. Their fights became legendary in the gossip rags." It was clear from his tone the violence against the woman sickened him. "Sunny had a run of bad luck. Her fame brought death threats, break-ins, maybe even mobsters. Before her death, the newspapers ran photos of her with a gun and a dog for protection."

Cami recoiled. Sunny had tried to fight back, and she'd lost. What were Cami's chances in her own struggle? Neil had threatened everyone in her family. She hadn't been able to risk getting a dog for fear he'd use her connection with the animal against her.

"How do you know all this?" Delia aimed her question at Sam.

He shrugged one shoulder. "I research local history for my brother's screenplays."

"Any films we'd know?" She'd adopted her prosecutorial interrogation intonation.

"Deals." Cami didn't need Sam to be cross-examined in his own place. She'd wanted to know more about Sunny Sol, but not with Delia quizzing him about his qualifications.

"Maybe." He avoided the question and left the bill after Delia requested it. His gaze never left Cami. "You want anything else?"

To touch the lock of hair that had fallen onto his forehead. To see more of his tattoo. To talk about his surfing. To ask him more about Sunny Sol's abusive past. She swallowed. "No, but thank you."

Someone called to Sam from the kitchen. "Let me know if you change your mind."

"We will. We most definitely will." Mina watched him go. Cami resisted the temptation. Barely. "He was totally flirting with you."

Delia tossed money on the table. "Work needs me. I'm heading outside to call the office. Mina, make sure you've eaten enough to replenish the you-know-what." She didn't talk about magic, especially in public. "Hey, Cami, your new boyfriend didn't charge for your drink. I left him extra tip. Mina's right. He's cute. Great ass." With those words, she cut through the tables toward the door.

"Sunny Sol." Mina dropped her napkin onto her empty plate. "It's always cool to know I saw a real deal. Creepy, but cool."

Cami put her hand over Mina's as much for her own reassurance as for her sister's. "I'll help you research her later if you want." It'd give her someone to concentrate on other than Sam, and now she felt a connection to the actress.

"Oh, a murder mystery. We can be the witchy version of Sherlock Holmes and Dr. Watson." Mina speared the last strawberry from her sister's plate.

"Let's not. After all the horrifying true crime stories you've heard from Delia, you still want to play detective?"

"It'll be fun," Mina dared.

"No way. Not happening."

Sam brought a tray of to-go drink containers to their booth. "I thought you might want this."

She thanked him.

Mina chimed in, "Cami is going to help me find out what happened to Sunny Sol." She slid from the booth and glided through the crowd, never stopping to check for dangers.

Sam grinned. "Let me know if you need any help with that."

"Uh, sure." She needed to stop staring. "We really enjoyed breakfast."

"Feel free to stop by anytime."

She watched him go. She'd always been a sucker for a man with natural swagger like Sam's. His walk boasted confidence without arrogance, ease in his movements, and comfort in his own skin. That kind of man could handle anything coming his way and not miss one sexy step.

She only glanced over her shoulder once on her way to the door. Sam caught her gaze and smiled. She slid the sunglasses on and slipped outside before she lost her stitched-together control.

Vet residency, board certification, family, avoiding her ex, investigating Sunny's abusive lovers. No sexy surfer in her safe plan. No matter how charming.

CHAPTER FOUR

CAMI TYPED A QUICK SEARCH FOR INFORMATION ON SUNNY SOL'S DOOMED love life into her phone and held the door so her younger sister could climb into the back of the car.

Mina stopped with her hand braced against the car's roof. "Thanks again for coming to get me."

"Anytime," Cami promised, tearing her mind away from the abusive cycle Sunny endured. She could research it later. "Sisters don't let sisters time slip alone."

Mina snorted. "You shouldn't be going home alone after flirting with Sam." She drew out his name.

Cami ignored the comment and buckled the passenger seat belt. She yawned, ready for much needed sleep after work and magic.

"He was totally into you." Delia hurtled out of the parking lot.

"I have over two years of my residency left, a paper to write for publication, board certification tests to pass." A bad choice with her last boyfriend to get over. "I've got lots of things on the list to check off before I flirt with anyone."

"Your life plan again," Mina mocked.

"The plan to keep my career. Sam isn't in it." No gorgeous guys with swagger had made the goal list. However sad that might be.

"Maybe you should add him."

Cami seized on the dreaminess in her younger sister's voice. "Mina, is there a guy in your life you're not telling us about?"

"Why would you think that?" Mina clicked her fingernails on the window.

"Because you're not usually a matchmaker," Delia said, her gaze on the rearview mirror.

Mina sighed. "Maybe I've never met a guy good enough for either of you."

"You sure this isn't about you?" Cami knew her baby sister well enough to suspect that everything eventually came back to her, and right now, she could take sister romance drama over magic messes.

"Maybe." Mina pulled a lighter with initials engraved into the silver finish from her shorts pocket. She clutched it in her closed fist. Cami had hit a nerve if Mina needed to cling to an instrument of her own element.

"Come on, Mina." Delia headed south toward Santa Monica.

"We're just friends." Mina's fingers flexed around the lighter.

Which meant the Zippo wasn't about her element at all, but about her mystery man. "You should bring him to Ama's…"

"No." Mina's immediate answer ended any further prodding. She slid the lighter back in her pocket. "It's complicated."

"Fair enough. No more talk about men." Fine by her. She didn't want to discuss Sam. Or worse, Neil.

Delia whipped across two lanes of traffic before their exit. "You at the same animal hospital tonight? You okay getting to work later if I drop you off at your apartment?"

"Yeah." She didn't have the energy to ride her bike back from the vet clinic this morning. "It's only a couple of miles away. I can walk it."

"You'll Uber it." Delia's tone didn't invite argument as she braked for the red light. "You're still worried about Neil. For good reason." She didn't know the half of it. "And it's not safe for you to be out walking at night."

Delia pulled to a stop by a fire hydrant in front of Cami's apartment. It was the only parking spot open this close to the ocean.

Her older sister eyed the square, squat building with disapproval. "We need to move you some place safer. This dump has no security."

"Love you too, Deals." She got the lecture every time Delia came here.

Mina slid across and climbed out of the car behind her. "Thank you, Cams."

She hugged her sister tight, taking the last bit of comfort from the embrace before Mina

scrambled back into the Mini and they were gone.

Fatigue weighing her down, she trudged up the narrow, unlit staircase to the third floor. She had long since stopped trying to avoid the noisy treads. They all creaked and groaned from years of warping. The building super never fixed anything, including the railing that wobbled under her hand.

She jiggled the key in the lock and undid the extra deadbolt she had installed at her own expense. The door knob stuck. Again. Using her shoulder, she shoved against the door once, twice, three times before it gave way.

She stumbled inside and twisted the deadbolt, listening for the solid clunk of steel before she flopped onto the futon mattress. Ignoring the groan of protest from the metal frame, she snuggled into quilts spelled by her mother and inhaled the comforting scents of sage and cedar. She should wash off the stink of scared animals, dog vomit, and probably cat pee. Those were her last thoughts before she woke hours later.

The setting sun cast long, dark shadows down the blocks of shops, restaurants, and bars of downtown Santa Monica by the time she left her apartment for work. Showered and as rested as she got these days, she checked her backpack again. She must've lost her sunglasses last night. A paystub, a paid utility bill, and lip balm had gone missing from the same zippered pocket. Maybe she'd ask to switch lockers at work. She swung the backpack over her shoulder and started the trek.

Less than halfway to the clinic, the charm around her neck flared with warning of nearby danger, and she remembered why she didn't go out anymore. She picked up the pace, checking faces as she hurried along. Not a single sign of her ex's tall frame in the last glimmering threads of sunlight.

She clutched one hand on the amulet and wrapped the other around her phone. The vet clinic was only about a mile away through residential, business, and industrial neighborhoods in the mishmash beach town.

She squinted to gauge the distance if she stayed on the path carved into patches of light and obscurity by streetlamps flickering to life. Cutting through one of the smaller side streets would be quicker, but should she risk it?

The necklace burned hot in her fingers. Picking the shortcut in a split-second decision, she dashed between the buildings. She realized too late she'd picked a deserted back alley of parking garages, trash cans, and loading docks.

A pothole snagged her shoe, and she barely managed to catch herself before tripping to the hard asphalt. Twisting to see what had triggered her charm, frustration mounted. There was nothing, and yet it blazed. Her heart pounded with the old panic setting in. She ran, her feet slapping the pavement.

The alley seemed to loom even darker and longer. She glanced over her shoulder, and her imagination raced to fill in the blanks of the shadows with the terror she'd known with Neil. Loud laughter and bright neon from the busy intersection ahead beckoned like a lighthouse.

Suddenly, the amulet chilled to its normal cool metal. She stopped, brushing her hand over the charm to double check. She only felt the carvings and cuts of the insignia. An anomaly. A misfire. Nothing more.

Embarrassment of how she'd overreacted chased the relief of knowing she'd been safe all along. Rubbing a hand over her flushed neck, she exhaled and ducked into a crowded deli.

The smell of freshly baked bread filled her senses, and her stomach grumbled. She waited in line for a sandwich, ordering an Uber for the rest of her commute. No need to risk activating the amulet again.

Four hours later, the tension in her shoulders popped as she shrugged the stethoscope around her neck. She reassured a pet parent whose cat had been stabilized in the ICU before excusing herself to see an emergency patient.

She flipped through the hastily scribbled admission chart. The notes read: basset hound. Approximate age, five years. Possible intake of poisonous household cleaner. No vomiting. Noted lethargy.

She pushed into the room. A familiar face greeted her.

"Sam." She blinked. His eyes so full of easy confidence and laughter earlier today now filled with worry and surprise.

"Cami?" He stilled his hands where they'd been stroking a long basset hound on the examination table.

"Who do we have here?" She rubbed the hound's head, checking his eyes for dilation, tears, or cloudiness. The dog rewarded her with a slow tail thump.

"Bogart." Sam's words came out rushed. "He stayed today with my sister in an office suite we share above the restaurant. She took him on a walk this afternoon, and he was fine every time I checked on him. But when I went up after closing, the safety lock on the cabinet under the bathroom sink had been broken, and I found drain cleaner spilled all over the floor. His bowl was full. He never skips a meal. He's lazy, but he always comes to greet me. Tonight, he just lay there."

She checked Bogart's muzzle and mouth. "Nose bleeds? Drooling? I mean more than normal basset hound puddles."

"No."

She moved further down Bogart's body. No blistered skin. No reaction to her careful compressions of the swollen belly. "Any digestion problems you know of?"

Sam shook his head. "My sister or I have been with him on and off throughout the day. We didn't see anything out of the ordinary." Sam's hand skimmed hers where she'd buried her fingers in Bogart's soft fur and rolls. "Please. I rescued him only six months ago, but I'm telling you this is not his norm."

Cami wasn't prepared for the sensation zipping up her hand to her wrist from his one simple touch. The demands of her magic flared in response to tug at him, and she pushed it down. Bogart needed her.

She bit her lip. Her elemental power had been the reason behind her breakup with magic, not the psychic bond. The elemental power she and her sisters possessed made up the crazy difference in her witchy family compared to other magical ones, not their psychic skills.

Asking her abilities for an answer so quickly after using her element would bring a higher toll for her to pay later, but it might save Bogart an unnecessary pumping of his stomach.

"Temperature?" she asked the vet tech who opened the door.

"Normal," he answered before gathering supplies and leaving again.

Cami plugged the tips of her stethoscope into her ears to block out the world more than anything else. She tugged the diaphragm down Bogart's torso. The dog's heart bumped in a steady beat. She pulsed one thread of magic into Bogart, focusing solely on him and not his owner.

Sorry about the bad touch with the thermometer, Bogie. I can call you Bogie, right?

The hound lifted his head and raised his eyes to hers. He sent anxiety and discomfort down the line, but no pain.

"Sam, I'm going to need you to stay calm so Bogart can do the same." She slipped the stethoscope out of her ears. Kneading Bogart's belly, she asked, "How did you know Bogart chose you when you adopted him?"

He rubbed the back of his neck. "My sister Lottie had been nagging me about living alone so I went to an adoption fair. Bogart came right to me. With his sad eyes, I couldn't leave him there. He was lonely." The way Sam twisted his last word, Cami wondered if he was only talking about the dog. "He already had a name from my favorite time period. He's a partially deaf, drooling goofball, but we're a perfect match. He loves people. I'm sure he would appreciate a visit from a pretty girl."

Cami jerked her head, breaking the connection with Bogart for a second. Returning her attention fully to Bogart, she listened for answers to silent questions. "Sam, any strain when Bogart's out doing his business?"

Sam's forehead wrinkled. "No. Although he hasn't been going as often now you mention it."

Cami smoothed a hand down the dog, checking one more time. She pinched a roll of fur, counting the seconds it took to fall into place. "Constipated, Bogart? Because you didn't lick any of the bad stuff." The dog whined. "Yeah, buddy. I know you don't feel good. Some pup's been indulging in too many treats and not enough water. Let's get you hydrated."

"He's okay?" Bogart bumped her hand for more petting and crawled to lay his head against her breasts. Sam huffed. "I guess Bogart's fine if he's flirting. He beat me to it."

Bogart licked her hand. *Gah,* one charming comment from Sam, and she'd lost her connection. She cleared her throat.

"Let me take him in the back to see if he'll drink or if we need to give him fluids. I'll try a simple medication once you approve the cost. Let's keep treatment as straightforward as possible. I'd like to order a blood panel to rule out any underlying issues. I can recommend a probiotic and diet to help in the future, and he'll need a follow-up with his regular vet."

"Do you make house calls? Bogart hates the vet, and it's obvious he adores you." Sam gestured to where the dog rubbed against her. "Or do you work another night? We can come back and see you?" He blew out a breath. "This has to be the least sexy way ever to meet up with a woman I already wanted to ask on a date."

The door opened, cutting off any response she might've made. The tech helped her get Bogart into the back for treatment after Sam signed off on the costs and chose to wait rather than leave Bogart behind.

She didn't see Sam again for almost two hours. She treated other animals and assisted in a minor surgery in the meantime, but Bogart's problem had been cured. He was happy, healthy, and ready to go.

"All right, Bogie. Let's get you back to Sam." *He's probably every bit as much of a heartbreaker as you are.*

The basset hound trudged along beside her, his ears swinging low enough to almost skim the floor. She took a deep steadying breath before pushing open the door.

Sam was asleep on the bench, his head slumped against the wall. Cami sighed and looked down at Bogart. She scratched the rolls of furry flesh at his neck. She needed to focus on the dog and not his handsome owner. Even one who made her catch her breath and forget everything else when he looked at her. She'd never felt a spark like this. It was enticing. And dangerous.

His tight shirt showed off the tattoo she'd seen edging out his sleeve earlier. There was the curl of another on his left bicep. It was artwork, a tribal pattern with clean lines and curves. She had to stop staring at him.

She shut the door, and Sam woke. He stretched and rubbed his sleepy eyes. "Sorry. Long day."

"Bogart is good to go for now." The dog sagged against her legs. She tapped on the computer to bring up his records. "No more poking and prodding tonight."

Sam reached for the leash. "Listen, I didn't mean to freak you out earlier."

"With what?" Rolling a stool up to the screen, she clicked through the blood work results. Bogart had no other issues she could find.

"However awful the reason I got to see you again, I'm glad I did. I wanted to ask you on a date this morning."

She swiveled to face him.

Sam scratched his jaw. "But the restaurant is my place of business." He looked around the office. "And now I'm hitting on you in your place of business. Great."

Even his awkwardness was charming. "Are you asking me out?"

He ruffled fingers through his messy hair. "Yeah. I know it's bad form." He dipped his head toward Bogart. "And with the most unattractive, uncool timing possible. I swear I'm not usually this weird." He spoke before she could respond. "What if I helped you look into Sunny Sol? Like your sister talked about earlier."

Cami petted Bogart, who bumped against her leg. "How so?"

He gave a lopsided grin. "I've got contacts in the industry. I can get you into private collections to research her. I don't know if you'd find anything new after this long, but I'm decent at digging through old resources. If you're interested in a study date."

If Cami could learn from Sunny's history of abusive and controlling relationships, it'd be worth a few hours of research. Especially if it'd prevent her repeating a bad choice, as Sunny apparently had. Plus, it might keep Mina from time slipping alone again on ground subject to rockslides.

Sam was offering her a chance to figure out who'd killed Sunny. Maybe she could discover if it'd been Sunny's violent ex catching up with her or something less sinister. With the hot surfer guy who had an adorable dog, no less.

"You're on."

CHAPTER FIVE

Sam circled the block where he'd agreed to meet Cami tonight for their first date. A research field trip still counted as a date, right? He'd called in favors to get private after-hours access to the collections library.

"To impress a girl?" Marilyn, the librarian, had asked him.

Yes, actually. It'd be worth it if Cami would go out with him again.

She'd been amazing with Bogart—kind, efficient, and professional when he'd been so damn worried about the basset. Usually, Bogart couldn't wait to bolt from the vet's office, but Sam almost had to drag the dog away from Cami. Bribes and promises of belly rubs had done no good. His dog had wanted to stay. So he'd finally picked Bogart up and carried him to the truck.

Sam's beat-up Land Cruiser was perfect for surf boards and Bogart to drool out the window, but maybe not for first dates. He glanced at the taped passenger seat and surfing gear in the back. Too late to worry about those things now.

He spotted Cami coming out of a 1950's apartment building with peeling retro lettering on the front and broken blinds in the windows. She strode down steps to the sidewalk in jeans, pink Converse sneakers, and another vintage graphic shirt. His memory hadn't exaggerated her curves in the least. She walked with purpose, turning her head back and forth. She'd scanned his restaurant the same way two days ago. Who was she looking for?

He rolled down the window and called her name. She jerked her gaze in his direction and grabbed for the chain around her neck. When their gazes met, her face softened, and her hand fell to her side. Sam pulled into a loading zone and parked.

Rounding the truck, he pulled open the passenger door for her and swiped at the drool stains along the side.

She grinned. Damn, she did have dimples. They cut deep divots in her cheeks. He wanted to stretch out a finger and trace those adorable dents.

"Bogart's favorite place to ride?" She touched the back passenger door.

"How'd you guess?"

Her eyes had been light brown, almost whiskey-colored the other night at the clinic before she'd treated Bogart. They'd glowed golden again afterward. Now, they were back to whiskey with hints of gold.

Her smile stretched wider.

"What?" She brushed a hand along her cheek before swiping a curl behind her ear. "What is it?"

"You've got dimples."

She tipped her head to the right. "Slept on buttons, my Gigi tells me. My grandma."

He offered a hand to boost her into the truck. She laced her fingers in his, and he resisted the urge to steal a taste of those knuckles. This close she smelled like crème brûlée. "Hope you don't mind a drive tonight. The GPS says the ten miles to Beverly Hills will take about forty-five minutes."

"Nice digs for a library," she said when he climbed into the driver's seat. "Those the private resources you mentioned?"

He reversed and eased into the street. "It's the best place to start a search for any information on past film stars. Did you eat tonight?"

She looked out the window toward the ocean. "No, I overslept after another long shift."

He'd have to feed her often. "I know a few places near the library to grab something."

She tugged on the hem of her shirt. "Nothing too fancy. I should've dressed for dinner instead of a study session."

"Nothing fancy." The perfect counter for comfort food was within walking distance of the library. "Your *Reading Rainbow* shirt's cool."

She narrowed her eyes. "My sisters hate it."

"What?" He disagreed. "That show had class. And the host was on Star Trek."

She grinned a bright cheerful sunbeam of a smile and nodded. "Vet school didn't call for many formal outfits. Most of my old clothes are still at my mom's house in South Pasadena."

She'd looked amazing in scrubs with paw prints and animal cartoons. He might have needed resuscitation and a new plan if she'd dressed up for their date tonight.

An hour drive and a demolished pizza later, the two strolled side-by-side through the courtyard leading to the library. Palm trees swayed before the large arched entrance with its round stained glass artwork, and a tower shot up out of the terra cotta roof. Cami moved closer to him as she took in the impressive façade.

"Was this a Spanish mission?" Her voice filled with the awe of facing a historic ecclesiastical site.

Sam chuckled. "It was the old water pumping station, actually."

She stopped mid-step. "But it's amazing."

"Wait 'til you see the inside." He trailed a finger down her arm to her wrist, traced the delicate coolness of her palm, and was rewarded when she slid her hand into his. He squeezed once before tugging her through the doors into the archive's formal lobby and upstairs. After explaining cell phones weren't allowed in the collections, he stopped to stash their phones, her wristlet, and his keys in a locker. He led her into the dim, empty reading room.

"Are they closed?" she asked in a hushed voice, sliding closer to him.

"Almost. No need to whisper." A beautiful woman dressed in a skirt, cardigan set, and double strand of pearls approached.

Marilyn had nailed the quintessential librarian look a decade ago.

She flipped a switch and light flooded the high bright arches of the ceiling. Sam kept his left hand in Cami's as he reached to pull Marilyn into a hug with the other.

"Privileges of the Corraza family being huge patrons of the foundation." Marilyn patted Sam's shoulder with sisterly affection. "Thanks to your father and asshole brother." She cast an appraising glance over Cami. "So you're the woman he wants to impress with private access?"

Cami didn't respond, but her grip tightened on his fingers.

"Marilyn." Sam shot the woman a look and drew Cami farther along the rows of tables and chairs lined with stacks on each side.

Cami's chin hitched upward a fraction, but Marilyn only returned a knowing smile.

"Smart woman, then. Kimmy, right?"

"Cami. Short for Camellia." She stood straighter.

The way she said her full name in an accent heavier than her usual Spanish-tinted lilt, with a take-charge tone, had Sam hoping she would repeat it. Or say anything, anything at all in the same strong, superior way.

"I can see we will be friends." Marilyn ran her hand along the glass covering movie memorabilia in the center showcase. "I hear you're interested in Sunny Sol's life and death. How would you like to begin?"

When Cami didn't respond right away, Sam answered, "We'll start with Sol's biographical file, if you have it. Periodicals of the time. *Photoplay, Silver Screen,* maybe *Screenplay.* Any photographs relating to her life and death." He studied the manuscripts and correspondence displayed with care under glass throughout the reading room. This place had earned its role as the world's premier movie research library. "Perhaps we can begin with the aftermath of her death and work backwards. Whatever Cami would like to do."

"Any screenplays?" Marilyn asked, gesturing toward back rooms he knew shelved thousands of scripts.

"You have scripts here? Originals?" Cami hovered above costume sketches so old the paper had started to shear at the edges.

Marilyn's noncommittal smile returned, but it seemed more

reassuring now. "We house over eighty thousand screenplays, forty thousand movie posters, and ten million photographs. If you're looking for movie star history, you've come to the right place."

"Can we start with Sunny Sol's love life after her move to Los Angeles and work forward to her death?" Cami sounded like she'd asked for the impossible. Sam wanted to tell her Marilyn specialized in difficult research missions. But why work forward?

Marilyn gave them a brisk nod. "Let me lock the doors downstairs, and I will head back to archives. Wait here. I won't be long. I took the liberty of running a general search in advance." She glowered at Sam. "Don't let him touch anything."

Cami spun on him as soon as Marilyn had gone. "What's she mean by that?"

Sam focused on the small circles his thumb traced on her hand. She hadn't pulled away. "Marilyn's known my family a long time. She dated my older brother, but don't tell her I mentioned it." He kept his answer evasive about his own history. Discussing his family was tricky business and a risk he'd known when he brought her here. "Just you and your two sisters in your family?"

She wandered along the framed movie posters. "There are five us of all together. Mina's the baby. Our older siblings are technically half-siblings. Same dad. Different mom." She stopped before artwork depicting Sunny Sol with the Marx brothers. Another showed the actress in a film called *Scoria*.

"You met Mina and Delia. Mina studies at USC. Delia is a deputy district attorney. Ruby, our oldest sister, works as a paramedic and has the most adorable baby girl. And my half-brother John, he..well...he's John." Her voice trailed off. He recognized the tone she'd taken when she mentioned her half-brother. He used the same to talk about most of his childhood. She raised her head to look up at him. "You mentioned a writer brother and a sister who helped you get Bogart?"

"Older brother Joe writes for television and movies. Baby sister Lottie is a personal stylist. She works mainly in show business. She's the best of us." Sam didn't want to talk about his parents. It'd lead to questions he wouldn't, or couldn't, answer. "Do you have a boyfriend?"

Her eyes widened. "No." She pulled her hand away. "I wouldn't be a very good girlfriend if I was, since I'm here with you. Do you have a girlfriend?"

A corner of his mouth twitched. "Not unless you're volunteering." He moved to the stacks, running his fingers along the spines of the volumes.

Cami hummed and she reached toward the stacks but stopped. "Are we allowed to touch the books?"

Sam laughed at her avoidance. "Even Marilyn will let you handle the books. She's probably read them all."

"I have." Marilyn's voice cut around the edge of the bookcase.

"God, Marilyn. Ninja much?" Sam grumbled. Her skinny heels made no noise on the carpet. He rushed to take two large boxes from her.

"Put those on the tables." Marilyn followed along to direct. "Have a seat, Cami. I'll show you what I've got." She spread the contents over the table. "Sam, grab legal pads and pencils from the first case. How much do you two already know about Sunny Sol?"

Sam would bet they didn't know half as much about her as Marilyn did. "She died at age twenty-seven." He listed off facts as he fetched items at Marilyn's direction. "Discovered Monday morning in her married lover's garage, dead in her convertible. A Packard Victoria. Awesome badass car with a V12 engine. The maid told the cops Sunny had worn the same clothes she was found in to a party across town at the Frontero Saturday night."

Marilyn stopped unpacking the files long enough to remark, "Read all that on Wikipedia, did you? So you know an infinitesimal bit about the maid's discovery of Sol's body, but nothing more substantial?" She arched a brow. "Cami, anything to add?"

Cami straightened in her chair like she'd been volunteered for a pop quiz in junior high. She touched the gold chain at her neck, and Sam's focus snapped to the delicate hollow of her throat. He could barely concentrate on what she said until she mentioned an autopsy report.

"Wait. You read Sunny Sol's coroner's report?"

Cami sharpened a pencil Marilyn had offered. "Of course. It's available free online along with crime scene and autopsy photos, which I found disturbing but unsurprising. The coroner ruled Sunny's death to be accidental carbon monoxide poisoning. They listed her under the name of her ex-husband. I dug up gossip about their short, ill-fated marriage and how he continued to abuse other women after Sunny died." She blew on the tip of the pencil, and he couldn't stop looking at her puckered lips. "I couldn't get to sleep after my last shift, so I spent some time researching."

Marilyn tapped a stack against the table to form another straight row in her neat, orderly piles. "Well done, Cami. We have an official copy of the death certificate here as well. I'll give you my card and a list of easily purchased quick references before you go. No library resources can be removed at any time." She stopped to glare at Sam before turning to Cami. "But you are always welcome back."

She finished organizing the documents. "Here's what I've pulled." She started from the left side and worked her way across. "Biographical file, magazine articles, press sheets, and photographs. I found one large special collection with multiple clippings of her death and the fallout afterward. That would take days to sort through, so I didn't bring it tonight."

She rapped the table sharply next to a smaller stack she'd placed in front of Cami. "I also retrieved the file on Joseph Corraza, Sam's brother, in case you want to know more about what you're getting into with their family."

Cami snickered.

Sam's jaw clenched. "Bye, Marilyn. We can take it from here."

She slid a sly glance between the two of them. "I'm sure you can. I'll be in my office with my blinds closed until you're ready to go." Marilyn stalked away on those razor-thin heels. "Don't make me check your pockets when you leave, Sam."

CHAPTER SIX

"I'D RATHER NOT TALK ABOUT MARILYN'S ISSUES." OR HIS, FOR THAT matter. He didn't thank Marilyn for alluding to them, either.

Cami's laugh floated light and effervescent, like bubbles from the champagne he served at his restaurant. He raised a hand. "Let's focus on Sunny. Where do you want to start?"

Cami scooted closer. "I'll take the biographical file." She plucked an accordion file from the folder box and rifled through the contents.

"All right. I'll go through the photographs." He opened the first envelope and flipped through images, stopping to read the descriptions. He tried to focus, but after a few minutes of watching her play with the chain on her neck, he couldn't resist breaking the silence.

"I like your necklace."

She shuffled to another page. "Thanks. My mother gave it to me."

"You get your good looks from her?"

"Wow." She looked at him. "What a pickup line."

Her deadpan tone and poker face revealed nothing. "Did it work?"

She gave a crooked half smile. "I thought you were going through old photographs?"

"I can study pictures and flirt at the same time. So far all we've got are film stills and promo photos." He turned another staged image over to underscore the point.

"Talented."

"I multitask." He stopped at the next picture of Sunny Sol, Bing Crosby, and celebrities in what looked like the Brown Derby based on the caricature drawings on the walls.

Cami leaned closer. "Who's the other actress?"

"Joan Bennett." Sam had watched enough film noir period movies and researched more than enough Hollywood scandals to recognize her. The label on the back of the photograph read: "Cast of *Three for Tomorrow*, fall 1933."

"Only months before Sunny died." She peered over his shoulder. "The Brown Derby Hollywood," she read out loud.

"It was the place to be seen and cut deals." He held the photo closer, squinting to see who might be in the background. "Probably a planned photo op to boost sales with the stars all dressed up."

He turned to ask Cami about her research, and her face was inches from his.

His gaze lowered to her mouth. A few minutes alone with her, and he was ready to lean in for a taste. The woman was the embodiment of temptation. He pulled back and looked anywhere but her lips.

He focused his attention on the photograph and cleared his throat. "Hey, you see this guy in the background?" He pointed to the booth behind and to the right of the one occupied by Sunny's party.

Cami hummed again, and it shot straight through him. "The man in the hat. Didn't all men wear suits and hats back then? Or at least they do in the movies."

"Yeah." He tapped the table. "But most didn't indoors. I recognize his profile."

She set aside her own paperwork. "Who do you think it is?"

Sam bit the inside of his cheek while he tried to think around his distraction. "He was part of the Davino crime family. They ran illegal gambling businesses."

"The police or maybe the press speculated Sunny's business was targeted by gangsters for illegal gambling, but Sunny refused to allow it." She sounded breathless with the possibility of a connection. He got it. The legend-meets-reality intersections of history never failed to thrill him. "Are there pictures of Sunny's café?"

Her breath tickled his ear. He sorted through the photographs until he found images of Sunny's restaurant in its prime.

"What's on the door?" She pointed to the etching on the right side. "Coral's? Wait, I just saw that word in a logo." She reached into the accordion file, spreading clippings and printouts. "Here it is. Sunny Sol's Seabreeze Café delights beachgoers and film fans alike, but the true recognition of success or fame is to receive an invitation to the exclusive Coral's Restaurant upstairs. Named for Coral Elton, Paul Price's wife. Her real name was Flora, I think." She skipped further down. "Sunny lived in an apartment above the café, adjacent to Paul Price's with only a sliding door separating the two flats."

"Scandal." Sam knew all about old celebrity scandals. "Hollywood was coming out of the notoriety of the 1920s. A married washed-up director and a comedy sweetheart living together down the hill from the wedded couple's mansion? That'd have been fodder for the press. Especially if Paul Price's wife had pushed it instead of agreeing to a three-way partnership in owning the restaurant."

Cami ran a finger down the list Marilyn had given them. "None of these titles and summaries even mention a wife. Maybe there's more in the newspaper articles."

He shrugged. "From what I remember she was a silent film star who couldn't make it once the pictures became talkies."

She wrote down the name on her list of topics.

"Might be a lot of research rabbit holes you'll be going down. Several will have dead ends." He tapped the handwritten note above Elton's name where she had scrawled, *Visit the location of the restaurant, exterior and environments.* "I'm down for this field trip. Tours of old restaurant layouts help remind me of the conveniences we've got now in the kitchens."

He picked up a laminated trifold Cami had put with the clipping on Coral's. "Is this Sunny's menu? She signed it. Good marketing strategy. Clean art deco design. Decent upscale entrée choices."

"You thinking of stealing some of the dishes for your own restaurant?" The teasing in her voice drew him in.

"Maybe. I could do a theme night. Offer old Hollywood classics and end-of-Prohibition-era cocktails. Host a costume contest. Especially if you would show up in something like this." He flashed a photograph of Sunny in an expensive satin pantsuit with gossamer sleeves.

"What is she wearing?" Cami leaned closer, leaving a trail of her sweet scent.

"Hostess pajamas." Sam assured her he hadn't made up the description when she stared in disbelief. "Those ladies knew how to lounge." He winked. "You'd always come out on top at my restaurant in some satin and silk."

"You're awful." She crumpled a scribbled page from the notebook and tossed it at him. He smoothed the sheet to find a long list of phrases.

"This your first plan of attack?" Similar to the one she worked on now, the prior draft lacked the organizational columns and boxes.

"Yeah." She hovered her fingers above paper-clipped bunches of news articles. "There's so much information here. I'm not sure where to start."

He nodded. Sunny Sol had led a busy twenty-seven years. "Her death has three possibilities—accidental like the coroners said, suicide, or murder. Why did you want to begin with the men in Sunny's life?"

She glanced away. "Delia, my DA sister, says to initiate a murder investigation with people closest to the victim. Sure, things can happen between strangers, but most of the time, crimes come from within the family or romantic relationships. If Sunny was murdered, we should start with those close to her."

He pointed at squiggled notations along her margin. "What's SS? Are we going sailing for one of our investigative trips?"

"No." She clucked her tongue. "It stands for spreadsheet. I need to organize those topics in spreadsheets to keep it all together." When he simply stared at her, she continued, "Don't you have a similar organizational strategy when you research time periods for your brother's screenplays?"

"Hardly. I read through all the sources I can find and paint a big picture for Joe, filling in small details wherever I need throughout the script to keep the plot moving and story authentic. History isn't statistics and numbers. It's real life people, the random stuff happening to them, and how they deal with it." He knew he should tone down the excitement and gestures, especially on a first date, but history was his passion.

She lowered her brows. "But there's a reason for the saying 'history repeats itself.' So I'm trying to pinpoint the patterns and repetitions in Sunny's history. Chances are she came from an abusive paternal relationship, which increased her likelihood of choosing abusers as romantic partners. If her death involved foul play, starting with the men in her family makes sense."

He read over her list again, noting how methodical and detailed she'd been. "All right. I'll take on the tangled history. You sort the data. Maybe together we can come up with some theories."

She pushed a stack of newspaper articles toward him. "These all relate to violence, death threats, even break-ins Sunny suffered because of her fame. One article talks about a fight where she got punched at the restaurant by her lover a week before her death because he'd gotten jealous when her ex-husband came to the café."

"Sounds like a good place to start." He gathered the articles. "We can make copies of these to take with us."

She added the photograph from the Brown Derby. "This stood out to you. It could be important somehow. I'll tag anything else we might use since we can't stay here all night."

"I'll take you home before it gets too late."

"Do you work tomorrow morning?"

"Yeah." He picked up a photo of the Frontero, the nightclub where Sunny attended her last party. "I hope to get a few minutes to surf before the breakfast crowd. You?"

She shook her head. "I'm up all night again. I'll sleep and study tomorrow before my shift."

"What are you studying for? You're already a vet."

She drummed the eraser against the table and paged through newspaper articles. "I'm completing a three-year residency to become board certified in my specialty. I have to take and pass the exam as well as publish in a scientific journal."

"Determined to become the top in your field?" He liked the way she reached for even more than she'd already accomplished. She ducked away from his appreciative scrutiny. "What?"

"Mina warned me not to discuss my life plan on a date. She said my checklists scare people off."

He frowned. Cami had purpose. She helped animals like Bogart, and she wanted to be the best at it. How the hell could her drive be anything but a turn on? "What are you supposed to do? Leave it all to luck?"

She beamed at him. "Exactly."

"Don't get me wrong. Getting lucky is incomparable." He could've groaned at how cheesy the line sounded now he'd said it, but a pink tint started at her neck and crept over her cheeks. That blush was hot. He'd have to make her do that again.

She hid behind a curtain of curls. The way she shuffled the clippings in a sudden jumble told him he'd ruined her concentration.

He needed to give her some space before he crossed the line from likeable goofball into stupid territory. "I'm going to make copies. You good?"

Her curls bounced in what he'd take as an affirmative. He bit back a grin. Apparently, he got to her the same way she got to him. He'd never imagined an enjoyable research date, but damn if he wasn't having fun. He was grinning like an idiot by the time he reached the copy machine.

She was beautiful with tiny brown freckles scattered across her face and the graceful way her head tipped when she was thinking or planning. Which must be all the freaking time since she could even make spreadsheets sound seductive. She'd twisted toward his chair with her pink Converse propped on the rung. Cami was cute and sexy, all in one clever package.

He couldn't wait to see her on a surfboard. Would she play it safe or tackle rough waters? Of course, those thoughts led to wondering how her curves would fill out a bikini. He pressed the copy button a little harder than he'd meant to. He needed to take this slow. She mattered.

Maybe for their next date, they could skip the fancy dinner for a picnic at the ocean, and he could get a glimpse of her in the bikini like he'd been fantasizing.

"Sam."

Shit, he hadn't shared the fantasy aloud, but perhaps his expression had given him away. "Huh?"

"Did you hear something?" She sat upright, staring at the staircase where they'd come in.

"No." The machine clacked and whirred as it spat out multiple pages. He strained to hear anything in the silence that followed. "What'd it sound like?"

"Almost like someone else was downstairs." She chewed on her bottom lip.

"It's probably Marilyn." The only sound he could hear was the air conditioner kicking on.

She went back to her research while he finished making copies. He laid the stack at the end of the table.

She pointed to the last photograph he'd set aside. "What's this?"

"The Frontero on Sunset. Sunny was last seen by her chauffeur after he drove her home from a party there." He studied the long building, a cross between a roadhouse restaurant and a barn. The beaming art déco font of its sign looked out of place. "I know The Front from screenplay research. It was a swank nightclub with an eternal line at the velvet rope, tuxedoed attendants, and a formal ballroom."

He ignored the vague description scrawled beneath. "The Front went bankrupt in the late 1930s after the owner sold to Alan Knapp. Alan was a seriously bad guy. He ran the Cosmo Club, an illegal gambling den in Glendale. Other than that? The man was an enigma. When a new political regime came into power in '38, Alan got shut out, and The Front got shut down."

"Why do you know so much about bad boys and scandals?" She wrinkled her nose in an adorable grin. "It's kind of hot."

"Yeah?" He checked to see if she was teasing, but watching her lips move, all he could do was imagine what they'd feel like on his.

He hesitated. What was it about her that made him doubt himself? Most women moved along when they saw he was already married to the restaurant. But Cami was different. She had her own ambition.

He brushed his knuckles over her soft cheek before skimming them along her jaw. She shivered, and he grinned. He wondered if she tasted as sweet as she smelled, but he didn't want to scare her off.

All he'd thought about this week were her golden eyes, her scent, and the pull she had on him. He'd never experienced a connection on this base level to anyone or anything other than the ocean. It was crazy how she made him think of the call of waves and swells.

She stretched her fingers to brush the nape of his neck. Sam stilled with every single nerve focused on that delicate touch. He almost lost control when she grinned a mischievous, sly smile and a dimple flashed. His breath caught as she pressed her lips to his and quickly deepened the kiss.

He'd been wrong about her. She might be reserved and serene on the surface, but her passion was wild and bewitching. She was anything but the calm cool waters he'd expected. She was a riptide. Sam's last coherent thought was how he'd be happy to drown in her before need took over.

CHAPTER SEVEN

CAMI SLID HER FINGERS INTO THE CLIPPED HAIR AT THE NAPE OF SAM'S neck, skimming upward to sink into his curls. Sudden hot desire flashed across her senses. She touched her tongue to his bottom lip and melted at his groan. He nudged her mouth open to tangle his tongue with hers. She smiled and nipped at him until she breathed in the smell of ocean air.

For a second, she panicked. Had she lost control in kissing Sam and drawn on her power?

She inhaled. This wasn't her magic. It was Sam, his scent of saltwater mixed with that spicy alcohol hint she'd caught at the restaurant when he was near. It was dark, delicious, and intoxicating. She needed more.

She reached for his shoulders to tug him closer and got distracted by the muscles there. She ignored the quick pulse of heat at the base of her neck. All she wanted to feel was more of Sam. She pressed against him and clutched his shirt.

A door slammed somewhere in the building. He tore his lips away and lay his forehead against hers. Cami's mouth trembled at the loss of his and the intensity of this newfound passion.

He lifted his head. "Was that part of the research? If it was, sign me up."

Cami suspected from the roughness of his voice she'd gotten to him as much as he'd consumed her. She wanted to do that again as often as she could. His kiss was sexy and tempting, yet tender and giving all at the same time. There'd been an underlying need for more than physical contact. The sheer hunger in his kiss had been enough to make her crazy. She hummed over the seductive mixture and licked her lips for one last taste.

Sam narrowed his eyes on her mouth, his gaze hot with promise. "If you don't stop looking at me like that, we are never going to be allowed back here again."

Cami swallowed. She had to quit replaying the kiss over and over in her mind. *Spreadsheets, lists, dead actress, abusive ex.* The last sobered her.

"Right. Back to research." She picked up her pencil, ignoring the fact she couldn't write a legible sentence the way her hands shook to get back on Sam's skin, in his hair, down his body. She picked a crisp copy sheet off the top and skimmed the page.

"Someone broke into Sunny's home less than six months before her death. They ransacked and burglarized the place. The papers reported it along with her full home address so anyone could find her. That's why she moved into the apartment above the café."

For Sunny to have someone paw through intimate belongings in her own home? Supposedly the woman's refuge from the world after she'd escaped one bad relationship? The invasion of the actress's privacy sickened her, and she fought the urge to rub her knotted stomach. Her sister's doubts about her apartment's lack of security echoed in her head.

Sam reached for her shoulder. "Hey, it's awful, but unfortunately, burglars targeted celebrities and the rich. The cops couldn't or wouldn't do much about it back then."

"The articles say she had no privacy at all above the café. People could simply walk upstairs and be inside her rooms. That's horrifying."

"Yeah, it is. It's important in the restaurant business to separate work from home. Or you never leave the job."

His home? Where was it? Here she'd been kissing him, and she knew almost nothing about him except he owned a restaurant and adored his rescue dog. "Where's home for you?"

He pressed his lips together. "My apartment?"

"Yeah." Although, now she wondered what home he'd been thinking of.

He relaxed, his features open again. "Santa Monica. Only about a mile from your place." He slid his warm touch from her shoulder to her waist. She could feel the press of each finger against her soft shirt and imagined what it would be like if he slipped his hand beneath it to touch her sensitive bare skin.

With reckless curiosity, she seized the file on his family.

He arched a brow over those dark eyes. "Careful. That's like Pandora's box. Once you know more about my family, you may not like me."

He had no idea how much of her own family she hid. *By the way, I come from a long line of matriarchal dynasties of magic on both sides of my family tree because power matches in arranged marriages still rule the witch world.*

Risking his scrutiny, she pulled a random article from the paper slips and frowned when she realized she held an obituary. "Akira Hiroyo Abrams. Famed botanist, survivor of internment camp during World War II."

"My maternal grandmother." His even and quiet voice held no trace of sadness.

"I'm so sorry." She gripped the paper. Pandora's box, indeed.

He hitched a shoulder. "She never liked me very much."

Cami glanced back to the article. "She is survived by her two children, two grandsons…"

"Wait. They got it wrong. My mom's an only child."

She continued reading. "Aretta Abrams Corraza and Michi 'Mitch' Abrams."

Sam stiffened. "Michi? Mitch?"

Had the paper made a mistake? Or worse, given his reaction, did Sam not know his own family? He took the clipping from her hand.

"I don't understand." He flipped to the paper-clipped photograph.

A ringing alarm screamed from downstairs. Cami jumped.

"You okay?" He slid his fingers along her arm, pulling her closer.

She nodded although her heart had kicked into a frantic beat. She reached for her phone only to remember he had locked it with his when they came into the reading room.

"I'm going down to check it out. Let Marilyn know when she comes through." He raced for the entrance.

She rushed after him.

"Stay here." He told her, raising a hand. "I'll be right back. I promise." Before she could argue, he was gone. Cami dashed back to the table for the key to the locker with her phone, grabbing the articles Sam had copied along the way. She shoved those under her arm and ran for the lockers at the top of the stairs.

She fumbled with the lock, but her hand shook so badly she dropped the key twice. When the locker finally opened, she snagged their things from inside. The amulet on her necklace flared.

"Sam?"

The lights in the library suddenly cut out, leaving her in complete darkness. Cami froze. A wake-the-dead shriek tore through the room, interrupted by a mechanical voice announcing "fire" and urging all occupants to please move to the nearest exit. A bright strobe flashed.

She could hear glass breaking downstairs. Her warning charm pulsed heat in a steady rhythm eerily in time with the flashing red lights.

"Sam?" Her voice echoed back.

A rush of footsteps from behind had her spinning to face her attacker. Wishing for a weapon or at least better lighting to run, she shifted the papers and phones to one hand so she could grip the keys in the other. She'd raised a jagged edge when Marilyn strode around the corner, a beaming flashlight in one hand and a small fire extinguisher in the other.

"Where's Sam?" The woman never missed a step.

"Downstairs." Cami ran beside her.

"Of course he is," Marilyn muttered under the piercing alarm.

They hurried down. Cami breathed a sigh of relief when Sam sprinted up the steps, scaling two at a time. He grabbed the fire extinguisher before running back down. They caught up to him as he pulled the pin on the extinguisher, aimed it at the burning contents of a tall, metal trashcan, and shot a steady stream into the flames.

Cami scanned the rest of the lobby under the glare of the strobe light. It was empty. She'd expected as much when her charm cooled. The back door stood open. Someone had vandalized the elegant room, shattering a glass display and throwing garbage on the floor, the shelves, even the walls.

Marilyn whipped out a cell phone, and her fingers flew over the screen. The deafening alarm stopped, leaving only the rhythmic blinding flash that gave the room the look of a garish night club or, worse, a horror movie.

Sam lowered the extinguisher nozzle and waved away the fumes. "You two okay?"

Cami opened her mouth to answer, but her throat went dry with the acrid taste.

"What did you see?" Marilyn was all business.

Sam dropped the extinguisher to his side. "Whoever it was must've heard me coming. By the time I got down here, they took off. I didn't chase after because, you know, fire." He ran a hand down Cami's arm, seeming to need the contact as much as she did.

"Police and the fire department are on their way." Marilyn toed a strewn ream of paper with her pump. "Sorry, you guys will be stuck here a while longer."

After Cami and Sam gave separate statements, the police released them to leave. They headed to the parking garage where they'd left his truck, Sam wrapped his strong hand around hers. His hold brought comfort. More distracting, a spark thrummed beneath the strength, an unspoken awareness with the silent question of what comes next even beneath the drama of the night.

"Some first date." Sam squeezed her hand. "I mean the kiss was awesome, but it certainly didn't end the way I'd hoped." He glanced her way, and a curl fell in his face. Part of her wanted to mess it again when he thrust it back into the tangle. "I'm guessing you won't be interested in a second."

She reached the fingers of her free hand to brush ash and powder from his dark hair. "Why wouldn't I be interested in a second?"

He flashed an incredulous grin. "Between my dog almost getting poisoned and tonight's excitement, I've got to have the worst streak of bad luck when I come around you."

She frowned, thinking of the way her charm had flared the first day she'd met him, only hours after she'd been at the restaurant and before he brought Bogart into the clinic. Then again, it'd signaled danger tonight. Maybe Sam wasn't the one with bad luck. Maybe it was her.

He must've read her pinched brows to mean she'd agreed with his theory. He dropped his hold on her hand, and the cool night air chilled her palm where his skin had been seconds before.

She fought the urge to reach for him again. "A second date, huh?"

His sure step slowed. "Yeah."

"With more kissing?"

The corner of his mouth kicked up in invitation. She wanted to nip the edge and see how the amused half-grin tasted.

"Definitely more kissing." He brushed his lips over hers.

"Deal." She bumped into his body, hoping to come off more playful than awkward. She didn't have much experience with flirting. She'd been too serious about her studies at school and her magic at home. In college, Neil had pressed her for a date and then a relationship until she found she hadn't said yes to any of it, but she hadn't openly refused either.

She glanced over her shoulder. She hadn't seen Neil since their last fight in a town hours north of here. He'd probably moved on to another naïve, vulnerable woman to push and grab, hard enough to leave tenderness and pain but not noticeable bruises. She touched the detection charm on her necklace. At least it'd stopped throbbing.

Who'd been in the library tonight? Teens pulling a prank or someone more threatening? Whoever it'd been, the permanent damage would've been worse than smoke and soot rings on the ceiling if Sam hadn't acted so quickly.

"You all right?" Sam's voice cut into her spinning thoughts. "You're checking behind you, scanning the streets. Tonight's got you rattled, huh?"

She nodded, not wanting to talk about Neil. She cringed inwardly. She certainly didn't want to remember how she'd weaponized her elemental call against him. Tonight, she'd been too paralyzed by the memory to consider calling on her powers to protect them.

Her history needed to stay history. And Sam? He didn't even seem to know his own.

"Could you have an uncle you've never met?" She snapped her mouth shut as soon as she'd asked the question. It wasn't her business. Not really.

To her surprise, he shrugged. In Cami's life, family meant everything. She couldn't imagine not knowing about a relative as close as an uncle. She stared up at him, watching his face drift into and out of the light between streetlamps they passed.

"It's possible." He rubbed the back of his neck. "I don't talk much to my parents. My dad only ever wanted a girl for whatever reason. He tolerated Joe. And I think I reminded my mom of someone she didn't like. They packed me off to a boarding school when I was nine. I caused some trouble. By the time I turned thirteen, they were done with me. I got sent to live with Pops, my grandpa who owned Corraza's."

"What do you mean trouble?"

He flashed a devilish grin, but it didn't meet his eyes. "I got into a lot of fights, and I was really good at stealing stuff. Not because I needed it, but because I could. I did it constantly, and never got caught until I wrecked the headmaster's Porsche. The school sent me home. I boosted my dad's Ferrari. They kicked me out. Pops took me in."

Suddenly Marilyn's comments made sense. Sam's parents had abandoned him after shuffling him out of their house as a kid. They'd denied him his own home, his immediate family. No wonder he hadn't wanted her to look in his brother's biographical file.

On the drive to her apartment, they discussed theories on Sunny Sol and further research ideas. Sam promised he'd email Marilyn for her list of recommendations, since they'd left without it.

"Thanks for getting us access to the library." He had gone out of his way to plan a first date based upon something of interest to her, and she appreciated it. "The files and sources will be helpful. I wish we could get something more personal, something that mattered to her. Like the witnesses and evidence my sister has access to in an investigation." Delia possessed psychometric powers to go beyond evidence and crime scenes, except she refused to use magic unless necessary. "It'd have taken me months to find all this information."

Stopped at a red light, Sam raised an uplifted palm. "Almost a century has gone by. The witnesses to her life would either be elderly or dead. Memories fade." He tapped the steering wheel. "But there might be something more out there. Let me think on it."

She waved his offer away. "You've already done so much." She tugged on the necklace where it lay cool against her skin.

"Call it self-interest." He smoothly shifted the Land Cruiser into motion. "I want to see you again. Maybe we could go surfing. Or let me take you out. Whatever you want."

Cami hadn't been on many dates, and she hadn't left her apartment for much other than work or family. "Another dinner together would be nice."

He laughed. "I think I can manage that. You forget to eat with work and all, don't you?"

What an understatement that was. She existed on cold cereal, microwave dinners, and handouts from Ama whenever she was lucky enough to score some. "Yeah. Even on nights off, I usually grab one meal a day."

He turned onto her street. "How about you come to the restaurant when you get a full twenty-four hours off. You can camp out in my office to study or sleep. I'll feed you. I'll bring Bogart. He's a champion napper."

"Can't say no to an offer like that." She smiled. Being with Sam would be easy and fun if they could have a simple drama-free date. She liked how he could be straightforward yet laidback. At that, she sobered. A kind, good-looking, successful guy like Sam could be easy to like. She'd have to be careful with her heart.

He parked at the curb and gestured for her to stay put while he came around to her side. She watched him walk to her door, appreciating the same swagger she'd been drawn to at his restaurant. Sam Corraza had a great walk. She could record that walk and watch it again and again. She fought a contented sigh as he opened the door.

Helping her step out of the truck, he leaned over her. "Call me if you want to meet up at the beach in the morning. Or anytime." He tipped his face closer to hers. "And for anything."

Oh yeah, she'd definitely need to put a heavy padlock on her heart before it floated away and followed Sam home.

He tightened his hold on her waist. Brushing his lips over hers, he teased her before deepening the kiss. He pulled away and grinned when she followed.

Right. End of the date. She wasn't comfortable inviting him up no matter how many times her younger sister reassured her it was totally fine to get laid on the first date these days. Old-fashioned or not, Cami wasn't a first date all-the-way kind of girl.

After kissing him once more with a sweet light touch, she slowly forced herself toward the door. She glanced back to where he stood, watching every step she took. She touched her lips where she still could taste him. Dashing up the stairs to her apartment, she didn't mind the creaking treads with the excitement and buzz of first kisses. She couldn't wait for the next.

CHAPTER EIGHT

Driving up the PCH before dawn, Sam wished for a third normal date with Cami without possibly poisoned dogs, fire alarms, or police questioning. He'd managed two drama-free dates in the twelve days since they'd first met.

The one evening she'd had a single shift off from her residency, she'd biked along the ocean path the four miles from her place to his restaurant. She'd gotten there around dusk and waited for him in the office with her laptop and food he brought up. He'd rushed through closing routines and cleanup with the mental image of tight yoga pants, the pink Converse sneakers, and the stubby ponytail he couldn't wait to tug out so he could tangle his fingers in those curls.

He'd taken her to watch the bonfires on the beach before they made out in his truck, fogging the windows. He hadn't wanted to rush. She'd mentioned taking things slowly. Something about getting in over her head in a past relationship. If he hadn't had a predawn delivery to meet at the restaurant the next morning, he'd have gone down on his knees to have her reconsider. Her golden eyes and sweetness reduced him to longings and nerves he hadn't experienced since his teens.

Another morning, he caught her getting off her shift at the animal clinic. Her face had lit up when she'd come out to find him propped against the Land Cruiser with a healthy, happy Bogart at his feet. Sam had shoved his hands in his pockets to keep from grabbing her. Not that it'd done any good.

She'd bounded out of the back door of the vet's office with tired eyes and smelly scrubs to wrap her arms around his neck. He'd loaded her bike into the truck and headed to Ocean Avenue for a tailgate picnic of leftovers. On the bluff above the beach, they'd talked about work, her family, and Sunny Sol before he'd gone into the restaurant and she'd headed to bed for the day.

This morning, he'd picked her up in front of her apartment building for an early morning date before he started work. He'd promised her a drive up to the building where Sunny Sol's restaurant had been before taking her to camp out in his office. When she climbed into the truck, she'd had the lines she got between her brows when she worried.

Before he could ask what was wrong, Bogart scooted between the front two seats to dominate her attention. Sam grabbed a flannel jacket from the back for her and cranked up the heater. The jacket fell past her thighs to cover the dress she'd worn over cropped tights. She slipped out of her sandals to prop polished toes on his dashboard. She hummed along to the radio, occasionally shared new trivia she'd learned about Sunny Sol's life, and stroked Bogart's head for the few miles along the coast.

He parked across the street from the old restaurant site. The place stood empty and under construction, having been sold a few months ago. The windows were covered in particle board, and a large gate stood propped open in front of the entrance. Maybe the building should've been eerie given Sol's death up the hill from her business, but it only struck him as a sad shell with a vibrant history of happy diners and bustling kitchens much like his own restaurant.

He opened the door for Cami. The sand spilled over the road in places, and the sound of the waves slapping the shore drew him in. The surf wasn't high enough to tempt him this morning. Plus it'd rained hard last night. While the water might be cleaner this far north, he couldn't risk exposing Cami to the cesspool of drainage and runoff.

An arched pedestrian bridge spanned the highway. When his

headlights swept across the steps, he'd spied the flash of glass or broken mirror and told Cami. He'd forgotten all about it as he helped her from the truck, distracted by her, but she hadn't.

She leaned into the back window. "Bogie, you can't go this time. Wait here for us, please?"

To Sam's amazement, his stubborn, un-trainable, "I do what I want" dog lay down and put his head on his paws as if agreeing with her. She pulled his favorite toy from the bag Sam had packed. "Pink pig? Really? This one?" Bogart's tail thumped when she eased the pig against him.

She lifted a hand. "Stay. We will be right back."

Sam chuckled. "I've taken him to classes, private training, you name it. Bogart's the most obstinate dog ever. How do you get him to listen? Magic?"

She didn't meet his eyes. Bogart bumped against her.

"My dog's as crazy about you as I am." He reached for her hand. "Back off, Bogie. She's mine for now."

He pulled her to the split in the sidewalk. Go right, and they'd be on the beach headed toward the waves. Go left, and they'd cross over to Sunny's restaurant. The garage where the actress had been found dead was up the hill from there with Paul Price's mansion even farther up the bluff. He looked down at Cami, her curls whipping in the wind. "Choose."

She walked toward the stairs. The grey tones of the breaking morning light cast a ghostly pallor over the pale concrete arch and abandoned restaurant building beyond. Sam had a sudden inclination to yank her back to the truck, but he resisted the stupid urge.

A gust of cool morning air, the precursor to the June gloom of SoCal, cut through the wire grating surrounding the overpass. Cami huddled in the flannel and clutched it tight. She looked good in his jacket. He slung an arm around her shoulders and held her close. It'd warm her, and he couldn't help but touch her.

He curled close to her ear to be heard above the whistle of the wind. "If you're up for a trek, we can climb the hill to the garage first this morning. The construction crews should be here in half an hour or so. The foreman is a regular at my restaurant. He's agreed to let us take a look around." Sam had at least an hour before he needed to be at Corraza's. Plenty of time to loop the site.

"Thanks, Sam."

Her soft smile made it worth the effort.

She pointed to the side of the building. "I've studied old photographs. Her apartment door would've been there with steps leading up. They added this retaining wall later. The old pedestrian bridge would've led straight to the restaurant."

They crossed to the east side of the highway, winding to the street level. Together, they walked before the empty structure where Sunny Sol's Seabreeze Café had stood. Its richly embellished entrance remained beneath the three-story hexagon-shaped center, and seven arches spanned farther in the two-story wing. Hazy light spilled through the windows. Security lights, Sam would guess since the sun wouldn't crest the bluffs behind the restaurant for another hour.

Cami led the charge up the side of the hill. "Sunny's maid told the grand jury she climbed over a hundred and fifty stairs straight up from the café to get to the garage's level. Then it was over a hundred and twenty more up an angle to Paul Price and Coral Elton's mansion." Cami swept a hand in the direction the staircase would've originally been. Her breath came in shorter puffs as they crested the top.

"Casa Oceana. That's what Price called the mansion." They kept their voices low in the quiet residential neighborhood, though the wind would likely muffle them.

He'd seen the photos she talked about and read the articles with details from the grand jury investigation. He'd spent as much time researching Sunny Sol for Cami as he had any historical lead for Joe's screenplays. Sam didn't need a guided tour right now so much as to know why she'd looked unhappy when she came out to see him.

"Something happen this morning at your apartment before Bogart and I got there?" He changed places with her to take the brunt of the next gust.

Her gaze snapped to his face before searching the hillside, then back again. "Yes. No. I don't know." She lifted her hands to tuck messy curls behind her ears but had to push back his sleeves first. "When I went to deadbolt my door on the way out, the key wouldn't go in. It's like the mechanism stuck. Or broke. I had it installed less than a year ago, and it's been working fine until this morning."

A chill having nothing to do with the weather went down Sam's spine. "You know I still haven't figured out how the safety latch got broken under the sink in my office with Bogart that day. He stays sound asleep under the desk or on the balcony most of the time."

She frowned. "Do you lock your office?"

"No." They walked the winding uphill road to the garage. "It's a big suite. I use the rear office and balcony. Lottie keeps her stylist stuff in the rest. The only access is up from the restaurant. Or the locked back door." He looked over the guardrail to the ocean below. "We had deliveries in the morning. Someone could've snuck in, I guess." They took the curve to the left. "Who'd want to hurt Bogart? Hell, who'd even know he was there?" He shook his head.

Expensive homes towered on either side of them with professionally manicured landscapes jutting up the hills and obscuring the dim light. Cami shivered. He needed to stop freaking her out on a darkly shadowed street, climbing to the garage where a woman had died.

"Your sisters seem cool." Maybe if he got her talking, it'd distract her.

She relaxed against him. "They're awesome."

Before she could ask about his own family, he continued. "What about your parents? You close to them?"

"No one is close to my dad." She sounded resigned to the fact. "His first wife, Susan, rocks. Ruby and Delia take after her. All my sisters and I call my mom Ama, which is our Mexican shorthand for mommy."

"What's Ama like?"

They headed into another curve in the road, looping back and up. "Ama's the best. She runs her doula practice and sells a line of hand-crafted soaps and candles, but she still makes time to keep us all in line. Don't get me started on her cooking. She makes tamales for Christmas better than any presents under the tree."

"Nice."

"Everyone loves Ama. She draws people in." Her voice trailed off, carried into the wind.

"So your parents still tolerate each other?" His own parents had stayed married whether or not there was any love left.

She nodded, and her curls bounced against his jaw. "Dad and Ama have been married over twenty-five years now. When he bothers to come up from his work, he is devoted to her."

An angel trumpet tree loomed over them, glowing pearly in the morning mist. "Ama must have some sort of supernatural hold on him. Some kind of charm or spell."

"She might."

He'd been joking, but she sounded so serious. "Do you have any gifts like that?"

"Absolutely not." Her words tumbled out, and she picked up the pace.

Sam chuckled. "Don't be so sure."

They rounded the final curb to the dead end in the road. A sign read "Formillo Way." They stood before the double garage doors with a smaller entrance and mailbox to the right. Huge walls stretched to either side, giving the mansion a looming appearance in keeping with the gothic hand-carved "Casa Oceana" sign above the garage doors.

Sam swallowed hard, unable to keep up the flirtatious banter in such a somber place. Cami walked to the garage door on the right, not touching the heavy studded panel designed to look like it would've kept invaders out of a fifteenth century castle.

"The apartment above it." She indicated the trio of windows over the doors. "The restaurant manager lived there."

Sam nodded. "Sunny's V12 in the Packard would've been a noisy engine, but if she hadn't opened it up all the way, and if the wind had been blowing like this…" He shrugged.

She wandered around the entrance a couple more minutes before heading down the hill, quiet and pensive.

"You want to try and get a look at the mansion someday?"

"Yes. Although I can't exactly walk up and ask to look inside." She glanced over her shoulder. "You said yourself, even the garage has become a macabre tourist attraction. No one wants strangers marching up to their door."

Especially not the woman who still scanned the streets when they were together, sympathized with break-ins and burglaries from almost a century ago, and worried about her deadbolt. He slid his hand down her back to ease away the fear in her voice and nudged her toward the restaurant's impressive entrance with intricate tile work he'd bet was original to the building.

Construction trucks now lined the road leading from the restaurant's small parking lot up the hill to the north.

"Sam!" A grey-haired man with work boots and a heavy tool belt called out to him.

"George, man, how you doing?" Sam introduced Cami, and George told them to feel free to wander the inside of the building. He'd be up on the roof doing tile repairs if they needed anything. Sam thanked the man and promised him a meal on the house the next time he stopped by.

George shook his head. "No need. What are friends for? Now, if you could get Lottie to help my wife find a dress for her class reunion, I'd be in your debt."

Sam said he'd see what he could do. He and Cami followed George inside before the man continued up the staircase. The large open space, broken up only by columns, would've been the dining and cocktail area for the café. Sam steered Cami around power lines, equipment, and debris. The kitchens must've been a cramped, hot area to work in with none of the modern conveniences he took for granted.

They moved upward, where Coral's upscale restaurant would have been, through an open courtyard, and past large arched windows before climbing to Sunny's apartment.

"Sunny would've had so little privacy." Cami ran her fingers along the metal balustrade. "But the 360-degree views are pretty amazing. I can see why gambling outfits were after it."

Some of the rooms had been stripped to studs, but Sam could imagine from photographs how the place had once looked. He checked the time. He still had twenty minutes, but they'd seen enough to bring the spaces to life when they researched.

They'd made it to the second floor when Sam heard Bogart barking and howling. Cami raced out of the building and across the street, not bothering with the pedestrian bridge. Sam chased after her, opened his mouth to tell her to be careful, and closed it again when he saw his rear tire was flat.

He let out a string of curses, but Cami's concern centered entirely on Bogart. She crooned to the dog, stroking and comforting him.

Shit, he couldn't even make it through another date without something going wrong. He moved to get the jack and spare tire from the back. Stripping out of his shirt, he got to work. His restaurant was only a mile down the road. They'd be fine on the smaller spare until he could get a replacement brought out during the day.

As he finished changing the tire, he looked to where Cami sat on the curb with Bogart's head in her lap. Her hand clutched her necklace.

He swore. "I promise my life isn't this messed up. My norm is restaurant, home, ocean, back to the restaurant."

She stared at his naked torso, blinked, and focused again on his face. "I don't think it's you."

Hallelujah, saved by the six-pack. At least Cami didn't blame him, even if he felt like a dating fail. "Damn bad luck is what it is. You still okay to spend the day at the restaurant?"

"Yeah." She ran a hand down Bogart's ears. "But if it's all right with you, I'll lock the door to your office suite."

A big wave smashed against the beach, drawing both their attention.

"You want to go surfing with me sometime soon?" None of the craziness. Just the two of them and the water.

She grinned and went back to ogling his abs and tattoos. "I'm in. I've got next weekend off."

"Next Saturday, then. I can arrange to start at the restaurant later in the morning." He put his shirt on, pausing only a second to flex for her. "It's a date."

CHAPTER NINE

An hour later, Sam's frustration had him deflated worse than his flat tire. He'd never had problems with concentration when it came to his restaurant. At least four mornings every week, while the prep staff worked in the kitchen, he hit the office to review receipts, supply lists, and inventories. He didn't pull many all-nighters at work anymore, and he employed a capable assistant manager, but the need still clawed at him.

A very different need clawed at him now, with Cami sprawled on a lounge chair at the open door of the balcony. She had a cold drink, a stack of books, Bogart asleep next to her, and the morning sun on her bare toes.

She didn't seem to share his trouble with focus, so absorbed in her reading she alternated between biting her lip and chewing on the cap of a pen. He stared at her mouth and lost his place in the order again.

After their tour of Sunny's restaurant this morning, she'd slicked on bright pink lipstick that begged to be smeared. In his office, she'd shrugged out of his flannel jacket and tugged off her tights to reveal a strappy sundress.

He wanted her happy, safe, and relaxed, but he also longed to hike the little dress she wore up above her hips and bend her over the desk.

She slid her legs beneath the flimsy fabric and reached for a different veterinarian journal. The sweep of bare thighs against each other damn near had him snapping the pencil between his fingers. He bit back a growl.

"Stop that or I won't get food orders in for next week." His voice came out lower and more forceful than he'd intended.

"Hmm?" She continued to flip through pages and reached again to pull something from the floor. The dress inched farther up her skin. He counted backward in his head, focused on next week's surf date, the flat tire repair, ingredients for upcoming specials, anything to stop thinking about her legs.

On a curse, he exhaled the breath he'd been holding. Almost an hour wasted with supply orders barely finished couldn't be a good sign.

"You okay?" he asked her as he shut down the program and started for the kitchen.

"Yep." She slipped on headphones and closed her eyes. "I'll take Bogart for a walk later."

Sam shook his head at her easy dismissal. The rush of the kitchen and restaurant got his mind back where it belonged as soon as he hit the bottom of the stairs. He remembered to send breakfast to her a couple of hours later. He'd meant to do it earlier, but the morning rush kept him busy. It should've been enough to know she was nearby, camped out in his office with his dog among his things, but it wasn't.

Their relationship had been easy. *Too easy*. Cami seemed happy with anything he did for her. *Anything at all*, he realized with irritation as he seated some regulars. Cami didn't come across as simply low maintenance. She had low expectations. He'd struggled not to take advantage of that when the desire to touch her made him crazy.

What had happened in her past with the ex-boyfriend she'd mentioned? Did she not want a serious relationship with work, the board certifications, and family? Or worse. Was it him? The possibility raised old fears of being unwanted.

The way she startled and carried herself like someone might dare to strike her, he'd question her attraction to him. Except she responded to him as though she craved it as much as he did when they touched. He had gone slow to give her some space, some time.

He straightened. Maybe his little fantasy of foreplay on his desk was exactly what they both needed. It'd been almost five hours since he'd sent her breakfast.

"I'm taking a break," he announced and prepared a heaping plate of food. He whipped up the creamsicle mimosa he'd made her the day they met. Smiling in anticipation of what might come, he unlocked the upstairs suite and carried a tray through. He'd expected her to be asleep. Instead, her whiskey and gold eyes stared alert the second he opened the door to his office.

"I brought you lunch." He set the food on a bookshelf, high enough to be out of reach for Bogart.

"But you made me breakfast."

"Hours ago. You've got to be starving." He pulled a bottle of water out of the mini fridge to add to her tray. "It's nearly three in the afternoon."

"No." Cami glanced at her phone in surprise, then stood to stretch. Her dress inched upward. "It smells good."

"An original Corraza's recipe." He tracked her movements as she set her headphones aside and checked on Bogart where he slept on the balcony.

"A meal not out of a box or a can." She met him by the desk. "You can't beat those relationship perks."

He stroked her cheek and was rewarded when she stilled beneath his touch, her pupils dilating to swallow all but a ring of gold. "Is the food really the best part of us?"

He could've sworn her breathing quickened, but she quipped, "No, your dog is pretty great too."

His fingertips trailed along her jaw. Her skin was so soft.

"That for two?" She nodded toward the tray.

"Nah, I grabbed a bite earlier." He moved his fingers to massage her neck, finding small knots, and tried to soothe them away.

She leaned into him. "Thanks for this."

"I brought you a creamsicle mimosa." Reaching for the glass, he pulled the long spoon from beside a straw. "It's still too thick to drink.

I wasn't sure how long it'd be before you could get to it." He held the spoon to her lips, cupping his other hand beneath it.

Her mouth fell open, her eyes slid shut, and a murmur escaped as she savored and swallowed. She licked at the sticky sugar remaining on her lips with the tip of her tongue. Damn, the temptation of her taste drew him in. He brushed her mouth with his own, savoring her natural rich sweetness chased by bright orange. Sam decided this mimosa rated as his best ever.

Stroking his thumb against her jaw, he smoothed light kisses from her temple to her closed eyes. Her breath hitched. A tiny, significant noise. He trailed fingers down her cheekbones to her neck before pulling away. She opened her eyes, blinked in confusion, and reached for him. It was all the encouragement he needed. He stepped back only to shut the door, and the relief apparent on her face would've been amusing if not for the desire that shot through him when he saw a wicked shiver race down her as he tripped the lock to the room.

In two steps, he gathered her body to him. His hands lowered to the hem of her dress and slipped it upward, his calloused palms rough and catching against the back of her soft thighs. She fisted her hands in his curls. Those dragging fingertips scraped so good against his scalp, and he wanted more. Now. He needed to stand between her thighs, to grip as much of her naked skin as possible, to mark and to own.

He slowly slid his hands up to cup her ass and bit back his delighted shock at finding bare softness covered in only a lace thong. Breaking contact long enough to shove paperwork onto the floor, he lifted her on top of the desk. The cold wood must've been a shock after the warmth of him because she gasped. He locked his lips against hers to swallow the sound. The orange mixed with the scent of her tickled his nose.

"So good," he whispered against her. "You always taste like sugar. Do you taste so sweet everywhere?"

Her sigh was the only answer. She parted her lips, and he inched back with a teasing grin. She nipped at him. Sam sucked her tongue in his mouth for a forceful tangle, and Cami's moan filled his head. *This.* This is what he'd been missing. Relentless yearning overwhelmed him with the need to dominate.

He managed to keep control until Cami kicked the sandals off her toes and hooked bare feet around his legs, bringing him flush against her body and between her thighs. His woman was fierce and passionate. He couldn't get enough. She bowed upward against him. There was still too much fabric keeping them apart.

He shoved up her dress. She pulled at his shirt at the same time he slid his grip from her ass to tug on the lace of her thong. Her quick fingers flew to his chest and struggled against the buttons there. He heard her suck in a ragged breath as she pushed the shirt down along his biceps. Her sexy sounds had him close. Too close. Too fast.

Sam exhaled heavily and said aloud the words circling in his mind, not caring how crazy he might sound. "Why do you remind me of the ocean? The same thrill and intensity? Like crashing toward home."

She froze, staring at him with eyes wide and unblinking. Damn it. He'd gone too far. Someone had hurt her before, and now somehow he'd said too much. He had to slow down.

He skimmed fingertips at the lace of her panties. "Tell me if you want me to stop."

She shook her head, her body relaxing around him. "Don't you dare."

He hooked his hands around her legs to pull her closer, wider. He inched his fingers back to the lace, darting in and then pulling away.

"Now?" He breathed against her temple.

"No. I want this. I want you."

Her gaze followed the direction of his hands. Lower and lower.

"Come for me. Right here on my desk. Now," he whispered. The shake of her head became frantic, curls bouncing hard and fast.

"I can't." She wet her lips with her tongue, and Sam zeroed in on the movement.

Her warm willing body and the way she leaned into him told a different story. He pinned both her thighs, but she hadn't pulled back. In fact, her hands covered his, gripping tightly.

"Can't what?" He breathed, concentrating on her eyes. He tried to focus on those huge golden pools, not the lust screaming through him.

"I mean I can't, you know, with other people." She glanced down, and he made the mistake of following her gaze to where he pressed against the damp heat of her. Her two front teeth sank into her bottom lip.

He dipped his fingers inside the lace to the crease. God, she felt so good. She shivered, and it took every bit of control he had not to strip her and take her right there.

"Never?" He stilled. What kind of selfish assholes had she been with?

"I can do it perfectly by myself." Now she sounded indignant, irritable, and irresistible.

"Want to show me that?" The mental image of Cami pleasuring herself had his dick going from already hard to rock hard.

"No." Her face flamed red.

He fought a smile. Her blush was sweet and so damn tempting. He kissed her gently and trailed a finger to one hip and then the other.

"Anything you want," he assured her, keeping his voice as light as his touch. He'd give her anything. *Everything.* She only had to ask.

She licked the edge of his tattoo at his collarbone in an impulsive flash. Her gaze never left his. The intensity of that shared hot look shattered Sam's self-control. He grabbed her hips before he yanked her panties down and hustled her back on the desk, stripping the lace to her ankles and off her feet in one quick motion, grabbing her thighs and jerking her toward him.

He needed her. All of her.

* * *

Cami gasped when her bare thighs hit his coarse jeans. She rubbed against the scratchy roughness before she could stop herself. She couldn't help but sigh at the friction. Sam kissed her again, stroking her as he did.

He swallowed the sounds she made as he alternated between fast and slow, delving deeper to circle her clit. She moaned again. Two fingers slipped inside. She shook from the vulnerability, but she wouldn't let him stop now. She'd never felt so insatiable.

"That's it," he told her between hungry kisses. "So hot, so wet for me."

She murmured an unintelligible agreement and rocked against his hand. Something was building. Something she hadn't shared, hadn't been able to do in front of anyone before. Her body screamed. Her legs jerked. She clutched his arms tighter to stay upright, feeling her short nails dig into his flesh.

Every nerve tingled, and her senses heightened. She could smell Sam all over her body, feel the cool breeze from outside anywhere he didn't touch her. The excitement of being open scared her, but she couldn't bite back the little sounds escaping her.

"I'm going to finish you like this." His forehead touched hers. "And then I'm going to put my mouth where my hand is." The image of him licking her there sent an ache through her. "Let me taste you, Cami." His fingers moved faster, demanding exactly what he would have her do. She rocked her hips against him, the hotness of his words driving her on. "I need to know what you taste like when you come for me."

Every sensation narrowed and focused on one sharp edge that splintered into a thousand pinpricks before her body clamped over his fingers inside her. Her breasts brushed his chest, and she came undone. Panting, she slowly lowered her legs to the ground to let gravity and reality sink back into all her senses.

She hadn't known she could do that. To lose herself? With the balcony door open so close by? On a desk? At Sam's work in the middle of the afternoon?

He stuck two fingers in his mouth. "What do you know? You do taste that sweet everywhere."

Lust shot through her. Trying to regain some composure, she fumbled to straighten the top of her dress and close her legs.

He swept away her hands. "I wasn't finished. Though I'm thinking maybe you finished for at least the first time. Am I right?"

Flustered, she nodded. That was one way to put it.

"Good." He trailed his hands up her thighs and started to lean down.

She jerked at his shirt collar to stop him, pulling him back to her. "What are you doing?"

"You know exactly what I'm doing. I told you I'm going to put my lips and tongue where my hand was. See if I can make you come again." He grinned, wicked and wild.

"But don't you want to..." She gestured toward his zipped jeans. Good Lord, she couldn't finish her sentence. What was it about Sam that stole every word right out of her head?

He chuckled. "Want to? Of course, I want to. Any man would. I've been dying to have you since you walked into my place. Your bossy little self telling your sisters what to do with all your curls and curves. And those golden eyes." He flattened his palms against her thighs and then stroked outward. "How could I not want to? But I need to do this first."

He knelt in front of her, his hands tracing lazy circles on her hips and thighs. She would have fallen off the desk if he hadn't shoved her so far back. How was she supposed to think with him touching her like that? He hadn't given her time to clear the fog of a climax, and here he was stroking and petting her again.

Harsh pounding on the inner door shook her out of the daze. She tried to clamp her legs together, but Sam hadn't moved. He stayed there kneeling with his palms forcing her thighs apart.

"Unless something is on fire, handle it," he snapped toward the door.

The beating stopped. His harsh domineering tone left no room for argument. She hoped he never took that authoritative voice with her. Or maybe, a part of her argued, maybe she hoped very much that he would.

"Boss, it was a little fire. In the kitchen. We got it, but...."

"Shit." He shrugged into his shirt and fastened the buttons quickly, not bothering to tuck it. He leaned over and stole a kiss from her lips.

"Gotta go, love." He snatched her panties from the desk where he'd tossed them. Tucking the thong into his pocket, he winked at her. "Stealing these." And with that, he was out the door.

CHAPTER TEN

SAM HAD BEEN GONE AND THE DOOR CLOSED AGAIN BEFORE SHE COULD even argue. Heck, she hadn't even tugged down her dress. She picked up the creamsicle mimosa with one hand and brushed her swollen lips with the other. The straw dangled dangerously against the side of the glass. The ice cream in the mimosa wasn't the only thing melted into a puddle.

Although she'd panicked when he'd mentioned the ocean having the same pull as she did, the anxiety had eased under his touch. Sam couldn't know about her powers, yet he'd felt it. She'd have to be more careful. The last man she'd invoked her powers around, she'd nearly drowned.

Golden light spilled over the cliffs outside when Cami's phone rang with the third blocked call of the afternoon. She had gotten a lot of unrecognized numbers, blank voice mails, and odd calls this week. The caller never left a message.

She stretched and checked the clock. At almost seven, Sam would need at least another hour to wrap up his long day here at the restaurant before heading back to Santa Monica.

"Come on," she called to Bogart, who'd been sleeping on the balcony. She hooked the leash, and Bogie loped behind her down the stairs and out the back door. Cami paced him toward the shrubs at the edge of the parking lot to do his business. Careful not to bend too far and flash anyone, since Sam had kept her panties, Cami rubbed Bogart's neck and ears before turning to head back inside. She whirled when she heard the squeal of tires speeding across the pavement.

A familiar turbo-charged red Mini Cooper with black racing stripes wheeled into the lot and whipped neatly into a parking spot. Mina bounded out of the passenger side in shorts and a tank top with a hooded sweatshirt tied around her waist. Delia unfolded from behind the driver's side wearing a long classy dress. Linen, Cami would bet. Delia smiled at her, a rare genuine melting of her wide mouth and lovely features under mirrored glasses.

Bogart wiggled excitedly. She looked down, and he fell on his rump with his tail thumping.

"Are you Bogart?" Mina cooed and bent to pet the dog. "Did she make you sit?"

"I didn't make him sit. I politely asked him to," she clarified.

"Think you can swing us a table at your new boyfriend's place tonight?" Delia asked.

"Deals, it's Friday night," Mina argued between fending off dog licks to her face.

Delia's arched brow threw down a challenge.

"Come on," Cami told them and gave a gentle tug on Bogart's leash. They rounded to the

front of the restaurant. At least the deck had open spots, though it looked like the bar had filled already. She caught sight of Sam and waved. He lifted his chin and flashed a smile before returning to a guest.

She requested a table for three, and the hostess pointed them to a quiet spot at the far end of the patio. After snagging menus, she steered her sisters to the table.

"What do you two want to drink?" She looped Bogart's leash around her chair and dug in her back pocket for a chew stick.

Delia slid her sunglasses on top of her head. "Do you wait tables for him now?"

Her sister's face had been expressionless, but Cami knew by the judging tone of voice Delia didn't approve. "No, but I thought you might be thirsty, and I could speed up the process by asking Sam at the bar."

Delia narrowed her eyes but asked for a water and a glass of whatever wine Sam recommended.

"Iced tea," Mina said.

Cami walked to the bar, her gaze never leaving Sam. He stopped to chat with a few customers along his way down the bar, topped off a drink, and cleared an empty glass like a dance in motion. She enjoyed watching him work. He answered a server's questions while pouring from three bottles for a mixed drink, but when his gaze met hers, his look said she had his full attention.

"Delia and Mina are here."

He handed the cocktail to a passing server. "What would they like to drink?"

"Iced tea for Mina, and Delia wants a water and whatever wine you recommend."

"Is the wine recommendation a test?" Sam joked. With Delia, she probably meant it to be. Cami shrugged and didn't answer outright. Sam sobered at her evasiveness. "What's she like to those of you she doesn't ignore?"

She considered before she answered. "Prim. Proper. More refined than the rest of the family. Nasty in a courtroom. Probably a volcano waiting to happen for the wrong guy."

"Or the right guy," he said with a grin that had her insides melting. "Chicken or beef kind of woman?"

"Steak. Rare."

He nodded. "Full-bodied, red, bold, a little dry. I got just the thing."

He reached for a wine bottle from the top shelf. The edge of his shirt rode up to show a sliver of tanned skin. His forearm muscles flexed as he uncorked the wine and took another order. She remembered that skin pressed against her, his mouth open and demanding on hers. Hot and intense. She leaned against the bar, her body weakening with the memory.

With a sly look in her direction, he popped a fingertip in his mouth and sucked. Her eyes damn near crossed. He kissed her cheek and nuzzled her ear as though he knew exactly what she was thinking. Then he patted the pocket where he'd tucked her panties.

"Later." He pushed a tray loaded with tall glasses of what her sisters requested and an extra glass of wine in her direction. She took a deep fortifying breath before lifting the drinks. Thank goodness he'd added some wine for her. She'd need it after that rush.

She managed on unsteady legs back to the table, and the server taking her sisters' orders plucked the tray from her with murmured thanks. He unloaded drinks and napkins before leaving the sisters to chat.

"Tell us about your restaurant-owning surfer guy," Delia said, taking a sniff and then sip of her wine. "Other than he has excellent taste."

Cami told them everything but the foreplay in his office because those were big bold conversation lines not to be crossed. By anyone. Ever.

"Have you slept together yet?" her older sister asked.

"Delia." She hissed. Thankfully, no one sat close enough to eavesdrop.

"What?"

Mina rolled her eyes. "At least our sex crimes DA didn't ask you about penetration or oral stimulation."

"Not having this conversation," she bit out.

Delia cocked her head to the side. Cami wouldn't budge.

"Come on," Mina pled. "You gotta help your loveless sisters live vicariously."

"That was a no," Delia told her baby sister. "They haven't. But she wants to."

"What?" Mina asked, her mouth falling open. "Why haven't you? It's been two weeks since you met, right? You two lip locked in a library. Like steamy hot bodice-ripper made out according to our phone convo. I would assume you've kissed him since. What's the problem?"

Cami took a long drink of her wine but not before a blush stole up her cheeks. *Sisters.* A girl's best friends and worst critics.

Mina wasn't finished. "Seriously, your new boyfriend is hot. You need to fix that." She wound her finger in a tight circle to suggest wrapping up the sexual situation. "Remember, chica, no one judges sex on the first date anymore. So the third or fourth or whatever you guys are on is fair game."

Cami coughed. "You better not let Ama hear you say that. Or worse, Ita." Their maternal grandmother was a scary force of nature.

Mina paled. "Ita doesn't play. She'd probably conjure me a chastity belt."

Delia pressed her lips together. "I think our Cami has already made some progress toward taking things to the next level. I'll have to shake hands with your Sam later."

"Don't you dare use your psychic powers to read my boyfriend," Cami whispered to Delia. She pointed at Mina. "You either."

Mina held up her hands in mock innocence.

Her youngest sister had double the psychic powers of the rest of them. She wouldn't be surprised if Mina hadn't already tried to read the past and any possible future of Sam's restaurant. Mina could also catch any loud thoughts he might focus on. *Please, don't let her see what happened on the desk earlier.*

Delia stared at her over the wine glass. "I don't ever use my powers if I can help it."

"You're no fun." Mina stopped short of a full eye roll.

Delia edged forward and dropped her voice. "It's not like we would use our elements on him. What good would that do, Mina? I might blow over some tables, and you'd set the whole place on fire. There's a reason for discretion, for the rules. No public exposure unless it's for a damn good reason."

Cami swallowed. She'd learned that lesson with Neil. Hopefully, he didn't remember the seconds before the water rushed over his head or the way her eyes had changed with the magic.

"It's not like I can control my time slips all that well anyway." Mina crossed her arms. "Why do you think I need all your help researching Sunny?"

"I know you don't have as much direction for your powers." She didn't want to imagine losing her ability to pinpoint her communication with animals. Ruby had the same precision over her healing powers. But Delia had almost no control. Her power of touch to read an object or a person didn't have a switch to voluntarily turn it on or off outside family immunity. Mina's power came when it wanted. Her only choice was whether or not to physically follow the visions from other times.

"Sam's researching Sunny to get closer to you." Mina set her jaw. "Why are you doing it?"

"To keep you off the bluffs another night. Or from wandering sightless down the Sunset Strip. Or breaking into the mansion." Cami didn't doubt Mina would try to slip again. She wouldn't risk her sister's safety. "Sam loves history. No magic necessary." She shot a hard look at Delia. "No attempts to read him are necessary either."

"You think Ama hasn't already run your new boyfriend's name through the witchy networking chain?" Delia asked.

"She's dating Sam," Mina protested. "Not agreeing to have little witch babies."

Cami's phone rang again as the server brought her sisters' food. She checked the screen–"No Caller ID"–before silencing it.

"Who's that?" Mina asked.

"Nosy," Delia accused, cutting into her steak.

"I've gotten blocked calls all week," she explained and waved it away.

Delia frowned. "Any messages?"

"No."

"You got a new phone number after you moved back."

She nodded. Of course she'd changed her number. She'd changed almost everything. After their last fight at the beach, she'd left Neil crawling out of the ocean gasping. She'd fled, abandoned her life there, and picked up the pieces as best she could.

"You haven't seen Neil, have you?" Delia asked sharply.

"No."

Delia's lips thinned. "You need to be careful. Change your number again. Better yet, get a different phone."

"I'm sure it's nothing."

"You're still running scared." Delia shook her head. "We should've made you go to counseling."

"It wouldn't have done any good. Stop worrying. Eat." She gestured toward their plates.

Delia took a bite, but clearly she hadn't finished lecturing. "You don't trust yourself anymore, little sister, and none of that with Neil was your fault."

"I know that."

"No, you don't," Delia argued. "Not really. You still blame yourself."

Cami looked at Mina.

Her baby sister forked a potato wedge. "I agree with Deals on this one. Neil the Eel was crazy and took advantage of your sweetness."

"I'm not that sweet." She tried not to think of Neil being dragged deeper into the coming tide.

"You are," Delia said. "You're the darling of the family, and we love you for it, but we need to know you're safe. You wearing Ama's 'alarm charm' everywhere?"

Cami touched the amulet at her throat. "Yes. Although it's misfired a few times."

Delia's brow furrowed. "Ama's charms don't misfire."

She curled her hand in her lap. "Can we drop this and talk about something else? Anything else?"

Delia stared at her a moment, obviously deliberating as she chewed. Finally, she said, "This food is delicious. You made a good choice with your new man."

She couldn't stop her smile at both her sister's double-edged approval of Sam and his food as well as the switch in topics.

"What'd you wear on the library date? Knee socks and a short schoolgirl skirt?" Mina snickered.

"What's it matter?" Maybe the switch in topics wasn't all that better.

Delia sliced her food into neat, ordered bites. "Clothes always matter."

She ducked her head. "Jeans, pink Converse sneakers, and my *Reading Rainbow* shirt."

Mina choked on her salad. "You did not wear that ratty old thing."

Delia's eyes widened a fraction, her equivalent of shock.

"What? It's vintage." Cami loved that shirt. She wouldn't be parted from it. "Besides Sam said LeVar Burton was cool. The man was on Star Trek."

"Stop it." Mina poked her fork in the air until Delia put up her hand. "Cams, you found a hot surfer geek. You cannot mess this up."

Cami stared blankly at her wine. "I'm not so sure about that." She'd screwed up her only other attempt at a relationship. Running away from Neil had been a welcome relief. Losing Sam would be more of a punch in the gut. How'd he manage to become such a vital part of her life in a couple of weeks?

"Wow. You've got it bad." Mina's deadpan tone did nothing to reassure her.

Cami chewed on her lip. "Not helping." She tugged Sam's flannel closer, telling herself it was only the clouds moving in over the water that made her shiver. "What brings you two out this way?"

Delia drank deeply of the wine. "Mina wanted to talk to you about the case you and Sam have been researching."

"Sunny Sol's death is not a case. The coroner said she died of accidental carbon monoxide poisoning." She had been sure the woman had died because of one of the violent men in her life, but maybe she was projecting her own fears on the mystery.

Mina shook her head and chased her food with tea. "Something feels off about Sunny's death. Unresolved." She lowered her voice. "I couldn't see what happened in the garage before that morning. Something about it blocks me."

"It's been bothering her, keeping her awake," Delia said.

Cami frowned. "You didn't tell me that."

"Way to rat me out." Mina pointed a knife in Delia's direction before quickly tucking it back into her chicken.

Delia gave her a scary stare over her wine. Only a sister would call Delia out on anything.

"Sorry," Mina said. "I didn't want to bother you about your research. I was hoping you were getting busy with your new boyfriend."

"Maybe you should reach out to that research group that contacted you last year about people with special talents." She tried to remember the name of the study.

Delia wrinkled her nose. "I still don't know how they found Mina. There's no reason for anyone to know what we can do. Parapsychology? What sort of freak study is that?"

"We aren't freaks," Mina snapped. "We're magical and awesome. It's a gift. Just because the two of you don't accept it as part of who you are doesn't mean I should have to hide."

Cami learned in those final moments, bloodied and beaten at the beach with Neil, that her own powers could turn into something ugly and unruly. She'd called on her powers to plunge him below the waves, and her magic had begged to drag him further down. The ocean had welcomed her to force him into its depths. She hadn't allowed herself to tap into the seductive pull since, except for a moment to track her sister the morning she'd met Sam. "There are rules and consequences for our abilities."

"Other than keeping magic on the downlow, the only big rule is not to hurt anyone," Mina snapped. "How hard is that?"

She remembered the overwhelming temptation, the absolute desire to use her powers against Neil and make her own pain stop. The first rule of magic to *harm none* wasn't so easy to keep. She had learned that the hard way. She didn't want her little sister to do the same. "I'm only trying to help. Maybe they could teach you some control."

Mina never looked up from her plate. "I study spells with Ama. I work with Ita and Gigi whenever I can. If our mom and grandmothers don't qualify as experts in the field, then I don't know who could."

Cami didn't argue. "So about Sunny Sol, why do you say the garage at Casa Oceana blocks you?" She could tell from Mina's blank look she needed to backtrack. "You mentioned you couldn't see before Sunny's body was discovered. The garage is down the hill from Casa Oceana, the mansion Sunny's lover Paul Price owned with his wife."

"I don't know. It just does. It's like a blank around the garage doors." Mina's face screwed up. "Sunny and Paul as lovers? So gross. He was way older—like three decades older—and totally creepy."

"Cami, how old was Sol when she died?" Delia interrupted Mina's coming tirade.

"Twenty-seven."

Delia pushed back her plate. "Way too damn young."

"Agreed."

"What else did you discover?" Mina asked, stealing leftovers off Delia's plate.

"You slip today?" Cami asked her. Mina always ate more after she used her powers.

"Can't I simply be hungry? Geez. Your Sunny research?"

Cami took a sip of wine before resuming. "They called her the Sunshine Sweetheart based upon her golden blonde locks and gorgeous face. She had impeccable comedic timing and bankable star appeal. She rocked a sassy smart mouth. The press went crazy at the discovery of her body and started spinning all kinds of stories. Sorting through the misinformation, false reports, and rumors about Sol's death took as much time as researching the supported facts."

"Did you find any other lovers?" Mina interrupted. "Any possible suspects?"

Of course, in her family's experience, it had to be a lover or crazed ex. "Other than Sol's short marriage to an abusive mafia-affiliate husband, she'd gotten death threats and extortion letters before her death. Someone even broke into her house." Cami shuddered at the invasion of privacy. "And a nasty rumor circulated about Felix Fortuno."

"The mobster?" Delia perked up at the mention of crime. "But I thought he was a New York guy. What kind of rumor?"

Cami didn't comment on how organized crime captured Delia's attention. "That Fortuno threatened her because she wouldn't let him open a gambling business above her café."

"Where did he supposedly do this?"

"At the Brown Derby."

Delia opened her mouth to say something to Mina, then snapped it shut. "Wait, aren't those all closed?"

Cami nodded. "The Brown Derby Hollywood burned. There's a luxury hotel built at the site now."

Delia smiled. "Maybe you and Sam should go research the location. Mina could stop by for a drink. She might slip."

Mina interjected, "*She* is able to speak for herself, and I don't mind Sam knowing." They both looked at her. "We can't hide our magic forever. He won't tell. He will have good reason not to, and we'll need him to figure out what happened to Sunny."

Cami held her tongue. Mina could see future as well as past. She didn't want to know what, if anything, her sister had seen about Sam. Sunny's past seemed a safer topic even if it paralleled her own worst experiences. "Sam and I are not detectives," she reminded Mina.

"But you two could be the closest thing Sunny'd ever have to a hope of solving the mystery," Mina pleaded.

Maybe solving the mystery would put her own paranoia to rest. Perhaps through researching Sunny, she could figure out her own life and where she'd gone so terribly wrong.

"We should talk with Ruby," Delia said. "She's got a good head about this stuff."

"Ama wouldn't mind seeing us all. She said so last week." Mina speared the last bite. "You should invite your new boyfriend so Ruby and Ama can meet him."

Cami refused to be bullied into taking him to be interrogated. "I'll ask Sam."

"Ask me what?"

She turned at Sam's voice, then smiled when he dropped a kiss on the top of her head and squeezed her shoulder before extending his hand toward her older sister. "Good to see you both again."

Delia merely nodded and kept her hands folded in her lap in a classic "don't touch me" distancing technique for the psychometric. Cami breathed a sigh of relief. At least Delia wouldn't read her boyfriend.

"Delia doesn't shake hands," Mina said around a mouthful. "Don't take it personally."

Sam ruffled Bogart's fur and put his hand back on Cami's shoulder.

"You're invited to come to our family's home in South Pasadena to talk about Sunny," Mina answered. "Maybe next weekend?"

"Can we make it two weekends out?" Delia interjected. "Ruby's working extra shifts this week, and I start trial Monday. Cami will need more time to research Sunny Sol on top of work and her new man." The hint at their sex life wasn't the least bit subtle.

She blushed, but Sam answered after a chuckle. "Sounds good. Let me know the times, and I'll arrange the restaurant schedule for a day off." He looked down at her. "I need to wrap some things up before I go. You good for another half hour or so?"

She nodded and put her hand over the one he rested on her shoulder. He picked it up and kissed her fingers. "You ladies have everything you need?"

"You bet," Mina said. "We'll keep her company for you."

Sam worked his way through the crowd back to the bar. Both Mina and Delia leaned over in their seats to watch him go.

"That ass," Delia whispered.

"Right?" Mina shook her head. "Chica, if you don't jump in bed with that man soon, some other lucky girl will."

Cami downed the last sip of her wine. "Working on it."

Delia raised her own glass in salute. "Make sure you do."

CHAPTER ELEVEN

Sam packed dinner and dessert with hopes of enticing Cami back to his place for the night. He'd finally finished up in the restaurant. He opened the truck door for Cami and loaded Bogart in the back. His dog followed her everywhere and was currently nosing through the center console for a rub.

"You okay to come over to my place for dinner?" he asked before closing the door.

"Sure." She never looked away from Bogart. How was he supposed to guess what was on the non-food menu tonight with that vague answer?

He started down the PCH. She was unusually quiet, staring at the dog or at her lap.

Was it the intense almost-sex on his desk? That foreplay would provide masturbation fantasies for many nights to come if he didn't get laid soon. He didn't think she was upset about the orgasm he'd given her. Maybe she'd wanted him to spend more time with her? Or even worse, what if it was something her sisters said? He got along with Lottie fine, and he tolerated Joe, but he could only imagine how out of sorts he'd be after five minutes with either of his parents.

"Your sisters okay?" he asked.

"They're good."

That was no help. "They wanted to talk about Sunny Sol? Mina seems really interested. Are we helping her cheat on something for school?"

"Mina would like that." Her voice lifted.

"This for a history project?"

She didn't meet his gaze. "More of an independent study for the end of her junior year."

"That's cool. She's a history major?"

The corner of her mouth twisted up. "Almost. Her minor is in forensics and criminality. Her major is more complicated. Let's just say she picked the closest to hacking she could get."

"Wow." He wouldn't mess with the Donovan women. "Anything else we can do to help her out?"

"Yeah, I may go with her to a luxury hotel in Hollywood next weekend. She wants to check an angle on Sunny's death." She paused. "I thought maybe..."

Sam leaned toward her. A hotel with Cami definitely had his attention, but her phone rang. She quickly silenced it and turned it over in her lap.

"Your other boyfriend?" he teased. She bit her lip and didn't answer. Now he wasn't so sure he should be joking. She looked nervous. She'd gotten a phone call this morning too, and she'd let that one go straight to voice mail. He started connecting the dots. "Ex-boyfriend?"

She didn't say anything for a minute. "I don't know. It's probably nothing. I figure it's a telemarketer, but Delia's worried it's more."

"Your DA sister's worried?"

"Yeah." She shrugged. "She's probably overreacting."

"But if she isn't, then you know who's calling?" He couldn't shake the sudden concern.

She nodded. "I had a bad breakup about a year ago."

Sam considered that for a moment. "Would he still try to bother you?"

She picked at her thumbnail. "I don't know." She looked out the window, crossing her arms, shutting him out.

"That must've been a really bad breakup," he said, prodding one last time.

"It was," she whispered.

He gripped the steering wheel. "Do you still have feelings for the guy?"

She turned, her eyes wide and blinking. "What? No," she said immediately. She sighed. "I didn't ever really, but he didn't understand." She went back to staring out the window toward the ocean.

How the hell was he supposed to respond without prying or having her completely shut him out? She'd had a bad breakup with some stalker guy she didn't even like? No wonder she researched Sunny's nasty romances, although from all reports, the actress had brawled herself a few times. He couldn't imagine Cami being caught up in a similar situation.

She still looked tired. "Did you get any rest?"

She nodded. "What happened with the fire earlier?"

"The inferno on the desk? Or the small one in the kitchen?"

She curved the corners of her mouth before answering. That was a good sign. "The one in the kitchen." She smiled outright then, dimples and all. "Though I preferred the one on the desk."

He grinned, brushing the back of his hand against her bare thigh before he remembered her thong in his pocket and that she was naked underneath the thin dress. She'd been without her underwear for hours now. Damn, he'd have to roll down a window as hot as that made him. Nothing like fighting an erection in traffic.

He shifted, discussing the flames in the kitchen which suddenly seemed safer for his driving than talking about sex. Still, his hand crept further up her thigh, and she did nothing to discourage it.

Bogart whined from the backseat and pushed his head between them to drool on Sam's arm. Cami laughed.

"Mood killer," Sam grumbled.

He pulled into his apartment's garage with the dog's drool still on his sleeve. He wiped it on his jeans and walked Bogart before heading in. Sam juggled the food and the dog while she checked her phone.

"Six voice mails," she said. "All blank."

"You need to follow up on that." Seriously, could she not see how dangerous that could be? "Want my help?"

"No, I'll deal with the phone service." She didn't sound concerned as she turned the phone off and reached for her backpack from his shoulder. But he worried enough for the two of them.

"Can you grab the keys out of my pocket?" He shifted the bags to give her access. He'd asked because his hands were full. The fact she'd be reaching her hand in to grope near his dick would simply be an added bonus.

She dug fingers into his jeans pocket, wrinkled her brow, and pulled out a lace thong. "Look what I found."

She turned it in front of his face. The scent hit him. *Her scent.* Lust took over, and all he could think about was her climaxing on his desk.

She sucked on her bottom lip. "Guess the keys were in the other pocket?" She reached her hand in for a quick feel.

He wondered if she could hear his heart pound, see his fingers twitch with need. He breathed in, trying to grasp any coherent thought. But he lost all hope of logic when she coaxed his face down to hers for a deep kiss and licked the tip of her tongue along the seam of his lips. All he could taste or smell or feel was Cami.

Sam took charge of the kiss even with his hands full, using his body to back her into the door. Not caring about the neighbors, he slanted his mouth over hers again and again, deeper each time, while pressing the length of his body against her. She wiggled against his erection, and he struggled to maintain control. He had to get her in the apartment.

He broke the kiss. "Inside," he demanded. "Now."

She grinned, this wicked woman of his. She took her sweet time getting the door open.

"Nice use of a door," she said over her shoulder.

He'd be happy to show her what he could do to her up against a door. A wall. Any surface, really. He stared at the way her hips swayed, summoning him forward.

Not looking away, he toed the door closed, flipped on the kitchen light, and unhooked Bogart's leash before she could set the keys on the counter. Overwhelmed with the need to touch her, he reached for her again.

"What about dinner?" she teased.

"It'll keep." He shoved the food in the fridge with one hand and touched her waist with the other. He inhaled, remembered to go slow, and then forgot everything when she curved her arms around his neck and crushed her soft breasts to his chest.

He groaned at the sensation and sucked her bottom lip into his mouth. She tasted like caramel and sea salt. She was all passion and sass as she snapped back at him with a grin and then a small squeak when he cupped her ass to lift her off the floor. She wrapped her legs around his waist and tilted her head back as he walked them farther into the apartment. Sam couldn't get to his bed fast enough and almost dropped her when she bit at him.

He staggered into the bedroom without breaking the searing kiss and pressed her against the door with the sole intent of getting her clothes off.

"Wait," she panted. He pulled back an inch. "Wait. I wanted to talk about..." Sam froze and hoped she wasn't about to tell him to stop when every nerve in his body was screaming for release. "I told you before," she whispered and then stammered. "I, uh, I hadn't, you know, done that."

"What? Orgasmed on my desk?" He chuckled. "I should hope not. I would've hated to miss it." He leaned back in until she stopped him with a fingertip to the lips.

"I mean sex before has been okay, but nothing special."

He frowned. "I'm having trouble concentrating with you all over me." All focus was gone when she reached for the buttons on his shirt. He worked on paying attention to her words and not her nimble fingers when all he wanted was to tug on the neckline of her dress to expose the silky skin beneath.

"I'd planned a much, um, uh, less physical setting for this conversation." Her words spilled faster and faster. "I wanted to ask what you enjoy, your turn-ons." He tightened his hold on her bare ass, and she gasped a hot huff of air against his cheek. "To find out what you like."

He struggled to remember what she'd said, and they weren't even naked yet. Her skin was so soft. "This," he said against her mouth and kissed her again. "This. I like this." His words were muffled against her lips.

She gripped his face and returned the kiss. He pushed his leg between hers, pinning her to the door. He dragged her hem up with one hand. The fabric caught on her ribs. He stopped, seized by the dilemma of letting her go or getting her naked as fast as possible. Wanting both at the same time, he whispered a curse at the sudden confusion. Her sexiness had short-circuited his brain.

With a shy grin, she tugged the dress off, tipping her head back as she did. He seized the moment to trail kisses down her neck, across her bare shoulder. The kisses stopped. He eased away from her to stare at her breasts. A pink bra with black lace matched the thong he had stolen. It was a mixture of sweet and bold, just as Cami was.

"Like it?" she asked and trailed a finger along the edge.

"I definitely like what's in it. I want to look at you. I didn't get the chance this afternoon." He started to pull away, and she stopped him.

"Later," she whispered, echoing his earlier taunt, and pulled on his shirt.

He braced her with his leg and jerked at his own sleeves, craving her bare skin against his. She made him crazy when she wrenched his undershirt away from his body. How was she so cool and calm on the surface yet this sensual when she touched him? He grabbed the bottom of the shirt and snatched it overhead in one quick motion to toss on the floor. She slid her legs down his and grabbed for his belt.

"Condom," he gasped as she unzipped his jeans and slipped her hand inside. They needed to slow down.

"On birth control." She reached for him again, shaking her head. "I'm clean."

"Yeah?"

"Yeah."

"Me too." The words came out raw. He couldn't think around the all-consuming undertow of Cami that was dragging him down to not caring about anything but getting inside her.

She tightened her hand around his cock. "Now, Sam. Now."

He heard the sharp demand over the whoosh of blood in his head.

"Hell, yeah," he muttered, any hopes of restraint gone. He leaned in to devour her mouth again while he kicked off his jeans. He needed to have his hands on her. Those little flicks she made with her tongue against his lips had him staggering with the desire to possess all of her.

In hurried motions between frantic kisses, they made it to the bed with her wearing only her bra and the golden pendant at the base of her throat. The heat of his body touched smooth skin everywhere as he stretched over her. He grabbed her and rolled so she was on top. He reached for her bra, and she batted his hands away. He stilled.

In the blue cast of the city lights that stole through the open blinds, Sam watched this gorgeous goddess above him. She reached toward his tattoos, and he sucked in a breath. He didn't move a single muscle as she studied him with her adorable head tilt, because if he gave in to the temptation, he wouldn't be able to stop.

The smell of the ocean and waves filled the bedroom. He braced for the staggering swell of the incoming tide that was Cami's seduction. He'd never wanted anything in his life so much as he wanted this woman right now.

* * *

Cami breathed in deeply and fought the raw power seeping through her pores and calling to the nearby shore. No reason to cause a freak storm just because she'd lost her mind over this man. Willing herself to gain control over at least her element, she studied his sculpted and golden upper body. A tan line rode low beneath his abs. She traced a finger there. He had another at his ankle, and the stark contrast tempted her to lick each line.

She turned her attention to the black tattoo racing up his left shoulder and down to the elbow. The design inched toward his heart but stopped before his collarbone. A smaller mate to it shot down his right biceps like a flame. The marks were vivid and bold against his skin, depicting water, sea turtles, a sting ray, and sharks' teeth. He'd mapped her source of power on his body. She followed her gaze with her fingertips.

"This is your story, isn't it?" Her voice was breathy. She swallowed again.

He nodded. Like a chart, she simply needed to read it. Those marks that called to her, singing her elemental source's hymn. There'd be time enough to decode his tattoos later. She unhooked the bra and slowly inched the lace away from her breasts.

His hands tightened on her hips. She darted her tongue out to taste the skin underneath those inked maps of the sea. Salt and Sam. He hissed, and then she lost all thought as he cupped her breasts. She rubbed against his erection, writhing in the feel of him.

Here was what she had missed. The intimacy and sensuality of connecting at such a base level that it was ingrained within her body how to instinctively move, how to tantalize while finding her own pleasure. The fingers digging into her hips, the swell of him against her most tender places as she leaned forward and rubbed her breasts against his chest. She reveled in the coarseness there that had her nipples swollen and aching within moments.

Sam fisted his hand in her curls at the back of her neck and brought her down for another kiss. She lost herself to the tangle of tongues and lips before reaching down to angle against his length and guide it into her body. Not all the way. Only the tip of his massive erection. Her focus narrowed to their joining. The intimacy of the act fast becoming the one thing she hungered for.

Her own body constricted and rebelled, unaccustomed to being used this way. She waited and allowed her body to stretch to take a little more. Fighting down the instinct to claim, she paused, lingered, let her body adjust before sliding further and taking him all the way in. She rocked again, finding a slow rhythm that built as he moved his hands to grip her ass. She wanted more. He raised up on his elbows, and she clenched around him as he thrust higher inside her.

Cami needed the connection, the power that came as she rose higher and fell back to take him further inside. She could feel the weight of his stare when he watched her breasts bounce. The heat and slickness from her core spiraled and grew, spreading through her entire body. She tried to fight it, to hold it off. To savor the feeling.

Then she chased it, needing to catch ecstasy before the exquisite moment was gone.

That overwhelming climax was almost upon her and yet just beyond her grasp. She moved faster, needing the intensity. Sam matched her pace, urging her toward it as he sucked on her breast. The heaviness and need pulsed through her with ragged breaths. Sam nipped at her wickedly, encouraging her to let go with feverish whispers.

"You're so close. I can feel you tighten around me. I've got you." He breathed the assurances against her neck.

She clutched at his shoulders, rising further but not fast enough. He seemed to sense the change in her rhythm, the uncertainty. He pulled her close for a deep kiss. That spicy ocean scent wrapped around her. Sam's scent. Her body relaxed even while the desire continued to build.

Taking control from her, Sam never let go as he rolled her to her back, his hands holding and roaming. He withdrew, leaving her empty and wanting, before reaching down to tease her with his fingers.

The memory of her climax on his desk had her twisting in the sheets, needing that same glorious release. She could hear her own sighs and pleading moans as she lay pinned there waiting for him to slide back inside her.

"I love hearing that. Open your eyes, Cami." The gruffness of his voice warred with the tenderness of his touch. "I want to see you when I'm inside you."

She blinked heavy, languid lashes until she could watch him. Sam was over her, his face expectant, his eyes filled with lust. He touched his forehead to hers at the same moment he inched inside. She writhed against him, begging with her body for more. He drove in again and again.

At first, she clung to the sounds he made, luxuriating in the power she had to push him to that. Then her center clenched around him, drawing him in as far and tightly as it could, pulsing against him. She reached for blissful release with a gasp.

Her body rocked against his. She clutched his shoulders to ride out the climax and felt when he let go. His face relaxed into the hottest expressions as his body spasmed with his own orgasm.

Her heart beat wildly in time with his as he rolled to his side, pulling her with him. She tried to catch her breath and then stopped caring how the quick shallow pants sounded because she lay there deliciously sated, wrapped in his body. Her hair stuck to her face and fingers when she pushed it back, having to first untangle herself from Sam. He turned to his back and took her with him in one motion. She draped over him, feeling his hands rub up and down her body.

"I definitely like it just like that," he said softly with a sweet kiss against her head. "More. Anytime."

Cami nuzzled into him. He moved his hand into her hair, lightly stroking her sensitive scalp.

She stretched and sighed in pleasure. "So much more to the point than the discussion I had planned."

He exhaled in a huff. "I had plans too." He shifted her so he could see her tipped up face. "I had planned dinner and trying to lead up to getting you in here sometime tonight. I didn't think I could take another night of kissing you and watching you walk away. Or being right there about to taste you and having the door pounded down."

"This way was much hotter."

"Agreed." He slid her damp body against his own. He held her like he wouldn't let go.

Cami breathed in the sea and salt, hoping he didn't notice the essence of it against their skin, and reveled in the magic filling this room. She'd been warned all her life how power had a lure. And a price. For this, she might pay any price.

CHAPTER TWELVE

SAM CARRIED TWO PLATES TO THE TABLE AND ADMIRED THE VIEW OF CAMI sitting crossed-legged wearing only his button-up shirt. She had pushed the sleeves back from where they'd fallen to her fingertips.

He had negotiated so she'd eat dinner in his shirt before they showered. Hopefully together. He'd made sure to bump into her often in the kitchen, and he'd had no problems when she told him he'd have to eat without a shirt if she ate without pants.

"I can do that." He'd pulled her against him for a quick kiss and a pat on the butt. He poured her a glass of wine before grabbing a beer.

"Such a surfer with your wetsuit tan line on your neck and those board short lines." She gestured toward his thighs with her fork before lowering it to his heel.

He glanced down to the white ring around his ankle. "Surf board leash." He dug into his food. "Don't you have one?" Come to think of it, he hadn't seen a single tan line on her skin.

She jerked a shoulder. "I don't guess you can surf naked."

He choked on his beer. "It's a little cold here for that, and board rash isn't so good in some places. But damn, I would love to watch you try."

She smiled, and his eyes locked on those dimples. Bogart lay across her feet. Apparently, his dog couldn't stay away either.

"The discussion with your sisters earlier seemed intense."

She chuckled. "You mean Mina grilling me for not already having sex with you?"

He swallowed and ran a hand over the back of his neck. "Awkward."

She wagged her fork. "My sisters think you have a cute butt. They're right."

He shook his head with a grin. "At least no one can say you guys hold back. You have a great ass too. Couldn't help but notice it that first day you walked in." He could tell by her expression that she didn't believe him. "It's true. Tiny thing with those hips and that wild hair. When you hit me with those giant golden eyes, I was done for. You started doing that thing with your mouth. You're doing it now." He touched her bottom lip. "You bite here when you're concentrating."

She stared at him, angling her face so a curl fell across her cheek. He brushed it away.

"Then there's that inquisitive tilt you do with your head like you're figuring out, organizing, and sorting the whole world. I watched you and your sisters. You all do it. It's just so much sexier on you. I mean, I respect your brains, your goals, and how sweet you are in every single imaginable way." He glanced down pointedly so she knew that sweet meant both kindness and how she tasted there. *Everywhere.* "Plus you're bossy in the nicest way possible."

She avoided his eyes, reaching for her glass. "You cannot mean that bossiness turns you on. I'm not bossy," she grumbled. "I simply like to get things sorted."

He laughed. "Hot little miss bossy making me crazy from day one."

"Obviously I'm going to need more alcohol for this conversation," she muttered, and he topped off her glass. She thanked him before protesting further. "I am not the bossy sister. Delia is. She says I'm the darling. She said so tonight."

"You are the darling, and I'm sure Delia can be a real ball buster. But you would sweet-talk her into getting your way if you wanted. Your older sister adores you. It must be hard being the favorite."

She rolled her eyes and paused between bites to shake her fork at him. "I'm not the favorite."

"You are. I'm the worthless flunky kid who got kicked out. Who knows why my parents couldn't stand me?" He let the cold beer chase the memory away. "Lucky for them, Lottie came along. She makes a good favorite."

She shook her head. "They were wrong. You were a kid, and whatever problem they had with you, it's on them. You didn't deserve to be abandoned by your crappy parents. No matter how you've convinced yourself it's somehow your fault. It's like you don't even know your own family because they shut you out."

She didn't miss a thing. Sam shifted uncomfortably. He wasn't sure he wanted her seeing through him, so he put on a front, swigged his beer, and grinned. "You could kiss me and make everything all better."

She frowned. "That how you avoid talking about it?"

"What do you mean?"

"Your family deserted you. That had to hurt. You don't even speak with your mother or father from what I can tell."

"I don't have anything to say to them." He set the beer down forcefully. "They don't have anything to say to me, so it works out well.

"Doesn't mean it can't still hurt."

Well, damn, she cut right to the point. He swallowed and considered. She didn't sound like she judged him. Maybe she was defending him in some ways. Being dumped by his own parents had sucked. It'd screwed him up more than he'd already been as an attention-seeking little prick. "You think you could've helped a stray like me?"

"I could have at least tried. That's what I do every day. Try to make a difference. Even a tiny one."

"I see that." He nodded. "I respect that."

"It doesn't mean I always succeed. I've had my own share of colossal failures."

"At work?"

She looked down at her plate. Maybe he wasn't the only one with hurt to hide. Finally, she nodded.

"At work. In life," she told him.

"How could you have ever failed at anything in your life? I mean, everybody makes mistakes. But you? Fail? Not hardly. You're so together." He waited and still she didn't talk. *Oh no, turnabout is fair play.* "You called me out on my parents. Come on. Spill."

"I didn't always have it together," she said quietly.

"You with the life plan? I don't believe it." This woman had a blueprint for every day for the next five years.

She paused. "I didn't plan much of anything until about a year ago. I had a general idea of what I wanted to do after vet school, but I took it day by day. I figured everything would just work out."

"What changed?"

She sipped her wine and gestured toward her bare legs and then his chest. "We're both half naked. This really the conversation you want to have right now?"

He knew evasion. He was a master at it. Something had spooked her bad enough to change her entire way of life. And if his hunch was right, it might be the same reason she watched the world like the big bad wolf would come around any corner. He stared at her until she sighed.

"It didn't work out with the ex-boyfriend I mentioned."

He shook his head. "One boyfriend didn't work out perfectly? That's the reason to change your whole life? I don't buy it. What else happened? You must've had a line of men around the block vying to be your rebound."

"No," she whispered to the table and swallowed hard. "That was it. I ended it. He didn't take it well."

Sam stilled. She'd been right. Half-naked and post-orgasm right after their first time together probably wasn't the best time to talk about this, but he needed to know. She looked like someone had sucker punched her. "Sweetheart, what did he do to you?"

Her head dropped, and she pushed back her plate. She struggled to pretend nothing had happened, but it was all an act.

He couldn't stand to see her hurt like that. He shoved back his chair and hauled her into his lap. He wrapped both arms around her and only relaxed after she settled against his shoulder. She fit perfectly there. Her personality was so big, sometimes he forgot how small she really was.

He rubbed her back. "How'd it start?"

She sighed. "He followed me around campus and asked me out until I couldn't say no. He was tall, blond, and a preppy kind of handsome."

Sam frowned. So far her ex was his exact opposite.

"He started making comments about little things at first like my weight, my hair, my clothes. It changed so gradually that I didn't realize how bad it was when he checked my phone every day and followed me to make sure I was exactly where I was supposed to be."

Sam breathed in the scent of her curls. At least there hadn't been any physical abuse. Not that verbal or emotional abuse was okay in the least, but he hadn't hit her. Had he? He needed to know. "Was your ex ever violent with you?"

She tensed in his arms. Damn, he ached to punch anyone who'd touch her and marked that gorgeous skin. He wouldn't pressure her. He waited until she started talking.

"It wasn't much at first. He'd pull my hair and of course it wouldn't show with all my curls. I wore it long back then. Down to my waist." Her voice trailed for a moment. "He started pushing. Or sometimes he pulled on my arm, grabbed, pinched. Nothing that left much of a mark. It got worse. Especially when I tried to leave him."

"He beat you." Sam said it out loud, needing her to know he understood.

"I hid it. I couldn't let my sisters see. They would've taken care of me, but they would also have wanted to retaliate. We handle our own." She didn't sound angry, simply matter-of-fact.

Sam could easily imagine the vengeance angle. No man in his right mind would screw with the Donovan sisters. They were a force.

"I didn't want a hero," she explained. "I got myself into the mess. I wanted to get myself out."

"So you left him?" His hold tightened on her.

"I did. Finally. After I caught him cheating on me."

"Son of a bitch." Sam hated this guy.

She laughed a dark, hollow chuckle. "Want to know the worst part of it? I was glad he'd been unfaithful because it gave me the excuse I'd needed to leave him."

"You didn't need any excuse to leave him.

"I know, but I blamed myself."

"Why?" He soothed hands up and down her back.

"I picked the wrong man. An obviously wrong man. I had to make sure I didn't do that again." Her voice rasped on the last words.

"That the reason for your life plan?"

She nodded.

"Your ex didn't just let you go, did he?"

She rubbed the heel of her hand against her chest. "We had a fight down on the beach. I ran there from the apartment in the middle of the night because the water makes me feels stronger. He chased me. At the water's edge, things got ugly. He threatened to go after my sisters, my mother."

She paused a few seconds before whispering, "I got really angry. I did things I regret, and I vowed not to do it again. To stick to a plan that's kept me out of situations like that one."

Sam didn't think she could do an ugly or regretful thing in her life. She was so sweet and strong. "Was I in your life plan?"

"No."

Her soft denial shot straight to his gut. When she shifted, her bare ass against him had him clutching her in place. "Then why are you here having dinner with me after crazy good sex?"

"Because I can't stop thinking about you," she admitted. "Because I need to be here with you more than I need my life plan."

With those simple words, Sam felt pieces of his heart fall into place as though watching the perfect wave peel along the shoreline like a zipper before taking off on the ride of a lifetime. *This woman.* How could he have ever fallen so hard so fast? And how would he ever keep her?

So far, she'd worked easily into his own plans, never demanding or too needy. He'd managed to juggle restaurant and romance without much work. He'd take it. He certainly was more than an upgrade over the abusive coward who'd done a number on her.

He didn't want to be that controlling prick, but the possessiveness was hard to beat back. He wanted her, and she needed to know that because she was worth it.

"I'm glad you picked me. I can be a control freak about the restaurant and an asshole in general, but I take care of mine." He stroked her thigh. "And you're mine as long as you want to be." He leaned back. "So tell me again what you could've possibly failed at, because attracting everyone including a spineless shit doesn't count."

Cami blinked at him. "That was it. The failed relationship and the bad way I ended it."

"Sounds like any way you end that would've turned out bad, and if you hadn't ended it, things would've been even worse."

"Probably, but it cost me leaving town before graduation. I had to cut off my friends and connections there to make sure he didn't follow me."

She gnawed on her lip, and he couldn't resist. He leaned in for a kiss. One of appreciation and tenderness. A more dangerous kiss than those that had come before.

They'd gone from sex to serious conversation way too quickly. He teased her to ease the sadness from those big golden eyes. "They can't all be a catch like me."

* * *

He was a total catch. She tilted her head, doing the considering quizzical look he liked so much before she realized he was watching knowingly. She straightened. "You *are* a catch. Why are you still single?"

He gave an evasive shrug. Her arms were wrapped around his neck and rose with the movement.

"I tried," he told her. "Sort of. Women wanted my money. Saw me as a piece of property in Pacific Palisades with a trust fund."

"You have a trust fund?"

"A small one. Dad's a jerk, but he's loaded. Entertainment lawyer. Eats small studios for breakfast. He's *that* guy. He set up a trust the minute he had kids to avoid taxes and other loopholes. He may hate me, but he hasn't written me out as far as I know. I don't have access to the principal right now, and I don't need it. That still doesn't keep people from knowing what I stand to inherit." His grip tightened on her.

"Which is really sad." She traced a finger down the back of his neck. "But what's it got to do with women?"

Sam blinked at her. "Money." He blurted the two syllables like his meaning had been obvious. It hadn't been.

"So?"

He laughed. "And this is why I need you. A woman who would say 'so' when I talk about money."

"That the only thing that held you back? That you're hot and loaded?"

"You think I'm hot? And loaded can mean so many dirty things."

She started to pull away and then overcame the embarrassment. Instead, she shoved at him and nodded to the bedroom. "I think you know I'm attracted to you, and we've talked enough about me. This is about you."

"I'm not over six feet tall."

"Seriously? I don't think real women keep a scorecard on stats of the men they date."

"You don't because you're miniature sized." He ducked to avoid the scrap of his bread she snatched from the table to toss at him.

"Lame excuse. What's the real reason?" She tipped his beer bottle for a taste, but he'd drained it.

He huffed. "They wanted to be first priority over the restaurant. They didn't understand why I worked all day, every day."

"Want another beer?" She stood when he nodded. "You worked hard to build a business. You have goals."

"I do. Which is why we work so well. You have your own goals."

Cami considered her life plan again as she opened the fridge and wondered where amazing sex was scheduled in. Maybe she should've planned for more of that. Perhaps somewhere between finishing vet school and the residency and board certification. Or every single day of her entire life. That sounded pretty good.

"We both have ideas about what we want in life." She heard herself say it, but did she mean it? Right now, she wasn't sure at all about her plan. She popped the bottle cap off.

"Exactly. And we don't get in each other's way."

She let the cap roll between her fingers. She was uncertain how she felt about Sam liking her for not getting in his way. Was that all she could hope for?

"What were you and Delia talking about?" Sam asked before she could think more about that. "Surely your older sister didn't discuss my butt. She seems way too uptight for that."

Glad for the change in subject, she decided not to argue about his assessment of Delia. Most people saw Delia as uptight and for good reason. Cops and coworkers called her the "Ice Queen," and she did nothing to dispel the reputation. "Mina isn't sleeping well."

"Is she staying up because of your random calls? I will, now you've told me about your ex."

She ignored the last bit, taking a sip of the beer before handing it to him. "She's worried about finals next month, a boy that she won't talk about, Sunny Sol." Magic. Lack of control over her time slips. Exposure of their powers.

"Really?"

Cami told him briefly about Mina's belief the death hadn't been as certain as the cops and coroner made it out to be. She didn't add that it wasn't a college project. Let him believe Mina obsessed over schoolwork. As far as her sister's mystery maybe-boyfriend, the only information she had was the letter "J" engraved on a lighter. They had more leads about Sunny.

"We both know what caused Sunny's death was never clear," Sam agreed. "It could've been an accident. Some people argued she committed suicide. The murder theory circulated from day one. Makes more sense why you're interested in the violent men of her life now I know about the creep ex-boyfriend of yours. Only you're completely different."

"Am I?" She stared at a scratch in the table's surface.

"Sunny went back to her controlling ex-lover." Sam lifted her chin. "You've moved on."

Not wanting to dwell on that personal connection, she broached her sisters' invitation. "Ama wanted us to come over. She wants to meet you. Puzzling out Sunny's death is a bonus. Ruby and Delia's areas of expertise can be helpful in any discussion, but talk about death is right in their fields, sadly enough. Plus, Mina will let us know if she finds something new."

"Sunny died decades ago. We've gone through most of the research. There's been no undiscovered information in years. How exactly is your little sister expecting to find anything new?"

She swallowed. "In her own way." She couldn't bring herself to say more about Mina's powers. "She needs to go to Hollywood for a research trip next Saturday." There. That was truth without revealing everything. "I can meet up with her after our surfing date."

"Where does she want to go?"

"The W Hotel." She took a sip. "Hollywood and Vine."

He made a noise of admiration. "Good location. Built where the old Brown Derby was."

"The Brown Derby is why Mina wants to go there."

"But it burned down years ago." He looked confused. "Wait, she's not researching the Felix Fortuno rumor, is she?"

"That's exactly what she is researching."

He rubbed his jaw. "She won't find anything. Fortuno was in New York most of that fall."

"Mina still would rather see for herself."

"What's she plan to do at the hotel?" He touched a fingertip to her hair.

"She has her own methods." She took her most assertive no-further-discussion tone. "She needs to be as close to the old site as possible."

He slid his finger through her corkscrew curl. "You and your kid sister will be chasing the Sunshine Sweetheart by tracking vibes at a hotel?"

"Yes." He didn't know how right he was.

"How can I help?" He took a sip from the bottle, and she watched his throat work. Why'd he have to be so darn sexy?

"Delia actually volunteered you by teasing we could spend a night at the W Hollywood together and maybe invite Mina in the afternoon for drinks before we went up for the night."

"I'm liking Delia better every minute."

She shook her head at his playful cockiness. "I looked at the reservations page. The hotel is pricy. Maybe Mina and I could do dinner there."

He ignored her comment about money. "How long do you two need to work your magic?"

She hoped her eyes didn't betray how very close to the truth he had come. Not sharing the secret was tricky, but she hadn't figured out how to do it. "It depends. Sometimes minutes, sometimes hours."

"Does Mina need company for it?"

"We don't like her to go alone. She can become very..." She searched for the word. "Introspective during her research."

He nodded. "Quiet space?"

She leaned back, crossed her legs. "It helps. We wanted to walk around the lobby, maybe sit and have drinks."

"I can do better than that."

"What do you mean?"

"I'll reserve a room."

"What? No. You don't need to do that. That place is expensive." Probably worth every penny with the luxury it advertised, but way outside budget.

"I have money, remember? Plenty for a night with you alone in a hotel. I'll have to make sure I get a room with a city window view. You don't seem to mind open balcony doors or window blinds."

She felt her cheeks turn pink.

He laughed. "There's that blush. I wondered how long you could keep from turning all shades. I'll have to see what else I can come up with to see just how red we can make you."

She cleared her throat. "I can handle it."

"Can you?" He smiled. "Don't worry. The trip is only for research purposes."

"Exactly. To research Sunny."

He chuckled, and her belly tightened beneath his shirt at the sound. "Sure it is."

CHAPTER THIRTEEN

WITH HIS RESTAURANT AND HER WORK SCHEDULE, SAM HADN'T SEEN CAMI in almost three days. He couldn't stop thinking about her. Her responsiveness to his touch, her vulnerability in how she'd revealed her asshole ex-boyfriend, and her honesty all undid him. He'd almost never sent a text in his life outside of work and quick answers to Lottie. Now, he couldn't control the constant urge to check his phone to see if Cami had texted or called.

The phone in his pocket vibrated with a local number he didn't recognize, but he answered anyway. Maybe she had gotten a new account to deal with the random calls. He walked into the hall behind the busy kitchen to answer.

"Bro!" Sam battled the urge to press "end call." Joe didn't know how not to yell. "Bro, you know why I'm calling, right?" He didn't, but his brother only called when he needed something. Without waiting for him to answer, Joe blathered on. "I heard you met up with Marilyn."

He winced. Talking about Joe's ex-girlfriend was even worse than him calling for research help. "I saw her at the library. I was researching a historical project with a friend." There. He'd been truthful, but vague enough not to invite questions.

"A hot friend?" Apparently, he hadn't been evasive enough. "I hope she's either paying or putting out if she's got you helping with her homework. Does she know how much your historical knowledge of Los Angeles is worth?"

Yep, there it was. His brother was a Hollywood asshole. "Do you need something, Joe?"

"Actually, yeah. It was the reason I called."

Of course it was. Sam waited, trying not to hold his breath.

"Listen, I've got a new project coming up. A film noir type thing with maybe characters from the mid-thirties or early forties I pitched off-the-cuff to some rich jackasses for a movie project. They bit. Who'd have thought?"

Only Joe would have such pull to mouth off about a script he hadn't even started and turn it into a funded project because of recent awards. "Anyway, I'm going to need to meet up with you in a couple weeks to get historical perspective on my ideas. I'd push for sooner, but I'm butting up against another deadline." Joe sounded like he was yelling down a tunnel. He probably had the top down on his convertible. "How's Marilyn? Did she ask about me?"

And now they'd gotten to the only question Joe probably cared about but was too self-centered to understand why Marilyn hadn't asked about him at the library or when she called earlier.

Marilyn had tediously sorted through a collection totaling eight linear feet of scrapbooks, correspondence, photographs, and documents to find newspaper clippings on reports of Sunny Sol's death. The librarian had invested her time because it mattered personally to him and Cami. She wouldn't be so patient with one of Joe's projects.

"Your name didn't come up in conversation."

"Huh. Well, I guess you had other things to discuss, with you looking into Sunny Sol."

How the hell did Joe know who he and Cami were researching? Sam opened his mouth to ask, but Joe paused only to breathe.

"Sam, you know I always appreciate you thinking ahead on projects for me. I did you a favor since you don't seem to know making reservations for the hottest celebrity restaurant or table service at a club is the easiest way into a woman's panties. Because it is. But if you're trying to impress some girl with your brain, I've got an exclusive for you while you research Sunny Sol for me."

Joe slammed the horn and yelled profanity at another driver before continuing the conversation like nothing had happened. "I called the man who bought Sunny's mom's personal effects in a lot at auction. He's agreed to give you access to his storage of collectibles in exchange for an acknowledgment if the story goes to print. Or a blip on the movie screen. Everyone wants to be famous, you know. But you gotta go tonight. He and his staff leave for Morocco for six weeks tomorrow."

After a brief exchange of place and time to meet the collector, Joe rambled about his current project. Before his brother could end the call without so much as a "later," like usual, Sam asked the question lurking in his brain since the library.

"You know anything about our mother having a sibling?" He thought about Cami's relationship with her older sisters. "Or maybe a half-sibling from a prior marriage?"

Joe's irritated snort stopped him. "We both know Mother is an only child."

Sam had believed the same, but some digging online for his grandmother's obituary had turned up the name Mitch Abrams in one other local newspaper. He had failed to discover any information on the man. It was as though he never existed before or after the one-line mention. "Does Mitch Abrams ring any bells? Maybe a brother she didn't talk about"

"You saying Mother has some kind of evil twin brother? That's soap opera shit."

Sam's eyes widened. He hadn't been saying any such thing, but now Joe had mentioned it, his mind seized on the idea.

Joe laughed. "Oh, that's rich, baby brother. This is why I'm the writer in the family. Do us all a favor. Keep to flipping burgers."

Sam wasn't surprised when the line went dead. Eight hours later, he'd gotten everything under control at the restaurant for his assistant manager to handle the few hours to closing. He pulled to a stop in front of Cami's building. When she came out smiling and swinging an overnight bag, he hurried out of the truck. He wanted to help with her bag, sure, but mostly he needed some of her refreshing sweetness. Talking about his parents always left him bitter.

"I'm so glad I had the night off so I could come." Cami swung into the truck. "How exciting to see Leslie Sol's possessions firsthand. Maybe Sunny's mom kept some of her things. Oh thanks." She leaned toward him for a kiss when he took her bag. Sam lingered over her mouth, letting each sensation pull him back to safer waters.

He hoped she wouldn't be disappointed in whatever they found. Celebrity auctions could be hit or miss. Much like the storage bidding reality television show that aired in a time slot behind Lottie's favorite show about the LaVay family of fake Voodoo priestesses, the lots of property bid off at a celebrity auction might contain a treasure trove or a load of useless crap.

The worry haunted him as the underpaid lackey shuffled to unlock the large storage rental. He pushed the creaky door and pulled the chain on the bulb. Stacks of crates, bins, and boxes towered haphazardly to the ceiling with only two narrow walking paths cut through the mess. Joe had called this guy's boss a collector? More like hoarder. How would they find the right parcels in this claustrophobic cluster?

"This way." The slight man with the pinched face continued down the right side. Sam followed, clearing a path for Cami while watching overhead to make sure the jumbled maze didn't topple on them. The precarious stacks constricted to a small opening.

Sam plunged ahead and found something wholly unexpected when the man flipped a switch. Dust particles danced like fairy lights through the illumination as a bank of ceiling lamps flickered to life. Blinking against the growing brightness, he faced three long rows of neatly shelved and itemized rubber bins. All the containers were stark grey or dark blue with small white labels taped on the side near the top. Only their sizes differed.

"Let's see." The man rolled a ladder down the left corridor. He quietly mumbled a listing which made no sense to Sam, but had him reaching for the middle shelf at the end of the center row. He tapped two different bins. "These are the items."

He stepped into the shadows for Sam to lift the heavy bins to the floor. "I must get back to my employer. I will lock the door from outside. There's a safety latch inside somewhere underneath the front unsorted collections. I'll leave a heavy doorstop to keep the entrance opened. Try not to get locked inside. My employer would be disappointed to find deceased family members of a favorite writer on his property."

The man sounded as though he discussed inconveniences, a worrisome bother, not death. How could the man be so pale beneath his mop of greasy black hair? Sam started to ask a question, but when he turned, the man was already gone.

"Well, that was creepy." Cami shuddered. "Do you feel like we've walked into the set of a don't-go-in-there horror show?"

He had, but didn't want to admit it out loud. "Let's get through these, and we can get out of here."

They each opened a bin and raced to sort the contents. Bundled clothes, dull costume jewelry, hair pins and clasps, dirty makeup brushes, and perfume bottles went into one pile. Framed pictures, photo albums, scrapbooks, tattered leather-bound notebooks, and twine-bound envelopes and papers into another.

"I read Sunny Sol's ashes were buried in her mother's casket almost thirty-five years after the actress's death." Cami brushed her hands against each other. Small dust clouds puffed and faded.

He nodded. "Leslie Sol loved her daughter. After she'd lost her son when he was just a kid and her husband's heart attack, Sunny was the last of Leslie's family."

She gestured toward the stack of papers and photographs. "Let's start there." They each pulled from the documents. She wrestled a bulky leather-bound book. "Articles about Sunny's career in this scrapbook. How she started out in a training school for actors." She flipped through the large volume. "Through her short films and supporting actress roles in male comedies." She flicked the flashlight from her phone over the yellowed pages.

Sam opened an overstuffed envelope. "Marilyn scanned a large collection of articles from the year or two after Sunny's death for us."

He flipped through bills, invoices, and receipts. "Nothing here except Leslie's finances."

"Marilyn's pretty awesome." She hefted another scrapbook with a torn cover into her lap, wiping away dark smudges and grime.

He agreed and started into another bundle of bills. "I'll forward you the scans and release forms the library requires." Two of the envelopes in his hand fell to pieces on the floor. Dangers of handling documents at least sixty years old. She started to reach for them, but he waved her off. "Huh." He held a fallen torn slip of paper to her bright light. "I'm sorry. F." The shaky scrawl smeared across the paper. "Wonder what that's about."

"Look. Here's the same photograph posed at the Brown Derby you found at the library." She spun the book in his direction. He brushed his hands over her fingers to steady the phone and resisted the temptation to linger. The faster they finished inventory of the collection, the faster he could get her somewhere more romantic than a cold, dirty cement floor.

He angled the light. "That's definitely Arturo Davino behind her. Otherwise known as Artie the Hat. He and his brothers ran a gambling business. After they were run out of Vegas by the East Coast Syndicate, he turned a heavy profit on offshore gambling on a couple of luxury ships he converted."

He searched his mental file cabinet of local historical facts. "Davino didn't get his biggest gaming ship going until the late thirties." He flipped to the back of the scrapbook. It ended before Sunny died.

She finished paging through the book, and they both searched invitations, promotional photos, scripts, and personal papers for clues. Finding nothing, he thumbed through small hardback volumes of poetry—Bronte, Dickinson, and Plath. He leafed through the first book only to find none of Sylvia Plath's poetry in the slim volume with the broken spine. On impulse, he checked the other two volumes.

"Cami." He tried to keep the excitement out of his voice as he scanned the long lines of neat cursive with strikethroughs and blots of hastily composed handwriting. Each had long narrative of personal reflections. What if these false-covered volumes had been Leslie Sol's secret hiding place to record her feelings?

"Hmm?" She pressed a fingertip against those pretty pink lips and dampened the edge with a flick of her tongue before turning a sticky page.

Every coherent thought flew from his brain except the need to kiss her, to borrow some of her sunshine and sweetness.

"Sam?" Her brows pulled together as she studied his face and looked down to the book he held. "You okay?"

He shook his head to clear it.

She tapped the book in his hand. "Find a favorite verse?"

"Even better." He held up the three books. "Leslie Sol's journals."

"No." Her reverent gush made him feel like he'd found a lost holy relic. She snatched one of the volumes from his hand.

He flipped to the end of Plath. "This one ends abruptly with a quarter of it blank. Maybe it's the last." It was hard to tell with the entries being undated and stream-of-consciousness free- flow writing.

For the better part of the next hour, the two of them read intently, sometimes sharing snippets out loud, other times flipping through rambles they couldn't decipher. The entries in the beginning detailed daily observations, recipes, and musings. Many of her accounts revolved around her daughter.

After Sunny's death, the journal seemed to morph into a more introspective function. In a few pages, it appeared Leslie used her writing as a sort of means to communicate with her daughter. In others, she scribbled accusatory rants in small, spiked handwriting. In the later entries, underlying threads of guilt and grief wove the passages together.

Cami bit the end of her pen. "Listen to this: 'They talk of suicide. My bright girl would never have taken her life. She had plans and parties. I knew from the moment I heard of her death, they'd killed my Sunny. Now they assassinate her character, and I cannot bear it.'"

He turned a page in the Bronte volume. "She says Sunny was worried about a gangster. Leslie writes: Sunny told me she'd been approached at the restaurant after their publicity pictures by an underworld fellow with such nasty countenance. He threatened to open a gaming din above her café. Possibly where she lives now with vile Paul. I worry for my lovely girl."

From the Dickinson volume, Cami read to him, "I cannot stop reliving the last night before my Sunny left to the party. Paul attacked her at the restaurant only a week before. I'd heard the rumors. Could I have prevented her death if I'd simply insisted she not go?"

She passed her cell phone to Sam as the flashlight dimmed. He glanced at the screen. No service. He checked his own phone and found the same. No wonder he hadn't gotten any calls from the restaurant.

Cami continued, "Aida has apologized profusely, dear girl, for inviting Sunny's ex-husband to the party. Mabel, poor woman, has written long letters detailing her affection for my daughter. I treasure these sentiments, but they can never bring my Sunny back.

The overhead lights flickered as they bent their heads, absorbing as much as possible of the journals. Cami rolled her shoulders and something audibly cracked. She groaned.

He reached a hand to massage away the ache. "Take a break. We'll get as much information as we can tonight. I'm sure Joe can get us back in here when the collector returns to the States. Or maybe he can arrange access somewhere not so gloomy."

She handed him her volume. "I'll go through the clothing and tidy things so it'll be easier next time." She knelt over the bundles, sorting through while Sam continued reading.

"I found a page in the Plath volume where Leslie says, 'One of the Davino bastard children has written me with slanderous accusations of my Sunny spending her last day cavorting with a lowlife criminal. He gives assurance she was delivered safely back to Casa Oceana. Preposterous.'" He snapped a photograph of the page with his phone. "It might be worth reaching out to see if anyone in the Davino family is still living." He took a break from reading. "Find anything?"

"These hair clasps and pins are so ornate. I think I recognize this one from a photo of Sunny." She withdrew plain hair pins from the same velvet pouch. "The way these were kept like precious jewels, I wonder if they all belonged to Sunny."

He stared at the jeweled feather shape in her fingers. "I remember the photo. Sunny wore the pin on the front of a dark hat." He looked back down at the journal. "She was convinced Sunny's death was a result of the men she knew. She says here, 'I blame Paul. I blame her ex. I blame all the men in her life and even the man in mine. Did seeing her father's firm hand lead her to these violent men?'"

Cami folded the rest of the clothing into the bin, cushioning the glass bottles and makeup pots with the fabric. She'd stored almost everything except a few small items on the floor. He packed away the scrapbooks and photo albums, leaving the journals for last.

"Look at this." She withdrew a small square of fabric from a silk pouch. The cutting shimmered in the light.

"What about it?" Clearly he'd not given the answer she'd been looking for based upon her insistent expression and the way she thrust the cloth at him. "It's silver?" he guessed.

"Exactly, and it sparkles with intricate bead and thread work. It's a scrap from an evening gown." She spun it in front of his face so close he could notice the loose threads at the edge held with a fabric tape or glue. "I've examined black and white photographs of the crime scene, and the material was similar to this. Reports said the dress Sunny wore to the party and was still wearing when Mabel found her was a silver sparkling evening gown."

Sam instinctively backed away. What a ghastly souvenir.

She must've seen the understanding in his face. "Yes." She folded the small cutting.

"Talk about bringing history to life." He stood to heft the document bin back onto the shelf. "You'd wanted to be closer to the mystery than clippings. Looks like you got your wish."

He cradled the journals, hesitant to part with them. "Good thing Marilyn's not here. She'd have me on monitored lockdown for sure with these treasures so close at hand and probably no one else knowing what they really are."

Cami didn't laugh. Hell, she didn't even smile. He reluctantly returned the journals to the plastic storage tote. "At least we know where they are for next time."

He reached for the other bin. She looked everywhere but his gaze. Was she nervous? Had the discovery finally made her jumpy? He opened his mouth to ask what was wrong when he heard it—a clicking noise like nails on cement. The light from the front room swung wildly, casting long shadows through the back room.

Sam jumped up. The man had locked the door. If someone was out there, they could be trapped in here with no cell phone reception. He grabbed for her and raced toward the entrance.

"Sam!" She dug in her heels stubbornly. Did she not know the danger they were in?

"We've got to go," he insisted and pulled again, only to be stopped by her stubborn resistance. Seeing no hope for it, he swooped her onto his shoulder in a fireman's carry.

Her short shriek turned into loud laughter before they reached the first shelf. She called his name through giggles. "It's a cat. Put me down, Tarzan. It's just a kitty."

A cat? How'd she know it was a cat? He stopped and slid her to the floor. "You sure?"

The clicking resumed, followed by a swish of fallen papers.

She nodded. "I'm sure. It's as scared as we are. I'll corral it while you get Leslie's things back on the shelf."

"Hell, no. I'm not letting you traipse alone into the unknown with whoever or whatever is between us and the locked door we need to stay open." He snapped the lid on the bin over the clothing and shoved it onto the shelf before stretching a hand toward Cami. She squeezed his fingers. "Let's go. I can't risk us getting locked in here with our luck. At least we'll be safe surfing Saturday morning."

CHAPTER FOURTEEN

"You're doing great," Sam called.

Cami sat astride one of his boards. She splayed her hands before her, counting in her head the reasons she shouldn't tap into her magic.

Her legs dangled in the water, the wetsuit she'd dug out of her closet snug against the chill. May mornings in Santa Monica brought cool air and even colder waters. The leash strap's weight tugged at her ankle, a security measure she hadn't needed before with her element.

"You've caught a couple of good rides." He flashed a quick thumbs up of encouragement. "Don't be nervous."

She couldn't tell him the real reason for her apprehension. The call to water overwhelmed her. She could do this. The ocean hadn't rebuked her the last time. Maybe it'd accepted what she'd done after she'd been provoked by Neil. When she'd almost killed him. She shook off the memory. She could do this.

She swam hard strokes, letting the waves carry her up and out. Sam bobbed in the water farther out alongside the other surfers waiting for their waves. The sun peeked above the mountains to kiss her face.

Sam caught a wave and paddled from where he'd been almost twenty feet away. Cami waited for the next and floated along the currents. He balanced on his board and rode a wave in, cutting the nose through the water in an impressive zigzag of ups and downs dodging other surfers. This morning, he'd already caught air, cut left and then right to show off his skill or maybe just his abs, and even wiped out impressively a couple of times.

The most amazing sight had been watching the way his hands trailed through the water, an intimate caress like his fingers on her body, with the same strong connection as she'd had with the ocean before she'd turned her back on it. Watching his touch, she was jealous of what she'd lost.

The ocean had welcomed her when she needed to find Mina. Maybe refusing her element had been her own mistake.

The water rushed toward her, picking her up and carrying her forward. With a laugh, she popped up on the board and rode along the shore as she'd done so many times before she'd locked her love of the ocean and her powers away. She could hear Sam cheering and clapping.

"That's awesome." He paddled close to her and pulled her in for a kiss. His damp hair slid between her fingers. Saltwater and Sam, the most potent combination of flavors.

They waited amongst the others for a wave to break closest to them with Sam paddling further out. She sensed the steady roll coming for them, to curl them into the wave. She couldn't hang the angle as well as Sam, but she rode until she had to bail. The water rushed to catch her, and she surfaced next to her board.

"Sweetheart!" He pointed to the swell forming behind her, but she had known before her head cleared the water. She scrambled onto the middle of her board and paddled straight into the coming crest. Other surfers on the lineup would be too far away to catch this one. It was all hers.

Glancing over her shoulder, she watched him grin before he duck-dove with his board beneath a smaller wave. She waited for the right moment, pushed up into plank, got her feet beneath her in a crouch, and slowly rose to a stand. Leaning into the wave, she let the water carry her toward the shore. Riding the curl proved impossible. The ocean forced her to shallow waters in a smooth, uninterrupted carving of the spray.

Standing, she snatched her board to start paddling out again. The water surged, and the board almost smacked her in the face.

On the third failed attempt, she mumbled to the ocean, "What gives?"

Swallowing the risk, she snuck a tendril of power into the waves around her and almost choked on the sense of completeness rushing over her. She wanted this as much as the sexy buzz she got every time Sam reached for her. But why wouldn't it let her back out in the waves? Back to Sam?

The roar of a small engine combined with slaps of water came to her above the normal "whoosh" of the waves hitting the shore. Her head snapped up. A jet ski raced along the waves, encroaching on the surfers.

She stopped grabbing at her board and pushed the tangle of wet hair from her face. The rider zoomed dangerously close to Sam. Her breath caught.

The tall, lean man leaning over the handlebars had a cap pulled low over his forehead. She couldn't see his face, and long sleeves covered his skin, but she could swear she saw twists of familiar blond hair beneath the hat. It couldn't be. Her imagination zipped to memories of her last night at the beach with Neil.

How could the rider not see Sam where he sat astride his board? Panic swirled through her.

"Sam!" She jumped on her board and pulled fast strokes.

Sam paddled toward the shore, whipping his head around to the jet ski.

Too late. She judged the distance between them, climbing to her knees to wave her arms in desperation. She had to get the rider's attention. She screamed Sam's name again.

The jet ski edged so close she could see the plume shooting out the back as it skipped over the water. Sam paddled harder, his jaw set in a tight line.

The motor blared louder. The bastard was accelerating.

She'd never get to Sam in time, and he was no match for an engine. A wave swept over his head. He rolled beneath it. The spray from the jet ski arced over him as the rider banked.

Her hand flew to her face. Relief poured over her. The jet ski revved again and rolled into a sharp U-turn straight for Sam.

Fear shot through her, surging her elemental magic perilously close to spilling over. Thrusting one hand into the water, she shoved hard. Her mouth curved downward. She pulsed a wave between Sam and the jet ski. One to stop the danger.

Power thrummed through her, and another pulse created a second wave pushing Sam toward the shore. She should stop while she still could, but the connection and clawing need rolled through her. The third push brought Sam almost even with her, a fourth wave capsized the jet ski, and a fifth tugged the menace further from his ride. She could scare him as badly as he'd terrified them.

Hurt him. Pull him under, hold him there as he would do to you and yours. The same hunger she'd fought when she'd held Neil's head below the tide tore through her. A heartbeat later, she could hear echoes of Ama teaching the first rule of magic. Ama's sweet brown eyes filled with laughter as she sang lullabies and kissed her to sleep with whispers of, "May you harm none. I love you, mija."

The water stilled beneath her fingers, rocking her tenderly. She wouldn't break the rule. Not again. Not for this.

Yet, her elemental magic rushed through her, more thrilling than any ride on a board. The call devoured every part of her, wanting to reclaim her as its own.

"Sweetheart." Sam reached for her. "You good?"

His hand brushed her waist, and the magic blazed. His fingers locked on her, and her magic blinked away to a calm, constant hum. She studied him, taking in every inch of him.

"Sam?" Her voice broke, and he gathered her close. She ran her hands over his head and down to his suit, checking for any injuries. Or at least she'd meant to simply assure herself of his safety. But magic had a price. An individual toll for each user to pay.

For Mina, it brought on hunger. For Delia, the power could send her into a blackout. For Cami, her magic had always craved affection, and right now, it wanted Sam.

She crawled from her own board until she'd practically climbed in his lap. He fumbled for a moment but adjusted to hold her against him. She brought his head down to hers and pressed her lips against his. Her kiss marked a claim, licking and teasing until the needs of her power subsided.

The demand for passion finally gave way to the catcalls and encouraging whistles from the other surfers. Cami ducked her head.

Sam snickered and bit his lips, clearly savoring the taste of her there. "Surfer girls are hot."

She smacked her hand against his slick wetsuit. "I was terrified."

He winked. "If we can do this again without me getting run over, I'm all for it."

Her grip tightened on him. "You sure you're okay?"

He glanced down before meeting her eyes again. "Maybe you can kiss me all better again just in case."

She brushed her lips against his before pushing out of the water. She heard his footfalls close behind her.

"Wasn't it insane what happened out there?" He laughed. "What a rush."

"A rush?" She spun so fast she almost hit him with her board. "Is that what you call nearly dying?"

"What? The crazy on the jet ski?" He planted his board in the sand. "He's probably a tourist."

"He could've killed you." She bit out every word, fear fueling her anger.

"But he didn't." Sam waved a dismissive hand toward the water. "It's all good. Karma took care of it."

"No, Sam." She couldn't stop herself from poking her finger into his chest. "I took care of it. *Me.*"

She stormed toward his truck, fuming with the entire situation. What if she hadn't been able to connect with the waves? What if her element had refused her?

She could've lost him in a split second, and his nonchalance meant he didn't realize how close he'd come to death. She snapped the key from where it hung around her neck below the inactive charm and jerked open the back of the truck. How many of their "bad luck" dates had been decided by fate?

Sam jogged after her. She yanked down the zipper of her wetsuit and peeled the fabric away to reveal a bikini beneath.

"What's that supposed to mean? You stopped it?" He braced his hand on the truck over her head.

"Nothing." She seethed and wrenched her feet out of the suit. She snatched a towel from inside and rubbed at her dripping hair.

He leaned over her. "Come on, Cami. What did you mean?" He didn't sound mad or even annoyed. The curiosity edged with concern undid her.

"Magic." She huffed a long sigh. "It was magic."

This was not the way she'd imagined the conversation happening. She'd planned to break it to him last night before clothes started coming off. Or maybe sometime earlier in the week. Certainly not hours before they planned to meet Mina at the hotel. She slumped into the gaping hull of the Land Cruiser.

"Sure it was." He huffed a laugh and dragged a hand through his curls, flinging droplets around them both. "More like dumb luck." He pointed toward the rider who'd treaded water back to the jet ski and attempted to mount it. "Or terrible operating skills."

She swallowed. She could retreat, say she'd made it up. Then what? The agitation and still-piercing need from magic expenditure seized her. "He didn't fall. I pushed him. If you want to get technical, I asked the water to nudge him."

"Right." He drew out the word. "The guy fell, sweetheart. I'm sorry he scared you."

"I did it." She bit back the aggravation. "Like this." She flicked her fingers toward the water. A wave popped and knocked the rider back under.

Sam shook his head. "Impossible."

She shrugged. "Or this." She glanced toward the beach and created three consecutive crests for the surfers to ride. Sam wouldn't have seen waves like those outside of Hawaii or Central America.

"Or that." She nodded toward a couple of teenagers making out near the water's edge. Spray caught them both, startling a shriek from the girl.

Sam's posture stiffened, his features shifting, eyebrows shooting up, lashes blinking like he couldn't quite believe what he saw. "It's not possible."

"You keep saying those words like it'll make it true." She rubbed her temples. "But it won't. This is what I do. It's part of me."

He gripped the truck so hard his knuckles whitened. "What are you playing at?"

Her shoulders sagged, and she ducked her face behind her curls. She shouldn't have listened to Mina. She'd broken another witchcraft rule. For what? For him to stare at her like a freak? A fake? She shimmied out of the wet bottoms and into dry shorts. "Can we pretend I didn't tell you?"

He stepped back. His hard gaze flicked from her fingers on the top button of her shorts to her face. "Is this some kind of trick?"

Her eyes burned and not from the salt water.

Sam's expression turned guarded, his eyes wary. "I thought we were having a good time."

"We were until some psycho aimed for you." She scrubbed her upper body with the towel, trying to wipe away her sadness along with the water. Ama would have a spell to erase his memory. She could pick one up after meeting Mina at the hotel. A few well-crafted drops in his food tonight would make this all a bad joke by the time he woke in the morning. "Surfing was fun. Like you said, the guy must have fallen."

"No." He gestured between them. "I mean *we* were working out."

She flinched at his casual use of a "good time" when he'd been talking about their relationship. She stared at him, watching the tension in his hands, the tightness around his mouth. "What are you trying to say, Sam?"

He shifted his weight from one foot to the other. "Are you...is this you pushing me away? Coming up with a reason to take off?"

The pieces clicked into place. He'd been left his whole life by anyone who mattered until all he had was a business he slaved to make successful. And her.

"No, Sam." She touched his chest, trailing her fingers there. "I didn't tell you to hurt you." She paled at the memory of childhood lessons of how witches must maintain secrecy, the need to protect the family, the threat of persecution from humans who'd always feared and tormented those who they deemed different.

Sam turned away, changing out of the wetsuit and into dry clothes in silence. He inclined his head toward the bluffs. "Get in the truck. I'll take you home."

She asked about their plans for the morning, but he only said he'd be spending it at the restaurant. Five minutes later, she climbed out of the truck onto the curb outside her apartment building. His focus stayed trained out the windshield.

She pressed her lips together. What could she say?

"I'll pick you up around two." His hands slid around the steering wheel. "I need to think."

She shut the door without slamming it and trudged inside, doubting she'd ever see him again. At half past two, she waited with her stomach in knots watching from upstairs for Sam, who'd never been late. Until today.

No matter. Mina called to say she would meet her at the hotel in an hour. When asked about Sam, Cami evaded, saying only he'd had to work. No need to disclose their possible breakup and the reason for it over the phone.

She searched her tiny apartment for missing earrings and clothes she could've sworn she'd put away, packed a bag, and plunged into gridlock traffic on the freeway. She realized too late she should've taken Sunset Boulevard instead. Add another slip-up in an entire day of regretful decisions she wished she could wash away. Her phone lit up with missed calls from an unknown number. Ignoring it, she cued up a podcast on Sunny Sol's prolific film history.

"You and me, Sunny. Crazy work life and the worst record with men."

CHAPTER FIFTEEN

SAM'S GAZE BOUNCED BETWEEN THE HOTEL'S WELCOME DESK WHERE HE'D checked in, the massive spiral staircase at the back of the lobby, and the large crowd around the bar, but none of those things held his attention. What if he'd fucked things up permanently with Cami?

He'd called his sister, because something Cami had said ate at him. *It's part of me.* Lottie had said those words before, explaining her gift for always knowing the perfect look for people she'd barely met. Those talents kept his sister booked months in advance as a wardrobe stylist, but she called it her magic touch. His mother and grandmothers used the same phrase describing their own individual abilities. He'd never given the casual expression a second thought until this morning.

Lottie had launched into a detailed inquisition the moment he asked. He'd shared as much as he could without sounding insane. But she'd interrupted, "Wait. Your Cami? You said her last name is Donovan? You're dating a Donovan sister? She's not a Nahualli-Donovan, right? Shit, no one knows about them. I'm not supposed to know. She didn't wipe your memory?"

When he'd finally gotten a chance to agree to at least the first question—because seriously what was the big deal?—Lottie had torn into a tirade so loud he'd had to hold the phone away from his ear.

"Thanks for being the second judgmental asshole big brother in the family. Upgrade to the hotel's best suite. Something with nature if they've got it. Get her a damn gift and grovel." She'd stopped the rapid-fire rant long enough to ask. "Haven't you ever wanted answers about our own family?"

He hadn't even had time ask her about Mitch Abrams or any sibling their mother might have before she had ended the call. That afternoon, Lottie had shown up in his office with bags in hand. "Clothes and overnight supplies for your witch and her sister."

"Don't call her that." He shoved away from his desk which had done nothing but remind him of Cami's moans and sighs all day.

Lottie had rolled her eyes. "Seriously, you're so dense." She'd snagged a water from his mini-fridge. "What time are you picking her up?"

He had answered with one eye on the restaurant's staffing schedule.

"You're late." Lottie had thrust the bags at him. "She'll be gone before you can get there. You better go straight to the hotel. Stay on the side streets. The freeways will be a mess." Lottie had thrown keys at him. "I'm stealing Bogart tonight. Now go. Don't screw this up. I can't wait to meet her. I've only heard hushed hints about the sisters from their grandmothers."

An hour later, gripping the single camellia blossom his sister had brought, he waited without knowing what he could say to fix this. He'd been so sure this morning Cami had been making it all up, trying to shove him out of her life as everyone else had. He'd run to the only refuge he'd known—work.

During the drive, he considered Lottie's words. What if Cami had been telling the truth? And what if asking more questions about the family who hadn't wanted him would've somehow prepared him for the craziness at the beach this morning? Cami had saved him, shared a deeply personal secret, and put herself out there. Then he'd shut her down out of his own fears.

He rubbed a hand over his face. Sunlight streamed through the lobby door but couldn't cut through the darkness hanging over him. He didn't have a clue what to say when he saw her. He turned the stem over in his hands and tried to stop his leg from jumping with nerves.

A crowd of young professionals in suits and dresses gathered at the bar. He glanced toward the mixer when a tall fair-haired prep brayed like a drunken donkey. The ass wrapped his arm around an equally towering woman whose stick-straight hair must've come straight from the salon. The gesture had Sam wishing for a pint-sized curly-haired goddess with golden eyes to arrive. What if she didn't come? What if he should've gone to her place instead?

Cami stepped through the door clutching an oversized tote bag like a shield. She craned her head to take in the towering lobby. The same immediate attraction he'd experienced the first morning he'd seen her coming through the restaurant flooded him all over again. She was perfect for him. How the hell could he go back to living without her now he knew how smart and funny and fucking magical she was? He wouldn't. He'd make this work.

He jumped to cross the room to her. His heart sank a little when she hiked the bag higher on her shoulder. She looked like a startled animal who might bolt at any second. Her irises shone darkly, more whiskey than gold.

"Wait." He held up his hand and approached slowly. "Let me explain. I got tied up at the restaurant. I ran late. There's no excuse." He rushed on before she could respond. "I shouldn't have shut you out this morning. I mean, what you said was huge and hard to take in, but I freaked and took my own issues out on you. Lottie told me she has two judgmental assholes for older brothers. I was instructed to grovel. I brought you a camellia."

She glanced down at the blossom in his hands. He'd managed to crush and mangle the thing.

He bit back a curse. "I didn't mean to ruin it." He poked at the petals in a failed attempt at revival. "The flower. Or us."

He could hear her deep inhale over his thumping heart.

She wet her lips before ducking her head. "We are going to have to talk about the whole..." She cut a look around the crowded lobby. "You-know-what thing if we are going to make this work."

He reached for the giant purse, waiting until she pried her grip loose. "Overnight bag?"

Her jaw tightened, and her chin jerked upward. "I had planned to get drinks with Mina. Possibly dinner. My mother and my two older sisters live less than ten miles from here. I figured I could crash with one of them."

He crowded her space, unable to keep his distance a moment longer. This was his chance. "Stay with me." His fingers traced along hers at her side. "Please."

"Sam."

She stretched his name into two syllables. Did he hear sadness? Or was it hope? He couldn't let her push him away. Not Cami. He couldn't lose her too. He inched closer, entwining his fingers through hers as he searched her face for a sign.

"It's not a good time. I thought I saw someone today. If it's who I thought it was, I don't know." Her babble had turned to mumbling too low for him to understand. She took a deep breath and released it on a frustrated rush. "Why do you have to smell so good?"

The corner of his mouth kicked upward. "Like what?"

She sighed. "Like saltwater and Sam," she whispered.

He tightened his hold on her. "Stay, Cami."

He couldn't let her go. Not when they were so close to something amazing. He waited, counting the breaths in the space between them.

Raising on tiptoes, Cami brushed her lips against his cheek. His eyes never left hers, pleading and seeking. She tugged him down to kiss his mouth. He couldn't stop the soft noise of pleasure that escaped him. He swept a hand against her curls and pulled her into his chest. She had to hear his heart pounding. For a few seconds, they stood silent in the embrace.

"How'd you beat me here?" Her voice sounded muffled against his chest.

"Shortcuts and side streets around the accident on the 10." He ran a hand down her back, escorting her toward a table tucked beneath the grand staircase. He pulled her down on the massive booth next to him.

"You haven't seen Mina, have you?" Cami scanned the lobby.

"No." He waited for her to text her younger sister. "I picked up our keys. I was being cautiously optimistic you'd still want to stay here with me."

"Thank you, Sam."

The happiness in her voice relaxed him. He leaned back against the booth. "I upgraded us to a suite, a floor above the old Brown Derby. Does Mina...can she do what you do?"

"Not exactly." She shifted in her seat. "She has her own talents."

He ran a hand above the hem of her shirt sleeve, careful not to cross any lines. "I'll listen this time. Promise." She lifted wide amber eyes to gaze into his face. "I swear your eyes change color. I know it sounds crazy. Maybe it's the lighting."

She bit her lip. "It's not the lighting."

He started to ask more, but Mina rushed up, sliding into the chair across the table from them. "OMG, what posh digs. Wow. This place is more club than hotel. Didn't you just love the VIP carpet strut-your-stuff entrance? And the enormous bright pink couch you two are sitting on? I need one of those." She sparkled and vibrated with happy energy.

Cami bumped against him. "I don't think it would fit in your dorm room."

Mina huffed. "Whatever. I promise to be out of here as soon as I get anything. I know you two need alone time to break in your room."

"Mina, filter."

Sam couldn't hold back the laugh.

"So very Hollywood," Mina observed in an upbeat gush. "And modern. Not much of the history left." She suddenly sounded much less excited.

"You'll...do it...if you're meant to."

Even with the gentle, measured tone, Sam could tell she had been about to say something else.

Mina pouted. "It never turns off these days. I walk around in a permanent half-slip. It gives me a headache." She rubbed the bridge of her nose.

Sam had no idea what they were talking about, but it sounded serious.

"Did you call the study we talked about?" Her voice lowered.

Mina's didn't. "The one Delia says will treat me like a lab rat?"

"We don't know that." Sudden tension zipped through Cami's body beneath his touch.

"I'm pretty sure Delia is right. She usually is. Don't tell her I said that." Mina looked from Cami to Sam and back again. "What have you told him about the reason we're here?"

"That you're researching Sunny, specifically what might have happened here with Felix Fortuno and the threat on her life." She leaned into Sam, and he put an arm around her.

"You didn't tell him how I research?" The corners of Mina's mouth tugged into disapproval.

"No. It's a secret for a reason."

Mina sighed. "You seriously need to learn to trust him more."

Sam flashed a smile. "I knew I liked this sister."

"It's not my story to share." Her voice had turned hard. "It's yours, Mina."

"But part of it is yours too." Mina folded her arms across her chest and waited.

Her shoulders slumped. "My part didn't go so well this morning." Sam could've kicked himself. Her eyes shot around the room, and she touched her necklace. He'd never noticed her younger sister had a matching charm around her neck. "I'm not talking about this here."

Mina slumped in her chair. "You should've told Sam at the ocean. You're strongest there. I thought we agreed you'd tell him about what we can do."

Cami stared at the table.

"She did. She tried." Sam couldn't let her suffer further for what he'd done. "At the beach this morning. I reacted badly."

Mina's brow shot up. "Define badly."

Now he wanted to stare at the table, but he resisted. "I didn't listen." She flinched beneath his touch, and he tightened his hold. "But I am now." Because he'd be willing to consider anything she said if it meant keeping her.

Mina studied him. "Not the reaction I'd anticipated. But it'll do for now. What changed your mind?"

His answer was immediate. "Cami."

"Lottie. His sister," Cami added.

He hitched a shoulder. "My sister reminded me I can be an idiot. And an asshole." He rubbed a hand along his jaw. "Speaking of that, who or what is a Nahualli?" When both sisters stared at him, he added, "Lottie mentioned it."

Mina smiled, and it wasn't altogether kind. "Did she now?" She cut a look at Cami. "Ama will definitely want to meet your Sam and his sister. What else does Lottie know?"

Cami lay her hand flat on the table. "Can we save this discussion for somewhere private?"

He flashed the black key cards. "We can go up anytime you like. There's plenty of room to talk in our suite."

"A suite? Fancy." Mina snatched one of the keys.

He swapped the one she had taken with the other envelope. "I got you a room as well."

Mina clapped. How could anyone ever stay irritated with her? Her older sister didn't seem to be able to. "Come on." He stood and tugged Cami's hand. "Let's go up. We're on the second floor. I booked the garden suite for us."

The look on her face when he opened the door to the suite and she stared out at the private patio made the upgrade worth it. She walked through the living and dining areas in awed silence, trailing her fingers along furniture and heading straight for the terrace.

She cut her eyes at him. "Thank you, Sam."

"Anything for my girl." He kissed her cheek and tried to ignore Mina, who was currently inside scouting the entire suite. She lay her head on his chest, and he swept a hand down her back, content to hold her.

Mina bounced out to join them. "Dude, you could fit three of my dorm rooms in here. Did you see the size of the tub? Oh my god, there's a fireplace out here." She stretched across the loveseat, which was plenty long for her five feet. "I'm moving in." Mina closed her eyes. Damn, if she didn't pass out on the spot.

Sam grabbed drinks and snacks from the minibar and sprawled across from Mina on the larger sectional, happy when Cami curled into his side. She cradled the battered camellia blossom in her palm. "Sam, did your sister say anything else after our...disagreement at the beach earlier?"

Honestly, he couldn't remember everything Lottie had said. He'd been too thrown by this morning. "She seemed to know your family. She kind of made it sound like your last name is a big freakin' deal, which is weird coming from Lottie, since she works with celebrities all the time. She doesn't give two shits about fame. Anyway, she said something about Nahualli and bitched me out for not trying harder to question my own family's past."

He swallowed past the difficult truth in Lottie's accusation, although how was he supposed to know the secrets of a family who'd never wanted him. "She called you a witch. Although I'm sure she meant it in the nicest possible way since she told me not to screw things up. She can't wait to meet you."

Cami smoothed each petal of the camellia, taking her time as though weighing what to do or say next. He waited, not wanting to risk another fuckup like this morning.

After a long minute, she nodded to herself. Mina's eyes flew open. Sam almost swore. The younger woman had never been asleep. She'd simply been waiting for some silent cue from her sister. She jerked her chin in assent. "Show him," she told Cami.

Cami tipped glowing golden eyes up at him. God, she was beautiful. He could float endlessly in those bottomless oceans. She smiled, and he felt the pull. Maybe he'd drown there. She spoke and broke the spell, tensing as though steeling herself for the consequences.

"I'm a witch descended from both the Nahualli and Donovan lines of power. Among the very few magic users who know my sisters or I exist, that makes me a big freaking deal."

CHAPTER SIXTEEN

CAMI COULDN'T BELIEVE SHE'D BLURTED THE FAMILY SECRET OUT SO bluntly. She'd been in shock Sam's sister had known who she was. Almost no witch knew the Donovan sisters, and Ama made sure they didn't know too many others of their kind. It's too dangerous, she'd say. Apparently Lottie didn't get the memo.

There was no going back now. She eyed the open water bottle on the coffee table between their two couches. "Remember what I said this morning about having an elemental power over water?"

"Oh, hell no." Mina dashed to the far side of the terrace. "I didn't mean demonstrate all over me."

Sam eyed them warily. Her sister's reaction and his own memory of the morning's display probably wouldn't help ease him into this.

Cami stared at the water in the plastic. It'd been a while since she'd concentrated on such a small elemental focus. She asked for movement, for swirls, for something creative. The bottle shook and spewed water toward the cushions where Mina had been.

"See." Her sister shouted.

"Stop." Cami urged at the same time. The water stilled, suspended in mid-air. She manipulated each droplet, deconstructing the spill and working it into shapes. Sweat dampened her face and back as she struggled to keep control. With an intense yank, she forced the water back into the bottle. Already exhausted from this morning's back-and-forth with the ocean and so little sleep, she slumped against Sam.

His muscles tightened beneath her, but he pulled her closer. "All right." The two words came out strangled. He breathed deeply against her hair. "Anything else to show me?"

Where was Bogart when she needed him? She searched the terrace and spotted a small bird searching for food in a planter. She gave a silent call. The sparrow landed on the table in front of them and cocked its head to study her.

Cami swung her index finger to the right. The bird hopped in that direction in time to her movements. She repeated it on the other side and again the wings fluttered to follow. She smiled at the sweet bright eyes. "We'll get you some snacks." She tossed a small bag of chips at Mina. "Stay out of the air for a bit. I sense a hawk nearby."

The sparrow bobbed from one side to the other and then darted to the feast Mina crushed and sprinkled beneath the dining chairs. "I love this part." Mina held out a hand of crumbs. "I feel like a freaking fairy tale princess."

"What just happened?" Sam asked. His arm dropped, and he gestured toward the bird. "Is it trained?"

"She," Cami clarified. "The sparrow is a girl, and she's not trained. I talk to animals. It's one of my two magical talents."

Sam pulled away and looked at her with doubt. She held her breath in dread and anticipation. He ran an unsteady hand through his hair.

She shot a glance at Mina and expelled the breath she'd been holding. What had she done? Her heartbeat kicked into a fast pace, and not in a good way. Sam didn't move away from her. That was a good sign, right? All she could do was wait to find out.

He rubbed the back of his neck. "Well, that explains you and Bogart. And your job. That's how you knew Bogart hadn't licked any poison. And about the cat the other night." He stopped when his neck cracked. "So water and animals. Any more, I don't even know what to call them, superpowers?"

"Hey, I like that. We've got superpowers," Mina crowed.

Cami glared at her and then shook her head. "I've only got two."

"Only?" he asked.

Some of the tension buzzing through her left as soon as he reached for her hand. "Mina has three. All the Donovan sisters are elementals. I'm stronger near large sources of water." She wanted so badly for him to understand, and she cared far too much what he thought. When had that happened? "We each have a psychic power as well."

He blew out a long breath much like the one she'd been holding. "You being tied to water and animals explains a lot actually."

She started to ask what he meant, but he turned to Mina before she could say anything. "So what's your power thing?"

Her sister flashed a big showstopper smile. "My element is fire, and I'm decent at reading thoughts thrown my way, but my real power is time slipping," she said and then explained the ability to him before adding why she'd come to the hotel. "I wanted to see the site of the Brown Derby and try to get back to that night in the thirties to see if the rumored threat with Felix Fortuno actually happened."

"Okay. All right." He leaned back and ran his other hand down Cami's arm for a few silent beats. "When you time…what do you call it again?"

"Time slip."

"Yeah." He reached for the bottle of water.

"Don't touch that!" Mina lunged to knock it over, and the liquid puddled on the floor. "What is wrong with you? Didn't you see her magic all those droplets? You could've died."

Her head hurt with the need to roll her eyes when Sam's hand stayed outstretched in the space where the bottle had been. "Cut the crap, Mina."

Her sister giggled so hard she choked. "I was just messing with you, Sam. You should've seen the look on your face. Like I'd said it was a radioactive nuclear meltdown coming at you."

She groaned. "Sam, did you have a question?"

The puzzled look on his face told her he'd forgotten whatever he'd been about to ask. He got up and crossed to the mini bar to snag another water.

There really should be a guidebook or something to presenting witch talent to non-magic boyfriends. Seriously. When their oldest sister Ruby had needed a baby daddy, Gigi had matched her with someone who'd grown up with magic. Someone likely to produce powerful magical offspring. Someone who wouldn't have fallen for Mina's gags.

"Ruby didn't have to explain this to Jared," she told Mina quietly.

Mina snorted. "That's an arranged partnership, no messy romance involved." Her sister jumped back to the magic conversation. "Surfer Sam, what do you want to know about time slipping?"

He sat beside Cami, opened the bottle, and offered her a sip. "How's it work?"

Mina shrugged. "It just does. I wander after whoever I'm tracking. I lose focus when I slip into someone else's mind from another period. It makes me vulnerable." She waved a hand at the patio around them. "Landscape and furniture aren't usually the same in the past I'm seeing and the present I'm walking around."

"Then why do you slip if you're not safe?"

"Because I'm nosy." Mina grinned. "But that's why Cami didn't want me to come to the hotel alone."

"My girl is smart and protective." He squeezed Cami's hand. "What else do I need to know?" He leaned forward.

"You can't tell anyone. We may be badasses, but the whole burning at the stake thing forbids future public reveals. We can be killed as easily as a regular human, and we're outnumbered by about seven billion." Mina brought her legs up into a cross-legged sit on the couch. "Oh, and we pay a price every time we draw on our magic."

"What kind of price?" He swallowed and choked.

Cami fought the urge to smack his back, barely snatching back her hand before he faced her.

The call to be savage. To become the ocean in a storm or one of the beasts she called. She pushed one truth aside for another. "Depends on the magic and the witch. Mina's hungry afterward."

"We are talking insane amounts of calories." Mina nodded. "I spent the night before you met us on the beach following Sunny Sol and fragments of her life. I was too damn tired to find my way home. Delia and Cami rescued me and took me to your restaurant to refuel."

"I'm lucky you came by that morning." He rubbed his thumb along her hand. "Do you all have to eat afterward?"

She shook her head. "We physically recharge in different ways. Mina eats. Delia sleeps. It depends on how much power we exert."

"And you?"

She looked away. Hers was more challenging. She could immerse herself fully in the ocean to recover some of her strength, but not all of it.

Her sister didn't hesitate. "Cami needs love. She replenishes through love."

"Ugh, you make me sound like a bad Valentine's day card." She wanted to crawl under one of these plush cushions.

"You feed off love?" Sam asked her.

Mina laughed. "Not off it. *From* it. Though I'm sure getting off doesn't hurt."

"Mina." She cringed.

"What? Our mother gets her power through a fertility and love goddess ancestor. You think those traits didn't rub off on at least one of us? We've always known it was you."

She stared at her lap, not daring to glance up at Sam. He traced long strong strokes along her palm and knuckles that quieted her nerves.

"I help you refuel?" She heard the sincere humor in his voice and looked up. "I can dig that."

Mina slapped her hands on her thighs. "That's totally my cue to go check out the view from my room."

Sam insisted on going first to scope out Mina's room. He wanted to make sure the hotel staff had delivered the small bag of clothes and toiletries Lottie had sent with him. He brushed a kiss over Cami's cheek and walked into the suite. She watched him move with possessive need. Why'd he have to be hot enough to make her crazy? After this morning and now this conversation, she wouldn't blame him if he kept going.

She shivered and touched her necklace. The pendant had burned in the lobby earlier, but that kept happening randomly. She'd need to talk to Ama about it.

Mina frowned at her. "You okay?"

"This morning at the beach I thought I saw...my ex."

"Neil," Mina hissed. "That skinny rat bastard." Her fists clenched. "You were so quiet when you were with him. We never once heard you laugh."

"I couldn't. Neil said his own laugh made him sound like an ass so no one else should do it either." She pushed aside the worry. "It doesn't matter. I'm probably imagining things. All the weird hang ups and blocked calls ringing on my phone lately. They play tricks on the mind."

"You're still getting those?"

"I'm going to the phone place tomorrow before work."

"Glad you're staying with Sam until then."

She sighed. "As long as the magic doesn't push him away. You should've seen him this morning."

Mina dropped her chin into her hands. "You've got to give him a chance. He's a good fit for you."

She pulled her knees to her chest. "I don't exactly have a good track record."

Mina groaned. "Cams, you don't have any track record. You dated one womanizing abusive nightmare. When will you realize you didn't do anything wrong?"

She bit her lip. She couldn't share the whole story. Not with Mina. Not with anyone. "Sam says I'm bossy. Maybe I pushed Neil to be controlling."

"Neil was born a controlling asshole, and you are bossy. That doesn't mean you're controlling. Maybe Sam has a weakness for cute bossy." Mina's lips twisted. "You're just scared."

She bristled. "I'm not scared."

Mina raised a finger in an eerie semblance of Ama. "You are, and it'll wreck things if you let it."

The admonishment stopped her. "What have you seen?"

Mina smiled sadly. "It doesn't work like that, and you know it. No shortcuts. No easy answers. Especially not the ones we would like."

She stared at her sister. When had Mina grown up? And was she right? "I will try."

With a loud click, the door to the suite opened.

"The room is good to go," Sam called.

Mina's voice dropped to a whisper. "You need to be proud you got away from a bad relationship and move on. On to Sam. All over Sam. All the time."

Cami tossed a throw pillow at her. Mina dodged easily and laughed before raising her right hand. "I swear I won't even leave my room. I'll put a chair under the door and lock every single latch. I might even take a nap." Mina dashed out of the suite.

Cami shook her head, not trusting those promises but unable to make her stubborn sister change her mind. And what the hell was she supposed to do about Sam? She dug the heel of her hand against the ache in her heart.

"You all right?" Standing behind her, Sam rubbed knots in her neck she hadn't even realized were there. A moan escaped her. "You've got to be exhausted after being up all day when you're on night shift schedule. And with all the magic you've used."

He sounded so matter-of-fact, like he'd been discussing normal boring non-witch things. She wanted to deny the toll today had taken on her. She even made it so far as to tip her head up to meet his gaze when the resolve crumbled.

"Anything I can help with?" He traced his thumb along her jaw.

She gave into the need thrumming through her. She climbed to her knees facing him.

"Actually, there is." Without giving herself time to second-guess the impulse, she grabbed him and pulled him down for a kiss.

CHAPTER SEVENTEEN

THE MOMENT CAMI'S LIPS LOCKED ON HIS, SAM TAMPED DOWN THE URGE to tug her body against his and hold her there until he could be sure he hadn't lost her. She'd stayed. She'd confided her own secrets. She needed him to recharge after all the magic—shit, he could barely think the word—the powers, the whatever she'd used today for him. To save him. To convince him. Damn, if he didn't need her too.

She kissed him with passion and ferocity, and he couldn't fight the desperate desire to return each lick and nip. It was as if he'd drowned this morning when he'd been stupid enough to leave her, and each pass of her tongue against his brought him back to life. When she dropped her hands from his face, he yanked her closer. He wanted her to feel how badly he craved her.

He grunted when she catapulted over the couch into his arms and slammed her sweet center against his erection. His hold tightened around her to keep them both upright because his control was slipping the more she wiggled.

Her chuckle vibrated low and wicked against his mouth.

"Witch," he growled.

She laughed, a happy sound of delight that went straight to his heart. He watched those shining eyes of hers glow and sparkle. He'd have to make her laugh with such glee again and again.

She shot her fingers through his hair and nibbled at his lower lip. Her greedy mouth bit at his, and the hunger there had him struggling not to drop her. Or worse, to toss her on the couch and finish what she'd started out on the terrace. He clenched his jaw, resolute in his determination to take things slower this time. Those little sounds she made when she rubbed her breasts against his chest weren't helping.

With his hands on her ass, he fumbled his way into the bedroom. "Not rushing this," he said against her mouth. Damn, if she didn't take his parted lips as an invitation to conquer. He moved quickly across the suite, wondering why he'd gotten them so many rooms and trying not to crash with her into furniture. Cami wasn't helping matters. She crawled up him, tugging at his clothes.

Finally, he hit the bedroom and thanked whoever had the foresight to leave the door open for them. A massive crescent-shaped white leather couch dominated the room before a wall of windows showcasing a view of the Hollywood skyline. He lifted his head from the kiss long enough to steer her into the room without hitting anything. A miraculous feat considering his current state of arousal.

Sheer panels of shimmering fabric hung from the ceiling in the middle of the room to barely hide the king-sized bed behind the couch. He aimed for the gap in the panels. "That bed was made for sex. Decadent, mind-blowing sex." She licked a sweep of her tongue over the shell of his ear, and the last word came out as a hiss.

"Indeed," she murmured. Her warm breath tickled the hairs below his temple, sending a thrill through him. He struggled to stay upright. Why'd the bedroom have to be so big and the bed so far away?

"Not going to make it to the bed." He dropped with her onto the couch, Cami straddling his lap.

She wet her lips, and his gaze locked on her rosy, swollen mouth. When she bit her bottom lip, he wanted to do the same. He needed to bite that spot, to taste her there. Leaning forward, he tried to do just that, but she arched toward him. She rubbed against him, all lush curves. He could taste the soft skin of her breasts instead. The sensitive spot that made her crazy, that would keep her writhing against him like this.

Determined, he slipped her shirt overhead. Her bra was red and lacy with hints of the awesomeness beneath. He dipped a finger to trace the lines and whirls and cutouts. He forced himself to slow, to still his hands that shook with need. She tipped her head forward and a curl fell against his forehead, teasing and light. He ghosted his fingers up her back, unhooked the clasps of her bra, and stopped at the catch in her breath.

"This okay?" Damn, his voice almost broke like a fumbling teenager.

"Yes." The word, whispered long and slow, tightened something low in his gut.

He slipped the straps from her shoulders and palmed the fullness of her breast, rubbing a thumb to circle her nipple in slow rounds to calm his own raging desire. Cami made a sound in the back of her throat that told him she liked this as much as he did.

He inched his hand back, and she moved into his touch. The noises from outside fell away. There was no traffic, no helicopters, no blaring music through the open suite doors. Only Cami's needy whimpers.

Her nipple peaked, and he touched the other to watch it do the same. He turned her toward the rosy light streaming through the window to study her curves. The colors painted her skin to perfection.

Her breath quickened when he skimmed each breast and ran his thumbs along the heavy crease underneath. His lips replaced his hands, and he sweetly drew the tip of each into his mouth, sucking and licking the tight buds. He wanted to taste every bit of her.

She moaned when he rolled her nipple between his thumb and forefinger. He needed more of those sounds. Her eyes slid shut, and she lowered and rocked against him, silently demanding he go further. Not yet. He couldn't. He would be lost before they started. He kissed her mouth, and she opened for him, drawing his tongue against hers.

Sam groaned as she circled her hips against his lap, his erection rock hard beneath her. He'd never last long if she kept grinding that gorgeous body on top of him. He stood without breaking the kiss, and she swayed off balance a second before he tugged her close. A mistake. Before he could take another breath, she managed to yank his belt off and reached for the button of his pants. He staggered them both to the bed.

He needed a moment to ground himself, to keep from throwing her on the bed and burying himself inside her until they both forgot their secrets or why they kept them. She was so damn perfect.

The change in her when they were intimate together was incredible. She went from calm and still lagoon waters, to a tempest at his touch. It was fucking amazing how she responded to him so passionately. He swept his fingers along her collarbone, lingering on the delicate curves and edges.

Cami unzipped his pants and palmed his erection, stealing all thought with her touch. He leaned into her, desperate for more. She danced her fingers there, teasing with a light graze before grasping him tighter. He groaned at the sensation. She was a freaking tsunami, and he had no chance withstanding her.

He took a steadying breath and glanced at the streaming rose and gold light filtering through the room to lick at her skin. Calling on all his diminishing willpower, he tugged her hand away and ignored the ache left behind. He needed all of her, every single gasp and sigh. He wouldn't waste a second of the promised satisfaction for a quick hand job.

She reached for him again, but he refused to rush. He wanted to enjoy the view of Cami in the glow of the setting sun through the large windows. He slowly pulled her shorts from her hips and slid them down her legs. She was glorious, all curves and dark skin spread across the white bed. Small chill bumps rose on her arms, and he kissed them away. He skimmed an unsteady hand up her calf to her thigh and then higher to her panties. He snagged the thong and inched it off slowly, his calluses catching on the lace. She toed his pants, restless and impatient.

"Your turn," she told him.

"In a minute." He slowed his breathing and reveled in her beauty, her powers, everything about her. He lowered his mouth and licked along her smooth thigh. He smiled as her fingers tangled in his hair to tug and demand. She didn't waste much time on foreplay. Cami wanted everything all at once. She couldn't be sexier.

"Now," she moaned and tried to force him up her body.

Not a chance. He licked and kissed between her thighs, savored her sweetness, and delighted in driving her mad until she dug her fingers into his shoulders and panted. No man could resist that. He jerked off his pants and underwear before climbing on the bed. He rose above her to look down at her. Her chest rose and fell with hard, heavy breaths, and she ran her hands over his arms. She clutched at him, trying to bring him closer.

"Tell me what you need," he said. He wanted to make sure they were together in this longing.

"You." Her eyes were dazed, her voice hoarse.

He shook his head, sliding a finger inside her. She was so slick and wet. Ready for him. "You have to tell me."

"I want you." He slid another finger alongside the first to stretch her, and she gasped. "Inside me. Now." She smacked his shoulder. Her need clawed at him.

He withdrew his fingers and slipped his erection over the slickness there. "Is this what you want?" He rubbed himself back and forth, so close but never entering.

"Yes." She hissed.

He almost slammed into her then, but teasing her, building the anticipation was so very satisfying.

"Feel how hard I am for you? How much I want to be inside you?" He knew she didn't want to wait. That she needed instant gratification because she told him in urgent damn near pornographic whispers. Such a dirty mouth when she was turned on. He loved it. Couldn't get enough of it. Couldn't get enough of her.

She wriggled, grabbing at his shoulders. "Sam, now," she insisted.

"So bossy." He started to laugh and stopped when she reached down and grasped his length and squeezed. Stars burst across his vision, and he couldn't hold back. He grabbed the nape of her neck in one hand and her ass in the other before sliding fully inside her.

Her body burned beneath him, so tight. Their moans mingled in the hot breath between them. She dug her fingernails into his back as the passion stormed through her in a shuddering climax that clenched him so hard he fought to hold back. The craving and desire took over when her body spasmed around him again.

He pounded faster while he caught her gasps of pleasure. He'd made her come again and again. It was his undoing. He'd never be able to let her go. Not when she made him feel so invincible. That was his last thought before he completely lost himself in her.

He stayed propped on his elbows above her while their breathing slowed. Both their hearts beat so heavily that he could feel hers against his own pounding pulse. He rolled to his side and drew her against his body. He shuddered when her foot ran up his leg, catching at his hip to pull him closer.

"Sam?"

How he loved hearing her sigh his name, feeling the weight of her head snuggled against his chest.

"This is too much." She waved a hand to sweep the room, but it was obvious she was too worn out to be more specific.

He almost laughed. According to her, anything he did was too much. "You stay with me tonight and it's not."

She ran fingertips over his ink. "My magic doesn't scare you away?"

He turned her in his arms, leaning close to kiss her forehead. "I can't stay away from you."

She trailed her fingers over his left bicep. "You never told me what your tattoos stand for."

"My life," he said simply. "My grandma Corraza is Polynesian. I learned the symbols from her."

"A sea turtle?" she asked. "A *honu* in Hawaiian?"

His muscles flexed under her touch. "How do you know that?"

"I vacationed with my sisters a couple years back off North Shore in Oahu. We rented paddle boards to go up the Anahulu river with guava juice and wine." He heard a smile in her voice. "We floated and enjoyed the view with the company of several honu."

"Several, you say?" He pressed her hand over the inked shell.

She tapped a finger silently against his skin, and he realized she was holding back.

"Did you?" He gave in to his need to know. "Did you and your powers have something to do with that?"

She pulled her hand along the edges of the shell pattern. "Perhaps." She looked up to meet his gaze. "Are you sure you're cool with this?"

"Definitely. So what'd you do? Call all the turtles nearby to come hang out?"

"Basically." She hugged him tighter. "They swam beneath us, waved a flipper or two, and popped a head up occasionally. It's already a safe haven back there along the river behind the bridge."

"Just you and your sisters paddle boarding?"

"We sat on the boards more than we paddled. Having wind and water powers in the group helped with drifting away from the rocks and other people."

"I'll bet." He grinned. "You're hell on a surfboard. Did you surf that trip?"

"No, I was busy playing with some spinner dolphins." She cleared her throat. She was still uncomfortable talking about her powers, but damn they were amazing.

She was amazing.

"We'll have to go to Hawaii together someday," he blurted out. Luckily, she nodded against him. He was going to have to get a better hold over himself around her. He was planning forever when he'd barely won her back for the night.

"Why did you choose a sea turtle?" She led the conversation back to where they'd been.

"They stand for longevity. That's for Grandma Corraza. She'll be full of life no matter what age she reaches. She dances every day to talk with nature spirits. See." He touched the tip of her nose. "You're not the only one with mystic stuff in the family."

"And what's all this below in the spiral pattern?" Her curls brushed his skin. She'd distracted him so much he had to look down at his chest to remember his own tattoos.

"A fishhook and a chieftain's club are signs of respect for my grandpa, Pops. The feather is for Joe since he's a writer. Shark teeth for power, spearheads for strength, and sun for success."

He dipped his head toward his right arm. "The stingray is for Lottie. She's fierce like your sisters."

"What about your parents? Are they here?" She slid her fingers down his chest.

"No." His voice was firm and unbending.

She kissed his shoulder before laying her head on him again. "And this?"

"The ocean. The first real home I had."

She burrowed against him. As her curls bobbed under his nose, he breathed in and could smell the familiar scents of the ocean—salt water, driftwood, seaweed. Sam recognized it as the same sensation he'd had the very first time he'd talked to her at his restaurant. Then again the first time they'd made love.

"The smell and feel of the ocean in my room the first night? That was you," he whispered. "The feeling of paddling out on the waves. The anticipation, the thrill. All of it? You created it."

She nodded. "The power can be harder to control or suppress with strong emotion. Desire, anger, fear."

He heard the change in her voice. She didn't want to talk about the anger or fear part. She lay her hand on his collarbone above his heart where ink curved away inches before the unmarked skin. "Why nothing here?"

"I'm saving that space."

"For what?"

The hell with it. Might as well tell her the truth. "My future wife."

She slid closer, and he curled her tightly against him.

"Thank you for this. The room, your understanding." She grazed her lips against his skin. "All of this."

He kissed her upturned face then brushed his lips down her jaw. He wrapped a delicate curl around his finger.

"Sam, can I ask you for something?"

Anything. He'd give her any single thing she wanted. "What is it, sweetheart?"

"I'd love a bath."

He chuckled. Here he was ready to hand her the world, and she simply wanted to soak in the massive tub. The visual image of her naked in a bath with bubbles popping over all the right places had him hard again. He rolled away.

"I'll go start the water. Be back in a minute."

He turned on both taps, poured soap, and watched the hot foam rise before striding to the bed to haul her up against him. She laughed and threw her arms around his neck. He jostled her, enjoying the bounce and jiggle of naked curves in his arms as he carried her to the tub.

She protested as he leaned to slide her into the water. "You'll get wet."

Like that would stop him. Especially when he heard her sigh as her skin hit the warm water. It was a sound of ecstasy before she slipped lower into the tub.

He took a towel to his damp skin and stood there without a stitch of clothing on, completely comfortable as he watched her bathe. The tips of her curls waved and tightened from the steam. She was adorable and so fucking hot. She ran her fingers down one leg and then the other, stretching and relaxing deeper into the water.

"A true water sprite. Nude and all."

She smirked and the next thing he knew, he had water splashed in his face. From four feet away. Without her moving. It was impossible. Or was it?

"Did you do that?" he asked.

She nodded with a wicked sly smile.

He couldn't help but grin back at those devilish dimples. "Do it again."

She raised a hand above the bubbles and flicked her fingers. The water in the tub started spiraling as though there were jets beneath, but there weren't. He'd checked. She snapped her fingers and another small stream leapt to splash him again.

"I'll be damned." He was amazed. He wouldn't believe it if he hadn't seen it, felt it. "That's unreal." He grabbed the towel again to dry himself where the drops had smacked against him.

She lifted a shoulder. "Tricks I've played since I was a kid. Nothing special."

"You underestimate yourself." He meant it. She bit her lip. Pink from the heat of the bath rose up her cheeks. He stopped and dropped the towel.

"Mind if I join you?" He didn't wait for a response before he walked the few steps to the tub to stand over her and watched the blush deepen in color. He was imagining the fun he could have with her in that tub when someone knocked loudly at the door despite the "do not disturb" sign. He'd decided to ignore it, but the beating grew louder.

"What is with people pounding on doors when I'm with you?" He couldn't stop the grumble.

Her gaze darted to the door. "Mina," she whispered and started to rise.

Enjoying the last glimpse of her naked wet body, Sam tugged on pants, padded barefoot to the door, and looked out the keyhole. "It's your sister," he called and drew the bedroom and bathroom doors closed before yanking the suite door open.

Seconds later, Cami rushed from the bathroom wrapped in a robe with her skin still glistening and damp. Her sister had the worst timing. He shifted uncomfortably and grabbed for Cami.

Mina seemed oblivious to whatever she'd just interrupted. She jogged inside and dropped to a chair.

"I've got it." The excitement in Mina's voice contradicted her closed eyes and the sag to her shoulders. "I saw Sunny Sol and her gangster at the Brown Derby a couple months before her death. Wait until you hear this."

CHAPTER EIGHTEEN

"That's incredible." Sam slid more cilantro rice across the table to Mina, who had already devoured the tacos, street corn, and carne asada fries he'd had delivered from a local trendy place. She'd chronicled what she'd seen through Sunny Sol's eyes at the old Brown Derby. "To be able to see history. To live it."

"I don't live it." Mina shook the hot sauce bottle with a vengeance. "I'm not actually there. They can't see or hear me. I only get one person's impressions of the moment. It's not for real time travel."

"You sense what Sunny was thinking. You're in her head. Can you not see how amazing that is?"

Cami patted his thigh. She'd picked through some ceviche while they listened but didn't say much. "Mina's been doing this her entire life. What is a true marvel for us is her normal. It's overwhelming to us outsiders, but not to her."

"But it's like a peephole into the past." He put an arm around her shoulders. "This is science fiction stuff. I can't even imagine what it's like to experience that for a day. Let alone an entire lifetime."

"I'm getting better at it." Mina grinned, apparently not completely immune to his flattery, and shoveled down rice.

Cami smiled. "Yes, you are." She tucked her legs beneath the robe on the seat next to him.

He refused to let either of them trivialize Mina's slip. "You know exactly what Sunny is observing, what she's feeling."

"Sunny had this intense fear of the man, and still she couldn't resist goading him on. I could have peeked in his head, but I got enough from Sunny and her sass."

Cami agreed. "That fits with our research as far as her personality. You're saying what you saw through Sunny's eyes in this slip happened a few months before her death?"

Mina nodded. "He told Sunny he'd open a few gaming tables upstairs above her restaurant. Sunny said something like 'over my dead body,' and Felix Fortuno told her that can be arranged. So Sunny told him to go tread water to his barge or crawl back to Vegas since it'd turned out so well the last time."

Sam scratched his jaw before glancing at Cami, who nodded. He reached for his phone, ran a quick search, and showed a photo of Felix Fortuno to Mina. "That him?"

"No." Mina frowned. She took the photo and zoomed in on the image. "The mouth and nose are wrong. The hairline too."

"Not Felix Fortuno."

Mina sputtered in response. "But he talked about making her see the value of the profit they'd make off illegal gambling. He threatened her. He came off total mobster. Sunny didn't think or say his name, but if he wasn't Felix Fortuno, who the hell was he?"

He understood why Mina was pissed off. Based on what she'd said, she'd tried so hard, fought until she was exhausted to isolate that one moment in history. "He wore a hat? At the table? Inside the restaurant?"

"Yeah. And a suit. A nice one."

"Any real man wore a suit in those days. But she specifically mentioned his hat? And you saw it?" He gestured for her to keep eating.

"Yeah."

He pieced through the rest of the conversation she'd recounted. "Sunny talked about something floating?"

Mina finished eating and tossed a napkin. "He was a dancer. She talked about his foxtrot, said she'd heard his foxtrot hadn't been so graceful of a float lately."

"He wasn't a dancer. Not foxtrot the dance. *Foxtrot* was the name of his ship. She was talking about his ship, an illegal floating casino." He searched on his phone and showed Mina another image. "This the guy?"

"That's him." She jabbed her finger at the photo. "Who is he?"

"Arturo Davino. Also known as Artie the Hat."

"Your hunch about the photographs with him in the background was right." Cami pushed curls out of her face. "Looks like Sunny's mother had good reason to worry."

He lifted his hand to tuck the wayward strand behind her ear. "I need to follow up on the lead. See if I can find us a contact."

"Think Marilyn or Joe might have connections to someone who knows the family history?"

He shrugged. "Maybe my family history as well."

Cami opened her mouth, but Mina interrupted.

"Who are you two talking about?" Her gaze cut between them.

Sam probably should've been sympathetic to the fact he and Cami had shared enough in only a few weeks, they could communicate without everyone else in the room understanding what they said. Perhaps he was greedy, but he loved knowing what Cami meant when even her sister didn't.

Cami left his questions about his mystery uncle alone. "Remember when Sam told us he works on screenplays with his brother? Sam researches the local history."

He stretched an arm over the back of her chair. "My brother Joe specializes in Hollywood noir. Mafia stuff sells, especially mob stories from about 1910 through the 1940s. He's a big picture thinker. Good at dialogue. Great at action scenes. Not so good at historical detail and accuracy. My sister Lottie keeps him in check on clothes, makeup, hair, all the fashion stuff. The important details that'll give away a time period if they're wrong. I work on the straight history part. Who knew who. Who ran what. Connections, how the system worked then in Los Angeles, people in the news. People like Artie the Hat."

Mina glared at Cami. "You apparently haven't told us everything about your research."

"I haven't had a chance to. I've been..." She paused, looking at him. "I've been busy." She cleared her throat and looked across the room at something else, anything else.

He grinned. Her evasiveness was cute, as she obviously thought about what they'd already done in this room and she'd immediately glanced at him when she'd mentioned she'd been otherwise occupied. Not her work. Not her board certification. She was as distracted from her regular life as he was by their intense relationship. Good to know. He tugged her closer.

"What do you mean by mafia connections?" Mina asked.

He shrugged. "Organized crime infiltrated all parts of Hollywood, police, and government in Los Angeles then."

"How so?" She settled back into her chair.

"Studios owned the actors and directors. Criminals either outright owned the studios or banked their films. Every movie needed stage crew and transport staff. Those were union. Guess who ran the unions?" He stopped Cami before she could pick up the dirty food containers.

"Mobsters."

He tossed everything from the table into a bin. "Exactly. Those are only a couple of examples in one industry. The crime organization was pervasive." Tying off the bag, he carried it to the door.

"What else do you know about Sunny Sol's death and the time period that my sister hasn't shared?" Mina asked. She and Cami moved to the couches in the living room.

He glanced over his shoulder from the mini bar sink where he washed up. "How long you got?"

Mina rubbed her hands together. "You're definitely coming to South Pasadena next weekend. Wait until Delia hears this. It'll be another murder case she can work up. Plus Ruby's got great insight on death and disease and maiming."

Sam laughed and sprawled on the couch next to Cami.

She groaned and buried her face against his shoulder. "Mina," she scolded. "Learn to filter that kind of talk. Most families don't have a

DA who specializes in sex crimes and homicides or a paramedic who talks about her gunshot wound victims and traffic fatalities every day. Sam's going to think he's dating into an insane family."

Mina rolled her eyes. "But he already knows we are witches."

Cami hid her face behind her hand. He saw the other tightened around the sash of her robe. "Mina!" She lapsed into fast Spanish, not sounding the least bit sweet.

Sam laughed and hugged her when she glanced up between her fingers. He shook his head. How could he not be crazy about this woman? "I'm in."

* * *

A week later, Cami wondered if Sam knew exactly what he had gotten himself into. He sat in the backyard of her parents' house in South Pasadena, surrounded by her mother Ama, her sisters, and little Rose passed out asleep in Ruby's lap.

Rose's flushed face was slack with a bit of drool at the edge of her rosebud mouth. Ruby rubbed her baby's back in soothing lazy circles. Ama went inside the house for a pitcher of sangria. Cami leaned against Sam with his arm around her shoulders. Bogart flopped at her feet. This was the life.

"Parrots are out," Delia commented. Yellow-headed Amazons called from the trees above the high plank fence.

"Of course they are," Ama said as she returned and passed the sangria pitcher. "Cami's here. The wild parrots flock to our home when she's around."

"Wait." Sam pointed to the birds. "Are you saying those parrots come here because of Cami?"

"Absolutely. There have been wild parrots in South Pasadena for years, but they go and come as they like. They are drawn to our girl." She turned and gave Cami a searching and censuring look. "Haven't you told him about your abilities? Mina said he knew."

"I did, Ama, but we can't expect people to know the oddities we've lived with for a lifetime in a matter of weeks."

Ama clicked her tongue. "There's nothing odd about magic.

Witchcraft is as old or older than humanity, and Sam should know more about his own people."

He leaned forward like he was going to ask questions. She certainly had some of her own. What exactly did Ama mean about his people?

"It'll keep," Ama assured them. "Today my Kemina wants to speak of Sunny Sol."

"But I want to hear about Cami and Sam," Ruby said and jostled Rose. "Come on. I don't have a romance, and my sisters haven't had love lives lately to share."

Cami shook her head. Ruby had experienced enough adventure for three lifetimes, but she'd matched for magical strengths to pass onto her children, not love.

"How did you two meet?" Ruby shifted Rose lower in her lap.

"Delia, Mina, and I had breakfast at his restaurant." She didn't mention Mina's slip or anything incriminating with Ama this close.

"That's it?" Ruby crinkled her nose. "That's all I get?"

Cami didn't want to talk, didn't want to risk what she and Sam had pieced back together after the magic reveal. No matter what this was to him, whether he considered it a fling or an infatuation, she liked it. Loved it really. But she needed to figure out where this was going before she let it go too far.

Her board certification was over two years and a whole lot of work away. She didn't know what she feared more—failing at her own plans or losing precious time with Sam? And that alone scared the crap out of her. She scheduled her entire day around a few extra minutes to spend with him.

What if he dumped her? Nerves shot straight to her stomach.

He apparently didn't share her fears. "Later the same night I hauled Bogart into the animal hospital, and Cami took care of him."

"Nothing wrong with Bogart, right?" Mina scratched the dog's head between his ears.

He shook his head. "I still haven't figured out what happened to spill drain cleaner in the bathroom, but Cami said he didn't lick any off the floor."

"My sweet girl would know," Ama said. "More sangria, Sam?"

"Please. I'd love to get your recipe if you'd share it, Ama."

Cami tightened her hold on his thigh at the nickname coming from Sam's lips. She tried to remember if she'd told him that Ama was their version of mommy.

"Of course," Ama said with a dazzling smile. "The trick's in the soak and the chill."

"What?" he whispered when Ama moved away.

"Did I mention Ama is what we call her for mom?"

"So what am I supposed to call her?" he asked quietly.

Nothing escaped Ama's amazing hearing. She should've known better. Her mother gave Sam a gentle smile. "My given name is Eleuia, but feel free to call me Mom if Ama doesn't suit."

"Ama," she pleaded. Comments like this were why she hadn't been sure about bringing Sam.

Ama frowned at her daughter. "What?"

Ruby laughed. "You and Sam are lucky Ita isn't here. She would've pulled out old photo albums and naked baby pictures by now."

"Where is Ita?" Delia asked. "Gigi is artifact hunting somewhere in Europe."

"Who's Gigi?" Sam asked.

"Dad's mom," Cami said. "Ita is my mom's mom. She's always been Ita. It's our short for abuelita, Spanish for grandma."

"My Mamita is off wandering the jungles to visit my sister." Ama added for his benefit. "My twin sister is a goodwill ambassador, working with indigenous people to bring clean drinking water and medicine."

Sam didn't seem surprised. Cami figured he had seen enough of powerful women in her family not to be shocked anymore. He looked more distracted by Rose, who'd tilted sideways in her mother's lap.

"Want me to take the baby inside?" He offered. "I saw a crib by the kitchen."

Ruby smiled. "That would be heavenly. While she is a doll, she's a lot heavier than she looks."

Sam hefted Rose onto his shoulder and rubbed her back. Rose never stirred, only smacked her lips and nestled against him. Cami knew the feeling, that pull toward Sam's warmth and scent for comfort. She wondered if he had a special power for putting people at ease. It certainly worked on her. Except when her brain got in the way. She watched him walk away holding Rose. It was hard not to notice the sculpted arms and strong shoulders even with the baby drooling on his neck.

"Does she need a baby monitor?" He called over his shoulder.

"Nope." Ruby laughed. "My child's got lungs like a banshee."

Her sisters craned their necks and tipped their upper bodies to get a better look at Sam's retreating backside.

Delia clicked her tongue.

"Right?" Mina whispered. "That ass."

"So tight," Ruby agreed.

Delia's mouth tipped up in an almost smile. "Does it feel as solid as it looks?"

"Guys? Seriously?" Cami hissed.

Ama chuckled. "They're not wrong, my Camellia." Then she frowned at Cami's concerned expression. "It's not as though he notices anyone else. You're the only one worried about the relationship here."

She paled. "Is it that obvious?"

"Yes." The unanimous response echoed around the circle.

She bit her lip and checked to make sure he hadn't come back. "I don't know, Ama."

"He looks at you in adoration, mija. What's better than a good-looking man who watches you like that?"

She listened to the chorus of sighs from her sisters. They were right. Sam was handsome, successful, and marvelous between the sheets. On the desk. Anywhere. Her cheeks heated remembering how good he was. "He isn't the problem."

"You don't like him?" Ruby sounded shocked. "How could you not like that man? Is he bad in bed?

"Of course not," she snapped and then remembered Ama was there.

Mina interjected. "She likes him. She's still hung up on her crappy relationship with Neil."

Ruby looked like she had swallowed something bitter. "Why?"

"That manipulative asshole." Delia's lip curled.

"We are not talking about him." She refused to say his name. "Why do you keep bringing him up, Mina? I swear your constant reminders have me seeing him when he's not really there. It makes me feel like I'm going a little crazy."

"Because you won't let it go," Mina snapped, breaking a tortilla chip. "Planning your life down to the tiniest detail started with Neil. Whatever happened that last night you broke up with him?"

"I don't want to talk about it. I picked badly. I moved on."

"Then move on," Mina hissed.

"I am not discussing this. Especially not in front of Sam."

"Haven't you told him about Neil?" Delia asked.

"I've told him enough," she insisted and remembered the half-naked conversation in his lap. It'd been comforting but embarrassing as well. "This conversation is over."

"What about the calls and hang ups?" Mina asked. "You thought you saw him at the beach?"

On a jet ski trying to kill Sam. And in the background constantly. She'd wondered about Bogart's attempted poisoning and the library fire. Hell, she'd even worried about things she'd misplaced in her apartment, even though she was a zombie from a year of night shifts.

She was seriously starting to question her judgment and sanity when it came to her past coming back to haunt her. Maybe she was paranoid about her ex-boyfriend. What if he'd forgotten her?

"What are you doing about the phone calls?" Delia asked.

"I've already checked into it," Cami told her. "I'll get the number changed again."

Delia's brow furrowed, but at least she didn't say anything.

"Are you wearing your charm every day?" Ama asked and nodded to the pendant at Cami's throat.

"All the time. Though I think it's been misfiring. It's burned a few days when I know there couldn't have been danger. At work, outside of Sam's restaurant, around my own apartment, at the hotel."

Ama frowned. "We can check it later, but keep it on for now. Do you want me to brew a protection ward to take home with you?"

She remembered the breakup with Neil. "No. Magic isn't the answer."

Sam swung the screen door open. "Rose didn't budge when I

settled her in. Is it okay for the big-eared fox toy to stay with her?" He ambled down the stairs, pausing when he reached the circle of women. "Did I miss something?"

Ruby recovered first. "The fox is her favorite. She'll be fine. Thank you."

He sat beside Cami and slid his arm around her shoulders. She tried to relax and inhaled deeply as he rubbed knots from her neck. Bogart whined next to her.

"Why don't you two wait here, and we will get lunch on the table." Ama gave a meaningful look to Cami's sisters who stood and filed into the back door.

"I'll help." Sam rose, but stopped when Ama held up a hand.

"You do enough feeding people. Let us treat you." With that, Ama followed the sisters into the house.

"Do you want to talk about it?" he whispered.

She shook her head, touched her necklace, and then watched her sisters carry platters out of the kitchen and set up the backyard table with practiced ease.

Maybe she could make this work despite the bad and violent breakup with Neil. She glanced up at Sam. Even in profile, he looked strong and sure of things. He grinned at her. Ama called it adoration. Cami almost believed her. She smiled back.

"Dinner's on. Down to the mystery," Mina called and rubbed her hands. Over the food or the drama she had stirred up, Cami couldn't tell. At least they wouldn't be talking about her love life if they were talking about Sunny Sol's.

CHAPTER NINETEEN

Sam took the chair next to Cami's at the table. He'd been out of his depth at first, surrounded by all the Donovan women. He'd never seen a tougher, more loyal crew of sisterhood. He was sure he'd interrupted a serious topic of conversation between the sisters. Cami wasn't sharing, which meant it'd probably been about magic.

"Why don't you two bring us up to speed?" Direct as ever, Delia prompted the discussion. "I understand you've both researched Sol."

Cami started. "Sunny grew up on the East Coast. She was selected for an acting school sponsored by a studio. I forget which one."

"The Paramount School in New York." He passed a salad bowl and picked up the conversation when she nudged him under the table. "An experimental project. No one ever knew if it actually worked. The studios wanted new faces to overcome recent scandals and bad press. Sunny's beauty and stage experience made her a good candidate."

He trailed off for Cami to take over and shoveled salad in his mouth. This dressing tasted amazing. He'd have to raid Ama's recipes. Even Bogart had perked up at the possibility of table scraps.

Cami dished sautéed zucchini and peppers onto her plate. "Sunny moved to Los Angeles under contract with Paramount when she was twenty, right after her father died of a heart attack. She starred in over a hundred films. Most were short comedies, but she appeared with big names and worked for other studios."

He nodded. "The studios owned the actors, directors, and any talent really. Studios dictated everything—clothes, hair styles, makeup required in public, weight restrictions. Especially for women."

Ruby huffed. "That's stupid sexist."

"Not saying it was right." He held up his hands.

"Sunny lost weight at the school, and they expected her to keep it off." Cami stabbed a cherry tomato. "Newspapers reported she was on crazy diets and speculated she popped pills to keep the pounds off."

"Diet pills were amphetamines back in those days. Speed," Ruby clarified.

Cami waved her fork. "No one ever proved she took diet pills. After some big successes, she veered away from comedy to try a more serious role in a movie with director Paul Price."

"*Scoria*." He supplied the title, remembering the movie poster at the library.

"Never heard of it," Delia told him, passing the tortillas.

"Not a success." He took the round ceramic dish from her. "Though Sunny may have thought otherwise, since she and Price had a thing."

Cami finished while Sam ate. "Sunny Sol and Paul Price had an affair while making the movie. He was controlling. He made everyone call her a new name, Aubrey. He even addressed her funeral wreath to Aubrey. Paul obsessed over wiping out her past."

"Sounds like someone else's boyfriend," Mina muttered.

Cami shot her a reproachful eye. He watched the interplay between the two and knew better than to ask her what that had been about even before she shook her head. He'd really need to pry into her past relationship with the abusive asshole if she was willing to talk.

Surely, the guy wasn't still a threat. She would've told him, right? He lost the thread of conversation as he considered that and only picked back up when she told the sisters Paul Price was married to former silent film star Coral Elton, born Flora Wright.

"At the same time he had an affair with Sunny?" Ruby sneered. "Did Coral know?"

They both nodded.

Ruby let out an indignant noise and swallowed a mouthful. "If Mina senses foul play, then my money's on the jilted wife."

"Marriage wasn't the same then," Cami argued. "Especially not in the movie business. It was considered acceptable for married men to have a girl or two on the side. I'm not saying it was right."

Ama clicked her tongue. "That's not a generational dilemma, mija. That's been going on as long as there's been marriage."

Sam heard the teasing but warning nature of Ama's tone to her daughter. Maybe Cami had good reason for not wanting to talk about her father. He looked at Ruby and Delia. They were both tall, thin blondes. Not his type, as apparently his type was all bossy, curvy witch, but those two were knockouts. He'd bet their mother was gorgeous as well.

Cami plunged ahead with the story. "Sunny Sol and Paul Price had their affair. The movie flopped. Price left with his wife on a cruise to forget Sunny, and she married a wannabe mobster." She paused, thanking Ama for a refill.

"The two separated within months from an abusive marriage by all accounts. They divorced after two years. Sunny hooked up with Price again when she joined him and his wife in their restaurant business. They changed the business name to Sunny Sol's Seabreeze Café."

"Wait." Ruby put her hand up. "Sunny went from an abusive marriage to own a business with the ex-lover and his wife? Some women can really pick them."

Cami stopped in the middle of a bite to stare at her sister.

"Not you, kiddo," Ruby clarified and gestured toward Sam with a spoon. "We haven't found anything wrong with this one. Yet."

He didn't know who'd been more insulted—him or Cami. He seriously needed to have a conversation with her about the ex-boyfriend they all hated. She looked at her lap. He could tell she was either hurt or embarrassed or both. *Screw that.* Nobody picked on his woman. Not even her sisters.

"Hey, Ruby," he said. "You can let me know if I pass or fail inspection. I really could care less, but leave Cami out of it."

The table went silent. Cami blinked at him. *Well, hell.* They might be leaving early. He squeezed her hand.

Mina grinned. "Good to know."

Delia nodded. "Very interesting."

Even Ruby seemed to realize she'd stepped out of line. "Sorry," she muttered. "I might need some sleep."

"Sam, why don't you continue?" Ama suggested. She passed a bowl of fruit and spoke softly in Spanish. Sam didn't know what she'd said, but the mood at the table immediately mellowed.

He tipped his head in her direction. Ama was a force. He'd do well to remember that. "Sunny's café sat straight down the hill from the not-so-happy Price couple's mansion, Casa Oceana."

Mina frowned. "But Paul lived in a second-floor apartment with Sunny above the café. I've seen him there."

Sam paused. *She'd seen Paul Price there with Sunny Sol?* He shook his head as if to clear it. "Mina, I don't know that I'll ever get used to your unique perspective on history."

"Join the club," Delia said. "It grows on you. Doesn't mean it won't still shock the shit out of you now and then."

"As Mina said, Sunny Sol and Paul Price continued to live and work together until her death in December 1933. Sol attended a party at The Frontero. We know some things about the party from the coroner's inquest transcript and grand jury leaks."

"Why only leaks?" Ama asked. "Where's that transcript?"

Everyone looked to Delia, who sighed. "Because the grand jury would've been investigatory. There wouldn't have been a court reporter. No official documentation. No transcript." She reached for her glass and looked at Cami. "I'm assuming witnesses talked after the fact even with an admonition not to."

Cami nodded. "Witnesses and grand jurors talked to reporters. There were so many contradictory statements." She pushed her food across the plate. "There's a lot of misinformation published about Sunny's death. Getting to the truth of it won't be easy."

"We know she went to The Front Saturday night," he said. "She left there about 3:00 a.m. Sunday morning."

Cami put down her fork. "Her chauffeur dropped her off in front of the restaurant. He saw her going up the stairs to the apartment she shared with Price. We don't know anything else until she was found dead Monday morning in the garage by her maid."

"Mabel," Mina said. "Mabel was her maid's name."

He realized Mina had seen that discovery by the sorrowful tone of her voice. He cleared his throat to break the sad silence. "The coroner said she died of carbon monoxide poisoning."

Delia interrupted. "Listed as accidental, suicide, or homicide by the coroner?"

"Why does it have to be one of those three?" Ama asked.

"It does." Both Delia and Ruby agreed.

Cami looked at Sam with large worried eyes. She must have still been upset over Ruby's earlier comment. Or maybe she was nervous he'd be creeped out by her older sisters' easy handle on death and murder. He wasn't. It was part of their jobs. He winked at her and was rewarded with a shy smile.

"The death certificate lists it as accidental," she told them.

Delia frowned. "So what's the problem, Mina?"

"They're wrong." Mina might be the baby, but he was happy to see she held her own. She didn't question her powers. He sure as hell wouldn't doubt it, though he wondered what else she could see. Cami said she could see the future. Had Mina seen his future? His and Cami's?

Mina never looked up from her food. "I've been to the garage. There's something wrong there. A dark, bad feeling. It's been blocking my vision."

"The speculation about Sunny's death started right away," Cami assured her sister. "Her body was cremated soon after. The coroner's inquest wrapped within four days of her death."

"Quickest damn work I've ever heard from the coroner's office," Delia said. Her fork and knife stilled. "Testimony too?"

"Yes."

Delia shook her head and continued cutting. "Apparently medical examiners had a lot less work then. Trying to get one to testify in four months now is difficult with tox screens and all. Four days? Impossible."

"The press and her fans screamed murder," Sam told her. "That sped up the process."

"But who could've done it? Who were the suspects?" Delia asked.

"The controlling lover who told her to be home on time from the party and locked her out when she wasn't," Sam offered. "Or the wannabe mobster ex-husband who may or may not have gotten into a fight with her at the Frontero party."

"Don't forget the jilted wife," Ruby added with her mouth full. "I'd resent some young thing shacked up with my husband in my restaurant if I'd been Coral."

"Not likely," Sam argued.

"Why do men never expect it to be the women?" she countered.

"I've seen plenty of violent women. Stone cold killers," Delia said and tipped back her almost empty glass.

"Coral Elton gave odd statements about seeing Sol around the estimated time of death," Cami said.

"When was that?" Delia asked.

"Twelve to thirty hours before discovery Monday morning about half past ten," Cami told them.

"That's overbroad and not helpful. What else did they find? Drugs? Alcohol?" Delia had clearly lapsed into prosecutor brain. Sam would bet she was intimidating in the courtroom.

"Alcohol."

"Level?"

"Point one-five percent."

Delia looked at Ruby. "Her blood alcohol level could've been on the rise. More likely descending. Forensic blood alcohol contents get tricky."

Ruby nodded. "Descending given the estimated time of death." Her fingers moved over the glass like she was doing math in her head. "It could've been higher than point thirty percent when she died. Girl would've have been barely functioning if she'd been that drunk."

"The chauffeur said she was sober when he left her," Cami corrected.

"We don't know what else she had to drink after he drove away." Ruby pushed back from the table. "Any food in her system?"

"Partially undigested peas and green beans."

"Peas and carrots," Sam said. That's what he'd read.

She tipped her head. "Misinformation again spread all over the internet, recordings, even books. The coroner specifically said peas and green beans."

Sam was impressed. Maybe he'd recruit her as part of the family research team for screenwriting.

"Any physical signs of abuse? Injury?" Delia asked.

"She had a loose false tooth in the front, blood on her face around her nose and mouth, and police found blood drops on the running board of the car," Cami said. "No one knows how much for sure because Price wiped some away."

He'd definitely ask her to be part of the family research crew. He grinned. There was nothing like finding a hot smart woman.

"What signs of carbon monoxide poisoning did they find?" Ruby wanted to know.

"Sunny was dead," Mina snapped. "How much more of a sign do you need?"

"Cut that out if you want help from this little Scooby Doo gang," her oldest sister told her.

"She had a red face." Cami paused, appeared to scroll through her mental feed. "The coroners said it was consistent with carbon monoxide poisoning."

"Also consistent with cyanide poisoning," Ruby said, reaching for the water pitcher.

Wow. Sam needed to hang out with these women more often. Maybe he'd need to consult with all the sisters for Joe's next project.

"All right," Delia interrupted. "Let's not go all Soviet spy theory. Stick with the most obvious reason. She was found dead in her car in a closed garage which strongly suggests carbon monoxide poisoning. They tested her blood, right?"

"Yes." Cami traced her finger along the edge of her glass.

"They found carbon monoxide present in the blood?"

"Yes."

"So was it suicide?"

"Absolutely not," Mina argued.

"Did you see that in a slip? Because I'm not the one jumping to conclusions here. You asked for our help." Delia's voice snapped like a cold wind through the warm afternoon air.

Mina didn't answer.

Cami added. "Sol bought Christmas presents, planned a New Year's party, and had contracted new work projects. That doesn't sound suicidal."

"So maybe it was an accident like the coroner said," Delia reasoned.

"Maybe," Cami conceded, reaching down to calm Bogart. Sam wondered if she'd realized she'd even done it as she sorted through facts. "It'd have been chilly out. It was windy. Sunny could've been waiting out the cold and turned the car on for warmth. But if it wasn't suicide or accident, then how did the drops of blood that tested positive for carbon monoxide get outside the car door?"

"Someone would've had to push Sunny back in the car," Mina whispered. "While she was dying. What about Artie the Hat?" Mina rubbed goosebumps from her arms. "The guy I saw from the Brown Derby?"

Sam shook his head. "I've put feelers out for leads on Arturo Davino's family, but no one is calling me back. I didn't push because it's been a crazy busy week at the restaurant."

Delia's head snapped up. "Davino?"

While the three of them explained who Artie the Hat was, Delia took her phone off the table. The woman was never more than six inches away from it. She touched the screen a few times and held it to her ear.

"Tony, it's Donovan. No, your guy's going down on the case. I hope he paid you well. Sure, we'll do dinner together sometime after the trial. Listen, you know anything about Artie the Hat?" She held the phone away from her ear. "Yeah? My sister and her guy would like to talk with you about your favorite subject when you've got time. You okay with them bringing their dog? They can be there in an hour. Thanks."

Delia hung up without saying goodbye and stared at Cami and Sam. "Hope you two like sailing."

CHAPTER TWENTY

"THANK YOU FOR AGREEING TO SPEAK WITH US, MR. DAVINO." CAMI TOOK the hand the man offered to board the massive sailboat. Sam carried Bogart aboard, wrapped in an obligatory life vest similar to the ones they all wore.

"Call me Tony, please." The silver-haired man gestured to a bench. "No rough waters expected today, and no racing for us either. We're merely observing a youth team out practicing for the upcoming regatta." He pointed to a sleek, small boat cutting through the waves. "I sponsor the *Fortune's Foxtrot*. We call it the *Foxtrot* for short. You could say seafaring and risky adventures are in my blood."

She watched with Tony as the five young men on the other vessel worked together to maneuver the bow through the water. "Your sister probably told you I work as a defense counsel. Most of those boys weren't cut from the same privileged cloth as the other kids hanging out in the yacht club. I give them purpose. They win me trophies and championship cups." He winked at her. "Now, what can I help you with?"

She decided to take the direct approach. Certainly it'd be expected if he'd worked with Delia. But how to ask a man if his father had been a mobster, possibly responsible for the death of Sunny Sol? "Mr. Davino…"

"Tony." He tugged on a pair of aviator sunglasses.

"Tony." She cleared her throat and tucked her blowing curls behind her ears, blaming the breeze for her nervous tics. "We read an entry in Leslie Sol's journal suggesting her daughter Sunny Sol spent her last day with someone affiliated with the Davino family. She also wrote your family assured her Sunny was returned safely to the address where she was found dead the next day." She almost had to yell to be heard above the water and wind. Unfortunately, the volume of every noise except her voice receded when she mentioned Sunny's death.

Tony smirked. The lines around his mouth suggested it was an expression he wore often. "So the old biddy paid attention to the letters my old man sent her. Uncle Joey drove him crazy 'til Pops wrote her. Or maybe she meant the one I mailed to her later as a punk orphan kid, trying to reach out to a mother with no surviving children." He squawked commands over a radio, and the other boat shot through the water with a full sail. "She never did ask any questions. Figure she got scared off by all the media attention."

"Your father was Artie the Hat?" Sam asked. "The bootlegger and illegal gambling criminal?"

"Alleged criminal. We prefer entrepreneur." Tony walked the boat with steady sea legs, monitoring the proficient sailors who operated it. He never interrupted or intervened, yet they seemed to read his body language. He folded his arms in the lightweight windbreaker.

"I could've gone back to the family name of Sabato after Pops got poisoned, but I figured why bother. Oh, and Pops didn't kill Sunny Sol. I don't know who did. But it wasn't him. And he didn't order it."

Cami couldn't hide the disappointment. They'd come out here for nothing more than a blanket denial and dismissal? Her face scrunched up against the sun and spray. "Can you tell us anything more about her last day?"

"You a reporter? Or you making a movie?" He stared at Sam. "Is he? Because I gotta say I don't owe Donovan that big of a favor."

"No, Mr. Dav…" She caught herself before she blurted the rest of his name. "Tony." She glanced over the water. It seemed fitting she'd admit to someone, anyone, why she felt compelled to find the answer to Sunny's death out here on the ocean. "Sunny Sol attracted bad men. Violent men. She loved men who probably couldn't give her the same in return. I guess what I want to know." She took a deep breath and pushed ahead. "I need to know what happened to her. And how could it not have happened." She swallowed the last word. "How a woman could've undone those choices."

Tony's eyes narrowed, and he studied her face. Hard. He jerked his head in Sam's direction. "He one of those choices?" His tone sounded like he'd fit Sam with some cement galoshes out this far from shore. Maybe Tony had inherited more than a love of the sea from his father.

"No," she admitted. "I'm hoping he's the answer to choices I've made."

Tony lapped the deck again. His eyes stayed trained on *Foxtrot*. His young apprentices were excellent sailors. The wind kicked up, and they'd taken advantage of the change.

Tony sat next to her, kicking one ankle over the opposite knee. "Pops wanted to open a gaming room upstairs at Sunny's café. A few guys in the business did. But in December 1933, Paul Price sold the rights to Alan Knapp because Coral Elton owed a gambling debt to the Cosmo Club, Knapp's gaming hall over in Glendale. Knapp also bought The Frontero in 1938 not long before it went bankrupt."

She leaned closer. "The club where Sunny went to her last party."

Tony nodded and wiped the spray from his glasses with the bottom of his shirt. "My Pops sent a note to Sunny at The Front, letting her know she'd been sold out. She never wanted gaming in her place. She planned to keep it reputable."

He stopped briefly to check on the other crew. They'd picked up speed. "Alan meant trouble for Sunny. More than he'd be worth. Because the local mafia planned to run all of Los Angeles when it came to gambling. Knapp had already cut into the business. Sunny's place would've attracted enforcers with the addition."

"No more reputable restaurant," she guessed.

"Not with Alan in charge." Tony's ankle bounced where it dangled. The wind had popped again, and the waves were getting choppy. "Pops ambushed Sunny on the stairs to her place after her chauffeur dropped her off from the party. Not to hurt her. Just to reason with her. Paul Price had already locked the apartment up tight, the little prick. Pops brought her to the boat to think it over and sleep off the mad. The next day he offered her a driver to take her out for errands and return her to her restaurant. End of story." He walked away.

Water splashed over the bow. Sam tugged Bogart closer. "Damn, the chop picked up fast. This would be shit surfing weather."

A tingle shot down her spine. She touched her amulet. Nothing. She tapped into Bogart. No anxiety there. The dog had been on the water enough to ride out a change. Yet the prickle slid along the slickness of her skin as sure as the sea spray. She closed her eyes and dared to send out a thread of connection to her elemental magic. *There.* In the distance, she could sense the dread.

Screams ripped her from the link.

"The *Foxtrot*," Sam urged. "She's in trouble."

Cami scanned the horizon. A sail had fallen. The boat listed dangerously to one side, throwing a young crewman to the edge. She jumped to her feet and rushed starboard alongside Tony, who barked futile orders into the radio. The roar of the ocean and static was the only response. Tony clung to the rail with a white-knuckled grip. The *Foxtrot* teetered perilously close to capsizing.

Cami clasped the same railing beside the hand of this man who'd taken a chance on some kids, who had shared his family history, who loved the sea. She met his terrified gaze for a moment before reaching for the gift she'd been born to wield. She didn't need to touch the water to connect. She would become part of it. She burrowed deeper than she had since the element had urged her to drown Neil. Or had she wanted it, and the ocean listened?

Still. She breathed in. *Easy.* The waves calmed. *May you harm none.* The shouts sounded like distant, faraway voices echoing through a tunnel. She pushed with her magic. A gentle force. Only enough to cradle the *Foxtrot*. She blew through pursed lips, shaking with the effort of holding back the tide inside her.

The vessel righted. The sail still hung to one side, but the crew scrambled to fix the failed equipment. When the *Foxtrot* floated safely on the water and the crew radioed an all-clear, Tony told everyone to head in.

He glanced down at her, his expression unreadable behind the aviators he slid back on. "I'm thinking about getting a new boat." His voice was soft, respectful. "Maybe I could call it *Golden Eyes*." Cami blinked away from him. "Or maybe *Sea Witch*."

"I will deny anything you may have imagined." She straightened her spine. "What if you tell me the rest of the story you know about Sunny, and we call it a truce we don't talk about again?"

She waited, hoping she'd been able to bluff this man into believing she was every bit as tough as Delia, even though her fists hid trembling fingers and her legs were about to give way from something other than the sea. Tony stared off at the *Foxtrot* until the crew waved. The pride and fearlessness of youth might turn this into a happy adventure those boys could joke about later.

Tony bowed his head. "Deal."

She walked on unsteady legs to Sam, who took one look at her magic-filled eyes and pulled her into his lap. When they'd docked and Tony had checked on the *Foxtrot* and her crew, he brought a blanket to wrap around her shoulders.

"I can't prove this. It's all hearsay, so I'd appreciate it if you keep it close. Consider it my family's gift to yours." Tony cut a look at Sam. "What did you say your name was, boyfriend?"

Sam hadn't given a name. She sent him a silent plea. "Corraza. Sam Corraza."

"And what is it you do for work, Corraza?" Tony rolled Sam's name around on his lips as though sampling it. "Something good enough to get you a Donovan girlfriend?" She smiled at the implication.

"I own a restaurant in Pacific Palisades. Feel free to stop by sometime."

"Huh." Tony sat down heavy. "Uncle Joey's youngest stepsister married a Corraza. She sent him a letter to say her boy opened a restaurant out here. A nice beachfront place. Of course, he'd be at least my age by now." He waved a hand and moved to sit across from them. "Must be a common last name."

Sam paled. "Is it?"

She reached for Sam at the crack in his voice, but he took her hand and tucked it against his chest. He gave a subtle shake of his head before Tony might look back at them.

Tony rested his elbows on his knees. "Pops took Sunny in her car down to the dock before dawn Sunday morning. Pops wouldn't have hurt her. It wouldn't have been any benefit to business. He wanted her to trust him so he could make a move on her place. She was angry with Paul Price, with his old lady, and maybe with Pops. But she slept on his boat. When she woke up, Pops offered her food, but she only picked at the veggies. She was on a diet, she told him."

"Peas and green beans. She'd only eat the green vegetables," she guessed.

"You got it." He lifted his hand. "Pops might've offered her a diet pill for a little pep and to help with the weight loss. You know how hard the studios were those days on their 'property,' right?"

"Yes." She leaned against Sam, filling the void left by the sudden, substantial magic she'd used with the comfort of his touch.

"Uncle Joey wasn't my blood though he loved me and looked after me when Pops died. He was out here in '33 because his family had run into some trouble back east. Mafia kind of trouble. On Sunny's last day, about eight in the morning, Pops told Uncle Joey to go out with Sunny and keep an eye on her."

"Did he?" Sam asked, pulling her even more tightly against him.

Tony chuckled bitterly. "Uncle Joey said until he died how Sunny had been the most beautiful woman in the world, like she was an angel come to Earth. He relived his couple of hours with her down to the smallest detail throughout his life."

Tony offered her a bottle of water. When she politely declined, he popped the top for himself. "He said they bonded over being east coast transplants who'd had losses in their family. Sunny drove them all over the city in her flashy convertible wearing the same sparkling silver evening dress."

"They went to a Christmas tree lot. Sunny ordered a tree painted silver, and he teased her for being so gaudy." Tony huffed a laugh. "They were headed for a party when she stopped at a drug store to use the phone. Uncle Joey relieved a closed liquor shop of a bottle of gin for her hostess gift. By the time she got back in the car, she was shaking and said she had to get to Casa Oceana. She nearly drank the whole bottle before they roared up to the garage about 10:30 Sunday morning."

She bit her lip. So many details of his narrative corroborated information leaked from witness statements.

Tony smiled, a faraway look on his face. "Uncle Joey said Sunny kissed him. Told me she tasted like Christmas morning."

She grabbed Sam's arm, sadness washing over her.

Tony glanced down at the drink in his hand, swirling the remains. "Uncle Joey waited down at the café, but she didn't come. He figured she'd changed her mind." He took a long last drink before tossing the bottle. "Joey always did feel guilty about Sunny's death. Wondered if he could've changed it."

She locked gazes with him and lay her head against Sam's chest. While the weariness of tapping her powers subsided slowly at his touch, the heaviness of the possibility Sunny had been a heartbeat from happiness crashed into Cami. She'd expected to uncover consequences of bad romance. Not an unhappy ending to a new one.

They'd reached the end of a promising lead. She shifted against Sam, remembering the sparkling silver dress Joey had described–the same shimmering fabric as the piece Cami had stolen from Leslie Sol's possessions.

CHAPTER TWENTY-ONE

"IF JOEY LEFT SUNNY WALKING INTO PAUL AND CORAL'S MANSION IN broad daylight, there goes the accidental 'trying to stay warm on a cold night' death theory. We don't believe she committed suicide based upon our research. So who killed her?" Cami snapped earrings into her lobes.

Sam leaned against the counter in his bathroom almost a week after their conversation with the gangster's son, watching her put on lip gloss and mascara from her duffel bag. Maybe he'd need to upgrade to a bigger apartment when he moved her in. Not if. *When.* He'd have to take that step slowly, since she'd turned down his offer for even a drawer he'd cleaned out.

What was the big deal about her keeping a damn drawer at his apartment? It was only space, and he was tired of wondering when he'd get to see her between long shifts at the restaurant. Wait, what had she asked? He didn't want to admit he'd forgotten what she'd said while he stared at her.

"If Artie the Hat didn't do it, who did?" She prompted. "Or do you think his son was covering for him?"

Sam's gaze met her questioning one. Oh, right. Murder mystery. "Artie's son loved him. That was clear enough. Even called him Pops like I call my Grandpa Corraza." Hell, maybe Pops was related to this Uncle Joey. How many ocean-side restaurant owners named Corraza could there be in SoCal? Pops always said his people had been a little shady, but loyal to family. Unlike Sam's parents.

"Must be an Italian thing." She ran a finger over her brows. "But do you think he was lying to us?"

Sam shrugged. "Artie the Hat was never connected with a murder, but he was a part of the crime family. After the casino in Vegas he'd started with his brothers failed because of Felix Fortuno and the East Coast mafia, who knows how desperate he got."

"I don't think Artie did it." She studied her reflection and scrunched her hair before dragging stray strands off her collar.

"Love the School House Rocks shirt," he told her.

She tugged on it, swinging her shoulders side to side.

He kissed her hair, breathing in the ocean scent. "Thanks for coming to the beach and the restaurant with me today."

He'd picked her up early and watched as she played fetch with Bogart in the ocean while he took a work call. He didn't know if she talked to Bogart or controlled the water around them or both. She didn't talk much about her powers. Or anything, he realized with a frown. He'd talked with her every night this week, but somehow the conversation always came back to the restaurant.

She packed her makeup in the bag. "You haven't told me what we're doing other than a night at the park. You sure I'm dressed for it?"

He glanced at his sweatshirt wrapped around her waist. Curves like a Coke bottle and wearing his clothes. Could she be any hotter? "You look perfect. We're headed to Will Rogers Park."

"Named for the cowboy actor?" She braced a hand on his arm as she stepped from one foot to the other, slipping on her sandals. He nodded and stared at the pink pedicure. There was something so sexy about a woman with painted toenails.

He followed her into the kitchen where Bogart rose to rub his head against her. She reached into the fridge for water.

She trailed her fingers over the silvery reflection of the door. "I still can't believe this is your place. Fancy stainless steel appliances. And you have a stove!"

He replayed her last words in his head. "Wait, sweetheart, you don't have a stove?"

"Nope," she admitted. "It's more of a wet bar than a kitchen. Mini fridge and all."

What the hell? "How do you cook?"

"Hot plate and a small microwave." She shrugged. "My starting salary doesn't go very far in Santa Monica beach rents, and I don't know how to cook anyway."

He groaned. Obviously, he needed to move her in with him as soon as possible. "Remind me to feed you more. Anything else your place is missing?"

"I don't have a washer and dryer in the apartment like you do. Or a bedroom with a door. Now that's sexy." At her suggestive tone, he skimmed a hand to her waist.

"The ways we have used my bedroom door? Beyond sexy." Memories of pressing her against the door for the first time and the sounds she'd made had him pulling her close. Cami hummed in a cute agreement before she brushed her mouth against his. She nipped at his lower lip.

He kissed her back, tasting her. His hands roamed to the sweatshirt draped over her butt. "Stop," he told her. "Or we won't make it to our date. We'll have one right here."

She kissed him once more and pulled away. "I can't wait to see what surprise you've planned."

He shook his head. "Such high expectations. Come on Bogie, let's see if we can deliver."

They piled into the Land Cruiser and headed up the PCH to Pacific Palisades with Bogart hanging out the rear passenger window. The park rolled in the hills off Sunset Boulevard, a green oasis of horseback trails and polo fields among the mansions packed along the ritzy street. Two lines of cars snaked the entrance. Sam pulled out a prepaid parking pass.

"Wow. I like a prepared man," Cami said.

The park sprawled toward a white ranch house flanked by a full porch that welcomed guests with rocking chairs and blooming flowers. Gourmet food trucks lined the parking lot behind the house. In the rolling front yard, hundreds of people lounged on spread blankets and lawn chairs, waiting for the show to begin on a massive inflatable movie screen.

"An outdoor movie night?" she asked.

"Given your family's exploration into the life and death of Sunny Sol, I thought a couple of her films might interest you. It'll be fun. Even with the creep factor that she and Will Rogers died fairly close in time, and we are basically watching her movies on his front yard." Sam's brow creased as he made that eerie connection.

He glanced to see if he'd freaked her out, but she was still smiling. "They're playing two of Sol's comedies. We get a double showing since they're only about an hour each."

She looked toward the waves of people and dogs lounging between coolers, picnic baskets, beach bags, and backpacks. A rock band jammed near the screen. Dogs roamed on leash back and forth between blankets, food trucks, and the ranch house. Every inch looked to be crammed with casual good times.

"It's perfect." She squeezed his thigh. "I guess we better hurry to mark our spot."

He kissed her knuckles before he let go to turn into the almost full lot. "No need. I reserved us VIP seating up front and packed blankets and a cooler in the back. I tossed in your favorites from today's lunch at the restaurant."

He pointed to the food trucks parked ahead as he let Bogart out of the back and clipped his leash. "For dessert, Drunken Cake Pops serves liquored cake bites, and The Recess Truck has ice cream treats."

She laughed. "Of course, you'd be after the sweets."

He slung an arm around her waist to pull her close. "Got my sweet right here."

She sighed, and her soft curves sank against him. Maybe he should've taken an extra few minutes and tried to get her in the bedroom. They'd never have left the house if he'd gotten her naked, and they would've missed the movies. Seeing her excitement he knew he'd made the right choice.

They held hands and walked Bogart among the food trucks.

"Any you want to hit up?" he asked.

"All of them?"

He laughed. His girl had an appetite, and he hadn't found time to eat with the restaurant so busy. "You don't have to twist my arm."

"How about a sandwich? Or maybe pizza? Oh look, lobster rolls!" She dragged him toward the Lobsta Truck and got in line.

"How about some lemonade?"

"Sounds good. Ow." She grabbed at her necklace, yanking the charm away from her skin.

"What's wrong?" He touched his finger to the pendant and jerked it back when the metal burned him. "Damn!"

He tried to make the connection between her normally cool golden necklace and the blazing hot coal he'd handled, but Cami only grabbed his arm to steady herself and tiptoed to scan the crowd.

"It must be misfiring," she muttered.

He had no clue what she meant, and she didn't look like she wanted to share.

"Want to take it off?" he asked. "At least until it cools down?"

She bit her lip and nodded. She turned and he undid the clasp, dropped the chain in his pocket, and trailed his fingertips down her neck while he checked for marks. Seeing nothing, he kissed her forehead and stepped up to order for them.

They ate a picnic feast on their fancy reserved spot near the front of the crowd. Sam laughed when Cami told Bogart to eat his own food and leave theirs alone, but then he stopped when Bogie immediately did what she told him. She worried he didn't want her using magic with Bogart, although he hadn't seemed to mind this morning at the beach.

She was searching for the right way to ask when her phone lit up. She figured it was family and glanced down. The old familiar number turned her stomach. How had Neil gotten her unlisted number?

She punched the power button on her phone to turn it off. This must've been why the pendant went off so suddenly. Maybe she should've taken a protection ward from Ama. She would ask about finally getting that restraining order. Anything to relieve the sudden knot in her stomach.

"What's wrong?" Sam leaned toward her. "You okay?"

She tossed her phone in the oversized bag he'd brought and plastered on a bright smile. "It's nothing."

He didn't look convinced. "You sure?"

She breathed, relaxed, and pushed aside the bad taste and worry. What could be better than movies in a park with great food, an adorable dog, and this amazing man?

"I'm positive." Her tone convinced even her inner critic that this date wouldn't be tainted by the shadow of her past. She'd left Neil four hundred miles north almost a year ago. She'd get a new, stronger lock for her door and be more vigilant starting first thing in the morning. She could call Ama for wards if necessary. Nothing would spoil tonight.

The lights faded, and the movie screen flicked to life to cheers. Laughter spread through the audience at the jokes and gags of the comics. Sunny Sol's beautiful face shone over her flawless timing. She'd been funny, adapting to each role effortlessly, and besting her male costars with downplayed wit and silliness. Cami was enchanted. How could a woman so amazing attract such awful men?

Minutes into the movie, Sam lay his head in her lap. She divided her attention between the screen and running her fingers through his hair. She could feel the tension melting with every laugh.

Almost an hour later, Bogart lifted his head from his paws and whined. She whispered to Sam that Bogart needed a walk and started to stand but he grabbed her hand.

"I've got him." He kissed her knuckles. "You finish the movie. We'll be back in a few minutes. Maybe with dessert."

She smiled and shook her head, marveling over how much she adored this man. She'd fallen in love with him. She couldn't begin to deny the feeling. How could she when he was walking away looking amazing in those jeans and coaxing Bogart through the crowd as the dog tried to stop for petting and snacks? She was still smiling when she turned back to find Neil next to her.

CHAPTER TWENTY-TWO

"HELLO, CAMELLIA," NEIL DRAWLED. HE STRETCHED OUT WHERE SAM had been seconds before. "You take playing hard-to-get to a whole new level." He propped on an arm and straightened the corners of the blanket. "You enjoying being the plaything to a new rich boy?" He whistled softly. "Sam Corraza. Way to aim for someone completely out of your league. What does he see in you anyway? You've barely finished school. You're boring. You can't cook for his restaurant, and you're not pretty enough to work there. Obviously, he hasn't fucked you more than once, or he'd be bored and gone."

Cami swallowed. She wanted to look for Sam but didn't risk taking her eyes off Neil. "Why are you here?"

"Not such a smart question for such a supposedly smart girl. You should've known I'd find you. I've been calling, and you didn't answer. Such a bitchy move. I thought I'd help you remember your manners." He reached for her arm.

She flinched. "Don't you dare touch me." Her voice didn't shake in the slightest.

Neil leaned away before the smirk returned. "He isn't here to protect you."

"Leave. Now." She pushed to kneel, but he yanked her back down. She froze at the vicious look on his face.

"I don't think so. I just got here." He poked at the remains of their dinner and ran his eyes up and down her body. "No wonder you've gotten fat. What's he letting you eat?"

"Go away." The harsh whisper didn't even sound like her voice.

"In a minute. Maybe. *After* you've learned I can always find you and your surfer boyfriend. His dog is a damn barker. Did he enjoy the drain cleaner? Fucking mutt almost bit my leg off when I kicked at him. I only wanted to see what your boyfriend kept upstairs."

Bile rose in her throat, gagging her. He'd tried to poison Bogart.

"Hey, who's the hot librarian? Friend of yours? And that hotel. Such a swank place. Did boyfriend sleep with you and your sister? Oh, I almost forgot to ask about your family. How's Ama been lately? I stopped by her house and saw her holding a baby in the yard. Cute brat. Ruby's? Hope she won't require as much discipline as you did."

"Don't talk about my family. Or Sam." She clenched her jaw. After their fight she'd been bloody with black and blue bruises that had turned sickening shades of green and yellow. He'd hit her so hard across the face she'd been knocked off her feet. He'd followed with kicks and fists.

It hadn't been the first time he'd left marks on her. Each time he'd hurt her before that night, she'd apologized for whatever she'd done to provoke him because she'd believed it would make things better. It never did.

She'd run scared of this man for months. She'd been afraid of how he could hurt her or how he would take the revenge he'd promised on her family. She was even more terrified of what he'd pushed her to do during their last struggle at the water's edge.

Neil wiped his hand on the blanket in disgust. "Is Corraza enjoying my leftovers? Maybe he won't be so interested once he knows you're a carnie sideshow."

"Stop." She breathed in, pushed away the fear, and reached for her powers.

He snarled. "You think I forgot what you tried to do to me, freak? You're going to tell me how you did it."

"Leave, Neil. Or I'll finish it this time." It wasn't an empty threat. She'd been taught from birth not to use her powers to harm, but because of Neil, she'd crossed that line.

He'd pushed until she'd lashed out. She'd forced the water over his head, heard him gasp for air, and tried to drown him. She could've backed off, but she didn't. She'd enjoyed it too much to stop. He'd almost died. She'd wanted him to die. The same darkness rose again within her now.

"No water here," he snickered, but he looked unsure. "I'd hate for your boyfriend to have another close call out on his board. I might have to tell the cops how you tried to drown me and threatened me again tonight. I bet your fancy frigid district attorney sister would just love that."

"The jet ski." Her stomach twisted. "That was you."

He flashed a savage bearing of teeth. "Not so stupid after all. Had a string of bad luck lately?"

He'd already come so close to hurting Sam and Bogart. What else had he done?

She started to press him for answers, but he yanked one of her curls.

"I'll be seeing you. You're mine. Never forget it." He strode away before she could lift her hand to her scalp to rub away the pain.

She wrapped her arms around her knees and took deep breaths to control the shaking that had taken over her entire body. He'd been to her family's home. He'd seen Rose.

Had he been following her this whole time, stalking her and waiting for this moment? The perfect time to strike? To make her feel small and insignificant. Panic spiked until eighty pounds of slobbering dog hurled into her. Bogart snuffed and licked every inch of her as he fought his way into her lap.

"Bogart!" Sam yelled and ran after the dog. She held Bogart with both arms, soothing and taking comfort at the same time. "I don't know what happened, sweetheart. He took off on me. He growled and ran through the crowd to get to you. He's never done that." Sam crouched next to her to check on the dog and stopped when he saw her face. "What's wrong?"

She sniffed and held the dog tightly. "Can we go?"

"Tell me what upset you." His tone was insistent, urgent. She couldn't bear to see something happen to him because of her.

"I need to leave." She tipped her face up to his. "Please."

"Back to my place?" His voice was rough, low, and sounded uncertain. She nodded and bit her lip to stop the trembling.

He hustled them to the truck and drove straight to his apartment. She struggled to find the courage to drag him into this mess. She already had according to Neil. God, what if he'd hurt Bogart, an innocent animal? Or Sam for dating the wrong woman? His words that Sam was out of her league and that she had nothing to offer him played again and again in her mind. Doubt silenced her. What if he'd been partly right?

Sam reached for her leg, and she jerked before forcing her body to relax. She couldn't give Neil power over her again. He'd taken too much already. She touched Sam's hair, brushed her fingers through his curls, ran her hand down the muscles of his shoulders, and tried not to imagine what it'd be like to lose him. For such a short romance, the possibility of an end shot icy fingers of a different fear through her.

He pulled her into a hug and got her back to his apartment, where she clung to him as he scratched his two-day scruff against her neck. She wrapped her arms around his waist, buried her face in his chest to steal some of his strength, breathed in his scent to calm her jagged nerves, and let his warmth seep into her so very cold body.

"Sweetheart, tell me what's wrong."

She tiptoed to kiss his lips softly. "Tomorrow," she promised. "But now, I need you to make me forget everything else but you. Please."

He stared into her eyes. It looked as though he was judging whether or not to push her for more. She pleaded silently that he wouldn't.

Finally, he nodded. "I can do that."

A sad smile stretched her lips before Sam made good on his promise until they both fell asleep wrapped in each other.

* * *

"Dream Weaver" blared through his bedroom. The ring tone meant one of her sisters was calling. He couldn't remember which woman matched the song. He groaned and Bogart huffed as she fumbled to answer.

"Ruby?" she grumbled sleepily.

"Cami, don't come home," Ruby barked, her hardass voice loud enough that Sam heard every word. If Ruby used the same tone to push through cops at an emergency scene, Sam got why her sisters said everyone did whatever she told them. Cami sat straight up, clutching the sheet to her breasts.

"Wait, what?" she asked.

"Is Sam there? Put him on the phone."

"Ruby, what's wrong?" She sounded frantic.

He raised onto an elbow and stretched a hand toward her. "Put her on speaker."

Cami hit the audio button before she continued in a hurried barrage of questions. "Why can't I come home? What's wrong with Mina? Ama? Is it Dad?"

"No. Dad's fine. Your mom, Mina, and Rose are all here with me. We stopped by your place to see if you wanted to come to the beach with us. The door was wide open."

"I never leave my door unlocked."

"We know. Delia tells us all too many serial killer rapist stories for that to happen. I got worried and told Ama to take Rose back to the car. Thank god you stayed with Sam last night."

Her face paled. None of the teasing blush she usually got with her family when her sisters talked about anything to do with the two of them sleeping together. He rubbed her back, trying to ease the shock even as he took over the conversation. She needed level-headed and competent right now. Her usual ability to handle emergencies with cool calmness had apparently deserted her, and he wanted to know what'd gotten her so rattled. But that could wait.

"Ruby," he asked. "What the hell happened?"

"Neil happened." Ruby sounded pissed. And deadly. He'd bet Cami's big sister would fight dirty. "Mina saw it when she stood in your doorway. The fucker broke the flimsy lock, forced his way in, and wrecked the place."

"But I don't have anything worth taking," Cami whispered.

Sam disagreed. She'd missed the greatest risk. *She* was definitely worth taking. He seethed. What if she'd been there? What if she had gone home last night instead of staying with him? What would the asshole have done to her?

"What did this Neil guy do to her apartment?" he asked.

Ruby didn't say anything for a long minute. "He tossed the whole place, knifed the futon, slashed her clothes, and destroyed the furniture. He even carved a warning in the table."

"Son of a bitch, what do you mean he carved a warning?" he growled. "What's it say?"

"Mine. It says mine. That bastard carved the word mine across the whole tabletop."

Screw this Neil guy. Cami was his. Sam wanted to fight, needed to beat her ex to a pulp to teach him he couldn't and wouldn't ever have her. He worked to relax his clenched jaw and curled fists. He knew better ways to vent his anger, but right now he couldn't remember a damned one of them. He hadn't burned with this kind of rage in years.

Ruby continued softly. "Cami honey, he tore everything to bits. There's nothing left."

She stared ahead blankly. He held her hand, squeezed as Bogart came into the room and cried forlornly at the side of the bed.

"Neil was there last night," she whispered.

Sam rubbed her shoulder. "I know sweetheart, that's what Ruby said."

"No." Her voice cracked. "At the movies. He was there. He's been watching us. It was him on the jet ski, at the hotel, at the library. He tried to poison Bogart."

"What the fuck? Why didn't you tell me?"

She flinched, and he immediately regretted the harsh words. She got out of bed, murmuring something to Bogart who immediately stopped crying and followed her. She reached for clothes and called toward the phone. "I'm coming, Ruby."

"All right, sis. Delia texted. She's almost here. She says you've got to call the cops and report his ass. You can't let him get away with this. I've got to go. Mina's back, and I need to check on Ama and my baby."

He had slipped into the closest pants and a clean shirt by the time the sisters ended the call. He ran his fingers through his hair and walked to the kitchen where Cami fumbled with her clothes. He was mad at Neil, mad at her for not telling him, and mad there wasn't a damn thing he could do.

"Why didn't you tell me?" he asked again.

She ignored him and clipped Bogart's leash.

"Were you going to tell me?" He flashed through memories of last night before the amazing sex, when she'd asked to be held and to make her forget. *That she'd tell him in the morning.*

She bit her lip. "I'm not fighting with you and handling this."

His jaw ticked. "I don't want to fight with you either. But I want to punch this guy."

"You may have to get in line for that," she muttered.

"I'm coming with you."

She didn't argue. She simply strode out of his apartment with his dog. She acted like this wasn't a big deal. How could she not see how much of a threat this guy was? She'd apparently scanned crowds like a sniper for the last year and jumped at every shadow. Yet when her ex actually approached her, she hadn't told him. Because he hadn't been around.

Sam was pissed he'd taken her to an unfamiliar place and then left her by herself. No wonder Bogart had gone crazy and torn through the crowd to get to Cami. His own dog had known, but Sam hadn't dreamed it could happen. Then she hadn't told him. Did she not trust him? Would he always come behind her family in her confidences? Or had she been that scared?

Questions spun through his head in the silent short drive to her house. He whipped the truck into street parking and got out without waiting for her. He stood on the sidewalk and stared ahead until she led the way into the apartment building with Bogart in tow.

Upstairs, Mina lingered in the apartment doorway. She moved to block the door. "You need to know before you go inside that Neil was out of his mind with jealousy. There's no telling how much he's followed you two in the last few weeks. He tore the place apart in a rage about two o'clock this morning. I don't know how he didn't wake the neighbors with all the noise."

She took the dog's leash. "Come on, Bogie." Bogart didn't budge. "Cami tell the dog to go with me. It's not safe in there."

Cami nodded to Bogart, and he reluctantly plodded down the hall after Mina. Sam watched Cami take a deep steadying breath before she walked the few steps into her apartment. He followed close behind.

It was destroyed, wrecked, ruined. His mind couldn't come up with enough words to describe the damage. Her place was tiny. He had stayed in budget hotel rooms that would swallow this studio whole. And what the hell was smeared on the walls? The whole room reeked. She put a hand over her stomach. Furniture lay askew, overturned and broken.

He looked down to the shattered shards and her skimpy sandals. He reached a hand to steady her. "Careful. Watch the glass on the floor."

She nodded and kept moving toward the ribbons of her clothes, the pieces of her pink sneakers, the smashed bathroom mirror smeared with lipstick. How long had her ex been here?

"It's like a nightmare," she whispered.

"What could this guy have wanted in ransacking your place?" he asked her. He didn't add that he would've moved her weeks ago if he'd known what a crap apartment she'd been living in. There was almost no security, and the rickety door wouldn't have stopped anyone, let alone a psycho ex-boyfriend who'd carved up her shabby table. Sick bastard wanted to mark her things, probably to mark her.

She tried to tip a broken chair upright before he stopped her. They'd need the cops to see everything exactly the way they'd found it.

She sighed. "He did it to remind me he can still get to me. As another sign of how far his control can reach." She wandered further into the room. "He has threatened everyone and everything I've ever cared about."

He took the two steps back to poke at the deadbolt she'd mentioned before. The keyhole had been glued shut. Stuffing from a worn-out futon mattress littered the floor among streamers of what had been family photos now ripped to pieces. She knelt to touch the edge of a photo of Rose, torn in two and crumpled with shredded ribbons of Sam's flannel jacket.

Tears slid down her cheeks. A long moaning sob escaped her. It damn near broke him. He pulled her into his arms and hustled her out of the mess. He held her trembling hand all the way downstairs as two police officers came up the sidewalk with Delia.

"Don't let Neil get away with it," Delia told her younger sister. "Report his ass."

Mina stood mere steps away, and Ruby was close behind Delia in moments with Rose on her hip. Ama reached for Cami. He could swear the air thickened around the women. It wasn't just the ocean smell Cami brought whenever she was emotional. That had spiked in his bedroom this morning when she'd gotten the call. But this, this power was more. They were more.

Cami rubbed her sorrowful face and followed the officers into the house. Ruby and Ama took Rose towards the pier to keep the baby away from the building. Who knew what powers little Rose might already have, Ruby had told him. No need to test them at a crime scene.

Sam took out his phone. He texted Lottie to ask for a favor only his sister could pull off, left a voicemail for the tire repair shop, and one more message with a request he'd never imagined he'd have to make. He'd finished by the time Cami came back with an emergency restraining order and thanked the officers.

"You'll have to tell people at work," Delia said. "Some patrol officers can stop by and do a welfare check. They've already offered. No going to the beach. No shopping by yourself. Nothing until he's stopped."

"Other than the animal clinic and my apartment, you won't be out of my sight." Sam didn't leave room for argument. He twined his fingers through Cami's and was rewarded by her quick squeeze of his hand. He kissed her knuckles to soften the nonnegotiable order before taking the key that dangled from one finger.

"I couldn't even lock up," she told him.

"Can't lock a door that's hanging off the hinges."

"I've nothing worth saving now anyway," she whispered.

He disagreed, thinking she had plenty worth saving as they headed toward the pier following Mina and Delia. She had family who loved her. She had her magic. She had his heart.

CHAPTER TWENTY-THREE

SAM STARED DOWN THE LONG PRIVATE TABLE HE'D SET UP IN THE BACK hallway of his restaurant for an emergency meeting of the Donovan women. He'd been happy to host, and they'd included him without hesitation. He swallowed hard at being accepted into this family as Cami's partner.

Weary from discussing Neil over breakfast, she had seized the opportunity to change topics when he'd suggested sharing what they'd learned from Tony Davino.

When she had finished, Ruby sighed and shifted Rose in her lap. "That Joey. I'd have followed him down the hill."

"You always did have a thing for bad boys," Delia teased around the last bite of her omelet.

He watched Cami tense and wondered if it was a shared family trait to want bad boys. He'd come a long way from the juvenile delinquent kicked out of his home. Granted, he'd been angry this morning, but he'd calmed down with her safe beside him and the clatter of his own kitchen behind him.

Ruby shivered. "Knowing how it's going to end, it's sad. It's like a 'don't go up to the house girl' horror story."

"Any chance no one was home and she went to her car? Maybe she fell asleep from the gin and never knew what happened?" Ama asked.

"No." The sisters agreed out loud.

"Didn't think so." Ama sighed. She turned and looked at Cami. "Mija, where is your necklace?"

Cami touched fingertips to the bare space at the base of her throat and froze at the emptiness there. He reached for his pocket. "It burned her last night," he told Ama. "I slipped it off before…" He trailed off, remembering the exact chain of events.

"Before Neil?" Ama arched one eyebrow.

Delia joined in. "That necklace alerts her to danger. It's why she's worn it every day since Neil. Why we all wear one. It flares when someone near intends to harm us."

"Son of a bitch," he whispered. "I had it."

"Did you have Bogart?" Mina asked him softly. "I can't imagine him letting Neil near her."

Pain shot through the new knots in his stomach. Cami put a hand over his. "This was not your fault." She straightened in her chair. "Not mine either." He couldn't decide if she was trying to convince him or herself.

The sisters argued whether Sam and Bogart needed their own charms. Ama pressed a temporary protection ward into Cami's palm, the red and gold charm glinting with no sun or bright light to cause the reflection. "Take this, Camellia. Better late than never."

The back door banged open, and his grandfather came through it with arms outstretched toward Cami.

"There's the girl with the gorgeous curls that's got my boy distracted." Cami stood to be wrapped in a hug. "I'd know you anywhere, he's talked about you so much. Renzo," he told her with another squeeze. "Or Pops. Your choice."

Sam saw that twinkle in his grandpa's eyes and eased her away. "Go grab your own girl. This one's mine." He didn't resist when Pops smacked his jaw playfully.

"Always been cheeky," Pops admonished. "Wait 'til Lottie sees her. She pulled in after me, but I wanted the first look."

Pops extended a hand toward Ama. "Ciao, Eleuia. It has been too long. My wife will be sorry to have missed you."

Ama kissed his cheek. How did she know Pops?

Before he could ask, Lottie bustled in the back door, shifting bundles and bags around her gypsy dress.

"Bro, I got what you asked for. Where's she at? Let's see this knockout." She dropped the bags and moved to Cami, skirting around Delia and Mina on the way.

"Very Rita Hayworth early period. Those big golden eyes you talked about, perfect olive skin, and all those curls. I'm Lottie. I brought you some pretty new dresses and makeup to replace what that asshole destroyed. Oh, who does your hair?"

Cami blinked a startled look, and he sympathized. Lottie could be overwhelming.

Ruby answered, "Susan Donovan. She's our mom." She tipped her head toward Delia who looked coolly at the commotion of the newcomer.

"Oh, I know her well. I've worked with her," his sister professed. "Worked for your grandmothers too."

The Donovan sisters looked at Lottie with new interest before staring at Pops and him.

"Huh," Mina said quietly. "That explains a lot."

"Give a girl some love, Pops." Lottie moved to hug her grandfather.

"She always this energetic?" Cami asked as Lottie stopped to purr over Rose's perfection.

"She's only warming up." Sam chuckled and kissed her head. She leaned back, fitting perfectly against him. She had to be tired after the trauma of this morning. It didn't help he'd kept her up most of the night taking his time with her in the bedroom, but he couldn't regret one minute of enjoying her lush curves and those sighs.

"So which one's the sister with the history visions?" Lottie gushed.

"What exactly have you been sharing, Sam?" Delia's tone bled thick with accusations.

Sam shrugged, never taking his hands off Cami. He had enough of a fight coming with this Neil guy and to get her to trust him. He wasn't arguing with her sister.

"Not enough," Lottie insisted. "You must be the one who fights her gifts." Lottie rounded on Delia.

Ruby snickered. "She's got your number, Deals." Rose giggled at her mother's laughter.

"Do we let them fight it out?" Cami whispered to him.

He leaned close to her ear. "Delia has the red turbo Mini Cooper, right?"

She nodded, and if he didn't imagine it, she shivered at his breath so close.

"Wait until Delia sees Lottie's car. She drives a blue Mini Countryman."

"No."

"Yep. Straps surfboards on top. Those two are more alike than they realize."

She cut a look at him from the corner of her eyes. "You have no idea."

"Do all of you have an extra special something?" Lottie asked the sisters.

"Boldness. Beauty. Brains," Pops said before nodding to Cami. "Sweetness."

"I'm a healer," Ruby told her. "Cami communicates with animals. We aren't sure about my baby's powers yet though Rose's already got plenty of personality. You know a little about Mina's gifts. Ama's talent is love and special brews."

"I knew those candles in your house weren't ordinary," Sam said. He'd sensed the magic trickling through Ama's home. It'd wrapped him in an embrace and danced against his skin in a comforting touch.

Ama smiled secretively. "Nothing in my home is ordinary."

"And you?" Lottie asked Delia.

"No comment," she snapped.

"Oh, cattiness." Lottie made pretend claws in the air. Rose gurgled adorably and shoved a fist in her mouth.

"Delia reads the history of objects like Mina reads places." Ruby bounced the baby in her lap. "Sometimes she reads people too. Through touch."

Sam turned to Delia, realization dawning at every snubbed handshake and crossed arms defensive posture. "That's why you don't touch anyone."

Lottie stopped making fun of Delia. "That's awesome."

Delia's stone face didn't change. The two stared at each other. Rose whimpered.

"Which one of you needed to see Casa Oceana? Visions girl, right?" Lottie turned to Mina. "I got you access. It's back on the market. The realtor gave me the key code. We can pop up for a look this afternoon if you want."

"How'd you manage that?"

"I promised him a day on set with me." She rolled her eyes. "Everyone wants to be in show biz in this town."

Ruby juggled Rose and her diaper bag. "Why don't you guys head on up? I think little one here is ready for a quick beach visit and then home." She turned to Ama and Delia. "You want to head back with us?" They nodded. It'd been obvious Delia couldn't wait to leave since his sister had started asking questions.

Ruby pivoted to Mina. "You got a ride home after your time slip?"

"Where you headed?" Lottie asked.

Mina sucked down the last few sips of her drink. "USC. I have class in the morning."

"I'll drive you," Cami offered.

"Not alone you're not," Sam answered brusquely and ignored the stare he got from her. He could tell she wanted to argue.

"I can do it," Lottie insisted. "If you don't mind questions."

Mina laughed. "Feed me again if I time slip, and I'll answer all you want. Or at least what I can."

"Then it's settled," Lottie said. "I'll take you on my way to our parents' house. I stay there when I need an easy commute to the sets in Burbank."

Sam stiffened at the mention of their parents.

Lottie kept talking. "Sam, I have bags of stuff in my car for Cami. Want them now or after Casa Oceana?"

"After," he said. "We will go to the house and pick them up when we get back."

"You should skip the coming back part. Go home and take care of Cami," his grandpa chided.

"Pops, I'll only stop by."

"I'd put that pretty girl first," Pops scolded. "You come back here, and you won't."

Sam hated when Pops said shit like that. He'd already put her first today, right? This was the third time in as many weeks he'd taken time off because of her. Before her, he'd never taken a single full day away from the restaurant.

"Wait. What stuff?" she asked, interrupting his thoughts.

"Clothes. Makeup. Hair product," Lottie replied. "You can't be expected to live like a savage just because you dated one. Although my brother's a caveman so I'm not sure…"

"Lottie," he warned his little sister. She held up her hands. He shook his head. "You two waiting here or in the office?" Mina and Lottie headed for the staircase with overflowing shopping bags. "I'll walk your mom and sisters out." He carried Rose while Ruby, Ama, and Delia followed. "You coming, Pops?"

"I'll be there in a bit. I got to say goodbye to this girl and look around the restaurant." He closed the door as his grandpa grabbed Cami.

Pops better not scare her off with talk of family or work. Sam planned to have her moved in by sunset. They could start plans about a life together. Just as soon as he drove them up the hill and stopped back by to check on the restaurant.

* * *

Pops lowered his voice so only she could hear while the others shuffled to get ready to leave. "I like you, Cami girl. You stay around. Keep our boy in line. He's got a soft spot, but he doesn't take rejection after his folks… Well, my son isn't the best father in the world. He married no better." He shook his head. "Our boy needs his loved ones close—me, Lottie, and you. Keep that in mind."

Before she could answer, the man they'd been talking about walked in.

"You good, Pops?" Sam asked.

His grandfather hugged him before ducking into the kitchen. Sam steered her away from the dirty plates on the table.

"Leave it," he told her. "I'll have someone pick up." He laced his fingers in hers, pulling her up the stairs to his office where her sister was quizzing Lottie about her connection with their family. They stopped as soon as Sam walked inside.

Bogart slept on the floor. Mina ran her hand over the desk. "Nice digs."

Cami cleared her throat and tried not to blush as she remembered what she'd done on that desk. *Please don't let Mina time slip in this room.*

"Where are your vet textbooks and laptop anyway?" Mina asked. "I didn't see them in the wreckage of your apartment."

Her blush faded at the reminder. Everything she owned had been destroyed except what few things she'd left with Ama or Sam.

"They're at my place," Sam answered for her.

"Good," Mina said.

Lottie touched her arm. "I'm so sorry, sweetie. That asshole never deserved you."

"Lottie, can you loan Cami your key to my place until I get one made for her?" Sam asked.

Cami's head whipped around, but Lottie had already agreed. What the heck? It's not like she'd said she would move in with him. He'd never asked. He hadn't even seemed all that committed to a long-term relationship before. She wasn't about to tell him she'd fallen for him.

"Yeah, of course." Lottie dug through shopping bags on the floor. "I've got her a few clothes in those." She pointed to the pile on his chair. "At least let her change before we go up the hill."

He held the door. "Could you give us a few minutes? I need to talk with Cami alone. It might as well be while she changes."

Mina giggled and got a nudge from Lottie who snickered and said, "Come on, I'm sure we can visit with Pops while these two 'talk' things out."

He pushed her out the door. Cami shook her head as the two left. She didn't turn when she heard the lock click.

"How are you holding up?" he asked and touched her shoulder on his way to his desk.

"I'll be fine." She surprised herself with the certainty in her voice.

He dug through the bags, pulled out a dress, and broke the tag off with his teeth.

"Lottie remembered wipes in case you want some since we missed our shower." He reached into another bag and tugged out a bra. He stopped. "What's wrong?"

"You bought me clothes? You want me to stay at your place?"

"You're my girlfriend, so yes, and yes. It's not like you can go home. It isn't safe, and you needed new things. Want to change clothes now?"

She grabbed the hem of her shirt. He watched every move. "Still not weirded out by my sisters and Ama?" The discoveries at her apartment this morning had been a lot. He would be in for even more surprises if they started asking how closely Lottie worked with her grandmothers, how Pops knew Ama well enough to call her by her first name, and why Sam didn't know about magic until she'd told him. Cami wasn't sure how to start that complex conversation about his family.

He shrugged, tilting his head for a better view as she stripped. "I've heard some pretty weird things in the weeks I've known you. I've been fine with that. Why would today be any different?"

She didn't say anything. She let her shorts slip to the floor knowing she was bare underneath.

"Damn, I stole your panties again." He ticked his tongue against his teeth. "Wish I'd known that earlier." He didn't look the least bit ashamed. She'd noticed this morning and had known he'd taken them last night, but with the drama over her place getting trashed, going without undies had been the least of her concerns.

"At least you'll have a full drawer of panties at my place now." He rummaged through another bag, not taking his eyes off her. He propped against his desk and hooked a thong on his finger. "It's so tempting to have you run around the rest of the day knowing you don't have any on."

She snatched them from his hand and slipped into the soft wisp of lace. "Perv."

"Guilty." He twirled his finger, motioning for her to turn and give him the full view.

She obliged as she hooked the bra and slid up the straps. He moved behind her, pulled her hair to the side, and pressed his lips to her ear. She leaned into his touch. She needed something strong and clean so badly after the ugliness of this morning. He took her necklace from his pocket and fastened it around her throat. The metal lay cool against her skin unlike his warm hands and breath.

"Too bad our sisters are waiting," he said against her ear. "Lottie's probably timing us."

She shook her head. "I hope Mina has blocked any time slips in this office. The last thing I need is for her to know what's happened in here."

He snickered. "If we had a few more minutes, I'd like to see what other little noises I can get you to make on my desk."

She sighed. "I thought we were fighting."

He tugged until she turned in his arms. "Why?"

"What you said at your apartment this morning."

"I was angry and honestly hurt you didn't tell me about him showing up last night."

"I wanted to." She had planned to tell Sam this morning before Neil destroyed her place.

He leaned his forehead against hers. "Don't you trust me?"

"Of course, I do." She bit her lip. "I want to. I haven't even learned to fully trust myself. Not since my ex. I'm working on it."

"We can work on it together." He kissed her temple.

"You still mad?"

"We had a disagreement. I'll get over it. I already did when I saw what your ex did. We will have more in the future." He rubbed his hands along her waist. "It doesn't mean we're fighting."

Their younger sisters started slapping at the door and catcalling.

"Ready?" he asked her.

He assured her Bogart would be all right napping. The dog had been walked less than an hour ago. But he locked the doors to his office and the suite before heading down to the Land Cruiser.

She got into the passenger seat. He slid behind the steering wheel and turned to Mina. "You want me to drive to the back entrance with the garage? Or up to the front door? The two entrances don't connect by one road, so I need to know where to go."

"The garage."

He nodded and started the engine. The trip up Castellammare Drive only took a few minutes. Cami watched Sunday afternoon traffic crawl along the Pacific Coast Highway below.

Sam parked on the curb of the narrow Formillo Way a few feet past the garage where Sol's body was found. Even without her sister's gift, she felt the chill.

They got out of the car and climbed the dozens of stairs to the front door. Lottie checked her phone for the access code to the key lock box hidden outside the entrance. "It's a six-million-dollar listing," she explained. "He changes the code at least twice a day."

"I'm thinking this realtor wants something more than time on the set with you," Mina muttered.

They opened the door and locked it behind them before following Mina through the house. She stopped in a massive room with huge ocean view windows.

"It's like a real-life castle," Lottie gushed. "Straight from the Amalfi coast. They brought old royal Italy to SoCal. Pops would love this. After an exorcism or whatever. Oh, there's a wraparound balcony with a view over the Pacific."

"The grand room," Mina told them. "Most of it is original. The exposed ceiling and hardwood floors are." She glanced over her shoulder. "So are the inset custom bookcase at the top, the massive fireplace, and the big entrance staircase. Only the furniture changed over the decades."

"Can you see the differences through the years?" Sam asked her, but Mina's eyes darkened into a slip.

Cami put an arm around her. "Why don't you guys take a look around? This could take a while."

"Call if you need us." Sam followed Lottie under the oak arch and down the hallway to the right of the impressive curved brick stairs.

She had been alone with her sister for almost five minutes when Mina wandered toward the staircase with outstretched hands. She hoped her sister could see the furniture as it stood in the present day to avoid running into anything. Physical alterations to a place presented a danger in any time slip. A change in landscape or interior design that might be gradual over the decades in real life could abruptly alter in Mina's view. She wouldn't let Mina crash into anything.

Her arms dropped to her sides. Mina angled her head, looking from the staircase to the middle of the room and back again as though watching a conversation from the past that Cami couldn't see or hear.

"She's leaving," Mina murmured. "She's really leaving him." She turned to the fireplace. "He's so angry. Furious," she seethed.

Her fingertips touched the end of the massive carved oak railing that curled along the palatial staircase. She took one shaking step up the brick risers. She never looked away from the center of the room, not glancing toward the windows or back where Sam and Lottie had gone. Mina focused on that one spot in the room and slowly made her way up three more treads.

Her attention snapped to the fireplace. Her brow furrowed, and confusion crossed her face at whatever past the room showed her.

Her mouth slackened and then jerked again. She scrambled back another step and stumbled.

Cami grabbed for her as her breathing turned raspy and gasping. "Mina," she called. "Come back."

Mina didn't respond. She stared blankly with horror etched across her face before keening a low and haunting moan.

She tightened her grip. "Let go of the slip. Please." Terror strangled the last word.

Mina grabbed the base of her skull and sagged limply toward the stairs. Her eyes rolled into the back of her head. Cami rushed to catch her.

"Sam." She screamed. "No, no, no. Wake up. Come on, little sister. Wake up." Her voice caught. Not now. Her sister needed them. "Sam!"

CHAPTER TWENTY-FOUR

Casa Oceana
Sunday, December 17, 1933, around 10:30 a.m.

SUNNY WHEELED THE PACKARD CONVERTIBLE INTO THE GARAGE AT CASA Oceana above the café and backed it into the stall with practiced ease. She left her purse and gloves on the seat to fetch after dealing with Paul.

She watched every step as Joey strode in front of the grill to open her door and help her from the car. He pulled the door closed and joined her on the small street below the house, walking with her to the stairs leading to Casa Oceana.

She had to look up to see his face he was so tall. She swayed to the side, and he put his hands on her shoulders to steady her. Maybe she shouldn't have drunk almost the whole bottle of gin. At least she'd saved a few swallows for the trip up the stairs. She pressed against Joey's chest to feel the rumble of the low snicker.

His hands squeezed her waist. "You sure you don't want me to come in?"

"God, no." She wouldn't taint whatever this was with the ugliness about to come.

"Want to leave? I'll take you back to Artie's. We can stop at your place for your things."

Tempting. So damn enticing with his warm breath on her brow. She could steady herself with the collar of his suit, tiptoe, and press her mouth against his. Something real and physical without attachments. Just for a moment. Her bottom lip caught in her teeth.

"Keep looking at me like that, and we're leaving. That's a promise." He dug his fingers into her skin, kneading and rubbing away the anxiety.

Dropping her face, she pulled her shoulders up and back to square off for the confrontation with Paul. "I've got to do this."

Joey nodded once. "I'm going down to the café to call for a ride. You come get me in the next half hour if you need me."

She didn't answer.

"I'm serious. One harsh word and you come get me. Understand?"

She bobbed her head and swallowed hard, forcing down tears and anger. She would get this done.

"I'll be working security tonight on Artie's *Foxtrot*. Come find me if you're interested." He winked and tipped his hat before strolling toward the steps to the café.

Oh, she was interested. He glanced over his shoulder and smiled. She lifted two fingers in a halfhearted wave. She told herself it wasn't weakness to watch him walk away and out of sight before heading up the stairs. After this, it'd be time she took a water taxi out to the *Foxtrot* to see what all the fuss was about.

The mansion Paul shared with his wife looked more to Sunny like a staged set than an actual home. Beautifully detailed, the grand room could have been transported directly from a Mediterranean castle with its double grand arched windows overlooking the ocean and imposing oak and brick staircase circling for the perfect entrance. An enormous stonework fireplace loomed at the far end.

Coral had selected furniture pieces from around the world that dripped in exotic extravagance. Expensive drapes, tapestries, and rugs muffled the echoes of footsteps and voices to draw focus to the intricate details, such as the leaded windows with castles and fantastic shapes designed by Paul himself. A masterpiece. A showcase. Never a home.

Sunny gripped the heavy carved railing and descended. The alcohol had gone straight to her head, her heart rabbited in her chest, and her balance was hindered by the evening gown swirling around her feet. Not to mention her patience and compassion had both reached their end. Gathering a handful of sparkling fabric, she teetered and cursed the loss of composure. She'd have no graceful presentation this time.

Paul sat on the couch, illuminated only by the rays of the sun filtering through the balcony doors. His fingers tightened over a glass as she came down the stairs and into the light.

"Where have you been?" He seethed. "Why didn't you come home like you were supposed to?"

She sauntered across the room, ignoring the lightheadedness that had her landing on the couch with a thud.

He wiped his sweaty brow with a crumpled handkerchief and fisted his hand around the cloth. "Answer me."

She crossed her ankles and composed herself, unwilling to entertain his demands. "Why don't you tell me how you've given away our business to Alan Knapp for a gambling den?"

"What are you talking about?"

"Don't play dumb with me. I hear Alan has you by the short hairs for Coral's debts. You know what I went through standing my ground to keep the criminals out of this place." Her words came so quick and emphatic that her curls shook from the forcefulness of her conviction. "You don't understand what they're capable of. I do. I was married to one."

He leaned forward, jabbing a finger into the air. "Don't you dare speak of your ex to me, and don't you presume to tell me what to do with my business. You're just a pretty face and a name. I've been getting the job done since before you were in your crib. You cannot understand the amount of money we stand to make from this." Paul swiped spit from his mouth. "We will work with Alan. I will make the decisions as far as the extra business. That's the end of it." He drained the glass and pushed out of the chair.

"No."

He stopped. "What do you mean no?"

"No. I won't do it."

"You will." His voice rose to a yell, echoing in the big room.

"No, I absolutely won't. I'm out. I don't want any part of this. Buy my share of the restaurant for a fair price." She waved a hand before clenching it. "Or I'll tell the studios what you've done, that you've conspired with a criminal to open a gambling den. They won't stand for the scandal."

"Who do you think you are?" He looked down his long nose at her. "You're just another face that will age and fade away. Only talent and conviction like mine remain. You'll do what I say. I *am* the café. You're only its name."

"Not anymore. I'm finished."

"You can't blackmail or threaten me." His voice shook more with each word.

She pointed to the bar cart. "Why don't you bring me a drink, and we will discuss terms."

He slammed his glass onto the floor, stepped around the shattered pieces, and stormed to loom over her. "You watch your tone. Both you and the business are mine."

She shoved her finger into his face. "We are done. Finished. In business. In bed. I don't want anything else from you except to cut me out of it."

He grabbed her arm and dragged her from the couch. "Look at you. Drunk. Stinking of gin. And high too. Look at your eyes. Your pupils swallow the green. What have you taken?"

She rubbed the skin over her skipping heartbeat. The diet pills. It had to be. They dulled the alcohol but sped up everything else. Pep, Artie had called it. She wished she hadn't taken the damn things.

He sneered at her. "That's what I thought. Go down to the café apartments and bathe. Put some clean clothes on. You reek." He dropped her onto the floor.

She picked herself up.

"I told you." She slowed each word, persisting until every syllable got through his thick head. "I am finished."

He snatched at her again. She evaded.

"You're leaving me?"

"That's what I said."

"Are you going to him? Or is he only a distraction for the day?"

"Who?"

"I saw you," he spat at her. "In the street outside. Ready to go after him?" He looked her up and down. "Slut."

She balled her fists, ready to fight. "What did you just call me?"

Paul scoffed and ambled toward the fireplace. "Slut. You've always been a slut. I tried to class you up, to make you an honest woman."

"An honest woman? If anyone made me less than that, it would be you. You with a wife you couldn't bring yourself to leave. You had to take off from the *Scoria* set to get away from me. How stupid was I to try and pick up where we left off? To want to build a life with you? A business?"

She paced as her words raced from her mouth, the bitter truth spilling out. "When Coral would always be in the picture? Standing by like some silent watchman over our relationship. She's not part of it. No, she's more. She's the dark cloud over it. I'm done with being the spare. What was it about her? Talent? She hasn't worked in ten years. Some sick sense of loyalty?"

Her fingers curled, nails biting into her palms. "Does she have something on you? Is that why you haven't worked since our last film?" She advanced on him. Unease flashed through his gaze before the anger returned. "That's it, isn't it?" How had she not seen it before?

His rage vanished in an instant, replaced by a cool mocking tone. "Did you even know his name? The man pawing you outside? I saw his hands roaming toward your ass."

She moved toward the stairs. She had to get out of here.

"He's none of your business." She tightened her arms around her middle, fighting to find any warmth in this cold shell of a home.

Paul chuckled.

She glanced over her shoulder.

He tossed a match onto the kindling "You seem to think you know a lot about what my business is and what's not today. Let me tell you, it's all my business." He stared at the spreading flames. "How many men have had you since we got back together? One a week?"

She rushed toward him on teetering heels. How dare he accuse her after consorting with criminals? She stopped a few feet away, unsure if she'd halted out of fear or because she'd stumble if she took another step.

"I'm done," she repeated. "You can find someone else to bully. I'm not your whipping girl anymore."

"I won't sell to you. You're in this business." He dug at the fire with the iron poker. "All the way in. Alan will have the gambling equipment installed within the week. Construction has already started."

Her hand slashed through the air. "You have no idea what you're getting yourself into with this. Cops will be the least of your problems. The crime bosses won't like your incompetent attempt at a power move. They will be on this place so fast you won't know what happened."

He jabbed the growing flames again. "It's been handled. Alan has prepared for all the possibilities."

"By hiring muscle? Bringing in guns?" She almost chuckled at his naiveté. "Because that's what it's going to take. Enforcers to return fire when the rivalry comes here in a turf war. This isn't the movies. It's real life. Do you think guests are going to risk bullets flying?"

"They'll come," he said with firm insistence.

Her tone hardened again. How ignorant could he be? "No, they won't. My name will come down. The business won't last the year. You will have to figure out another way to maintain your lifestyle with all the luxuries you think you deserve. This house? It'll be the next thing to go right after the café. You won't have anything left."

His grip tightened on the poker with his knuckles flexing one by one. "It won't happen. You'll stay."

She laughed so hard she tilted on her heels with the alcohol still swirling in her system. "No. No, I won't. I'm done with your games." She glanced up and down his body, wasted from years of hard drinking and harder living. Gone was the handsome man who she'd met years ago. "I can't imagine what I ever saw in such a washed-up remnant of a mean petty nothing."

He rounded on her, the poker still in hand. "You bitch. You can't leave me."

"You're a failure." She jabbed at his chest with a finger at each word.

He jerked the poker toward her.

She swayed to the right, avoiding his swing. "You going to hit me with that?"

His grip tightened.

She pointed a finger at him. "How will you explain it away to the studio? That'll take longer to heal than bruises from your fist."

He threw down the poker with a clatter. "I'm going to have to remind you of your place."

"My place? *My* place?" She spat at his feet.

He flinched.

She snarled at him. "I am finished. Finished." She turned to leave. It was over. She had told him in no uncertain terms that she was out. The liberating headiness of it made her giddy.

She would head down to the café, find Joey, and ask him to stay while she packed. She knew he would. Then he would either take her to her mother's or she could go with him and explore his dark curls and wide sensuous mouth. Every step away from Paul would be closer to Joey.

Paul grabbed her bicep and yanked. She lost her balance and stumbled into him. He pushed her to the ottoman. *So different from Joey. Paul's blond leanness contrasted to Joey's muscled darkness.* She staggered to stand.

"Don't touch me again," she hissed.

"I own you," he snarled.

"Talk to my lawyer."

"I'm talking to you." His finger flew at her face, an inch from her nose.

She stepped back. "I'm through with you, and by the time my lawyer's done, you'll be finished. Your marriage. Your career. Your stake in the business. It will all be gone."

"You can't."

"Oh, but I can. Gambling is illegal." Donning her most innocent schoolgirl face, she mocked him. "Officer, I didn't know. I did everything I could to stop them." She smiled. "You're finished."

His arm snaked out lightning fast. The alcohol and diet pills slowed her reactions. He backhanded her hard in the face, hitting her square in the lower lip with his ring. She recoiled and pressed her fingers to the ache. She would bruise. Again. It was past time to go.

She would get Joey, maybe even find some retribution for what Paul had done. He deserved to know what it felt like to be smacked around by someone stronger. She folded an arm protectively against her waist and withdrew. She eyed the distance to the stairs. Could she outrun him? In heels? Inebriated?

She looked back at him. He had murderous rage in his eyes. She froze, trapped like a hunted fox waiting in the bushes for the hounds to come. Taking her chances, she lunged toward the stairs, sprinting as best she could with the dress tangling her legs.

He clutched her shoulders and yanked her to him. "You're not going anywhere."

She stepped into him. He hadn't expected that. She shook off his hold, and he staggered two steps back. Touching her tongue to the loosened cap on her tooth and the tender spot inside her lip, she tasted for blood and broken skin.

Every previous attack ran through her mind. She had relented each time, accepting what he said as right and acquiescing that he was better or smarter or superior. Her skin reverberated the sting of every other pinch, each slap, the hard hand clasp on her to keep her in check.

He had never been as open as her ex-husband. Paul was sneakier with the pain he caused, the taunts to belittle her, and the control he had over her. Until last weekend. Until he came after her in the restaurant in front of witnesses. Now he smacked her around to stop her from leaving him. He had become bolder, meaner. It would never stop until she stopped it.

She attacked. It was a last resort. She knew it. She planned to use her hands, fists, nails, and teeth if necessary. She would get free of Paul. Her ride to safety and escape waited only a short distance down the hill. She would make it out. She had to. She could not endure this any longer. She launched herself at him. His hands shot out and shoved.

She lost her balance. The fleeting moments paused and materialized in her mind in drawn-out slow scenes like a flickering movie reel winding through a broken projector as she felt the momentary wobble of teetering on her heels. The lovely heels she had asked Mabel to send out for dying to match this beautiful dress that snarled and caught between her wobbling legs.

She shunned the scorching heat of the fire at her front even as the chill of the room from behind bit at her. The long mink coat, so soft, so delicate like a child's sweet touch brushed against her skin. Her arms shot out into the open empty air to grab hold of a piece of this house that would never be a home. The rings on her fingers slid and jostled together with a clink. She reached for something, anything to break the fall.

Her fingers clutched and finally fisted on blank space. Her hands curled back into her body, and her knuckles brushed against the delicate fading petals of the camellia pinned to her dress before scraping against the hard diamonds.

Sunny saw a flash before the back of her head hit something solid with a muffled thump. Darkness descended.

CHAPTER TWENTY-FIVE

Casa Oceana
Present Day

CAMI SCREAMED HIS NAME, AND SAM'S HEART STOPPED. HE SPRINTED INTO the grand room, frantically searching for her. She sprawled on the spiraling stairs with Mina in her arms. It looked like Cami had managed to get beneath her sister before any fall to cushion the blow.

"What happened?" He hurried to them.

"Her time slip turned violent. She blacked out. She's not responding." Her words came fast.

He took Mina's weight while Cami skimmed her hands over the younger woman's body before running deft fingers through the long curly tumble of hair.

"No blood or broken skin. No obvious signs of injury," she said. "I wish Ruby was here with her healing abilities."

"You're here. You have magic and training. What do we do?"

Her gaze met his. "We get her out of here and away from the source. Now."

"It can't hurt." He swung Mina into his arms before heading for the door.

Lottie ran in. "Oh. no!"

He dashed by her and sprinted like a man from a fire. Cami chased after him.

"Check the house," she shouted to Lottie. "Lock up. Please. She's done here today." On the stairs behind him, her soles slapped the concrete with her flimsy sandals. He didn't slow. She opened the back of the truck and helped him ease Mina inside. Lottie joined them breathless and panting a moment later.

"What happened?" Lottie echoed his earlier question.

"She time slipped." Cami ran her hands over Mina's face. "She watched something happening in the grand room. I think the action moved toward the fireplace. There were at least two people the way her attention divided."

"Did she slip to the time she was looking for?"

"I don't know. I can't tell. Only Mina can see and hear the slip. She said something about a woman leaving and a man being angry. But if it was Sunny's last day or an argument from twenty years later, I don't know."

"She didn't make a sound as I carried her," he said.

Cami clambered into the back with her sister. "Help me roll her onto her back. Elevate her legs higher than her heart. It should help if she's simply fainted."

Sam helped her position Mina's limp body and moved to allow her access. She checked her sister's airway.

"No obstruction." She patted down her clothing. "Everything's loose." She unhooked Mina's bra beneath her shirt. "Ruby would open up the airways. Maybe a strong smell? Where's your board cleaner?"

"What?"

"Your board cleaner?"

Sam frowned, wondering why in the hell she'd want to shine his surfboard and then realized. A strong smell, she'd said. "Mineral spirits. Paint thinner."

"Strong chemical smell, right?" She tilted her head toward Mina.

"It's worth a shot." He scrambled to the toolkit, uncapped a small bottle, and handed it to her. She waved it under Mina's nose. Once. Twice. Three times.

Mina sputtered to life and pushed away the scent before grabbing the back of her skull. Cami gave him the bottle to close and wrapped her arms around Mina. "Welcome back, little sister."

Mina bolted to stand, swayed, and went down on Cami before he could reach them. "I've got to get back in there. I almost finished. It was all there. It was horrible. I only need a few more minutes to sift through all the memories."

"Absolutely not." Cami tightened her hold and nodded when he moved to block them.

"I have to put it together. I'm so close."

"No. I shouldn't have let you go in. You're never going back in that house. You want to stand out here again another day, we can do that. Or you'll figure it out tonight. Or maybe over the next few days."

"But it's right there." Mina struggled.

Sam put a hand on her arm, and she shrank in fear. He saw the flash of fright go through her eyes and slowly lifted his hands, palms outstretched. Damnit, was this the terror Cami felt with her ex-boyfriend?

"Easy," he said. "I'm not going to hurt you."

Mina trembled, and Cami pulled her close. "It's okay. You've had more than enough to handle. You go ahead and shake it out." The shivering escalated.

He draped a blanket around them. "She saw too much," he whispered to his sister.

"Not enough," Mina answered hoarsely. "It's gone now. I can't feel it. It's like the stations all turned off."

"Too much for one day." Cami smoothed Mina's hair. "You'll get it back. Just not right now."

"I can't feel it at all." Mina looked lost. "This is so frustrating. How can you stand it?"

Cami chuckled. "You can't miss something you've never known." She held her sister through the low sobs, accepting the tissues Sam offered.

"Wow." Lottie whispered. "You two have had a rotten day. I still think Cami wins."

Cami scoffed. "It's not a contest. She's short circuited her powers with an overload. I've got nothing to go home to."

Sam set his jaw. What did she mean nothing? "You've got my place."

She nodded and checked her vibrating phone. She turned it off before Sam could take it. He wanted nothing more right now than to have a nice chat with Neil and arrange a meeting where Sam could tear him apart piece by piece for what he'd done to her.

"The creep?" Lottie asked.

"Probably." Cami helped Mina into the backseat. He stopped her before she climbed inside.

He kissed her forehead. "Hey, you handled that like a pro." He touched his thumb to her cheek and enjoyed the way she melted at the gentle sweep. "Lottie's right. You've had a shit day. Let's get back and pick up the things she brought you."

He drove downhill, switched the clothing bags from Lottie's car to his, and helped the women into his office before stepping into the kitchen.

Fifteen minutes later, he returned in a temper. His restaurant was understaffed due to a stomach flu, filled with high-maintenance customers, and running short on inventory that'd been fully stocked when he'd checked yesterday. Pops had taken over the bar, falling into the role with practiced ease.

Normally, the sight of his girl and their sisters chatting easily in his cramped office or Bogart snoring at Cami's feet would've made him smile, but not with the disaster brewing out front.

"What's wrong?" Cami asked.

"Problems in the restaurant."

"Let your assistant manager take care of it today," Lottie said. "That's what you pay her for."

"I can't." He shook his head, already done with this conversation and ready to get back to the kitchen. "We're short on staff."

"I can help," Cami told him. "I know the layout as well as any hostess, and I can fetch orders and drinks."

"You're a risk out there with your psycho ex. I can't watch over you and run the restaurant too." The hurt in her eyes made him suspect he'd vented too much, but it was gone so quickly maybe he'd been wrong.

"We can go then." She nodded toward the other two women and knelt next to Bogart. Sam figured she'd done that telepathy thing because his dog was instantly awake and ready to go.

"You're an asshole," his sister hissed in his ear. He ignored her.

"I'll only be a couple of hours tops," he said to Cami who hadn't met his eyes. "Stay locked inside my place. I'll bring home food."

She pushed shaking fingers through her hair and lifted her chin. "We'll be fine." She and Bogart rushed down the stairs. Lottie shook her head at him and followed with Mina in tow.

He didn't even wait for them to hit the door before he was in the kitchen fixing all his staff's screwups. Almost eight hours of hard work later, he'd closed out another successful night at Corraza's.

Pops had taken off hours ago, calling him a stupid kid. But this kid had turned the business into a thriving success. Sam tossed extra food in the bag and headed out the back door.

"Samuel."

The deep voice from the parking lot played like a censuring soundtrack from his childhood. He managed to bite back his father's name, which would piss the man off. Not a good move on the eternal chess board between them if he wanted to ask for the favor he'd called in earlier. He almost wished it'd been Cami's ex. At least then he could've vented the day's disasters with a fight.

He glanced toward the dark Ferrari with its headlights still on. "Did my mother come with you?"

"Of course not." His father stepped into the light. The older man's eyes cut through him. "Seems you've gotten yourself in some trouble. Again."

He swallowed. He could ask this man for a favor if it meant Cami's safety. "Someone threatened my girlfriend. I need to borrow the villa for a week or so until the danger passes." The family's guarded, gated vacation home further up the coast would be the perfect place to keep her out of sight until he could deal with her ex.

His father's lip curled. "What kind of street trash did you pick up? Some thug's ex-wife? Does she know anything about you except dollar signs and real estate?" The man cut his gaze to the restaurant. "I'm betting she's not from people like us."

Sam's fists clenched around the bag of food he'd packed for her. "She's a good person, so no she's not like us. And her family is far more functional than ours. Is that a yes or a no on the villa?"

"Absolutely not." His father opened the door to the Portofino. The quarter-million-dollar car got more care than his own son.

Sam chided himself for even asking. No matter. He'd take care of Cami himself. He wouldn't let the man who'd tried to kill him and Bogart, burn down the premier collection of cinematic history in the world, and knife his tire, according to the repair shop, have a shot at her. Maybe even the villa wouldn't be safe enough.

He spun to walk away, but he stopped. He wasn't a little boy anymore. He could ask the hard questions. He lifted his chin. "Why'd you do it? Why could you two never accept me? I was just a kid. Was it something I did?"

His father shrugged. "More it's who you're not. I knew from your birth you'd never inherit the greatness we needed in our family. Your mother tolerated you longer."

"Who's Mitch Abrams?"

The anger in his father's eyes flashed for a fleeting second. "What makes you ask?"

Secrets and lies were all his father knew. "Because my siblings and I deserve to know our own uncle."

"I'm not saying any Mitch Abrams exists." His father leaned against the expensive car. "But if he did, he was a smart-ass upstart who couldn't respect family heritage and stay out of trouble. Sound familiar? We couldn't have you reminding everyone of our line's damaged goods. Authority mandated we remove the bad in our family to allow for the good."

"What authority? I'm not some rot in Mother's garden. I was your kid." He hated this man. He'd been tossed aside, unwanted from the day his shrew of a mother and this horrible prick had conceived him. "What are you ranting about? Family heritage? Damaged goods?"

His father sniffed and straightened. "There's a legacy running through both sides of your family tree."

"The money." He resisted the urge to spit. "Screw it. I don't want it."

His father shook his head and laughed a nasty, bitter sound. "Power. Lottie inherited. Joe fell in line. You didn't. Mitch Abrams hadn't, and it almost wrecked our family. You were just like him. We cut you out to protect ourselves."

"And the possible mafia connection to Pops? Was that an inconvenience like me?"

His father slid into the driver's seat. "Stay out of trouble, don't ask questions about things you wouldn't understand, and don't call again." He slammed the door.

Sam stood frozen to the same spot of pavement while the throttle of the twin turbo rumbled into a low roar through his lot and shot out onto the PCH. He hated his parents, hated the power plays in his own family, and hated himself for giving a fuck. He slapped the side of his already battered Land Cruiser before climbing in.

He needed to ask someone about his failure of a father's vague references to powers. Cami might know. She'd said magic was a secret. Apparently it wasn't as unique as the sisters thought.

Heading home to his girl, he tried to shake off the tension in his muscles. He snatched the bag of leftovers from the passenger seat and tromped through the apartment complex. He pushed open the door to find the apartment dark except the streetlights through the open blinds.

"Sorry I'm late. I brought dinner." He dropped his keys on the counter and the rattling thud shot through the empty room. "Cami?"

This hadn't been the welcome he'd hoped for. He flicked on the overhead light and pushed into the bedroom, holding the pasta peace offering outstretched.

Bogart lifted his head from his paws with a whine. A sparkling gold and red tag dangled from his collar. Cami's protection charm, but no Cami.

He checked his phone, the personal one not the work cell. It was almost midnight.

He'd missed calls and a couple of texts from her. She'd gone to her mother's house.

Refusing to believe she would leave this late and alone, he punched the screen to return her call. He was tired and not ready to deal with more drama. One of the best things about their relationship had always been her not demanding more from him. He would simply explain things ran long at the restaurant and she'd understand.

"Sam?" She sounded tired and uncertain.

"Why'd you leave?" He rubbed his eyes and dropped to the couch.

"I'm heading home."

Her mother's. Not theirs. He leaned his head back, the weight of the day catching up with him. "No, this is your home. I was going to ask you to move in." He probably should've done it today, but there had been a lot going on.

"I can't." Her voice caught. Had she been crying? "My charm went off. Neil knows where you live. I'm not bringing you and yours into this." Her words tumbled out faster. Bogart launched into a howl. Damn it, he couldn't think with Bogie making all that racket.

"Bogie, hush." He scratched the dog under the chin. "What are you talking about? I'm already so deep in this." Apparently, he'd been born into the witch thing according to his father.

"Today was too much. I need some time. To think."

The finality there worried him. "To think about what?"

She was quiet so long he checked the connection. "About us. About what's best for us."

No, this couldn't be happening. He should've come home with her. The restaurant could've waited. Hell, hadn't Pops tried to warn him? "How much time?"

"Until it's safe." Her voice sounded small, scared.

"Right. Safe. Your ex is dangerous, which is why you should be staying with me. I'm coming to get you."

"I won't risk you, Sam. I can't do this anymore."

"No, Cami." He could hear a tremor in his own voice and hated it. He breathed to steady himself. How'd they gotten to this in only hours? Every fear roared to life in his head. "Don't do this. Don't push me away too."

His hands clenched into fists with the unsettled rage of the horrible day and the nasty meeting with his father. He wouldn't be left this time. He was done with being abandoned. "There's no coming back if you leave me."

Her voice caught on a sob, and he wanted to swallow his words, but it was too late. The call failed.

"Cami?" He dialed again, but it went straight to voicemail.

What the hell was he supposed to do now?

He rang to her automated message a few more times before dialing a different number. "I need your help."

CHAPTER TWENTY-SIX

CAMI SHOVED THE PHONE IN HER POCKET. USELESS THING COULDN'T HOLD a signal even in the city. Or maybe Ama's wards interfered with the reception. Either way, the dropped call had stopped her from saying something stupid. Like telling Sam she loved him.

He'd worked late. Her charm had burned a steady thrum all afternoon, increasing in frequency after the sun set. She had called Sam to warn him, but he hadn't answered his phone because the restaurant came first.

His need to take care of what he considered his was part of what had attracted her. Her heart had never stood a chance. She'd probably fallen for him the week they met. She loved him and that hadn't made leaving tonight to protect him any easier.

She hadn't thought this through, only wanted some sanctuary from the tide of emotions. Fear had been circling her all day, and she was starting to choke on it. What if Neil made good on his promises? What if he finished what they'd started that night on the beach?

The pulse of the charm had echoed the noises she heard from outside Sam's apartment and the constant calls on her phone. She had broken down and answered, but no one talked. She wouldn't turn the phone off because what if Sam called? She'd heard a knock on the door, but there had been no one in the peephole. The hallway had been empty. She put her back to the door only to hear a crying cat that sounded like a human child screaming. Yanking open the door again for a second, there was nothing there. She couldn't think, couldn't concentrate.

When she'd left the apartment after looping the protection spell around Bogart's neck, she had been hoping for a short break, some time to sort things out. But then Sam had called. She hadn't known how to explain, couldn't push the words out through threatening tears that burned her throat. He had said there'd be no coming back. Not from this. He couldn't stand to be left behind and she wouldn't risk putting him in danger.

She wiped her cheeks with the back of her hand and knocked on the door to the home where she'd grown up, counting on Ama to open it. Ama would fix everything.

Only she didn't answer. Ruby did. She ran an unyielding gaze over Cami's tear-stained face.

"You left Sam."

She nodded, not trusting herself to speak.

Ruby held the door open and stood there blocking it. "Because you're scared of what Neil might do, and Sam has his head too deep in his restaurant to see it."

She nodded again, raising a hand to cover her quivering mouth.

Ruby shook her head. "You're both idiots. Come inside, little sister." She led the way to the kitchen where Ama fed Rose in her high chair. With Ruby's odd hours, Rose slept and ate on an adjusted schedule.

"My recipe is a hit," Ama said before looking up to see Cami. "Oh my sweet girl, what have you done?"

Cami couldn't fight the tears. Ruby handed her a wad of tissues and steered her toward the back door. "I've got her, Ama. You watch my baby, and I'll take care of yours."

Ama's brows lowered, but she nodded to Ruby.

Outside, Cami looked for somewhere to sit that didn't make her think of the last time she'd been here with Sam. Ruby pushed her down on one of the steps and filled a wineglass for her as she settled on the same stair.

"Why won't you let yourself be happy?" Ruby asked.

Cami stammered. She'd been happy. Lots of times.

Ruby slowly shook her head. "Not until Sam. I've seen you happier in the last five weeks than your whole adult life. That man makes you happy."

"I'm not. I didn't. He's..." She stopped.

"Sam is amazing. Hell, if you don't want him, Delia or I might take him."

Cami narrowed her gaze.

"That's what I thought. Not that he'd be interested anyway. He's crazy about you. And you're in love with him."

"I am," Cami whispered. She stared at her shoes.

"Did you tell him that?"

"No."

Ruby huffed and leaned back. "Then you're a bigger idiot than I thought. You're supposed to be the smart one of us."

Cami choked as she sipped the wine. "No, I'm not. You're all badasses. And I'm, well, Delia calls me the darling. I'm the weak one. I keep messing things up."

"I'm going to stop that pity party right now. We are all badasses. That much is true. And you boss us around. So what does that make you?"

She shrugged. "Sam calls me Little Miss Bossy. Like the book."

Ruby's mouth quirked. "Haven't read it, but sounds like he's right."

"I'll buy it for Rose."

Ruby set her almost empty glass on a step. "Great. Stop changing the subject. You're the one who takes care of us. You're not the weak one. You're the sweet strong bossy one who holds us together. You're everyone's favorite, our anchor. You and Ama."

Ruby glanced back toward the house, lowering her voice. "But we are sisters. Everyone else will fade. There will come a time when we will be the only ones to remember Ita, Gigi, Ama, and their magic. We are the next generation in the legacy. It's part of life. I count myself lucky to have all of you. But you, Cami, you're going to be the one who makes sure we can still stand each other in twenty years."

Cami started crying again for an entirely different reason. "I was so scared."

"Well, you're safe here. Ama's house is spell guarded better than a maximum security prison." Ruby topped off her wineglass. "Now get your shit together so you can go relieve Delia."

"What?"

"Mina showed up damn near hysterical hours ago. Lottie did her best to feed her and get her home safely without our girl jumping out of the car to go back to that house. Ama called us for reinforcements as you've had more than enough to deal with today."

Cami drained her wineglass and stood to go inside. "I'll take care of her."

"I'm sure you will. Now hand me your phone. There'll be no drunk dialing on my watch."

She could argue, but it'd be a waste of time. No one talked down Ruby when she was adamant. She needed to get to Mina anyway. Pulling the phone out of her pocket, she winced at the multiple missed calls and texts from Sam.

"Don't touch those. Give it over," Ruby ordered with an outstretched hand. "What the hell is this phone case? Is it kid proof? I need one of these." She pocketed the phone and tipped her head toward the door as she sipped her wine.

Cami slipped inside and past Ama.

Delia came out of Mina's room. "Oh good, you're here. I can't deal with all her emotions. No way I was this big of a drama diva even at her age." She rubbed her forehead above the bridge of her nose. "Your problem now."

Cami bit her tongue. Delia's coworkers called her Ice Queen for a reason. Her sister's back remained arrow straight as she stormed down the hall, likely in search of Ruby and wine. But both had dropped everything to come at Ama's call when Mina needed them. Because they were sisters, and sisters took care of each other.

Mina called out from inside the room. "I know you're there."

Cami pushed through the door, put her back against the knob and slowly closed it when she saw Mina's ravaged face. She was contemplating the gentlest way to comment when Mina said, "You look like shit, big sister. Rough day?"

She sighed. "Yeah. Yeah it has been. Some asshole destroyed my apartment. He's stalking me. My little sister passed out because she has incredible powers she can't control, and I think I might have broken up with the love of my life."

"Sam?" Mina looked appalled. "I did not see a breakup coming, and I see everything. I saw you two together in the future. Like married together. I should've come up to his apartment when we dropped you off. Maybe I could've seen it hours before and talked you out of it. How'd it happen?"

"Ruby says it's because I'm an idiot." Her shoulders slumped.

Mina patted the space on the bed next to her. "I'm thinking in this one limited instance she's right."

Moving to the bed, she hiccupped from either the sobbing or the booze on an empty stomach.

Mina frowned. "Can you fix it? I mean you fix everything. It's what you do. You can fix this, right?"

"I don't know. I may have screwed this one up too much to undo." She sniffed. "He pleaded with me not to push him away. Pops even warned me today. Sam's been rejected by his own parents. He told me there'd be no coming back, but I kept driving."

Mina put an arm around her. "Why?"

"Because he puts the restaurant first, and I get what's left. Because I'm not sure where our relationship is going. Mostly, because I'm scared shitless."

Mina cocked her head. "What are you going to do?"

"I'll figure that out tomorrow. I can't face it tonight."

"Me either," Mina whispered. "Maybe if we don't say it out loud, then it's not real."

Cami sat up straight. "Say what out loud? What did you see?"

Mina dropped her gaze and picked at her fingernails.

"Mina, what you saw today, you've put it together?" Her sister's bent head nodded. "You know what happened?" Another nod.

"Not her death." Mina sniffed. "But I think I saw everything just before."

"Let's finish this." She grabbed Mina's hand and dragged her toward the backyard to find Delia.

"You mean finish the wine?" Mina croaked.

"That too." She stopped to grab the scrap of fabric and pins she'd stolen from Leslie Sol's possessions. "You can tell us what you saw. But the rest, we need to know the rest, and Delia might give it to us."

With Mina in tow, she pushed into the backyard and thrust the pilfered loot toward Delia. "These belonged to Sunny. Can you try for a read?"

Delia flinched as though Cami shoved hot pokers instead of innocuous-looking objects at her. Her gaze bounced between the hair pins to the shimmering silver material. "Do I even want to know how you got these?"

"No." Cami lined them on the table. "Please. I wouldn't ask, but we need to know."

Delia stared at her tear-stained face and glanced at Mina's trembling mouth before turning to Ruby.

Their oldest sister grinned. "Come on, Deals. You want to find out what happened too. Don't pretend the mystery doesn't call to you." Ruby yanked up her sleeves and wiggled her fingers. "My magic will bring you around afterward."

Delia sighed. "Fine. Wine first." She beckoned for her glass with a quick flex of her fingers. Ruby obliged. Delia took a long swallow, staring at the items. "No guarantees. You know my psychometric power shows only what it wants, when it wants."

Cami's heart thumped as Delia's slim fingers hovered above the fabric, stroking a featherlight touch before yanking away. Delia sucked in a breath. "Heartbreak and possibilities."

Her hand shifted to the hair pins. She touched the first. "An older woman." Moving to the second, she murmured something about a maid. Her knuckle brushed the third. Her head shot up. The grey-blue of Delia's irises glowed silver.

"Not Sunny."

CHAPTER TWENTY-SEVEN

Casa Oceana
Sunday, December 17, 1933, around 11:00 a.m.

CORAL HURRIED TO THE LANDING OF HER HOME'S GRAND STAIRCASE, THE perfect showcase entrance to frame her tall, statuesque beauty. She'd heard Paul raging from four rooms away and had tied her hair in a knot to hide there were more grey strands than ebony these days. She didn't need reminders of her age when she confronted her cheating husband.

Paul wasn't the handsome heartthrob he had been when she married him, the powerful director who had promised her decades in the pictures together. Drinking and debts had taken their toll. In the room below, he hunched next to the enormous steamer trunk she had decorated with displays of antique silver and first-edition books.

She clasped her hands and opened her mouth to ask what he was doing. Probably selling more of her valuables. But she didn't get the words out before he moved to the side. Sunny Sol slumped against the steamer with her hair in her face. Her hands lay open and outstretched.

"Paul." Her voice cut through the cavernous room. "What did you do?"

He rubbed his forehead, blinking bleary eyes at her. "She made me. Look what she made me do."

Coral clamored down the stairs. Her heels clacked with each step. Bracelets jangled on her arms. Her breathing turned harsh, but she didn't stop until she loomed over him.

Sunny's cheeks were pink and her lipstick smeared.

"Is she?" She swallowed. "Is she dead?"

He continued arranging Sunny's curls back where they belonged. "No. She's drunk and high. She hit her head and knocked herself out a bit."

"What really happened?"

"She fell."

Coral didn't believe him. She'd been pinched and pushed by Paul. "How did she fall?"

"Why do women question everything?" He rubbed his eyes. "We argued. Sunny was leaving me, leaving the restaurant."

"What?" She clutched her necklace. "She can't pull out. She's in too far."

"Sunny was going to the studio."

"The studio?" That little bitch couldn't tattle to the studio. There would go Coral's chances. She'd been working with a voice coach and a stylist who was supposed to do something about her thinning hair. She was on the verge of a comeback. "But why? You haven't made a movie in years."

"Sunny knows about our agreement with Alan. She threatened to go to the police."

She gaped at him. The studios would be the least of their problems. "We would be arrested, questioned, and all of our dealings aired out in the press for a public trial by media."

"I know. I lost my temper. We were arguing, and she started fighting. She pushed me. I pushed her back. I didn't mean to hurt her." He patted Sunny's cheek. "What have I done? What do we do?"

She wrung her hands so tightly a knuckle cracked. "She was going to leave the business?"

He nodded.

"And leave you? She told you this?"

He nodded again.

She bristled. "If she tells people of our agreement with Alan, it'll ruin us."

He continued to touch the unconscious woman. "Sunny won't tell. I just need to get her to see reason. Help me wake her. Do you think I should bring her some water? If it's the alcohol, maybe bread would help. Something to soak up the spirits."

"She will take everything from us." No amount of talking by Paul would change that.

"She won't. We will wake her and make her understand. Maybe I should take her to the doctor. To a hospital. No, a private physician. Someone who won't tell the studio."

Coral put her hand on his arm. "Of course. I know a doctor." She needed a plan, something that would keep Sunny quiet. But who could they trust? No one. The woman knew too much.

"You do?" He clutched at Sunny. "You'll get her some help?"

"I'll take care of it. Help me get her to the garage. I can use her car, right?"

"She wouldn't mind. Why won't she wake up?" He jostled her slightly. Her head bobbed against his chest.

She needed to get him moving. "Please, Paul. I can't carry her to the car."

He shifted Sunny's weight against him. Her head lolled. "No," he repeated again and again.

"You have to get her downstairs. Then I can take care of everything." Coral cajoled, coerced, and prodded until he shouldered Sunny's weight. It wasn't dignified, but it'd be the only way he could carry her. He panicked when Sunny's shoes fell from her feet.

"I've got them," she assured him. "Keep going."

It took long minutes and several pauses for him to carry the one hundred and twenty pounds of unconscious woman down the stairs. In the end, he heaved Sunny onto the front bench seat of her Packard Victoria. He wiped the heavy sweat from his brow, cheeks, and neck.

Coral tried not to gag on the stench of perspiration mixed with her perfume.

"Are you sure?" he asked, struggling for air. "Maybe I should go with you."

"And invite even more questions?" She shook her head.

"What if Sunny wakes, and I'm not there? She'll never forgive me." He reached into the car to straighten the blonde's curls. "She'll come around."

"She needs a doctor right now. Some space. Some time to think before doing anything rash."

He shook his head, nodded, then shook his head again. "I should go. I can't believe I shoved her so hard. I didn't mean to."

She patted his arm. "She knows."

"Will you tell her?"

"I will." She put Sunny's shoes in the car. "You better get back to the café."

"I was there all yesterday."

"It's Sunday. You always say they can't run the business on a weekend with both you and Sunny gone."

He stared at her, his gaze losing some of the dazed dilation. "I do say that. All the time. It's nice someone pays attention. Sunny and I need to be at the café. The accounts improve when we are there to greet guests and keep the staff in line. Weekend sales suffer when she shops and parties instead of working. I told her that."

"Don't worry." She pushed him toward the door. "Straighten your clothes and go down to the café. I'll handle everything."

"You promise you'll take care of it."

"I promise." She watched until Paul walked out of sight down the stairs. She turned back to Sunny. It was all a mess and left for Coral to pick up the pieces.

She closed the garage and leaned through the passenger side inches away from Sunny. Taking a deep breath, she considered her options. She could take Sunny to the doctor and risk difficult questions. What if the woman woke to start spouting the venom she had raged at Paul earlier? She talked, knowing Sunny couldn't hear her, but needing to reason aloud through the choices.

"You'll ruin us. Our careers. Our living. We'll become headline fodder, and we'll be lucky to stay out of jail. Or worse, if Alan Knapp learns we've been exposed. He doesn't take kindly to people who interfere with his business." She rolled her shoulders to shrug away the memories of rumors about how illegal gambling handled people who owed petty debts. Sending out enforcers to beat a few dollars out of a person's flesh.

Clara Bow, a former costar of Sunny's, had never recovered from the career-crippling headlines when one of the Davino brothers dragged her name through every newspaper in town with his lawsuit to collect a gaming debt. Clara had insisted she didn't owe the exorbitant sum the Davino criminal claimed. Still, the lawsuit made headlines, and the studios could not afford another scandal. The actress had retired shortly thereafter. No movie exec came calling for a leading lady associated with crooks like the Davino family, and the public had little sympathy for a welsher.

A woman needed her work and her marriage. Sunny had bickered with Clara on the set while that farce unfolded. The two had gotten into a scripted fight that had come to actual blows on screen. Typical of Sunny to incite even a coworker to come undone.

Coral wiped the smudged lipstick from Sunny's cheek. "You're a bad luck charm for everyone unfortunate enough to have you ensnared in their lives. Look what you did to my marriage. I had to drag Paul from that damned set to get him away from your web. I thought we were done with you when *Scoria* flopped. I was certain he'd see his little prodigy had failed him."

She dabbed away the smeared mascara. "You got married, and I was sure his fascination with you was over. I would get another chance at my marriage. That Paul and I could come up to this beautiful place and fall in love all over again. That we could manage a lovely seaside restaurant to cater to the stars and get back into the movie world." She smiled wistfully at the memory of a promise almost realized.

"But then you divorced, and Paul ran right back to you. I had to stand by and watch you fornicate with my husband in the business we had built as a couple, steps away from the home we shared. It was your name that went up over mine in neon lights. It was you in his thoughts. You in his bed. You stole my life." Coral could feel angry tears well in her eyes, and she blinked furiously to keep them from falling.

"Everyone loves you, Sunny. You could have had any man. Any life. Why did you have to take mine?"

If she drove Sunny to the doctor, the woman wouldn't be grateful. She would find a way to turn this all around to point at Paul and Coral. She would drag them down with her and then dance away like nothing could touch her. Coral knew it. She had seen it before. In the past five years, she had learned a lot about what havoc Sunny could wreak with the slightest crook of a slender finger.

"I can't let you do it this time." She pushed Sunny into an upright position, ignoring the way her head lolled to the side. "You would destroy everything I've ever worked for, and still the public would love you. I'd never known true jealousy until I met you. The anger and humiliation. The shame."

Coral straightened the expensive, unspoiled silk hosiery over Sunny's polished toes and slipped the heels on her feet. "You don't even know what damage you do." She arranged the gloves and purse left behind on the bench seat, pulled the mink coat around Sunny's breasts, and tapped a falling petal of the flower pinned to her.

A camellia. A pretty delicate thing. "I won't let you live my life any more than you already have. I'm taking it back."

She could tell Paul that Sunny had never woken. That she had died from the booze. Or even the blow to the head if he pushed the issue. Maybe she would have died anyway. She had told him she would take care of everything. This was the only way to ensure Sunny's silence.

Nodding, the decision set in her mind, she rounded to the driver's side to sit beside Sunny. The key was already in the ignition. With a deep breath and a final resolve, she reached for the ignition button and fired up the big V-12 engine, a flashy car with a powerful thrumming energy. It matched Sunny's personality. It was a fitting end.

She took care not to open the engine all the way, keeping it as quiet as possible. She slipped out of the car and closed the door. Looking back, it appeared that Sunny slept peacefully.

Before she could second guess herself, she hurried from the garage and slid the door closed. She knew from films that carbon monoxide could kill fairly quickly. A painless sort of death supposedly. A person drifted into a permanent sleep. Sunny would simply not wake up.

She waited and worried, practicing all her voice exercises in a hushed tone to distract herself from the steady rumble of the engine and the underscoring screech of her nerves. Lighting a cigarette, she wondered how long she should stay outside. What if she was caught? What was she doing? Why had it come to this? She had never been a spiteful person. But what if Sunny brought them all down?

Coral had been steadfastly loyal to her husband whenever it mattered most. Couldn't she do him this one final service? What if Sunny being gone brought them back together? Paul would never forgive her if he knew what really happened. Or maybe he would thank her.

Oh no, what had she done?

She paced in front of the door, her thoughts tangling. Could she still undo her actions? She finished a second smoke, slid the garage door open wide, wrapped her scarf around her face, and hurried inside. The car still idled. She rushed to the driver's side. Sunny's face had turned dark pink, a macabre rouge smeared like a horror play.

Coral unlatched the door. Sunny's eyes flew open, startling green against the unnatural blush of her skin. Coral hesitated in fear. Sunny heaved toward the driver's door. Coral rushed backward two paces. Sunny pulled herself up with the steering wheel and slid toward her. She gasped and jumped out of reach.

"No," Coral protested. She recoiled from the judgment and condemnation in Sunny's eyes. The woman would talk. She would tell Paul and the press. Coral would be destroyed. She'd be blamed for it all. There would be no coming back from this.

Her heart raced, the terror of being discovered and of devastation rippling through her. She clutched her stomach with one hand to press down the nausea, never letting go of the scarf held tightly over her face.

Sunny hauled herself to the driver's side and struggled toward the door in a fight for her life. A trickle of blood descended from her nose. The startling red so vivid and pure.

It dripped and spattered on the running board beneath the door. The one single ruby spot like a tear, a stain that spurred Coral into action. Using her palms, she pushed Sunny back into the car.

Coral could feel tears pool in her own eyes. Sunny would be her downfall. "Why can't you just leave us? Why won't you just go?"

The woman's eyes slid shut again. The blood snaked down from a nostril. Coral ran from the garage, slid the door shut, and counted her own hoarse hard breathing. Her heart galloped as fast as her thoughts. The horror over what she had done screamed in her mind.

Disgust and dizziness overwhelmed her, and she sank to the ground outside the garage door. A kernel of self-hatred rooted inside her and bloomed a bit more with every passing moment.

She couldn't catch her breath. Her entire body flushed and tingled. It was too late to go back. She could never undo this. Sobs in great gulping heaves racked her. Her hair had fallen, the pins probably scattered in the scuffle. She buried her face in her knees and wrapped her arms over her head.

When her own moans became whimpers, she cracked the door. The wind outside whipped and wailed, but there was no noise or movement from inside other than the running engine. She opened the door wide.

She paused. There was no smell, nothing to indicate what had happened here. And yet she waited. Counted to one hundred before stepping a single foot inside the garage. Clutching the scarf to her nose and mouth, she crept closer to the car, pulled the key, and killed the engine.

Sunny was still. Slumped. Reaching for the door. Coral put the key back in the ignition. She hovered near the driver's door and listened. No noise. She watched for the rise and fall of Sunny's chest, but she wouldn't ever draw breath again.

It was done. Coral got in the car and righted Sunny in the seat, straightened her clothing, and tenderly placed her hands in her lap. She made sure Sunny's shoes and stockings remained neatly in place, arranged her gloves and purse next to her, and smoothed her hair into its lovely curled style. It looked like Sunny slept. Except for the redness in her face and the trail of blood from her nose and down her mouth.

Coral took the scarf from her own face and moved to wipe the blood away before she remembered maybe that could be used as proof against her. She recoiled. Realizing she could be discovered at any moment, she scrambled out of the car and ran for the door. She slid it closed and backed away from the scene.

She rubbed her hands together, trying to wipe away the magnitude of what she had done. She shook her head to clear her thoughts and rushed toward the house smoothing her dress and tucking her hair. She would need to stay somewhere else tonight. She had to get out of here and far away from this as quickly as possible. She had to escape.

Stopping at the door to the house, she looked to the ocean where the waves crashed and the wind howled, and then down to the café below where Paul and their future waited. She breathed a long deep sigh. She had taken care of everything just as she had promised.

CHAPTER TWENTY-EIGHT

THE SISTERS TALKED LONG AFTER MINA AND DELIA'S RETELLING OF THE events surrounding Sunny Sol's death. Hearing it retold from the killer's point of view had been chilling.

"Crazy bitch," Ruby summed it up. "She and Price deserved each other."

"Both had some extent of a nervous breakdown and went into seclusion," Cami said. "The rumor was Price confessed on his deathbed that he killed her. People figured he'd simply locked Sunny out."

"No one can be more violent than loved ones." Delia shrugged. "Daily story of my job."

Cami stilled. Her head pounded. She'd had enough of abusive relationships for a lifetime.

Ama touched her shoulder. "It's not the same for you, little one. You got out."

She had to tell them she'd never really gotten out. Not all the way. The shadow of her abusive past still loomed above her. "He threatened you, Ama. He threatened all of you if I didn't stay with him. He controlled everything I did, what I said, what I ate, where I went, who I talked to. He made me feel like I was crazy and paranoid. I second-guessed everything I did or said. I couldn't take it anymore, and then I found him in bed with another woman."

"I can't believe you didn't lash out at him," Ruby said. All the sisters nodded.

Cami struggled with the secret weighing her down, the reason she'd shunned magic and planned her life.

"I did," she whispered. "I knew Neil would follow me, so I ran to the beach. He knocked me to the ground and beat me, probably trying to knock what I'd seen out of me."

Mina covered her mouth. "That's why you wouldn't let me go near the beach when we helped you move. You were afraid I'd see him beat you."

"No." Cami's voice grew stronger. "I was afraid you'd see what came next."

"What happened?" Delia clipped her words. She'd slipped into her interrogation mode. No judgments. Just the facts, ma'am.

"I almost drowned him," she confessed. "I wanted to so badly. I called to the water to have the ocean drag him down and hold his head beneath the surface. I broke the first rule of magic to harm none. I didn't just want to hurt him. I wanted to kill him."

The silence roared through her head. She looked straight at Delia. "The monster you're so afraid of becoming? I've already embraced her. That darkness never leaves." There. It was out in the open. They could condemn her for it.

Ruby spoke first. "Fuck him. He got lucky you're strong enough not to have finished it."

She stared, shocked at the nods and quiet reassurance. Even Ama refused to judge her.

"He never deserved your attention, mija."

Delia alone didn't move to join in. "How close did you come to killing him?"

She cringed at the memory. "Close."

"How'd it feel?"

"Exhilarating. Vengeful. Powerful. And dreadfully wrong."

"Cams, you didn't do anything wrong. It was self-defense. Neil is a master of messing with your mind, but you stopped yourself and your powers before you went too far. I don't know if I could." Delia breathed deeply and rolled her shoulders. "Let Neil try to come for us. It would not go well for him. We stand together."

"Agreed. Bring it." Mina nodded.

She shook her head, overwhelmed by the outpouring of support and affection. She'd carried a fraction of the terror Sunny Sol must have gone through.

"Sunny knew she would die," she whispered. "The pain and fear she'd have known those last seconds, fighting for her life." She shivered before she could finish. "Mina, when you slipped into Sunny's time, was she afraid every second?"

Mina shook her head. "Her vivaciousness started the chase for me. Not fear."

Ama smiled. "It must've been the longing for love sustaining her. She needed love like oxygen. Just like our Camellia." Ama passed a hand over Cami's curls.

Tears stung her eyes. She couldn't remember crying this much before. She hadn't even started grieving the loss of Sam. She'd push that until later when she was alone.

"I'm hoping Sunny found Joey after all," Ruby said, their eternal optimist under all her tough exterior.

"That would be a sweet ending for our tale," Ama agreed. "Bedtime, lovelies."

CHAPTER TWENTY-NINE

An hour before dawn, Sam met Lottie at the back of a nondescript building in the Valley. Her gaze darted around the empty lot and street outside. She locked the door behind them. Her hair was tucked under a baseball cap pulled low over her brow.

He followed her down a narrow hallway to a large open space filled with green screens, camera lighting, and backdrops. "What is this place?"

"Rental studio." She clicked on a single light. "I know the guy that owns it. I'm dressing Witch's Bane for a music video here tonight after my day gig."

"Then what are we doing here now? Playing dress up?" He snapped his mouth shut. He didn't need to inflict his foul temper on her. It had already gotten him in enough trouble.

"I couldn't very well discuss this over the phone or at our parents' house." She poked around each corner as though checking for surveillance before swinging her giant purse off her shoulder and pawing through it.

"What's with all the secrecy? You wouldn't even let me bring Bogart." He gestured toward the bare studio, the dim light, and her ball cap. "I only called to ask about our pathetic excuse for a father's ramblings and Mitch Abrams."

She hurried across the room and clapped her hand over his mouth. "Don't speak until I tell you."

For such a small woman, his sister had a huge personality. Much like Cami. Even the thought of his girl had him longing to drive the short distance east to her mother's house and beat on the door, begging her to forget the last thing he had said. But Ruby had called. After cursing him with some creative names for stupid, she had told him to give Cami the night. The sisters had her. She was safe, and she needed the space.

Against his better judgment, he would give her the time when all he wanted to do was plead with her to come back. But right now, he needed some answers himself. Answers he hoped Lottie could give.

He nodded once, and she removed her hand. She yanked chalk and candles out of her bag. Not the scented pretty kind she had tried to put in his apartment. These were votives in glass cylinders like those used for prayers or altars or shrines. Pacing the concrete floor, she drew a smooth, fluid circle. She must have done this a thousand times as easy as the sketch came.

Grabbing his sleeve, she dragged him into the center of the circle. She rummaged through her purse. What all did she have in there? Fabric swatches, tape measures, a sewing kit. He straightened before she could catch him staring. She shoved a charm into his palm. He turned it in his hand. It looked a lot like the one looped on Bogart's collar except this one was blue. She held a finger to her lips.

She took out a lighter and lit the votives, spacing them in equal distances around the circle. Snatching the charm from him, she whispered something in broken pieces of Latin and Japanese. He frowned. Lottie didn't speak foreign languages.

A pulse went through the room. Nothing he could see except for flickers of the flames, but his gut tightened. What the hell was going on?

She gripped his arm and counted aloud to ten. "All right. The protective circle should hold. Maybe. I mean mostly this is doing the work." She held up the charm. "I'm shit at spells. We can talk now."

He touched the metal. "What is that?"

"A privacy ward made by the best spell crafter in the country, Eleuia Nahualli Donovan." She smirked. "I believe she lets you call her Ama."

He lowered his hand. "About that. I might have screwed things up with Cami."

Lottie narrowed her eyes. "What did you do?"

"Can we just talk about the family stuff?"

She moved to flick his forehead, but he dodged before her hand caught him. "Sam Corraza, you need to fix things with Cami."

"I will." He hoped. He prayed. He couldn't risk believing otherwise.

"You better." She ran her tongue over her teeth.

He pointed at the circle, seizing the opportunity to change the subject. "So you know magic?"

"Welcome to our witchy family secret." She stretched her hands.

"And you couldn't tell me this before?" Maybe when she found out he was dating a witch?

She winced. "Forbidden."

"By the authority?" He was joking, but she wasn't laughing.

She nodded.

"Wait, seriously?" He couldn't believe it. "Who are we talking about? A witchy ruler or Congress?"

"The Senate," she whispered. Her eyes had gone wide. She was afraid.

He rubbed the back of his neck. He'd already mishandled one frightened woman tonight, and it'd been a disaster. "Lottie, are you saying a witch Senate passed a law that said my own family couldn't tell me?" He swallowed, unsure what to say. If Cami's family was an example, the powers were inherited. Hell, his own father had told him the powers went to Lottie. "Couldn't tell me you're a witch?"

"Exactly." Her voice was low and urgent. "They told our parents to cut you off. But now you're dating a Donovan sister, which makes talking to you an even bigger no-no."

He blinked. He must have missed some key pieces of information.

"Lottie, I own a restaurant. I fell for a pretty girl who walked into that restaurant. I don't think that rates as a terrorism threat."

She swallowed and stayed silent.

"All right," he said. "If this Senate—"

"Shh."

"Okay." He stretched out both hands, palms down. "If this authority doesn't want me around the family or to know about your powers." She frowned. "Your special needs." She slapped his shoulder. "Your abilities," he concluded. "Then why wasn't Joe cut out?"

She snorted. "Please, as if Joe notices anything outside his own little narcissist bubble. Joe believes what he is told to believe about the family."

"But I wouldn't?" This guessing game was getting difficult.

She bit her lip. He needed to change tactics. Gesturing to the candles, he flicked a finger at the lighter. "So if you've got magic, why not just twitch your nose and light the wicks?"

She heaved a sigh that was much more like the little sister he knew and not this crazy super-secret Senate stuff. "It doesn't work like that. You've watched too many movies. Not even the elementals who are one in a million can create their elements from nothing."

He froze. "Cami is an elemental. Are you saying she's...?" He couldn't finish the question. What? One of a kind? He already knew that.

Lottie grabbed his hand. "Since the inception of the Senate, the Donovans are the only known set of sister elementals to have existed. They're a first in two thousand years of witch history. So yeah, she's one in a few billion. There's a reason no one knows they exist. It needs to stay that way."

Sam swore. It sounded like Neil wasn't the only threat to his girl. He didn't let Lottie pull out of his grasp. "Then how do you know who the sisters are? What they are?"

Lottie's expression went blank.

"Classified?" He guessed. "Or something else I'm not supposed to know."

She jerked her chin once.

"What can you tell me to protect her?" Because he needed to keep Cami safe from her stalker ex and whoever this Senate was.

Lottie lifted sad eyes to his. "You can stop asking about our uncle who never existed."

"Mitch Abrams?"

She flinched. "Yes. Him. He was gone before I was born, but he was a good-looking, smart son of a witch who did some seriously bad shit."

"So I got banned for reminding people of someone I happen to look like and pulling some juvenile pranks?"

"What I'm about to tell you?" Her gaze burned into his. "I will deny saying it and you need to forget you ever heard it. Swear to me you won't repeat it. To anyone. Ever. Not even Cami."

Shit, could he promise that? He would if it would get Lottie to talk. "Yeah."

She dug her fingers into his skin. "Swear it."

His throat went dry. "I swear."

Lottie closed her fist over the charm and dragged Sam closer. Her voice was barely audible. "You got banned to protect you and our family. There are prophecies. Mitch never had children, but if he had, we were told his son would betray the Senate. But you, Sam, you'll orchestrate the event that will seal the Senate's downfall."

CHAPTER THIRTY

LOVE LIKE OXYGEN. CAMI HAD WHISPERED HER MOTHER'S WORDS THROUGH the sleepless night. She rubbed the grit in her eyes and headed toward Santa Monica the next morning in stop-and-go freeway traffic. She planned to pick up the paperwork for an extended restraining order, meet with an insurance adjuster about the damage at her apartment, and return to Ama's house for the night. Mina shuffled music, scrolling through playlists.

Cami's phone lay silent in her bag. Ruby had deleted the messages from Sam last night, and he hadn't called or texted again.

"How's your life plan working out?" Mina interrupted her spiraling thoughts as they waited for the interchange from the 110 to the 10 westbound.

"Crappy," she admitted. "Other than Neil, it's all going to plan. Work is great, studies are fine, and I'm on track to certification. I should be ecstatic. But I'm not. Plans are boring."

"Sam's not boring." Mina flipped the fancy engraved silver lighter in her hand, dancing it out to the crook of her ring and pinky fingers. The lighter flicked the opposite direction toward her thumb.

She sighed and switched lanes. "No. He's not."

Mina snapped open the Zippo with a loud click.

"No open flames in the car."

Her sister clapped it shut and stuffed the lighter into a pocket. "Sam's dog is cool too."

"Yes." She held back the tears, unwilling to start another flood. She took the exit for Ocean Avenue.

"We going to your apartment after the courthouse?"

"Only long enough to meet with the insurance person. My lease is up soon." She pulled into parking. "Time to find a new place. Maybe further down the coast."

"Somewhere away from Sam?"

Without answering, she shut the door and reached for her necklace as they walked into the courthouse. Half an hour later, she had applied for a more permanent protective order.

"I'm hungry," Mina said for the third time in the last ten minutes. "How about the chicken shack by the beach? You hungry?"

She wasn't, but she couldn't let Mina starve either. It would be a short walk in broad daylight through a busy populated part of town. "Sure." She tossed the paperwork in her bag and glanced toward the police department.

When they got to the restaurant, the patio was full. They ordered at the curbside window, and Mina pushed to look for a seat in the back. Cami waited on the sidewalk for the order. Should she call Sam? Would he answer?

Her amulet flared hot and blazing. She spun to find Neil hurrying toward her.

His fingers closed over her upper arm. "Let's go. Don't make a scene."

"No." Her stomach pitched and rolled with the memory of every time he had bruised her. She yanked out of his grip. "Don't touch me."

His hand moved to cup her face. He squeezed her cheeks hard. "I said, let's go, bitch."

Adrenaline rushed through her, the tingles firing as hot as his hold on her face. She stomped on his insole. "No."

He stumbled back but regained his footing and yanked her off balance. Her world tilted. He hauled her against him. "It's not like you've got a home to run to anymore," he seethed. "Don't make me do something you'll regret."

"Stop." She dug her nails into his arms and squirmed out of his hold. He backhanded her to the pavement. Her forehead banged against the curb. Pain, sharp and overwhelming, shot through her. A hot rush of blood streaked into her eyes, and her cheek stung. She tasted a coppery tang in her mouth.

"No! Cami!"

A high-pitched scream had her struggling to her feet. *Mina.* Her sister had thrown herself on Neil who shrugged her off. Mina landed with a thump on her butt. A man rushed to help, but Neil hit him in the face. A woman yelled she was calling the police.

Neil seized Cami by the hair and raised her off the ground. She punched the heel of her hand into his crotch. He doubled over.

She saw fast movement out of the corner of her eye and whirled. "Stay back, Mina."

He took advantage of her distraction and wrapped his hands around her throat. He squeezed. She kicked, and he lifted her to dangle over the street. He'd kill her. She could see it in his eyes, the bulging vein in his neck, the stark redness of his cheeks under his blond hair. Sunny's face interposed over his features. *Sunny.*

Sunny had endured this. She'd fought back. So could Cami, and she'd win vengeance for all the times she'd run scared, for the Sunnys of the world.

She closed her eyes and called to the nearest water source—a fire hydrant two feet away. Gathering her magic, she pulled as hard and as fast as she could. The hydrant shook and trembled before erupting, the water exploding outward to break the cap and blasting straight into Neil.

With a startled shriek, he let go of her and flew backward. Drenched and slipping, he fell to the ground with three men piling on him in a wet wrestling match. At least two people had their cell phones out videoing.

"Cams!" Mina launched herself toward her sister.

Mina probed the cut on Cami's head, and she jerked. She swallowed past her sore throat. "I'm fine. I promise."

Sirens blared and lights flashed as police arrived. After a few shouted instructions from bystanders, officers hauled Neil against the hood of the car and handcuffed him. Before officers could question them, Delia's bright red Mini screeched to a stop.

"Paramedic," Ruby called and pushed open the passenger door.

"Donovan?" An officer must have recognized one of her older sisters.

Cami sat on the curb and put her hand to her head. The altercation with Neil had lasted maybe three minutes. The paperwork took much longer. An officer photographed her cut which had finally stopped bleeding. The matted blood down her face was gruesome enough according to her sisters. The police interviewed everyone separately. Ruby stayed with her, and Delia went with Mina.

Ruby hurried the officers, saying she needed to take the patient for treatment. All four sisters loaded into the Cooper for the dash to Cami's car. In the court parking lot, Ruby tipped Cami's head to the side. "It's a nasty gash, but it's not deep. Head wounds bleed like a son of a bitch."

Ruby rubbed her hands together, and her blue eyes darkened. She touched her fingers to the wound and hummed.

Cami breathed deeply, the sting intensified for a second before dulling to an ache. Ruby's healing hands moved to her chin, neck, and collarbone. A few moments later, she couldn't tell she'd been hurt in the first place.

Ruby winked at her. "All good. Although maybe we could call Sam to come kiss it better."

Her mind flashed to Sam teasing her about the same thing on the beach. She'd been so mad at the time, but the memory triggered a rush of others. She paled even under Ruby's care.

"No." She took the wipes Mina offered and mopped away the blood smears. "Thanks, but he doesn't want to see me." She stared at the red and black streaks, stark against the white cloths.

"Can't you have the happy ending Sunny should've gotten?" Ruby rubbed her shoulder. "You stood up to Neil. We're proud of you."

"I'm lucky you and Delia came so quickly." She crumpled the wads in her fists. "Why were you both in Santa Monica anyway?"

"We didn't want you going back in there alone." Ruby squeezed her hand, and the last of her soreness ebbed away.

Right. The apartment. She nearly groaned. "Delia, do you think the insurance adjuster you talked with is still available?"

The blonde arched a brow. "You sure you're up for it?"

She nodded. "I might as well finish it today."

Delia took out her phone and tapped against the screen. "You are set. Why don't you head over now with Mina?" She gestured toward the police station the next block over. "Let me check whether anyone captured your powers on video and keep your name out of public records. I'll come with Ruby right after."

Mina threw her arms around Cami. "You don't have to do this alone. We're here to make sure you're never alone again."

She gave her a wobbly smile. Her heart might be broken, but her sisters had mended her as best they could. She'd taken down Neil with a water shot to the gut. How much more challenging could facing her apartment again be? "Let's see if there's anything worth saving."

CHAPTER THIRTY-ONE

CAMI TOOK A DEEP BREATH AND PUSHED THROUGH THE BROKEN DOOR. HER apartment was a total loss. A complete disaster.

Clean slate. Only a few minutes to meet with the insurance agent today and she'd be rid of the place except for taking care of the mess. "Too bad I can't shoot water through here without losing whatever's left of the deposit."

Mina snickered. "You could do it. You showed hella control today. More than I've had lately." She rubbed her temples. "If I'd have called my element, I'd have probably burned the whole block down."

"I doubt it." She tried to right what was left of a chair. It teetered for a moment before falling again. She started a scrap heap in the middle of the room. "But why don't we avoid any fires here just in case?"

"I emailed Ita," Mina told her quietly. "She'll help me work on better control of my abilities as soon as she gets back. Gigi agreed to train me over the phone." Mina admitted in the silence of the ruin. "I called the research group."

"The one for parapsychology?" She picked up a single unbent fork with thoughts of saving it before tossing it in the trash pile.

"Yep. Lab rat reporting for duty in two weeks. Got to get through finals first."

"How are your grades?" She wandered through the small living area, searching for salvage and finding none.

"All A's except a B in econ. The professor is a tool. He'll mark down my paper on technicalities and will grade on the wrong curve."

"See all that using your powers, did you?" She hid her smile.

Mina's idea of studying obviously differed from others. "Why work harder than I have to if it's not going to change the outcome?"

"So what do you see for this place?" she asked, gesturing around the room.

Mina stopped, stared, lost focus, tried again, coughed, and laughed. "Same thing I've always seen. I'd say enjoy it, but I know you will. Damn, sis."

She frowned. "What?"

Mina pointed toward the empty doorway.

"Uh, Mina. I don't see anyone." Had her sister's powers expanded to include ghosts or non-corporeal entities now?

"They're on the stairs. Give them a minute." She calculated. "Three, two, one."

She turned to greet the insurance rep. Sam stood there. Sheer joy at the sight of him filled her before the memories of his words last night flooded back. Ruby and Delia moved in behind him.

"Sam?" She stammered, trying to recover. She couldn't. All the air had left her lungs.

"I called him as soon as I took your phone. You should really password protect it better," Ruby said. "Delia and I were on our way to pick him up when Mina called about Neil attacking you."

Sam exploded. "What?"

Delia tutted and typed something into her phone. "Calm down, lover boy. She kicked ass. She's fine. There were no cell phone captures of her, only a drenched Neil getting tackled by concerned citizens. Neil's locked up for now and hopefully he'll stay there. They'll issue a criminal protective order for you, Cams."

She couldn't breathe.

Ruby simply pointed at Sam, then at Cami. "You two need to fix this. You're both expected at Ama's Memorial Day cookout this weekend. Our mom is bringing ribs. I'm making spiked lemonade. Don't be late. Or no later than Delia always is."

Delia cut a sideways glance but didn't respond.

"I thought…" She swallowed. She couldn't take her eyes off Sam. Not for an instant. She pointed mindlessly at the apartment somewhere over her shoulder. It had to be back there. She'd sworn she'd been standing in her apartment a minute ago before Sam walked in and the whole world narrowed on him. She gestured again in the general direction. "Insurance."

"I've already scanned the police report and photographs to the insurance company." Delia flicked imaginary dirt off her shirt, not daring to touch anything. "They will send a check soon for the entire insured amount. Which wasn't much. We need to discuss that later. The check's going to Sam's place. As should you. Let this dump and any security deposit go." She spun on her high heels and left. Ruby followed.

"Gotta go catch my ride," Mina said, grabbing her in a quick hug. "Sam, stop being so afraid of rejection. She is your family. We are your family. You're not alone anymore. Put her first in your life before the restaurant, where she belongs."

Sam's head tipped in Mina's direction, but he never looked away from Cami, who hung onto sanity by a mere thread. Her breath hitched, shallow and needy.

Mina hadn't finished. "She is trying to sort you in her mental catalog of life. It's what she does before she bosses us around. It's out of love."

She reached for the door. "See you both this weekend for the cookout. Thanks for bringing desserts, Sam. The brown sugar coconut pudding thing you're going to make? So good. You'll need to bring the recipe for Ama." She fled before Cami could ask when she'd seen all that.

Her hands fluttered around her, reaching for him. She stilled, remembering his words. She bit her lip and worked not to stare at him. Failing that, she tried to memorize his black curls, the strong jaw, the rich brown of his eyes that had redness shot through them and dark smudges beneath.

She breathed in. How would she ever put the pieces of her life back together? Without Sam?

"You okay?" Sam took a couple of steps toward her.

She swallowed past the sudden lump in her throat. "I, uh, I blasted Neil with water after he slammed me on the pavement and tried to choke me out." She babbled, but she couldn't stop. "Delia says it's self-defense. I fought back, but he kept coming. So…" She lifted a shoulder, but the movement was jerky. "Magic."

His jaw ticked. "He hit you?"

"Ruby healed it." She swept her curls away from the spot where she'd hit the concrete, hoping she'd cleaned all the blood. He hurried to her side, his gaze searching her for injuries, his fingers reaching to stroke her face. He caught himself and stepped back. His attention shifted to the damage around them.

His ultimatum rang through her mind, and she stilled, unable to close the distance between them but unwilling to shy away.

He ran a hand over the back of his neck. "I tried calling and texting. I had almost followed you when Ruby called and said to give you some space. I brought all the clothes Lottie bought inside." He stopped in front of the remains of her cabinets.

Her eyes closed. She couldn't do this. He had probably destroyed those clothes like the torn rags thrown around this place. She couldn't blame him. Maybe he'd simply sent them back to Lottie. Sensible Sam moving on the same way he fixed problems at the restaurant.

"I folded each for you to try on. I put the makeup in the bathroom drawers I'd cleared for you." He moved to the one small window. "I fucked up yesterday. I knew the second the call failed."

She stared at his back, the slope of his slumped shoulders, but she didn't dare say anything. Not until he'd finished.

"I'd called my parents to see if I could get a safer place for you to stay. The conversation with my father didn't go well. He let me know they never wanted me. I talked with Lottie. Apparently, there's magic in my family too, and I remind them of my evil uncle who we're not supposed to mention." He shook his head. "Anyway, I was already frustrated about the shit day you'd had and stupidity from the restaurant. When you said you needed time and you were leaving me, it all came out."

Her mouth quivered and tugged downward. She couldn't control it any more than the shakes seizing her body. She folded her arms and hugged herself to stop the violent quaking. She had to handle this before the sobs forming in her belly could make their way out.

He looked over his shoulder at her. "Bogart cried all night at the door. He fell asleep with his snout on his paws looking for you. I found the School House Rocks shirt you left yesterday in my office along with The Reading Rainbow one you'd forgotten at my place before. I could smell you on them."

She clamped her lips together. She couldn't take much more of this. The mental image clearly stamped in her mind. Trying to protect him, she'd ruined it, and still he was here. She focused on his words, not even caring about her raspy breath and the escaping whimper.

He picked up the remains of her pink Converse. "Ruby told me how messed up you were about all of it, but she wouldn't let me come to you. She said you were trying to protect me from your coward chicken shit ex. That you..." His voice broke, and he cleared his throat. "She said you protect and boss around everyone you care for."

"I did. I do," she whispered, wiping a hand over her face before a tear could snake down it.

He dropped the torn pieces to the ground. "What Mina said about you trying to process everything and boss us around out of love? That true?"

She nodded.

"Sweetheart, you can't catalog this. Love's messy. Our love will never go into a neat little box, but our relationship is a hell of a lot easier than most."

She heard him say "our love," and her mind spun with hope. "What did you say?"

"I said it's too messy to be all organized."

"No, the other part," she interrupted.

He stopped and stared. "I love you."

She froze. "What?"

paddle out and a wave the size of a building comes up, I'm terrified then too. I'd be stupid not to be, but my choices are either try to tackle it and completely wipe out or to go with it and maybe, just maybe, get an awesome ride out of it. I've learned that being able to hang with the scary is part of it for the amazing things you want. I want you."

"I thought you said there was no coming back." Her sad gaze flicked upward.

"I was mad and hurt and scared. It was wrong, but I couldn't think straight with the possibility of losing you."

"I didn't know what to do," she admitted.

He tightened his hold on her. "I'm sorry. Ruby called and gave me an earful about it. I should've gone straight home with you after Mina's time slip. I put work before you. I didn't realize how much you were still in shock over what that asshole did to you and your place. That you were shouldering it for the rest of us and then came back to fall apart alone."

He moved away, grabbing the side of the door where it hung askew. "I'd never have guessed you thought he would come after me or you'd try to protect me from such a coward. When Ruby put it that way, it was sweet. Not smart, which is unusual for you, but sweet." He shoved the door closed as best he could on the one remaining hinge, flipping the lock in a useless circle.

"Ruby told me I'm an idiot."

He lifted his brows. "Delia called me worse. For such a priss, she has an astounding mastery of profanity."

"We had a long night too."

"I heard. You can tell me about it later." He didn't say anything, couldn't say anything about the prophecy Lottie had shared. That didn't matter now. Nothing mattered but Cami.

It was warm in here, an upper-level room baking steadily in the eighty-degree heat without air conditioning or an operable window. Let's see if he could make it hotter.

He righted the broken table and wedged it against a somewhat intact part of the futon frame. It'd have to do. He stalked back the three long strides to her, watching her wide, bright eyes. He wanted to see the beautiful whiskey and gold combination dazed and glossy with passion instead of tears. With sweat breaking out over his skin from the heat and the desire, he dipped his fingers into the low rounded neckline of her dress to tease and stroke the upper part of her breasts.

"What are you doing?" Her pulse quickened. He could feel it under the tips of his fingers as he rubbed them back and forth across her heart.

"Making up. Best part of an argument." He tugged at the collar of her dress. His hand caught on a zipper pull between her breasts. "Where'd you get this?" The fabric was worn soft and tissue thin.

She shook her head with a frown as though she had trouble concentrating on the question. "It's an old one of mine."

"Mine," he repeated. He glanced at the table and that damned carving. *Mine*. Cami was his, and he was hers. Nothing her ex did could change that. He nodded at the table. "We're going to take care of that too." His hand trailed lower, palming the heavy fullness her breast. She leaned into his touch. "Does the zipper down the front of your dress work, or is it just for show?"

Her brow wrinkled and she told him she'd never tried, that she didn't know, and was he considering unzipping it? All the way down? With those innocent questions contrasting the temptress dress, he had trouble focusing on anything except the heat from her body as his hands moved lower. Her breath caught.

He brought his mouth down over hers. Consuming. Devouring. That low burning from the first kiss caught fire and ripped through them. Every nerve ending felt the spark and crackle of the wicked tangle as he pushed past her lips. She opened for him. He could feel her welcome the invasion and plunder. If their earlier kiss had been a promise, this was a claim. A brand. Marking both of them.

He hiked her up against him by her hips, and her legs wrapped around his, clutching him, embracing him. Savoring the feel of her bare thighs under the dress against his rough hands, he carried her to the carved table and gently eased her down. Her curls and curves spread out before him like a feast. She was gorgeous and the love of his life. He'd make damn sure she knew that before they were done here.

* * *

The wood was hard and uneven beneath her back, and the fabric from her dress bunched and dug into her skin, but Cami didn't smooth it. She reveled in the slight discomfort there compared to the way her body hummed in anticipation. She wouldn't tug or fuss to fix anything this time. She wanted it all burned into her memory. She busied her hands running over the warm muscles of his chest as he unbuttoned his shirt to expose the naked skin beneath. The dim light of the window licked the curve of his jaw, and she wanted to do the same.

She kissed his neck, breathing in his scent, letting it wash over her, comforting the aches of yesterday. It soothed the hurt but not the desire scorching her skin. He claimed her mouth, deeply at first and then tenderly as he eased her down until she lay flat on her back. The small broken table barely fit her upper torso, and her legs dangled over the edge. She ran her feet up the backs up his legs to pull him closer and to revel in the power and the strength there.

He leaned over her, grabbed the top of the zipper, and toyed with it. He kept a steady pressure, pinching with his fingers. The fabric stuck for a long moment before giving to his demands. Slowly, so agonizingly slowly, he tugged lower. The metal grazed her skin, cool and biting as he pulled the zipper's teeth apart one by one. When he finished, he splayed the fabric open wide to reveal her nakedness except for her bra and panties.

He trailed his fingers down her body from her collarbone to her thighs. Skimming. Studying. Exposed and vulnerable, she reached to cover herself, but he looped fingers in the fabric over her hipbone.

"I see no one stole your panties today." His eyes darkened. "Let's see how long you can keep them." His voice deepened. His fingers lingered, caressing the flesh there. "But first." He peeled the straps of her bra down her arms, catching on his fingers.

Laying her back, he pushed the bra down to take her nipple in his mouth. The roughness of his tongue and teeth made her shiver. Her back bowed off the table in pleasure. She moaned with the sensations his mouth sent through her body. Her toes curled where they dangled in midair. The table rocked and righted. She gasped but arched again when he did the same to the other nipple.

He stroked and cupped each breast, running his thumbs along the underside. It wasn't enough. Not now. Not with the evidence of his desire pressing against her.

"Sam." His name fell from her lips, low, demanding, insistent. She reached for him but slipped on the table. Damn the slick fabric of this dress.

He kissed her gently before working his hands back down her body. His fingers ignited the desire as they slowly descended. He slid her panties down her hips, nudging her to lift her ass. She gasped when his fingers and the fabric rasped against her skin. His gaze met hers while she watched the slow pull of her panties along her legs before he tugged them over her feet and stuffed them in his pocket with a sly grin.

He pulled back to stand over her and stare at her, and the smile became one of tenderness and adoration. When he sighed, she could feel his hot breath on her skin. His hungry gaze moved lower. He stared at the slit between her thighs, and his eyes sparked. She wiggled, and his fingers gripped her, holding her in place. Her eyes slid shut, embarrassment at the exposure taking hold.

"Cami, look at me." His throaty, rough words had her skin prickling.

She met his gaze, held it before he turned his attention back to her center. He traced a blunt finger over her folds, and her muscles tightened under the feather-light touch.

"You are so damn beautiful," he whispered. "Splayed out like this. Eager for my touch."

Her belly quivered.

"So responsive." He touched his lips to her collarbone before kissing a path between her breasts. He nipped her left hip bone. The stubble on his jaw scuffed the sensitive inside of her thigh before he put his lips on her. His curls teased her belly while his mouth...oh his mouth did incredible things. She writhed as much as she could on the teetering surface without toppling. When his tongue licked flat against her clit, pinpricks made her shiver despite the heat.

"More."

The scent of ocean and salty air swept the room.

"You feel that?" He sounded breathless, awed. "Did you do that?"

"Love me, Sam."

"Always."

He stood, and it was her turn to admire him. The way his shirt fell open to reveal the muscled, tanned chest beneath and how the edge of his tattoo played at his collar. The way his cock stood straight, ready for her. She moaned, urging him on.

He stroked a hand down the front of her body, and she arched into the touch.

"I want to make you bow off this little table like that again and again. To obliterate what's carved beneath it. Because you're mine, and I'm yours."

He stroked her folds with his fingers, and she ached for release. She was so very tender there after his touch and his mouth and now his fingers doing things that made her rock against him, made her sink her fingernails into his arms.

"Trust me?" he whispered. He rubbed his cock against her.

She nodded. "I trust you."

"You want this?" Arousal made his throat thick, the demand a supplication.

"Yes." Flexing her fingers on his skin to claim, she gave control to him, lost herself in the need that built with each thrust. The craving for him climbed and built. His scent wrapped around her. The feel of his warm body against her chest and the hard wood against her back excited her in its contrast. The thump of the table against the wall thrilled her before she caught herself. The sound reminded her of where they were.

"The neighbors will hear," she whispered. She wasn't sure if she cared. Or if it didn't turn her on more. Her body seized on the possibility and tightened around Sam.

"Let them," he growled. "They didn't bother when he was destroying your place and could've been killing you if you hadn't been in my bed."

She ached at the fierceness in his voice. She gave her body over to the frantic fervor that had them both moving faster, harder. The table wobbled and snapped beneath her. Her breath caught as he clutched her to him, still buried inside her. He pulled at her legs, and she wrapped them around him. Tossing the broken remnants of the table to the side, he pushed her against the wall.

"Don't let me go," he clipped out.

He slammed fully into her, making her gasp and sending her spiraling upward in a shot toward ecstasy. He pummeled in and out of her. She clutched at his flushed, slick skin. The building carnal passion soared and surged inside her, a wave building too big for either of them to ride alone.

"I'm yours, and you're mine," Sam repeated between thrusts. "Say it. Now. You're so close. Say it while you come around me."

"I'm yours," she panted between ragged breaths. Her voice became stronger, feeding off the strength of the mounting intensity. "And you're mine."

With the possessive declaration, her body clenched over him. The climax tore through her body. She opened her mouth to scream. He clamped his mouth over hers, swallowing it down as he pumped his own release inside her with one final slam against the wall.

Her heart raced against his. She could feel both their pulses sprinting in unison. He kept her pressed against the wall. Her legs dropped, but he yanked them back in place. "Bare feet, broken glass."

She looked down the length of their bodies. He still had his shoes on. His shorts too. He hadn't stopped in their frenzy to do more than shove fabric down far enough to enter her. She smiled, taking pride in the power to make him crazy enough for her that he couldn't wait. Yet still protected her.

He carried her to the wet bar and sat her on the edge. He fastened his shorts while kissing her. He found her sandals and carried them to her. With strong hands, he ran his fingers down her legs to her ankles. Taking one sandal, he crouched and held her foot in his palm. He slid the shoe into place, cupping her heel and massaging her arches as he did. Their gazes locked. He kissed the inside of her knee and slipped the other shoe onto her bare foot. The tickle of his lips and quick scrape of his teeth had her body melting. The movement was so possessive and protective it was almost as intimate as the sex.

Turning away, he looked around the room. She surveyed the destruction as well. The pieces of the table had rolled to a stop against the wall. They'd snapped the flimsy tabletop in half. The carving lay broken.

"Let's get out of here."

"Your place?" she asked.

"Our place," he said, not meeting her eyes. She had put that uncertainty there. Had made him doubt her desire to be with him.

If she agreed, she had to be all in. She owed it to him to commit completely or not at all. Not only because of his history of people pushing him away who were supposed to love him. It was more than that. He was worth more than that. She sorted through emotions to find what was stopping her.

Sunny had been a heartbeat away from a happy ending. Cami had overcome her own past. Could she embrace this hope as her future?

Her heart said yes. Her body said hell yes. Her eyes grew. Fear had been the only thing standing in her way of happiness, of a future with Sam. She was better and stronger than that. She looked at the broken tabletop. She was fierce.

She touched his face. "Let's go home."

He moved between her legs where she sat and caressed her sides, pulling her closer. "I've been looking for home all my life. And it's been here all along." He kissed her lips softly, touched her breast. "In your heart." He dug his fingers lower and nipped her bottom lip. "In these hips."

She laughed, caught his mouth in a kiss before sliding down his body. Feeling loved. Treasured. Home.

CHAPTER THIRTY-THREE

CAMI PLAYED WITH BOGART. THE FOAMING WAVES LAPPED OVER HER BARE feet and his paws. She'd called the water forward to tease and play before pushing it back. Bogart was happy gnawing on his piece of driftwood. She wrapped the magic around her like a childhood security blanket she'd rediscovered.

Not that she needed to scan the beach as carefully with Neil's plea deal the day before. The phone had rung with the call when she'd been in the kitchen with Sam.

"Ignore it," he'd said.

"Can't." She'd reached for the phone blasting "Witchy Woman" by The Eagles. "That's Delia's ring tone." She ignored his snicker. "Hi Deals."

Delia did all the talking. "Neil pled to a felony domestic violence charge and a couple of assault counts. His counsel told him nobody would buy his 'she conspired with a fire hydrant to kill me' defense. You need a new phone. They found spyware on his linked to track yours."

Cami sucked in a breath, but Delia hadn't finished. "He will do three years state prison. Well, he'll actually do part of it, but you've got a protective order for the next ten years. He so much as shows up and you call the cops. Or blast the shit out of him again. Either way."

After Cami hung up, the muscle in Sam's jaw ticked. "I can't stand to think of him touching you. I hope prison is hell for him." He'd pulled her close. "No one will ever hurt you again."

"Because you and Bogart will protect me."

"Damn straight. Not that you need protection, but I've got you covered." He took her to bed to prove the point of how well covered she could be.

She smiled with the memory and watched him rinse off under the outdoor showers at the beach after a morning of surfing. She'd unpacked her few belongings at his place. *Their place.*

She had three days off at the animal clinic. She'd be content to sit here on a beach towel in her bikini the entire time, watching the water bead down Sam's bare chest. She'd expected to miss the tiny apartment, her first place of independence. But she hadn't. Not for a single minute.

It could be the amazing company and great sex. The gourmet food every day didn't hurt. Neither did Bogart's constant affection. She stroked his long ears, and he snuggled against her leg.

Sam walked toward her, toweling off his curls after shaking them in a very good imitation of Bogart. She grabbed another towel and started to dry Bogie and herself.

She peered up at him over sunglasses through her lashes. "Nice ripping." She'd watched him cut through the water, adjust into the curl, ride along the waves and topple eventually only to paddle back out with strong sure strokes and wait to pop up for another crest to glide with practiced ease.

He shrugged, too modest to accept the compliment. Her gaze moved downward. Maybe not so modest. His board shorts hung perilously low on his hips, and she admired the taper from his muscled shoulders down to a slim cut waist. His tan line fade flirted with the waistband and teased that she knew exactly what was below. "You looked good."

"You look better." He lowered next to her and dug through the bag for a container of kulolo. The fudge-like squares of taro, coconut milk and brown sugar had been a huge hit at the Memorial Day cookout the weekend before.

Mina had been right. Ama asked for his grandmother's traditional Hawaiian dessert recipe. Luckily, Sam had known to bring it along. Ama had thanked him and replied she knew his grandmother. He had asked Ama about any rumors she might have heard about the Senate, and his family or prophecies. She'd disappeared into the house, refusing to say more. Cami had assured him the Senate was older and stronger than any human government, but she'd been glad he hadn't asked more pointed questions about the witch matriarchy. The Senate preferred to rule silently.

He popped a bite of kulolo into his mouth. "Sweet like you." He nuzzled the sensitive spot behind her ear. The dampness from his body dripped onto her swimsuit. She started to protest, but why bother when she didn't mind. He lay her down on the beach towel.

She kissed him and asked Bogart to stay as she pushed at Sam's hands, got to her feet, and pulled him back into the water. She sprinted down the wet sand knowing he would catch her with a laughing spin that turned into kisses. She eased the weight of the last year off her shoulders, holding on to his embrace while the water rushed over their legs.

When their kisses turned so passionate that she'd used her power twice to keep them upright, he suggested they head back to shower together. They packed the bag and trudged through the sand to the Land Cruiser with Bogart.

"Need to go by the restaurant first?" she asked.

"Nope. I took the entire day off. I worked last night until close anyway."

"I know." She squeezed his hand. "I met you in the garage and lured you upstairs for a quickie."

"It was hot." He raised their joined hands and nipped at her knuckles. "You can do that anytime you like."

She climbed into the passenger seat and slid into a cover up. She enjoyed the show as he hung a towel from the window for privacy while he changed into dry shorts. She tangled fingers in his hair before running them down to the short-clipped sides.

"Do your curls always go back to the right place?" She teased.

He winked at her and tugged a shirt over his head. The curls fell right back into order.

"Some of us have to work for good hair," she muttered.

He loaded Bogart in the back seat and swung that door closed.

"At least I stashed a hair tie in the glove compartment," she said as she reached for the latch.

"Cami, no!" He scrambled for the passenger door. The glove compartment fell open. A small box tumbled to the floor.

Her mouth rounded. She leaned down as he reached to snatch the box off the floorboard. Their heads collided. She pulled back to rub her forehead.

"Ow." She opened her eyes to see him staring at her. He looked mortified and reached for her face with the hand not holding the suspicious package.

"You okay, sweetheart?" He pushed back her hair.

"You smacked yours too," she reminded him.

"I've got a hard head. I'm fine." He touched her cheek and angled her chin to check for injury.

Her hand snaked out and closed over his fingers clutching the box. "What's that?"

He gently pulled his arm out of her grasp and tucked it behind his back. His mouth opened and snapped shut again.

"Don't tell me I didn't see it, because I did." She fought a smile. "What's going on?"

He looked nauseous.

"Hey, it can't be that bad." Now she was worried. "You all right?"

"This isn't at all how I was going to do it. I was going to plan it all out. To make it right for you."

She gnawed her lip. Was Sam worried? She'd never seen him anxious like this. Irritated, yes. Angry, of course. And completely devastated when she'd left and come back. But not this nervous energy that vibrated off him now.

This couldn't be so bad. She'd simply stumbled onto a box he seemed direly interested in. A box she hadn't even seen except for a streak of color. She reached for him. "Sam, whatever it is, tell me. You don't have to make things right for me."

"I was going to wait until the end of the summer. I planned to give you time to get whatever boxes you wanted checked off that list of yours. Hell, I had to at least give you a few months to adjust to living with me and Bogart."

"I love living with you and Bogart. So what has the man I watched take on waves bigger than a truck all stressed out?"

"They weren't that big."

"Sam."

He took a deep breath. "This wasn't at all what I'd imagined. I thought I had more time but now I don't want to wait." He glanced down. "For sure, I thought we'd have more clothes on." He touched the bikini string at her hip. "Though maybe I should've been thinking less clothes. Maybe no clothes."

"While I'd love to get naked on the beach with you, I don't think it's such a good idea this close to the highway." Bogart whined, and she reached through the back seat to pet him. "In a minute, buddy."

She looked back. Sam wasn't there. She glanced down to find him bent on one knee.

"I'm going to do this right," he said.

"Sam?" Realization suddenly crept into the recesses of her brain. That had been a small box. A very small box. A square shaped box.

"Marry me." He pulled the box from behind his back.

"What?" She gasped in a sound more of wonderment than inquiry.

He laughed a nervous, uncomfortable huff of air. "Will you marry me?" He opened the box. A beautiful two-carat diamond solitaire with jewel-studded scroll work on the band was nestled inside. "I'll love you forever, Cami. I promise. There's a guaranteed life plan for you. If you'll say yes. Will you marry me?"

She stared at him from the passenger seat, listening to the roar of the waves in the silence between them. He'd proposed at the beach with her barefoot and perched on the taped seat of his beat-up Land Cruiser. Salt from the ocean stained her skin white. She had rough bits of sand all along her toes and legs. Her hair was a disastrous mess of curls. Bogart drooled out the back window. Propped on the rear quarter panel, his board listed precariously to the right from all the commotion. Her head throbbed from bashing into him. And Sam knelt in the dirt, sand, and gravel, looking hopeful. It was the perfect proposal.

She leaned down to seal this with a kiss. "You couldn't have planned it any better than this," she whispered against his mouth.

"Is that a yes?" he asked against hers.

"Yes." She smiled and kissed him. He grabbed her hand and slid the ring into its place on her finger before hauling her out of the truck and into his arm for a spin. He kissed her soundly. She laughed as her body slid down his, her toes sinking into the warm sand. He took her hand and kissed the ring on it.

"Where did you find this?" she asked. "It's gorgeous."

"Mina told me."

Cami stared at him in shock. "Did she see it in a slip?"

"She did. She told me the day we all met at Ama's that I'd better plan to marry you or walk away. Because she'd seen us married. Normally I would've run in terror." He raked a hand through his hair. "I know it's fast, but I wanted that future as our reality."

"You've known since then?" She looked up in astonishment. "And I took off. Oh, Sam."

"No, we're not going to replay that. We were both scared. She told me. I believed her. I even asked her what ring to get you."

She gazed at the ring. "It's divine."

"It's a two-carat Asscher-cut solitaire with a scrollwork band. I designed it with a local jeweler and picked it up yesterday."

"You custom designed it?"

"I did. I showed the sketch to Mina, and she said that was it."

"I couldn't have imagined anything so perfect." The diamond glistened and sparkled in the light. "Wait. Why was it in the glove compartment?"

"I'd just gotten it yesterday before work. When I got home, you were there waiting all sexy smiles. I tossed it in the glove compartment before you could see."

She stilled. "You left a two-carat custom Asscher-cut solitaire in the truck?"

"Yeah."

"And it was sitting here on the side of the road all morning?"

He grinned. "It's usually not locked when I surf. Or I put the key in a magnet box in the wheel well. You were here to keep the key today." He shrugged. "So I locked it."

"I could have watched the truck for you."

"The whole point was for you not to know it was there so I'd have time to plan." He laughed until she cut it short with a kiss.

They had a lifetime to plan. Together.

THE END

Thank you for reading! Did you enjoy?

Please Add Your Review! And don't miss more paranormal romance novels like, BLOOD KING by Amber K. Bryant. Turn the page for a sneak peek!

SNEAK PEEK OF BLOOD KING

Unlike most of the people in attendance, Sybille Esmond hadn't come to the county fair to watch a rodeo show or stroke the glossy fur of ribbon-winning show rabbits.

She came to be hypnotized.

Sybille stood among the selected volunteers as the would-be hypnotist, Elis Tanner, circled them, his scrutiny of his subjects aided by a flourish of his hands to the waiting crowd. Their environment presented a jarring mix, up-tempo techno music blaring like a nineties rave set against rainbow-themed carnival tents and food stands hawking deep-fried butter.

Elis raised his uplifted arms higher, mimicking a conductor about to direct an orchestra. As he closed his hands into fists, the music cut out. The crowd stopped their chatter, blueberry snow cones lowered, gazes raised as the man on the stage commanded their attention. A chill ran up Sybille's spine.

They were ready to be entertained and mesmerized, and though Elis Tanner had yet to do either, people were already leaning forward, hushing young children, silencing their phones.

The music came on again, another driving beat. Its vibrations tickled Sybille's toes.

She couldn't blame the crowd for wanting to be tricked in exchange for a bit of harmless fun. Only in this case, they weren't being tricked, not the way they imagined.

And Elis Tanner was far from harmless.

"How many of you have been hypnotized before?" He spoke with a vaguely British inflection, like someone who had lived stateside long enough that only scraps of their original accent remained. It reminded her of black and white movie actors. Cary Grant but a bit less Bristol.

A few people raised their hands, garnering a knowing smile from him. Sybille kept hers down. "The truth is, you've all been hypnotized multiple times. Every one of you."

The audience shifted. Sybille remained still. Elis was right: hypnotism was no magic. Not under normal circumstances. Today's show would present a different story, however. If he was nothing else, Elis Tanner offered the most abnormal of circumstances Sybille had ever come across.

"Hypnotism is simply another state of consciousness, no different than the ones we pass through on the way to and from sleep," he explained to them.

He searched the audience with clear grey eyes and then turned his gaze to the volunteers, stopping at her. It was a slight hesitation most would have missed, but Sybille was determined to miss nothing. In the briefest of pauses, perhaps there lay a hint of recognition.

Or perhaps not. Either way, Sybille must tread carefully. The enraptured audience had made themselves totally vulnerable. She glanced at her fellow stage-mates. They'd been naive enough to volunteer in handing their will over to him to play with for an hour. Sybille volunteered as well, but unlike the others, she did so with full knowledge of what she was getting herself into.

The music continued to blast. Intolerably loud, it forced its way into her, her head throbbing within a wall of sound.

Elis asked the volunteers to take seats in the metal folding chairs set out on the stage. "Are you ready?" He looked at her when he said this. Eleven volunteers nodded. Sybille smiled. She was ready. It was Elis who had no idea what was coming.

* * *

Elis spotted her as soon as she'd pushed through the crowd to take a seat midway from the stage. She wore sunglasses even though the day was never going to be anything other than dull and overcast. All day, he'd watched fair-goers glance towards the heavens, shaking their heads and cursing the weatherman. It could rain any moment and then their day would be ruined. For Elis, the clouds were welcome. This sort of sky kept the elements close, blanketing them low to the ground. A dark sky meant a world thrumming with electrical charge. He gathered this power on his tongue, like a child catching snowflakes, and then licked his lips.

Even with the weather in his favor, the woman in the sunglasses was an odd presence Elis was ill prepared for. She was as steady as a ticking clock where those around her, himself included if he was to be honest, registered as jumpy and nervous. Either she really was this calm or she hid anxiety well—he determined then to find out which was the case.

She would become one of his volunteers. She'd raise her hand, without a doubt. She was here for a purpose beyond entertainment—beyond a carnival sideshow act. She sought something. Something from *him*.

His heart strummed, fear of her unknown intentions making his palms sweat for the first time in ages. This was unacceptable. His act necessitated that he command the stage and here he was already having to work to maintain composure.

Elis shouldn't pick this woman. He already doubted his ability to control her, which made no sense—he had no reason to doubt himself.

He shook free of his mind's pointless meanderings, asked for volunteers, tried to select a diverse group—a girl wearing a state university sweatshirt, a man in his thirties with a goatee, a few middle-aged folks. Not wanting to seem too obvious, he picked the woman neither first nor last. He led his volunteers up onto the stage and instructed them to sit on rickety chairs.

The woman still had her sunglasses on, the audience visible in their reflection. Maybe she was one of *those* people—the skeptics who believed they could not be hypnotized, who assumed it was possible to hide their thoughts behind a layer of cheap plastic.

He didn't need her to remove the lenses, but he wanted her to. He wanted to see her without their interference. Maybe her eyes would tell him something her emotional restraint was able to hide.

"If you could take off your sunglasses, miss." He kept himself turned to the audience, his words, as always, spoken with a smile. "I bet there's more than a few men present who'd like to see what's behind them."

"Including you?"

His smile nearly broke at her words. There was a heat behind them, like an appetizer with a kick to it.

The audience laughed at her insinuation. She'd be great for his act. Her punchiness, conveyed in just two words, already made her a crowd favorite. He could use that.

"I'd be lying if I said no." Only now did he step in front of her, crouching near her chair. He breathed through his mouth, afraid her scent would be too distracting. Reaching forward, he lifted the glasses from her face. Now there was no breathing at all. Large hazel eyes looked right at him, olive green with a circle of warm brown framing her pupils. She was the strangest of strangers to him, yet her gaze was oddly familiar.

The steadiness he'd sensed in her earlier hadn't gone anywhere. If his touch affected her at all, she didn't show it. He could have studied her eyes for the rest of the afternoon, but he had a show to run. Besides, *he* was the one who did the mesmerizing, not the other way around. Elis placed the glasses in the woman's outstretched hand and stood again, twirling towards his audience.

"A beautiful woman has been revealed. We've gotten what we wanted." But he wasn't sure that he had.

* * *

It was foolish but necessary to let him come close. Could he truly not remember her? She had to be certain and now she was. A man capable of hiding such things from himself—who knew what else he was capable of?

The music no longer pounded in Sybille's ears. Instead, it cascaded into a repetitious and melodic raga. A flute quipped out note after note. It warbled gently, the underlying drone of a sitar making the piece quite mesmerizing, as was surely the intent.

Elis' voice was like the music—soft but intentional, magnetic, enticing. From her position at the end of the row of chairs, Sybille eyed the other volunteers. Their limbs were already relaxed. The girl next to her, dressed in her school's colors, nodded in rhythm with the music.

"…wants what's best for you." Sybille's attention returned to Elis' voice mid-sentence. "Your fear is floating away as you bob along the current, but you make no attempt to reach for it. You watch it go. Let it go…let everything go…"

She did her best to relax her limbs, allowing her shoulders to curl forward while loosening the tension in her neck, but no way in Hell was she going to let herself go.

"I'm going to take you deeper, farther away from your fears and closer to who you truly are. Each word I speak calms you, gives you back a piece of yourself you'd thought was gone forever."

That sounded nice. If only she could believe him. The girl next to her had no trouble. She sighed, her lips curled up into an easy grin. Sybille kept her mouth open slightly but made no attempt to smile. At this point, it would feel too strained. If she let anything break the pace of her mind, there was no telling what he would do to her.

* * *

Elis strode back and forth in front of his volunteers. He paused when he came to her chair. Her head tilted forward, it was impossible to see if her eyes were closed or not. She appeared like all the others, which of course meant little. If there was one thing he'd learned in life, it was that a surface often hid what lay beneath.

She was so steady, so unmoved. So unexpected.

"Many extremely intelligent people have said to me that they believe they cannot be hypnotized." He spoke to the audience, to the hazel-eyed woman slumped behind him. "There is a common misconception that only the weak-minded can be put under, but I assure you, the opposite is true." He turned so that he could see her reaction, if there was to be one.

"I have hypnotized doctors, lawyers, physicists, all at the top of their fields. It's the weak-minded who can't achieve this state of consciousness, not the reverse."

He imagined she raised an eyebrow at this, knowing his words were spoken for her benefit. One thing was certain: she was no feeble-minded townie. And even if she had been, it shouldn't have mattered. He played at being a mentalist; it's what everyone assumed he was. His act was a good one, but it was *his* show and he knew what lay behind the scene. Elis was no humbug on the other side of the green curtain. His abilities were fool-proof—that's what he had believed until today.

Elis led his subjects into a deep sleep. The hazel-eyed woman slumped to the side, resting her face on the back of her neighbor's chair, her breathing relaxed and even.

One by one, he tapped the sleeping volunteers' shoulders, giving them make-believe scenarios to play out for the amusement of the audience. At Elis' suggestion, a young boy believed himself to be a carrot about to be eaten by a rabbit. The college student transformed into a dental hygienist who cleaned people's teeth by singing Broadway show tunes.

The audience roared. Elis was a star, a marvel, a wonder.

He tapped the woman's shoulder last.

"You are at a fancy ball. When I ask you to dance, you're thrilled, but when you move to the dance floor, you realize you've forgotten how."

He tapped her shoulder again, a light and uncertain pat. There was no explanation for how this woman had avoided being mesmerized. Was she doing this to make him look the fool?

She raised her head, her eye blinking open. He offered his arm to her. "May I have this dance?"

The audience sat with rapt attention as she rose to her feet, a congenial smile on her face. She moved aside an imaginary princess skirt from her imaginary gown so that she could step forward. "I thought you'd never ask."

They took a few steps to the front of the stage. He calculated his reactions to his own movements, his hand placed on her lower back, the other clasped in her own. As he tamped down the thrill of it, he tried not to wonder what she tasted like, immediately finding he couldn't help himself.

Cinnamon…it would be cinnamon.

He stepped forward to begin the dance. She shuffled awkwardly to the side. The audience's laughter grew as she stumbled with every move until, while attempting to get her feet out of the clumsy position she'd found them in, she stumbled and collapsed against him. He caught her and for a moment, his lips were near enough to whisper something to her. If anyone caught him doing so, they'd assume it was part of the act.

The woman's hands crossed in front of her, pressing against his chest as though she was using him to regain her balance. She paused there, her hand to his heart—his unnaturally slow beating heart. She took a step back from him and he snapped his fingers.

"You may sit down now." He turned away from her, hoping he came across as aloof and unphased. "Wasn't she amazing, ladies and gentlemen?"

The audience broke into applause. She *was* amazing. They had no idea how much so. Elis twitched behind his calm façade as he swept his hand in the direction of the volunteers, giving them their due. They were awake but still mesmerized, still without memory of the events that had unfolded over the course of the show. He walked behind them, again tapping each on the shoulder, this time releasing them from his hold and giving them back the past hour of their lives. They laughed behind their hands and shook their heads in disbelief, all skepticism vanished. Eleven charmed people returned to their seats. The twelfth stepped away seemingly unchanged, the steadiness of her gate a stark contrast to the clumsiness she'd allowed people to see during their dance.

"You are an impossibility," he'd whispered to her. Now as he watched her sway towards the back of the benches lined up to face the stage, the urge to follow her came on him like a hunger. But he had enthralled this audience for a reason and now his ability to pursue her was hampered by a throng of admirers who couldn't help but want to purchase his CDs. He collected their money and steered several exceedingly eager people to the pricy hypnotherapy course on his webpage. He encouraged them all to make an appointment—first consultation is free! By the time his newfound fans dispersed, his impossible woman had disappeared into the crowd making their way to and from the midway.

The disappointment at her departure sparked an uncomfortable memory from a time he'd believed was well behind him.

* * *

Don't stop now. Keep reading with your copy of BLOOD KING available now.

And visit LunaJoya.com to keep up with the latest news where you can subscribe to the newsletter for contests, giveaways, new releases, and more.

Don't miss more of the Legacy series with book two, MAGIC TOUCH, coming soon!

Until then, try BLOOD KING by City Owl Author, Amber K. Bryant, and find more from Luna Joya at www.lunajoya.com

* * *

While the Blood King lives, no one is safe.

Sybille Esmond never wanted to inherit her family's weird business: summoning spirits of the undead and guiding them to the afterlife. While it pays the bills, dealing with supernatural monsters comes with colossal risks, including becoming undead herself.

When tall, dark, and undead Elis Tanner, a reformed member of the soulless ever-after, invades Sybille's life, bringing with him a possessive, disembodied ex-wife, those risks get complicated, and those complications become dangerous.

Sybille must aid Elis in confronting his jealous ex while also investigating the Blood King, a beast who refuses to die—by stake or by poison.

After a harrowing possession leaves her burned and bruised, Sybille finds herself drawing closer to the tempting Elis, who may be the only one capable of helping her kill the unkillable. With the Blood King and his legions of undead closing in, she discovers her own life is far from the only thing in jeopardy.

* * *

Please sign up for the City Owl Press newsletter for chances to win special subscriber-only contests and giveaways as well as receiving information on upcoming releases and special excerpts.

All reviews are **welcome** and **appreciated**. Please consider leaving one on your favorite social media and book buying sites.

For books in the world of romance and speculative fiction that embody Innovation, Creativity, and Affordability, check out City Owl Press at www.cityowlpress.com.

ACKNOWLEDGMENTS

Writing is a solitary adventure. Publishing is not. Thank you to everyone who helped bring the Legacy sisters to the page. First, thank you reader for spending time with my witches.

Thanks to Heather McCorkle for believing in Cami, Tee Tate for being #TeamSam and providing editorial guidance through my panics, and the rest of City Owl's team and authors. You are an awesome publishing family.

For all the pep talks and "let's add magic" conversations, thanks to the Tips. Megan, Summer, and Lana—you are my elemental sisters. A huge shout out goes to All the Kissing and #RChat. A very special heartfelt thanks to my sister-in-crime Hannah Felicia for getting my introverted stealth ways. Also, a special "you guys" to my paranormal pack Kat and Nadia, Jen who brings the tough guys, and Poppy who gets my favorite heroine.

A big kiss to my husband for putting up with plot brainstorms and me living in my head. You and Tiny Editor are my heart.

A million hugs to my parents for supporting storytelling so much my mother snuck me in to see Eudora Welty and other authors at symposiums, armed with crayons and snacks.

Finally, thanks to the County of Los Angeles Norwalk Public Library special collection, UCLA Library, and Los Angeles Police Department for access to their resources as well as the Margaret Herrick Library for helping me dream in technicolor.

ABOUT THE AUTHOR

Award-winning author LUNA JOYA writes hex and sex in The Legacy Series, a witch family saga of romances about kickass heroines and the men who love them.

Fluent in sarcasm and penal code, she prosecutes sex crimes and homicides by day and writes paranormal romance at night. She loves history, especially Los Angeles and Hollywood lore. A survivor of traumatic brain injury with steel body parts, she lives in SoCal with her combat veteran husband and their two-pound terror of a rescue pup.

www.lunajoya.com

facebook.com/lunajoyawriter

twitter.com/lunajoyawriter

instagram.com/lunajoyawriter

pinterest.com/lunajoyawriter

ABOUT THE PUBLISHER

City Owl Press is a cutting edge indie publishing company, bringing the world of romance and speculative fiction to discerning readers.

www.cityowlpress.com

Made in the USA
San Bernardino,
CA